10 DAYS TO SURRENDER

OZEROV BRATVA
BOOK 2

NICOLE FOX

10 DAYS TO SURRENDER
OZEROV BRATVA BOOK 2

I had a plan to make a mob boss hate me.

Good news: It worked.

Bad news: I'm pregnant with his babies.

Remember when I had ten days to make Sasha Ozerov hate me?

Well, I succeeded.

Just not the way I planned.

Now, I'm hiding in France with his unborn twins,

Trying to forget the monster who stole my heart.

The devil who betrayed my sister.

The man I can't stop loving.

But when Serbian hitmen track us down,

Guess who shows up to save the day?

Then Sasha insists we go with him to a remote Italian villa.

For our own safety, he claims.

Just me, my sister, and the father of my child.

For ten weeks.

Until the babies come.

Sasha says he's changed.

He says he loves me.

He says he wants to make things right.

Problem is...

I might actually believe him.

Ten weeks to resist a reformed villain.

Ten weeks to guard my heart.

Ten weeks to choose:

Run from the man who betrayed us...

Or surrender to the father of my children?

10 Days to Surrender is Book 2 of the Ozerov Bratva duet. The story begins in Book 1, 10 Days to Ruin.

1

ARIEL

The sun is such an innocent thing.

It just hangs up in the sky, all cheerful and naive, happy to do what it's always done. It doesn't know much about much and it doesn't care too much about that.

For instance, it doesn't know that I'm a liar. My passport says I'm a twenty-eight-year-old Canadian named Emily Carter, but the sun doesn't know that's fake.

It doesn't know that I'm a runner. My feet still hurt from sprinting through the Manhattan snow and the cut on my hand from the broken library window throbs constantly—but the sun doesn't know those reasons.

It doesn't know that I'm here to dig up one part of my past and bury the rest of it. The sun is just all *bonjour* and *ça va* and *mon Dieu, quelle belle journée !*

Thank God for that.

Because the thought of explaining myself to anything—person, plant, or inanimate object alike—is enough to make me sick to my stomach. Even as I pass by the most beautiful people I've ever seen, sipping cappuccinos at wrought iron tables outside the cafés of Marseille, I feel fear thrumming in me. When a Russian accent rises from the mix, it takes everything I have not to scream.

I've spent the morning asking around. *Do you know a violin teacher with bright green eyes? American accent, maybe? A few years older than me?*

That's all Kosti gave me to go by. He didn't know much more than that. *She's by the beach, I think.* Then he pressed the tickets into my hand and told me I had to hurry if I was going to make it out.

Now, I'm left to wander and rely upon the kindness of strangers. Half the people I asked either didn't understand English or didn't care to speak it with me. Seeing as how my grasp of French is limited to the toast, the fries, and the braids, that was a non-starter.

Most of the rest didn't know. But one said something about their cousin's daughter's friend or whatever who used to take violin lessons from a pretty lady in a blue building down by the water in Roucas-Blanc.

So I set off in search of that.

It's not like I had anything else to do or anywhere else to be. I'm all alone in a foreign country, with a few hundred bucks in my pocket and a prayer in my heart.

Jasmine's here. Jasmine's close. That's all I need to keep me going.

I spend the whole morning searching. Most of the afternoon, too. By the time the tourists have traded their cappuccinos and croissants for rosé and cheese boards, I'm exhausted, but no closer to finding my sister.

Until, suddenly, like it was waiting until I truly needed it, I turn the corner and see a blue building with a picture of a violin painted on the wooden sign.

I touch my belly in silent gratitude. Less than twenty-four hours since I found out there's a baby in there, I've caught myself touching it again and again. When the plane took off without incident from JFK, I touched it. When we landed safely in France, I touched it.

Now, I'm looking up at the building that—hopefully— contains my sister, and I'm touching it again and again.

But I'm here—so unbelievably close—and yet suddenly, I'm terrified. What if she hates me for not searching for her? What if she wants nothing to do with me, with New York, with our family? How could I possibly blame her?

What if she shuts a door in my face, or screams at me that I never should have come here?

What if she doesn't forgive me for giving up?

I don't know how long I stand there, one foot in the street, one foot on the curb, weighing a thousand different possibilities in my head.

Then I see a figure pass behind the window, and my heart starts to strangle me from within.

A bell over the door jingles as I enter. There's a small foyer, and then a flight of narrow, rickety stairs leading to the second floor. Another hand-painted violin points me up that way.

So up I go. One stair at a time. Each one is somehow more exhausting than the last, more exhausting than any of the other fifty thousand steps I've taken today. I reach the top landing and feel like I could curl up in a ball and sleep right here.

A curtain separates the stairs from the room within. Pretty green satin with a slight sheen to it. Like her eyes. *Our* eyes.

On the other side of the curtain, I hear the scratchings of an amateur trying to make their instrument do something right. A bit of it sounds like music, but most of it is fumbling and awkward.

Then: *"Bon travail, Alain!"* Chairs screech and pages flap. I hear the zippers of an instrument case open and close as Jasmine's voice flows melodically, praising a little boy who mumbles back, *"Merci."*

Her French has gotten good. Good enough to my ear, at least, although that bar is admittedly very low.

I reach out to open the curtain. Before I can, it gets whisked open from within.

And for the first time in fifteen years, I'm eye to eye with my sister.

My throat closes.

Fifteen years.

Fifteen years of funeral-black dresses and phantom phone calls where I'd dial her old number, just to hear *"this line has been disconnected"* in English and Greek. Fifteen years of wondering if her ghost resented me for staying with Leander. For becoming Ariel Ward instead of joining her in the grave.

"Jas," I croak.

The violin in her hand hits the floor with a thunk. "Ari."

Time takes on a funny quality. Molasses-slow and somehow taut at the same time. The girl in my memories—nineteen, trembling in fear as our father and Dragan bundled her into a black-tinted van—is gone. This woman has crow's feet and calloused hands, a bolt of gray shot through her caramel hair. But her eyes…

Her eyes are still green, just like mine.

"Jas," I say again.

"Ari?" Her voice is a shattered thing. "No. No, you're—"

"It's me, Jas. I'm here."

The boy at her side—Alain, I'm assuming—is baffled. He looks up at Jasmine and says something in rapid-fire French that means absolutely nothing to me, except for the very last two words: *"Madame Morgane."*

My eyebrow raises. "'Morgane?'"

Jasmine laughs and winces at the same time. "Like the fairy, yeah. It's… I don't know. Cheesy, obviously. I needed something to make me laugh when I picked it, because otherwise, I was going to cry."

"I know the feeling."

She bends down to touch the boy's back and whisper back to him. He nods, grins, hoists his violin case, and scampers down the stairs and away.

The bell chimes.

Then we're alone.

Jas looks at me sidelong. "Do you… I mean, you can come in if you want. But it's my last lesson for the day, so if you're tired, my apartment is—"

"Let's just sit for a second, if that's okay. I'm… It's been a very long few days."

"Of course. Yeah, come in." She holds open the curtain and I duck through.

I sit on the first thing I come across, which is an overstuffed armchair, formerly red, now faded to a pale pink by sun slanting through the windows. Jas takes a seat on a wooden stool across from me.

"You look awful," she remarks.

I look at her. She looks at me. I look at her some more. She squints back at me…

And then we both burst out laughing. It pours out of us, fifteen years of laughs we were robbed of, laughs we should've gotten to share, that we *would've* gotten to share, if it weren't for stupid, power-hungry men playing stupid, power-hungry games.

I'm laughing so hard that I slide off the armchair. Jasmine comes tumbling down off the stool and hugs me. We end up in a Chinese finger trap of crisscrossed limbs, hair tickling each other's noses, as we laugh and laugh and laugh.

Eventually, though, the laughter fades. The inevitable tears start to well up.

I grimace and wipe my eyes. "I don't want to cry."

Jasmine, shoving herself to a seat against the wall, nods. "Done plenty of that."

"More than plenty."

"You can if you want to, though. It'd be okay with me." She pulls my head to rest against her shoulder. We sit in the sun for a while as she strokes my hair.

I'm so, so tired. My whole body is one giant ache and the slice in my hand hurts as bad as it does the moment I got it. I don't have a home anymore, or a fiancé, or a father, or faith that everything will always work out and love will win in the end, like Mama always said it would. I don't know what the next hour holds, much less the next day or year or the rest of my life.

But I have my sister back.

That's enough.

2

ARIEL

Her apartment is a few blocks down from the music school. When I'm ready, we lock up the studio, then go there, holding hands the whole way. It smells like her when she opens the door and welcomes me in. Like *jasmine*.

"Cute place, Jas." I mean it. It's tiny, but drenched in sun. Window boxes spill rosemary down stucco walls.

She sets about making us two cups of tea while I wash off the grime of airplanes and taxis in the sink. She presses a mug into my hands when I emerge. Both of us settle at her kitchen table.

"I can't stop looking at you," she gushes. "You're a woman now."

I scowl at her. "Don't start. It's not like I was a baby when you were— when you left."

"Not that far off!" She reaches out to pinch my cheeks. "Little baby Ari. Couldn't *stand* being left out of the fun. Always wanted to play dress-up with her big sissy."

"More like 'big sissy always wanted to use me like a mannequin."

"Mhmm." Jasmine sips her tea. "And then you'd throw a fit and I'd have to go steal cookies from the pantry and force-feed you until you calmed down."

"And then Baba would—" I freeze before I finish the sentence, because a rush of such thorny, twisted, complicated pain hits me that my mouth momentarily stops working.

Baba, slumping to his knees. The hole in his forehead weeping blood. Then crumpling, tumbling, like a wadded-up receipt, and falling into the orchestra pit.

Suddenly, nothing seems quite so funny.

I look up at Jasmine. I can tell there are a million and one questions burning on the tip of her tongue. I can hardly blame her for that. Why am I here now? What's happened? What changed?

But the thought of unloading it all is so much. I don't even know where to begin. Which loose thread do I pull on? Will the story unravel first, or will I?

I suck in a deep breath. Jas, sensing what I'm going through, reaches out to cup my wrist in her delicate fingers. "Take your time," she says. "We've got that now."

I nod, swallow, and start. "Baba's dead."

Jasmine goes still.

"Dragan shot him." Then, because if we're doing this, we might as well rip the Band-Aid clean off, get all the trauma unbagged and laid out in front of us as soon as we can, I add, "And I'm pregnant with Sasha's baby."

She looks at me for a long, long time.

Then she turns to look out the window.

I follow her gaze. She's got a decent view from here. Half of it is blocked by a neighboring building, and she's only on the fourth floor, but there's still a beautiful slice of the city to be seen. Marseille sprawls down the coastline like a dropped dollar-store necklace—tawdry and harmless and bright. Beyond it, the sea beckons.

Finally, she sighs and turns back to me. "How... how are you here right now, Ariel?"

I shrug helplessly and let out a laugh to match. "I wish I knew. I mean, the x's and o's of it are pretty straightforward. But it just... It's all spiraled out of control so fast."

"How'd you find me?"

"Kosti," I tell her. "You called him; he gave me the tickets and told me where I could go. Honestly, I just didn't know what else to do. So I came."

She shakes her head in disbelief. "I didn't know what I was doing, either, when I called. I just saw that newspaper article and I freaked."

"That makes two of us," I mumble. "Honestly, it's felt like a bad dream ever since Baba told me what he'd done. About the marriage."

"Like mine?" she asks.

"Yeah," I say. "He wanted to do it just like yours."

Her lip twists in a disgusted sneer. "He didn't learn anything, did he?"

"No. No, he didn't."

Another lull follows before she looks at me again. "Why are you *here,* though? If you're pregnant, that means you must have—"

"I'm here because I can't be there." It's hard enough to say the words. I feel like I'm betraying something, although I have no idea what that something might be. Sasha? My baby? Myself? "I can't be with him. Not after…"

Not after everything.

Jasmine studies me—the reporter-turned-runaway, the little sister she left behind. Her eyes narrow. "What did he do to you?"

"Nothing."

"Bullshit."

"He saved me, in a way," I croak. "Over and over. But he lied, too—over and over. And… and…"

The apartment goes hazy at the corners. I grip the table's edge.

"Ari?"

"I can't." I press my forehead to the cool wood. "Not yet."

Silence. Then her chair scrapes back. She rounds the table and crouches beside me. Her hand finds my hair—gentle, like when I was a little girl with a skinned knee. My big sister again.

"Just tell me this: Did he hurt you?" she asks.

At that, I recoil. "Sasha? No. God, no. He just…" My words

falter again as I search for what to say and how to say it. "He was supposed to be *better* than them."

Jasmine shakes her head as she returns to her seat. She runs a finger round and round the lip of her tea mug. "They're all like that, Ari. Even the ones who play hero. Maybe even *especially* those ones." She frees a long, shuddering exhale. "I've had a long time to think about everything. It's hard to hate them. Well, hard to hate Sasha and Baba. Dragan is pretty easy to hate."

"Yeah," I mutter, feeling at my throat where he'd held me in that alley, before Sasha came to the rescue. "I don't have any problem hating that one."

"He's a violent, cruel, sadistic son of a bitch," Jasmine snaps. Hints of venom seep into her face and the whites of her knuckles where she's clutching the table's edge. "If he'd had it his way, he would've beaten me senseless, then hung me out to dry. Just a used-up husk of myself that he could move here and there like a doll. I'd have been a leash in his hand that connected to a noose around Baba's throat. That's what Dragan wanted." Her eyes flit to mine. "If it weren't for Sasha, he would've gotten it."

It's my turn to close my eyes. That prickly, complex pain is rinsing through me again.

You knew.

You knew and you lied.

"He's not a good man, Jasmine. Better than Dragan, maybe, but if that's the standard of comparison, Satan's not so bad, either."

She laughs bitterly. "'Good'? Maybe not. Not in the ways we're used to thinking about that kind of thing."

"Not in any way."

"In at least one way. He *saved* me, Ariel. He—"

"And lied about it!" I cry out. I leap to my feet, and the motion makes tea go sloshing over the edge of my cup. It puddles and starts a sad, brown waterfall off the lip of the table, but I don't care. "I've spent fifteen years thinking my sister was fucking *dead,* Jasmine! We had a funeral! Did you know that? Baba even insisted on a goddamn casket. I sat in the front pew in a dress I stole out of your closet and looked up at an empty fucking wooden box covered in flowers. There's a graveyard in Brighton Beach right now that has your name on a headstone. And yeah, sure, Sasha didn't know me until this whole marriage deal became a thing. But once he did, he could've told me at any time. When I was falling for him—when he was twisting and manipulating me and playing me, because apparently, that's just so fucking easy for him—he could've told me and ended fifteen years of my heart hurting so bad that there were nights I thought about trying to rip it out of my chest. But he didn't. He lied. So no, Jasmine, he's not a good man. I don't care if he saved you. I don't care what he did, what he's doing, or what he ever does again. Sasha Ozerov is not a good man."

I'm sweaty and breathless by the time I'm done. Jasmine, in classic big sister fashion, is unfazed by my eruption. She sits there the whole time, calm and cool as could be, nodding until I run out of steam and sink back into my chair, still jittery at my fingertips.

Sighing, she reaches behind her to pluck a dish rag off the counter. She bends over and dabs up some of the spilled tea. "Is—*was*—Baba a good man?"

"Is that a trick question?"

"No." She stoops to mop up the rest of the mess I made. "I'm asking if he was all good or all bad."

"He married you to a monster and then tried to do the same thing to me. He chased Mama out the door and broke her heart too many times to count. Which part of that is supposed to be 'good'?"

She keeps nodding for a while. Then she returns the rag to the counter and laces her hands in front of her. "When you were four, you fell off your bicycle. I was supposed to be keeping an eye on you, but I got distracted doing I-don't-even-know-what. He saw, though. He came charging out of the house—I remember because he'd been in the middle of shaving, so half his face still had foam on it—and he scooped you up right off the asphalt. You were throwing one hell of a tantrum, so he sat down with you on the stoop and sang you a lullaby until you calmed down. You don't remember that, do you?"

I hesitate before shaking my head.

"I know what Baba did to me, Ari. It horrified me that he thought he could get away with doing the same thing to you. That's why I called Kosti. I knew it was a risk—but at least I tried to say something."

"What's the point of all this, Jas?" I wipe my nose and try to sip at what's left of my lukewarm tea.

"The point, *neraïdoula mou,* is that no one is all good or all bad. We've all got a little bit of everything in us. Even Baba. Even Sasha. If I'd tried to hate either of them, I'd have been dead a long time ago. Fifteen years of clinging onto something that poisonous just eats a person from the inside-out." She reaches over the table to squeeze my hands again.

"Hating them lets the bad stuff inside you win. Don't do that. It's such a terrible way to lose the war."

I want to believe her, but it's not that easy. Every time I picture Sasha, I get filled with such a burning sense of overwhelm that I have to change the mental channel or else I'll go insane.

He ruined my life in ten short days. I hated him, then I wanted him, then I loved him, then he broke me.

Now, my big sister is here, telling me to simply… *let that go?*

Maybe the last decade and a half has wizened her a hell of a lot faster than it did me. If I was that enlightened, there'd be religions with my face on their altar.

Her face, though, is full of such patient hope.

"I'll try," I croak. "No promises."

"You always were stubborn," she laughs. "Just like Mama." She rolls my knuckles between her palms, then sets my hand back down gently on the tabletop. "Go take a shower. Let me make you something to eat. We can talk about everything once you're fed and clean and rested. We've got a lot of time for that now."

"But—"

"No buts," she says with a wink. "Honestly, you smell like B.O. and airplane pretzels. It's hard to have a serious conversation."

I snort a teary, snotty laugh and flash her a middle finger. "Still a bitch," I murmur.

"Still a brat," she replies, winking.

But she's right about one thing: we do have a lot of time.

We have the rest of forever.

3

SASHA

SIX MONTHS LATER

The cinderblock slips from my grasp, crashing into frozen mud with the sound of a skull hitting pavement. It tears my hands open as it goes.

"Goddammit."

I stare at the jagged, red groove carved across my palm. As I watch, blood pearls along the seam, brighter than the June sun bleaching the sky as it rises.

"At it again?" Kosti calls from the porch. Steam rises from his chipped mug as he sips his morning coffee. "You'll reopen the gut wounds if you go too hard."

I toe the block toward the firepit. Kosti's safehouse in Vermont is as well-equipped as they come: thirteen crates of Soviet AKMs buried beneath behind the toolshed. Six kilos of C-4 molded into hollowed-out encyclopedias in the root cellar.

But not a single fucking barbell. I'm left to lug around rocks like a fucking caveman for exercise.

"Better infection than weakness," I mutter, stripping off my sweat-soaked t-shirt. The barbed wire scar around my neck twinges as I haul the cinderblock back up, rest it on my shoulder, and start to squat.

Every inch of motion is fucking agony. My thigh screams; my torso screams. Most of all, my head screams. Two syllables on endless repeat.

Ssyklo.

Ssyklo.

Ssyklo.

I keep my mouth clamped shut, though. Even though there's only me and Kosti out here in the Adirondacks, with no one else for dozens of miles in any direction, I'll be damned if I let so much as a single grunt of acknowledged pain slip past my lips.

Only cowards show pain.

Six months of isolation and this place still hasn't grown on me. I despised it in those first few weeks in the dead of January, when I couldn't even sit up in bed without assistance. Pine boughs would scratch at my window all night long like feral cats. Snow rose and fell and rose again.

The whole time, I laid flat on my back and buried my agonized moans.

Doctors came and went. Secret doctors, discreet doctors, the kind who accept cash in unmarked envelopes and know to keep their mouths shut if anyone asks where they've been. Down to a man, they told me the same thing:

Your femur is broken and your femoral artery was nearly shattered. Your A/C joint and the tendons attaching your pectoral muscle to the bone are both in ruins. Most likely, you'll never walk again.

The doctors were wrong. Even when every inch of me bellowed in pain, I found a way to struggle upright. That turned into standing, and standing turned into timid steps to my door and back.

All day and all night, I'd do that same ten-foot walk. My socked feet sliding across the thick carpets of the safehouse bedroom. I'd be woozy and sweating bullets by the time I got back to my bed—then I'd turn around and do it again.

And again.

And *again*.

The winter eventually petered out. Spring came in, but the robins pecking at the window glass were just as annoying as the pines. Eventually, I conquered the stairs the same way I conquered the stretch from my bed to my door.

Fuck knows how many bloody bandages I went through. Kosti shuffled in daily to empty the trash cans and leave food for me to eat. He never said much in those first few months. Didn't explain why he'd damned me by showing Ariel proof of Jasmine's survival, only to save me from Dragan. He'd just look at me, nod, and say, "Hm. He lives another day." Then shuffle right back out.

It's summer now. The sun is a bitch, viciously hot. I'm sweating bullets and the cinderblock is numbing my wounded shoulder. But I keep going.

I squat.

I stand.

I squat.

I stand.

Somewhere along the way, I lose count of how many repetitions I've done. Kosti's chair creaks protest as he rises and saunters over to me. Grass whispers under his Italian loafers—still polished daily, even in this backwoods shithole.

He pauses in front of me and watches for a while.

I lie down and start to bench press the stone. My pecs hate it, but since when the fuck did I give a damn what my body cares for?

Three sets of thirty. Burn through the pain.

Kosti rolls a cigarette and lights it. I grimace. The smell of it makes my mind go to Feliks. Kosti got word to him for me, somehow, some way. He's camped out in a Bronx safehouse, living under cover of darkness, waiting for my orders.

What those orders are and when they're coming is a mystery to us both. I've been foaming at the mouth with thoughts of getting back to New York and putting a knife through Dragan's throat.

The first time I snatched the car keys off the kitchen table and tried to go do exactly that, Kosti told me it was too soon. "Your body is broken, Sasha. Push too hard and it'll fail on you when you can least afford it."

"My body will do what the fuck I tell it to."

He found me an hour later, kneeling in the dirt, unable even to finish the walk to the truck.

I had no choice but to acknowledge he was right—I'm not strong enough yet. Not sharp enough to do what must be done.

My body will heal eventually, though.

My mind?

That's another question entirely.

Six weeks spent aimlessly horizontal gives a man too much time to think. And I had too much to fucking think about.

Well, too much and not enough. Because ultimately, all roads led to the same place.

Ariel.

Try as I might, I couldn't keep my thoughts away from her. Even if I started with schemes of how to root out Dragan, where he might be vulnerable, how to reach him… inevitably, I ended up thinking of her.

Let me—

No, Sasha. You had your chance.

I stand, spit, and start to curl the rock.

"The demons are alive and well today, I see," remarks Kosti. The sun coming up over the treetops has his face glowing pink now.

"The demons can go fuck themselves."

I watch him out of the side of my eye as I keep curling the rock up and down. He's a difficult man to figure out, and he has shown little interest in answering questions.

Why'd you save me?

You seemed like a worthwhile investment.

Then why'd you fuck me over in the first place?

Family is a funny thing, Mr. Ozerov.

I can make neither head nor tails of the old bastard. As far as I can tell, he's content to rot in these woods until my beard is as gray as his.

"At least give me some news," I say between grunted exhales. "It's been a week."

He shrugs. "I've given you all I have."

"Bullshit. 'The Serbians think you're dead' came five months ago. 'Things have stayed quiet' was four. 'No sign of her' hasn't changed since the first time I asked."

I don't have to explain who "her" is, thankfully. I have no intention of ever saying her name aloud again.

Kosti puffs on his cigarette and gazes thoughtfully into the rising sun. "Would you like there to be some sign of her?"

"I asked for news, old man, not psychiatry."

"You mean 'psychology.' 'Psychiatry' would involve drugs."

"I'm going to *need* drugs to stay sane if you don't give me some fucking morsel to think about."

Kosti chuckles as he taps his temple. "Feisty, feisty demons." After a pause, he adds, "I did get this, though. Not much, but it's something."

I drop the block and snatch the offered cell phone out of his hand. On it is a picture of a man in a nightclub booth.

Dragan Vukovic.

He's got a magnum bottle of champagne clutched in one greedy paw, some silicone-enhanced blonde in the other. The arrogant sneer on his face makes my stomach curdle. Even worse is that I recognize the club name scrawled in neon over his head.

"That's *my fucking club.*"

Kosti accepts the phone back and tucks it into his pocket. "He thinks you're fish food in the Hudson, Sasha. He's gotten comfortable."

"Comfortable men make mistakes."

"So do angry ones."

I grab the block and start doing lunges in place. "Dead men don't, though."

Sighing, Kosti rubs his beard. "*You'll* be joining that club if you don't take it easier on yourself. You are still healing, Sasha, and you have a long way to go until you're—"

"Rest is for corpses. I don't intend to be anything of the sort." I ignore the lightning bolt of pain shooting up my leg as I keep touching my knees to the grass until my quads burn like hellfire.

"Stubborn bastard," he accuses.

He isn't wrong.

"It's kept me alive thus far."

"Oh, I'm sure you'll correct that oversight soon enough. Now, why don't you have mercy on that poor cinderblock and come have a glass of water?"

He rests a wrinkled hand on the block cradled in my arms to make me pause for a moment. His eyes flash as he looks at me and arches one thick, hairy brow.

With a grimace, I let the block fall to the grass between us.

We thump up the stairs. Kosti steps into the kitchen to fill two glasses of water. He reemerges and hands me one, then we each take a seat in the rocking chairs.

The cabin looks out on a long, flat stretch of valley. It's mostly grass, ringed with a few clumps of pine trees. Deer are grazing in one of the fields to the north. For a while, I let myself begrudgingly enjoy the silence.

Kosti, of course, can't bear to let me do that.

"If you knew where she was," he interrupts, "would you go to her?"

I grip the glass in my hand hard. "How many times do I have to tell you I don't want to talk about it?"

He waves a semi-apologetic hand. "I'm an old man. Very forgetful."

I don't buy his bullshit for a second. "Very annoying, too."

"Gratitude is not one of the virtues of today's youth, is it?" he teases.

"No more than brevity is a virtue of the old."

He laughs. "You know, I've enjoyed these months with you, Sasha. You're an interesting character. Full of contradictions."

I rock back and watch as the grazing deer get spooked and go dashing over the fence, up into the foothills of the Adirondacks beyond. "Nothing about me is contradictory anymore. I've got one goal: kill Dragan Vukovic."

"So it's a no, then? You wouldn't go to her, if you knew?"

I turn and stare him dead in the eyes. "No."

"Liar."

My teeth grind together. It doesn't take much to piss me off these days, and the old man has become an expert in mashing those buttons repeatedly. "I'm not lying."

"Yes, you are. You'd go find her and drag her into this self-loathing grave with you, if you could."

I don't answer. Instead, I look down at the chessboard that rests on a small folding table between the two rocking chairs. It's in the middle of a game, one that Kosti and I have played on and off for six months running. Weeks pass between moves sometimes. His white is hemming in my black pieces. Pawns have fallen on both sides. My queen is stranded in a distant corner of the board, but my king stands tall alongside a rook.

It looks bad for me, but I know better. I have a move waiting that will flip the game on its head. As soon as it's my turn again, this will all come to a swift and bloody conclusion.

"She is no longer a part of my life," I say tonelessly. "It's best that way for both of us."

I notice Kosti purse his lips, but he's quiet for a while. Eventually, he offers up, "You'll have to choose at some point. Two roads diverge in a yellow wood and all that."

"We're doing poetry now?"

"No, Sasha, we're doing truth." He cranes his neck to catch my eyes. "Dragan lies at the end of one path; Ariel at the end of another. You can't walk both at once. You can't turn back once you've chosen. But at some point—maybe not today, maybe not tomorrow, but *at some point*—you'll have to choose. For your sake and for hers alike, I hope you choose right."

Then he reaches down and makes a move with his knight that I never saw coming. My plan goes up in smoke.

And so the king remains poised between squares. Stuck. Cornered. Waiting.

Across the board, the queen waits, too.

4

ARIEL

The gel is warmer than I expect. It's a relief, really—the waiting room's air conditioning had turned my skin to gooseflesh.

"Ah, there's *Bébé A*," the technician murmurs in a thick French accent, pointing to the leftmost blob on the screen. "Kicking up a storm today, *non*? *Très bien. Parfaits.*"

I squint. To me, it just looks like static with a pulse.

Spat. Spat. Spat.

The Doppler picks up twin heartbeats. One is steady as she goes, the other staccato as rain on a tin roof. My own heart stumbles over itself trying to match their rhythm.

This is real. This is real. This is real.

I glance down at the swell beneath where my sweater is hiked up to my ribs. I'm as surprised as always by what I see there. Twenty-five weeks in, and I've gone from looking moderately peckish to smuggling cantaloupes. Still, my brain hasn't quite caught up to the math: *two* cantaloupes.

Twins came as a surprise the first time a technician spotted them. I made him go get the doctor and check again, and when that doctor said the same thing, I made her go get *another* doctor for triple confirmation. But when the dust settled, they all agreed.

Twins. *Two* babies. *Two* Makris-Ozerov-Ward angels-to-be.

God help us all.

Right on cue, I feel a pang and I bolt upright, sending a glob of ultrasound gel flying. The twins have been staging an MMA fight in my uterus for weeks now. I'm just the unwilling arena.

"Soon, *Maman*," the tech tells me with a broad, toothy grin. "Are you ready?"

I laugh politely and tell her the same thing I tell everyone who asks: "Not even close."

The woman grins, then leaves to fetch the doctor. I hear a knock on the door a second later, and when I look up, I see Jasmine slipping into the exam room.

"Sorry," she says. "Lesson ran late. Isabelle is getting better, though."

"Well, she can't get much worse."

"Hey!"

"No offense to her wildly talented instructor, of course," I hurry to say. When Jasmine continues to pout, I add, "… who is also wise, beautiful, and has an ass you could bounce a quarter off of."

She nods primly. "That's more like it." She plucks a pair of tissues from the box on the counter and helps wipe the gel off my belly. "Any motion in the ocean?"

"They're right where they're supposed to be. Still kicking me like Pelé."

Jas frowns. "Like who?"

"Isn't he a soccer player? I thought he was. Could be wrong."

"It's *football* here," she reminds me with a grin.

I roll my eyes. Six months in Europe has mostly gotten me acclimated to life across the pond. Some things are more adjusted than others, though. You can take the girl out of New York, but you can't take the New York out of the girl. And the distinct lack of good egg-and-cheese bagels is giving me conniptions.

"Any names come to mind yet?" Jasmine asks as she goes to stand in the corner. Like every other one of the visits she's accompanied me on, she leaves the husband chair empty. We haven't talked about that gesture, what she intends it to mean, what it might mean to me. I have no plans to ask.

"Thing One and Thing Two."

"Ah, yes, such a rich etymological history to those. Full of culture, tradition, and yet also forward-thinking and contemporary."

I stick my tongue out at her. "No, smartass, I have not yet decided on names."

"Hm. How about *Leon* if there's a boy and *Leona* for a girl?"

"'Leon'?"

"Greek theater muse and French lion. It's balanced."

"It's *tragic.*"

"Says the woman who named herself after a fairy."

Jasmine—excuse me, *Morgane*—lobs a peppermint at my head. "Rude. Also, moving the goalposts. Again."

I catch it, unwrap it, pop it in my mouth. The sharp coolness cuts through the hospital's antiseptic gauze taste. "That's a bad name and you know it. Sounds too much like…"

Leander.

The mint cracks between my molars.

Jasmine cringes at the sound. "Too soon?"

"Only by a century."

As often as possible over the last six months, we've talked about the future, not the past. Leaving Marseille was easy for Jas; she'd been ready to run for a long, long time. We packed up her apartment, got in her car, and drove west. When we hit the Atlantic coast of France, I said, "Good enough," and we found a little bungalow in a tiny beach town called Moliets-et-Maa.

It was simple enough to focus my attention on the little things. Get food to eat, a job to make a bit of money, stuff like that. Most words having to do with recent history are verboten: Leander, Dragan, and most of all, Sasha.

That hasn't stopped him from coming to me at night. More than once, Jas has shaken me awake with concern in her eyes. *You were moaning his name.* I could even feel the sticky residue it left behind on my lips.

Sasha. Sasha. Sasha.

And whenever I do dream of him, my ears catch odd little noises the whole next day. I'll hear a seagull squawk and I could swear it's saying, *Ptichka, ptichka!*

Jasmine reaches over to the ultrasound printer and plucks off the hard copies that the tech made for me. She studies them. "They have your nose."

"They have alien noses."

"Your *alien* nose, then."

I scowl at her, but before I can reply, the doctor shoulders through the door. She's a broad-hipped, no-nonsense woman with an elegantly gray ponytail and a clipboard she wields like a battle ax.

"Madame Ward, vos tests sont bons, mais votre tension artérielle..."

The French rolls over me like a poorly dubbed movie. I've gotten better, but I'm a long way from fluent. I do catch the highlights: *hypertension. Bed rest optional but recommended. No flying internationally.*

I look at Jas, who repeats all those things just to be sure I understood.

The blood pressure has been a recurring nuisance. Occasional headaches and swollen feet are just the name of the game so far as pregnancy goes. It's the spotty vision and the sudden dizziness, like someone whacked me in the back of the skull with a bat, that are driving me insane.

Not much to do other than wait it out and be careful, though. And, apparently, don't pilot any commercial aircraft.

I give the doc a thumbs-up. "Don't worry; I wasn't planning on going anywhere."

I've had to lie about a lot of things in my time as a fake Frenchwoman, but that part is true. As far as I'm concerned, Moliets-et-Maa will house me for the rest of my days. It'll be me and Jas, Jas and me. Two mobster's daughters lying low in the French Riviera with a double stroller and a lifetime of trauma that we refuse to face.

What could possibly go wrong?

~

"Lunch?" asks Jas.

"Duh. Crêpes. And a gallon of Orangina."

"Such refined tastes you have."

"I'm eating for three," I remind her. "You're not allowed to make fun of me."

She snorts. The sidewalk ahead shimmers with heat and promise. Our apartment's three blocks east and the beach is three blocks west. Tourists clot the sand beyond, broiling themselves in oil. We veer north, toward the market stalls.

We've fallen into this rhythm—mornings at the *marché*, afternoons teaching violin students (her) and freelance editing for expat magazines (me), evenings bickering over whether we're watching *Bridgerton* or *Emily in Paris*. It's so aggressively normal it feels like playing house.

Today, though, I can't stop thinking about that chair.

That stupid, empty husband chair in the corner of the room. It's been empty for six months; why am I fussing over it now?

I know the answer. It's because of two silly little words I can't stop rolling in my head over and over again.

What if...?

That's as far down that road as I dare to go. If I start filling in the blank that comes after "What if," they'll have to institutionalize me.

Because I can't let myself think, *What if that chair were filled?* I can't wonder, *What if* he *was the one handing me tissues to wipe my belly off?* I can't ponder what names he might suggest, what jokes he might make, what smiles might spread across his face when he hears the proud thump of our children's hearts.

What if is a dangerous, dangerous game.

It's also a pointless one, because in many ways, there *is* no "what if." France is home now. The twins will be born in the same cream-colored hospital complex currently shrinking in our wake. They'll speak Franglais, suck down sugared churros, throw sand at German toddlers building drip castles in the shallows.

They'll live their whole lives here. A world away from smoke-choked alleys and doorway bloodstains and men who hoard power like pocket change.

The crêpe stand guy knows us by now. "*Les sœurs américaines!*" he calls, already slinging batter.

"*Grecques,*" Jasmine corrects lightly, like she always does. He never listens.

The two of them banter as I gaze out at the navy blue ocean lapping at *la plage*. It's hazy on the horizon. Might storm later, another afternoon sprinkle to take the edge off the heat for a little while. I rub my belly absent-mindedly and try not to think about empty chairs anymore.

I look up to see the crêpe guy holding out a Nutella-drenched monstrosity for me. *"Merci,"* I tell him as I take it off his hands and give him a fistful of euros.

We go find a bench and sit. In the distance, seagulls chatter and families laugh. I lick Nutella off my thumb.

"You're spacing out a lot lately," Jasmine says, bumping me with an elbow. "Something new on your mind?"

"Checkbook trauma." I lift the crêpe. "These things are bleeding me dry, but I just can't stop."

"He's ripping us off because we don't haggle," she tells me. "Act like prey and they'll eat you alive."

"Said the sheep in wolf's clothing."

"A sheep would've fainted at your first pelvic exam."

I can't decide whether to chuckle or shudder at the memory. Both seem appropriate. *The most fun you never want to have again,* promised the doctor who performed it. I think she might've slightly upsold the procedure.

My crêpe disappears in the blink of an eye and I'm left mournfully picking crumbs from the wrapper. Jas eyes me warily, but she knows better than to begrudge a pregnant woman her sweet treats, so she says nothing.

When she's done with hers, we start the slow walk home. We pause at a crosswalk to wait for the light to change. Across the street, two kids are arguing over a melted gelato. A terrier pees on a hydrant. Normalcy settles over me like a too-small sweater.

It's not New York, but I've learned to love that about it. Sometimes, you don't realize how much you've started to call your cage "home" until you finally get the chance to walk around outside the bars a little bit.

"Uh-oh. We've been spotted," Jasmine mutters.

Madame Duvall hobbles toward us with the grim determination of a gossip bloodhound. Her toy poodle, Pierre, beats her to us, circling around and furiously yapping at our ankles.

"*Mes chéries!* How is the little whale today?" Her knuckles dig into my belly before I can dodge.

"Great," I grit out.

"You must rest more! My niece's neighbor's cousin, she ignored her hypertension and... *pop!*" She mimes an explosion.

Jasmine steps between us, forcing a polite smile. "We're heading home for a nap right now, actually."

"Good, good. Remember, rosemary tea with—"

"—with honey and lemon, twice daily. Got it."

We escape into a side alley clogged with linen dresses flapping on twine. Jasmine fake-gags. "Only eleven more weeks of that."

"Sounds like hell."

"No, hell would be Baba breathing down your neck all the time, telling you to—" She stops. "Sorry. I don't know where that came from."

"It's okay."

The grief comes at odd moments. Usually, it's manageable,

but every now and then, the weight of the lives we left behind hits us like a truck with the brakes cut.

That's when the *What if* game becomes harder and harder to ignore.

We resume walking. Jasmine's quiet for a while. "You could call him, you know."

"Pass."

"It's not just your secret, Ari."

My toes scrunch in my sandals. "I don't owe him a damn thing."

"Fair. But you might owe *them* something." She taps my stomach. "He's still their father."

Spat. Spat. Spat.

"And Baba was ours. Look how that worked out."

"So you think turning your back on the whole concept of a dad is the right response?"

Heat pricks behind my eyes. "We had a deal, Jas."

She holds up her hands. "Silence. *Verboten.* I remember. I'm sorry; I'll drop it."

She sighs, the sound swallowed by the crash of waves. We've had this argument weekly since I showed up on her doorstep. Her optimism versus my spite, round one million. Neither one gets out alive.

"You don't have to forgive him," she says carefully, unable to help herself. "But those babies… they deserve more than half a story."

I swipe at my face with the back of my hand. "Since when are you the wise one?"

"Since I realized running only works if you unpack the baggage first." She tucks a curl behind my ear. "You're still carrying his."

That night, I dream of the library.

Sasha's breath hot on my neck, his hands spanning my hips. *"Marry me now,"* I'd whispered. *"With nothing to gain."*

In the dream, he says yes.

I wake up pawing at sweat-damp sheets, the twins somersaulting like they're trying to kick the memory out.

I shove myself to my feet and go tiptoeing down the hallway. Through the crack in her door, I see Jasmine is still sleeping. I keep going, into the kitchen, where my laptop rests on the table.

When I open it, a folder titled *Thing1&Thing2* stares back at me. It's filled with half-written lullabies, scanned sonogram selfies, and lists of potential godparents (Gina, Feliks, a startled-looking barista from Rue de France who made me the best chicory root coffee I've ever had in my life; I almost proposed on the spot).

I open a new document. I feel like telling stories tonight.

Once upon a time, there was a girl who loved a wolf...

The cursor blinks.

She knew his teeth. Knew his hunger. Knew she should stay away. But one day, the wolf said—

I highlight the lines. Delete.

Another draft:

A queen once told her daughter, "Love is war waged softly." The princess didn't listen. She followed a soldier into the fog. When she returned, her crown had rusted, but her sword...

Delete.

Third try:

Dear Sasha,

They have your nose.

I shut the laptop.

Outside, waves erase the shore. Somewhere beyond them, my father's body cools in a grave. Maybe Sasha's is beside him, or maybe not. Maybe Dragan has killed him, or maybe not. It's impossible to know.

What I do know is this: here, in the dark, two heartbeats sync with mine.

Spat.

Spat.

Spat.

5

SASHA

The knock comes at three in the morning.

Sleep and I parted ways months ago, so I'm already awake, shirtless and drenched in sweat, doing push-ups on the warped cabin floorboards. My left shoulder screams like a gutted animal with every dip, but I keep count through gritted teeth. *Forty-seven. Forty-eight. Forty—*

Knock-knock-knock.

I pause and look at the door.

"We have a situation." Kosti's tone makes my spine stiffen. In six months, I've never heard him sound this grim.

I go back to work. *Fifty-three. Fifty-four.* The scar around my neck pulls taut. "Speak."

"One of my contacts in Marseille just reached out. Dragan's men have been asking questions about a violin teacher."

The air leaves my lungs. For fifteen years, I've maintained a careful network of watchers around Jasmine. Not close enough to compromise her new life, but near enough to warn me if trouble ever came knocking.

Now, it has.

"How did they find her?"

"Does it matter?" Kosti's voice carries an edge of impatience. "What matters is that they have."

I'm already reaching for clothes. "How long ago?"

"My contact spotted three of Dragan's men at a café yesterday. They were showing her picture around. Old picture, but still recognizable."

"Fuck." My hands shake as I pull on my boots. Not from fear —from rage. Pure, molten rage that burns away six months of careful healing and planning. "I need transport. Now."

"Sasha, is that wise?"

"Is that—" I stop and do a double-take. "'Wise'? Fuck 'wise,' Kosti. For six months, I've stuck around this godforsaken fucking pit in the woods, waiting for a chance to *do* something. I won't sit around anymore."

"But to go in guns blazing—"

"Do you see a choice? I don't." I slam drawers and start filling a duffel with everything I'll need: knives, pistols, magazines. Static crackles across my vision.

He stays mired in the doorway. "You could choose to wait until you don't have to crawl down the stairs, for starters."

"I don't need my legs to put a bullet in a Serbian's skull, Kosti." I zip the duffel closed. "I just need a trigger finger."

Kosti sighs. "Is this really about Jasmine? Or is this about—"

"Don't say it."

"Because if it is about—"

"Don't fucking say it, man."

"—then do you really think Ariel would want you to risk—"

Three strides take me to him. I fist his collar and lift him off his feet, slamming him hard enough against the wall for the hung mirror to wobble.

"I warned you not to say her name."

He doesn't struggle. Just watches me with that infuriating Mona Lisa smirk. "You think I can't see the wheels turning in your head, son? Save Jasmine; earn sainthood in Ariel's eyes. Return triumphant. Disney fucking ending."

"Fuck. You." My spittle dots his glasses. "This is about stopping Dragan and nothing else."

"Then why," he wheezes, "are your first words always about *Ariel?*"

The gun is in my left hand before I realize it's moving. Barrel pressed to the sagging flesh beneath his jaw. Kosti's pulse drums against cold steel.

"Say her name one more time," I snarl. "I fucking dare you."

His Adam's apple bobs. "This rage isn't Serbian blood on your boots, Sasha. It's *her* blood in your veins. You miss her. You—"

I roar and drop him. He crumples to the ground and I loom over him, breath sawing, finger white on the trigger as I aim it down.

"Make the calls. Get a jet ready."

Kosti laughs. "Or what? You'll shoot me? Go ahead. Faster than waiting for Dragan to end your farce." He spits on the floor, then wipes his mouth on a sleeve. "She won't take you back, you know. Even if you save her sister."

I turn away in disgust. "Jasmine's mine to protect. My debt."

"Since when?"

"Since I made her a corpse in her sister's eyes."

Kosti staggers up and gestures to the duffel I just filled with weapons. "If you go like this, you'll get them all killed. Dragan's expecting—"

I silence him with a stare. "Dragan isn't expecting shit. As far as he knows, I've been dead for six months. Let me stay that way a little longer."

The cabin door slams behind me. The moon bleeds white through pines. In the northern fields, deer freeze at the stink of murder on the wind.

I climb into Kosti's truck and twist the keys, bringing the engine roaring to life. But a moment later, the passenger door opens and Kosti gets in, groaning softly with the effort.

I eye him. "Are you sure?"

"I'm old, not dead," he snaps. "And besides, Jasmine is my niece, not yours. Drive the fucking car."

6

ARIEL

I'm up in the middle of the night again, blue light from my laptop painting my face. Sleep was too full of dreams and the summer air is too sticky to be comfortable for a beach ball with bladder control issues like me.

The cursor on my screen blinks. It hasn't moved in three days.

Dear Sasha,

They have your nose.

"Fuck this," I mutter under my breath. I pause to make sure Jasmine didn't hear me. But the steady murmur of her breathing continues unbothered.

I rise, careful not to scrape the chair over the floorboards, and waddle to the door. It's surprisingly smooth to slip out of the apartment, given my current girth. I may be a whale, but I'm a ninja whale.

Once I'm outside and down the stairs, I can breathe again. I just needed a little distance from that folder filled with bits and pieces of love I'm going to give to children who will never know their father. It was suffocating me, full-on claustrophobia.

Out here, though, the world is wide open. The breeze is cool and salty and the sky is filled with stars.

I make for the beach. No one and nothing else is out, not even clouds, so the sea churns with shards of white glass that get consumed and born again with each new set of waves.

The sand is cool between my toes. Midnight tides hiss and retreat, hiss and retreat, like the ocean is trying to scrub the shore clean. My flip-flops dangle from one hand, a half-melted Snickers bar from the other. The twins have been demanding chocolate all day, and I'm nothing if not their humble servant.

I press a palm to the side of my belly where a tiny heel juts. "Easy, slugger. Mama's walking."

The kick softens.

I take another bite of Snickers and stare at the black water. Back in New York, the Hudson never looked like this—all hungry and endless. Here, the Atlantic is a living thing. It breathes. It watches. It knows.

Just like him.

Stop it.

I crush the candy wrapper in my fist. Six months. Six months of pretending the ache in my chest is heartburn, that the hollow behind my ribs is just the twins stealing all my organs for legroom. Six months of biting my tongue every time Jas says, *He deserves to know,* like it's a fucking Hallmark card I'd be sending him and not a live grenade.

Another kick, harder this time. "You, too, huh?" I mutter. "Taking her side already?"

I keep walking, but when I reach the pier, I decide that's far enough and I turn back toward home. I see my first creature —a ghost crab—but it scuttles away across the white sand as soon as it hears me coming.

He'd hate this place, I think, crunching a seashell underfoot. *Too quiet. No shadows to own.*

My cell phone vibrates in my pocket. I pull it out to see Jasmine's name lighting up the screen.

JAS: *Where'd u go?*

ARI: *walking on the beach. be back soon.*

JAS: *You scared me. Woke up and you weren't here.*

ARI: *I'm fine. go back to sleep, worrywart.*

JAS: *Mkay. Love you.*

It's another few minutes of quiet walking, my bare feet skimming across the sand, before I make the turn inland, crest the dunes, and go down our street. The moon is behind me now, casting a silhouette that somehow manages to make my belly seem even bigger than it is in real life.

I laugh, rub it, and ask the night, "Does this shadow make me look fat?"

I'm still chuckling as I round the corner of our block—when a double flicker of orange snags my eye.

I freeze.

Cigarettes glow. Three of them. Three orange pinpricks, floating in the dark at the foot of the building's stairs.

For a second, I'm fifteen again—standing in the cathedral, looking at a casket that didn't hold my sister's body. It's the same icy trickle down my spine. The same copper stink of *wrongness* in my nose.

The twins roll, a slow, tectonic shift that leaves me breathless. "You're being paranoid," I tell them.

Their silence isn't reassuring.

I peek out again. I don't see anything at first. Are they gone? Were they ever even there in the first place? Am I hallucinating, dreaming, or—?

There.

I lunge back behind the corner of the building, out of sight. This time, I'm sure I saw them. A trio of shadows too tall for the squat French buildings. Parked motorcycles glinting under the moon.

I pick up a broken bottle lying in the gutter and use it as a reflection so I can peer around the corner without sticking my head out. It's shoddy, but good enough to confirm everything.

My blood turns to slush. The Snickers wrapper slips from my fingers.

Serbian license plates. Black leather jackets. The glint of a gold chain—

No. No, that's impossible. We've been careful. Changed our names. Paid cash. Never stayed anywhere more than—

One of the men turns. Moonlight slicks across the tattoo crawling up his neck.

A double-headed eagle.

Dragan's mark.

I grab the stone wall of the fish market to keep from falling. My pulse thunders in my ears, drowning out the waves. They found us. They fucking found us.

Move. Move, you idiot.

But my feet are concrete. My lungs are origami. Half a block away, in the bungalow, Jasmine is sleeping with her bedroom window cracked open, utterly exposed behind a door that we never bother to lock.

I text Jas with fumbling fingers.

ARI: *GET OUT NOW*

She doesn't answer.

The man with the eagle tattoo says something in Serbian. His companions laugh, low and mean. They're looking at our door. At the easy latch. At the dark windows.

My hand flies to my belly. "Okay," I whisper. "New plan."

The dumpster yields a splintered oar. I heft it like a baseball bat. It's heavier than my old Louisville Slugger from my high school softball days, but weekly prenatal yoga must finally be paying off, because it goes smoothly when I give it a test swing.

"Stay with me, guys," I murmur, creeping along the wall. The men haven't spotted me yet. They're too busy arguing over a crumpled photo. Even from here, I recognize Jas's smile.

Rage burns through the fear. These pricks took my father. My career. My whole damn life.

They don't get to take her, too.

But even as I approach, I think the name I swore I wouldn't let myself think anymore: *I wish Sasha was here.*

He'd know what to do. He'd bash these bastards' skulls together and make lasagna of their brains. He'd stand between me and danger, between Jas and danger. He'd keep us safe. He swore he'd always keep us safe.

But he's not here, is he? He isn't here and he isn't coming. It's just us. Just me.

I take a deep breath and heft the oar high.

Ready.

Set.

G—

Then hands reach out to drag me backward into the dark.

7

SASHA

This French village stinks of fish markets and diesel. A far cry from the Adirondacks' pine-scented purgatory.

I'll take it.

Fuck, I'll take anything that's not sap and summer grass. If I stayed in that shack for another day, I might've gone insane. This is better. This is good.

This is what I was born to do.

It was embarrassingly easy to pick off one of Dragan's men in Marseille and make him talk. I've had six months to plan what I'd do when I got a Serbian rat in my hands. He sang like a fucking canary.

When he'd given us everything he knew, we dumped his body in the Seine and followed the trail he drew out in his own blood. From Marseille to Montpellier, through Toulouse, into Bordeaux country. A handful of hostel owners along the way added to the story—some from bribes, some from brutality. It all led us here.

Moliets-et-Maa. A mistake on the map. Not even flyover country; it's really just nothing at all, a place for people who want to be nowhere.

It makes sense that Jasmine would come here.

Why, though? Did something spook her? Why'd she run? How'd she slip away?

I suppose those answers don't matter. She *is* here; that's what matters.

And so are men who want to kill her.

Kosti and I waited on the outskirts of town for night to fall. He smoked cigarette after cigarette while we sat. I just brooded. When the dead of dark was finally upon us, I stepped out of the car and started to walk.

Now, I'm crouched in the darkness at the foot of a three-story apartment building. At the far end of the block, Kosti is circling from the other direction. I don't intend for him to do much—any drop of Serbian blood that I don't get to spill myself is wasted, in my opinion. But it doesn't hurt to have him there to ward them in my direction instead.

They're so close. Ripe for the plucking. I want to gut them all now. But I have to wait until the time is right.

Patience, I tell myself. *Your body is not what it was six months ago. Give yourself the margin of error.*

It's hard to preach *patience* when every cell in that body is wired with adrenaline. I've sat on my fucking haunches for six months while the world kept spinning without me.

While Jasmine lay unguarded.

While Ariel—

Patience, Sashenka. That won't help you now. Focus on what's in front of you.

As I watch, the Serbians drop their cigarettes and grind them out beneath their heels. One man's shirt raises and I see the glint of a gun. They turn as one to start the trek up the stairs, clustered close together like invading roaches.

Patience...

Patience...

Then—movement. A scuffle at the far end of the block. A muffled cry. Alley cats squabbling, probably.

The Serbians snap toward the noise.

They never see me coming.

One second, I'm shadow; the next, I'm storm. I'm on the tallest one before he can turn back. My blade slips between his ribs like butter. He chokes, warm blood spilling over my knuckles.

The second man spins and cries out, swinging a crowbar at my head. I duck, sweep his legs, and bury my knife in his throat before he hits the ground.

Blood sprays the stucco.

But I'm already moving, pivoting left to face the last man standing. He fumbles to unholster his gun.

Idiot.

I kick his wrist. Bone cracks. He screams and the gun goes flying. I catch the pistol mid-air, spin it around, and jam the barrel under his chin. *"Gde je Dragan?"*

His eyes go wide at the Serbian coming from my tongue. He probably thinks he's seeing a fucking boogeyman. All things considered, he's not so far off.

"F-f-fu—"

No more patience.

The shot paints the wall. Then—silence.

Blood drips from my fingertips. It's a mess, a bloodbath at the foot of these stairs, but I've done the world a service. Three fewer Vukovic men is a good thing.

My shoulder screams and my knuckles are split, but fuck it— it feels good to be a monster again.

A crash echoes from the alley. Distant shouts—female, strangely enough. I frown. But that's Kosti's problem. Surely he can handle one Frenchwoman.

I take the stairs two at a time. The door opens easily. Not even locked. I growl in displeasure, low in my throat, and slip inside.

The smell is strong. Cleaning product base, with notes of jasmine and—surely that's not fucking peaches, is it?

No. Of course not. I'm hallucinating, smelling what I want to smell. I need to get my shit together. The rust might not be all gone after all.

It's quiet and still inside, which is surprising, given the ruckus of murder that just took place right downstairs. My heartbeat quickens. They didn't take her already, did they?

You're too late, ssyklo. *She's already gone—*

A floorboard creaks behind me.

I turn.

She comes at me in a blur of curls and fury, a kitchen knife aimed at my heart.

Fuck.

"*Nyet!*" I snarl, slamming her against the wall by her wrist. Plaster dust rains as she struggles to bring the blade down into my chest. Her heartbeat thrashes against mine. Violin-calloused fingertips.

Jasmine.

Alive.

"You fucking bastards!" she rasps. "I'll—"

"Open your eyes, Jasmine."

She freezes. Blinks. Peels her eyelids apart.

When she does, recognition floods her face. "... S-Sasha?"

I twist the knife from her grip. It clatters to the floor. She stumbles back, chest heaving, hands raised like she's waiting for the blow.

"I was starting to think you might be dead."

"That's a piss-poor '*thank you for saving my life,*'" I growl.

She rubs the sleep from her eyes. "I never know what to thank you for, honestly. Some days, I appreciate what you did. Others... I'm not so sure it was for me."

"Somehow," I snap, "your gratitude got even worse the second time around." I grab her by the upper arm and start to drag her to the door. "Regardless, we don't have time for this shit. I just killed three Serbs on your doorstep, and if I know anything about Dragan, there are more coming. We need to go, now."

She digs her heels in. "I'm not leaving Ari."

"I don't have time to deal with your—"

Wait.

Wait a fucking second.

Icy dread strokes down my spine. I feel graveyard chill all over, head to toe, inside and out. My mouth hardly cooperates, but I manage to rasp out, "… Who?"

Before Jasmine can answer, footsteps thunder up the stairs. I shove her behind me and turn, bloody knife clutched tight in my hand, to face the doorway.

It bursts open. Kosti charges through first, face stricken with something I can't explain. His eyes find mine. "Sasha…"

More footsteps sound out behind him. My gaze flits from Kosti, to the black rectangle of the entryway.

It fills slowly. A white linen sundress stretched to its absolute maximum in the attempt to contain the belly beneath it.

Then bare feet. Female. Dainty.

Above that, the tip of a broken oar. I trace up the oar, to the hand holding it, to the tanned arm, the familiar shoulder curve, a collarbone I've spent hours nipping and kissing…

To a throat I once looped a belt around.

To lips I've kissed, lips that have whispered my name after the words *I love you.*

And last of all, to green eyes that stare back at me with a hate I put there myself.

No.

No.

No.

Ariel stops in the doorway. Shock melts to horror melts to rage. Her grip tightens on the oar.

"You," she spits.

For six fucking months, I've done my best to bleed this woman out of my head. To cut memories of her out of me, stitch by painful stitch.

I should've known I'd meet her here, in this forgotten corner of the world, my hands dripping red for her again.

"Ptich—"

"Don't." She swings wild. The oar catches my shoulder. Agony explodes. My vision whites out. "Don't you *dare* say that to me!"

Jasmine grabs her arm to stop her from swinging the broken oar again "He's here to help!"

"He's here to *lie*!" Tears streak Ariel's cheeks. She jabs the oar at my chest. "Another rescue? Another *favor*? What's your angle this time, Sasha?"

I don't flinch. Let her project her hate onto me. I deserve it, every last drop.

Footfalls echo on the street. More Serbs. A lot fucking more.

"We need to get out of here first," I snarl, ripping the Glock from my waistband. "We can bicker after."

Ariel's laugh is broken glass. "Fuck you."

Bang.

A lamp disintegrates as a bullet clips it from the open window. Jasmine yelps. Ariel freezes.

Instinct kicks in. I tackle them both behind the couch and spread myself over them for cover as the rest of the window shatters. More bullets chew plaster.

"Back door!" Jasmine wheezes.

"Covered," I snap.

"So we die here?!" Ariel's eyes are bright green in the midnight gloom.

I press the Glock into her palm. Her fingers tremble. "Trust me."

She spits at my feet. "Never."

Growling, I grab her face, and *fuck me,* it's so soft between my fingertips. She's sun-kissed now, but still velvety to the touch. I look at her eyes because I can't bear to let my gaze drop to her pregnant belly and all the implications it holds. "You can tell me to go fuck yourself once you're safe. For now, though, I need you to trust me."

She searches my face. For once, I let her see it all—the fear, the want, the rot left by my father's hands.

Her resolve cracks. "One time only."

"That's all I need."

Ariel hesitates. Then she slips her hand into mine.

It fits.

It *fits.*

We run.

8

ARIEL

When we finally reach the highway at the edge of town, I rip free of Sasha's hand.

He turns and glowers at me. "The car is ten feet away, and *now*, you're stopping?"

Blood is rushing in my ears as I square off with him, my belly jutting between us like a physical reminder of all the reasons that I need to stand my ground. "We're safe now. You don't get to drag me back into hell just because you've got a hero complex."

Sasha's stare drops to my stomach for half a heartbeat—the first real acknowledgment—before snapping back to mine. "We're not anywhere near safe. You think your self-righteous tantrum matters right now? Get. In. The. Car."

"No."

Jasmine steps between us, hands raised. "Ari, please—"

"We're not going with him, Jas!" My voice falters. The twins kick hard, like they're trying to burrow out. "We'll find another way."

Sasha's jaw muscle thrums as he glares at me. I try not to catalog him the way he's clearly doing to me, but I can't help it. I can't help the sinking gut feeling I get when I see scars I know weren't there before. His posture is stiff, like he's been pieced back together with masking tape and hope.

What broke him?

"You're pregnant," he snarls.

"Observant."

"For how long?"

"Long enough to know you don't get a say in what I do."

I resent the implication that they aren't his—and then I resent myself for resenting that, because it's not like I owe Sasha anything. We weren't married. We never made promises. If I wanted to get pregnant by some other man, that would be well within my rights.

But you didn't *want that, did you?* croons the voice in my head that belongs to a sniveling little instigator who likes stirring up drama for no good reason. *You still felt that tether to him like you'd never left. You thought putting an ocean between you would sever it, but it didn't do anything of the sort. If anything, it only made you feel that much more how deep his hooks are buried in your heart.*

I tell that voice to shut the fuck up.

Sasha steps closer. I smell blood on him—Serbian blood. Old violence, fresh sweat. "You think I'd hurt my child?"

"I think you'll use anything you could get your hands on," I fire back. "Just like you used me."

His scowl deepens. He opens his mouth to reply—but before he can, a thunderclap of distant motorcycles grabs all our attention.

In unison, all four of us look down the road. It's a long, straight highway, so we can see a mile or so into the distance.

And in that distance, headlights shine bright.

More Serbians.

"This is fucking ridiculous," Sasha growls. He stomps away and yanks the car door open. The lights flick on and catch the scar around his throat, pulsing red as his jaw clenches. "You can argue, but you're going to do it in a moving vehicle. Not standing on the side of the road like a sitting fucking duck."

"Or what?" I jab a finger into his chest. His scarred, ruined chest. "You'll drag me? Chain me to your bumper?"

"I'll do what's necessary to keep you safe."

"Try it."

He does.

One second, I'm glaring up at him; the next, I'm scooped up in his arms like a baby. He's careful to keep my belly safe—but I have no intentions of treating him anywhere near as carefully.

"Put me down!" I beat his back. "You psychotic Neanderthal—"

"Keep hitting me," he interrupts calmly, striding toward the car. "You might fix all the shit that's broken."

Engines snarl in the distance. Closer. Too close.

Over Sasha's shoulder, I see Jasmine and Kosti looking nervously at each other. Then, as the bark of accelerating motorcycles rings out again in the night, they both jump into the car.

Sasha dumps me into the passenger side, then slams the door and locks it before I can crawl my way out.

"Seatbelt," he orders, sliding into the driver's seat.

"Go to hell."

He reaches over and yanks the belt across me himself. As he does, his knuckles graze my belly—and we both freeze.

His eyes meet mine. It only lasts a second, but some seconds last centuries. This is one of them. I feel like I'm hallucinating as the last six months replay in my mind—only this time, Sasha is there for all of it.

Hugging me to his chest when I bring out a pregnancy test cradled in my palms. I can feel his proud grin without having to look.

The first scan—fingers interlaced with mine, patting me on the thigh. "It's all gonna be okay. We get to meet our baby soon."

The reveal of twins. Twice the amount of love to give and share. Not shock, but pride and joy doubling, just when we thought we'd already maxed out on both emotions.

Sasha doting. Sasha guarding. Sasha loving. Sasha there.

I see all of that in his eyes. I don't know what he sees in mine, and I don't want to ask. I'd rather just rip my gaze away so these visions I didn't want disappear.

The engines roar louder.

"Sasha," Kosti warns.

He snaps the belt into place. Peels out before I can breathe.

Tires screech. The car lurches forward, throwing me back against the seat. Behind us, headlights swarm—motorcycles, four, five, six, more—charging down the one-lane highway like a horde of wasps.

We've got a hundred yards on them, maybe less, and this rental car isn't exactly *Need for Speed* material. Sasha guns it even harder.

"You're going to kill us!" I scream.

"You'd prefer Dragan does it?" He downshifts, veering onto a coastal road. Cliffs drop to our left, hungry waves below.

Another bullet shatters the rear windshield. Jasmine screams, ducking. Glass rains.

"Hold on!" Sasha wrenches the wheel. The car fishtails, tires spitting sand. For one heart-stopping second, we teeter on the cliff's edge.

Then he mashes the gas.

I close my eyes and scream. Sasha's hand flies to my knee, squeezes once—*I'm here*—before snatching back like I burned him.

But the maneuver works. We straighten out and take off like a cannonball, soaring down an adjacent road that the motorcycles can't follow. For a few minutes, there's no sound but the tires chewing up highway and our own softening breaths.

The road curves inland. Olive groves whip past. Finally, Jasmine speaks up. "Where are we going?"

"East," Sasha grunts. "Geneva. There's a plane—"

"No."

Sasha looks at me, brow furrowed. "Ari—"

"Stop the car."

"Ari—"

"Stop the *fucking* car, Sasha!"

Gritting his teeth, he finds a side road, pulls off, and cuts the headlights. We're still out in the countryside, so darkness plunges around us. Clouds block out most of the moon. It's vague suggestions of shapes around us, nothing more.

Sasha's voice, though, is very clear. "What the fuck, Ariel?"

"We're not going east—or north, south, or west, either. We're not going anywhere with you." I reach out to find Jasmine in the darkness and clutch her close to me. "Come on, Jas."

She hesitates. "Ariel, be reasonable—"

"He's the reason we're in this mess!" My voice breaks. "He's the reason Baba's dead!"

Sasha goes very still. "Leander knew the risks."

"He knew *you*!" I shove the door open. Cool air floods in. "You're a plague, Sasha. Everything you touch dies."

His face shutters. "Then run."

"Gladly."

"But," he adds, "if you run, I'll chase you. Is that what you want our kid's first memory to be? Daddy tackling Mommy into a ditch?"

Daddy. What a fucking word.

I jump out of the car and stride away. Sasha follows, leaving Jasmine and Kosti marooned in the car behind us. "They're twins," I say quietly when he catches up to me. "And you don't get to call them yours."

"Twins." Sasha's voice is stunned. Then the bite comes back. "Fine. Twins. They're mine, aren't they?"

"Says who?"

He's close enough that I can feel his breath pluming across my face. "Look me in the eye and tell me they aren't."

Tension ripples between us. I don't have to see Sasha to know he's brooding, glaring, that slanted V of his eyebrows sharpening to a knife tip.

"I hate you," I whisper.

"Don't bother. I hate me enough for the both of us." He shifts, gravel stirring under his boots. "But I'll be damned if I leave you out here to die, Ariel. Like it or not, you're coming with me. At least until I can ensure you're safe."

"Sash—"

"You owe me this," I say. "If those are my children—and I know in my bones they are—then it falls to me to keep them safe. Let me do that much. Choose us. Choose *them*."

His hand—just one fingertip—kisses my belly. For as long as it's touching me, I let myself hope.

Then he pulls it away. Tears sting my eyes. "Fuck you, Sasha Ozerov."

A cloud thins out and lets enough moonlight through to pick out the blue of his eyes. They're locked onto mine like they'll never, ever look away.

He nods once. Then he turns and stomps back to the car.

And, God help me...

I follow.

9

ARIEL

The engine hums a lullaby. My head lolls against the window, glass cool on my cheek. I bite back a wince every time that a bump in the road jostles the babies into a fresh revolt.

But even if the little ones weren't crying wolf over and over again, I'd still be uneasy. I feel like a bug getting thrown around by a wind that doesn't give a damn where I go or how unpleasant the journey is. I'm the Itsy Bitsy Spider, and this car ride here is just another trip back down the water spout.

Sasha's aftershave clings to the cramped air—cigarette ash, mint, and cedar. Familiar. Safe.

I hate how it steadies my pulse.

Jasmine pretends to sleep in the backseat. Kosti doesn't pretend at all—his snores are the loudest thing in all of southern France. At least that's the same as it's always been.

I do my best to keep my gaze fixed on the rearview mirror. The bullet hole in it soaks up moonlight and cracks jitter across the reflective surface. I don't think Uncle Kosti is getting his rental deposit back—this car's as battle-scarred as the man driving it.

Sasha radiates heat from the driver's seat, grip tight on the wheel. It's hard not to look at him. He's always seemed to have a gravity of his own. I fought against it for a while, then danced in it for a while after that. Now, I just want it out of my life.

The twins kick again, sharp and sudden. I stifle a gasp, though I can't stop my hands from flying to the swell.

Sasha's gaze darts to me.

"Don't." I turn away from him. "Just drive."

He sighs and looks back at the road.

I wake up with a jolt when I feel the car leave the road. First, two tires, then four, go from asphalt to bumpy dirt. I look out the window to see the dullest gray light beginning to leak over the horizon.

Shit. I slept for longer than I meant to.

"What? Huh—Where—?"

"They'll be on every major highway looking for us," Sasha explains without shifting his eyes to me. "And even if we duck Serbian eyes, driving a Peugeot with bullet holes in it doesn't exactly scream 'under the radar.' Do you want to explain to a French cop where we're going and where we're headed?"

I cross my arms over my chest. "A simple 'resting for a while' would have sufficed."

He steers us through a gap in some collapsing wooden fencing and then behind a farmhouse set half a mile from the road. The thing has seen better days. Half the roof is caved in and bird shit cakes the siding in streaks of white.

"Not exactly the Four Seasons Paris," he murmurs. "My apologies."

I roll my eyes. "I'll survive."

I glance in the back. Jas is asleep, effortlessly beautiful, like she's ready to star in a shampoo commercial as soon as she opens her eyes. Uncle Kosti, on the other hand, has his mouth wide open. Only when the car comes to a final stop do they both wake up.

"Eh? Eh?" mumbles Kosti.

"We're resting here until sundown," Sasha says, opening the door. "Get comfortable. More importantly, stay the fuck out of sight."

"He's got a way with words, doesn't he, girls?" grumbles Kosti as he emerges from the vehicle.

Jasmine, with one look at the tension on my face, comes to give me a reassuring squeeze of the hand.

Sasha told us to get comfortable, but comfort doesn't come easy. The four of us disperse to different corners of the barn. Jas and Kosti go up high, bedding down in haystacks. I'd follow them, but rotting ladders seem like a bad idea in my condition.

Instead, I try to sit propped against a barrel, a tractor wheel, and a pile of old saddles, but each one is more uncomfortable than the last. I can't stop thinking about how many critters must've called this place home over the years, and how many might still. Every time I think I'm about to drift off, an itch or a tingle sends me jolting back upright.

Sleeping during the day is odd, too. Sun peeks through the gaps in the roof like it's squinting in, trying to see who's here and why. I throw an arm over my eyes to block it.

But lightning bolts go racing through my hips when I try to adjust my position, and just like that, I know sleep isn't in the cards for me tonight. Today. Whatever.

I open my eyes...

... and across the room, I see Sasha looking back at me.

We stare at each other through the dusty gloom. His gaze drops to my belly first—always the belly, an instinct he can't seem to quit—before dragging up to meet mine. For a few thundering moments, I'm back in his penthouse, tangled in sheets that smelled like his stupid cologne, whispering promises we both thought might actually stand the test of time.

I wrench my gaze away before he says something. Seeing him here, now, like this—it's too much. It would be too much if it were just him, without all the baggage he's brought along for the ride. But for it to be him *and* Dragan's reaching, grabbing fingers, the ever-present cloud of danger that hovers over Sasha's head... That's far, far too much.

I close my eyes and pretend I'm sleeping again.

Fabric rustles. Footsteps approach. I tense as Sasha's shadow falls over me. He drops a canteen in my lap. "Drink."

"I'm not thirsty."

"Your lips are cracked, your voice is hoarse, and I know you haven't had a sip of anything in at least twelve hours." When I still don't move, he crouches—slow, predator cautious—and unscrews the cap. "Sit up and take one sip."

I stay wrapped tight around my belly. "Make me."

His throat bobs. Then, with a growl, he slides an arm under my shoulders and hauls me upright. Through the gap in his shirt, I see a bandage I hadn't noticed before—with fresh blood blooming through the gauze.

"Christ, Sasha—"

"Drink. Don't worry about me."

I swallow a few bitter gulps just to wipe that look off his face —some unholy mix of concern and possession. The water's warm. Tastes like his sweat. Like shared air in a car that's waiting for one or the other of us to drive it right off the edge of a cliff.

His thumb touches my lower lip, catching a stray droplet. "Better?"

Electricity arcs where skin touches skin. I jerk back. "Don't touch me."

His jaw clenches, but his hand falls. He rises and steps back. "Try to sleep."

"Where are you going?"

"Perimeter check." He tosses the words over his shoulder. "Stay put."

The barn door screeches open, then slams shut. The silence that follows washes his absence clean. My fingers drift to my lips, still tingling from his touch.

"Asshole," I tell the twins. "Your father is a total fucking asshole."

Their answering kick feels suspiciously like laughter.

Twilight finds me perched on an overturned crate, squinting at a tractor operator's manual by the watery light filtering through filthy windows, just to take my mind off things. Unlike me, Jasmine has had no problem sleeping. I can hear her breathing soft and even in the shadowy corner overhead.

A wooden creak signals Sasha's return. He's shirtless and covered in a light sheen of sweat from whatever the hell he was doing out there. The sight of scars and scabs rippling across his torso makes my heart clench up—but I tell myself I'm not allowed to ask questions.

What's the point? Would you sympathize with him? Do you feel as if the man you knew, the body that gave you these babies... Do you think that man is gone? Damaged? Broken beyond repair? Or worse—what if you're the only one who can repair him? Can you? Should you? Is it your job to save him?

Can you, Ariel?

Should you, Ariel?

I pretend to be consumed by the technical ins and outs of the T293's instrument panel, as described in French. I can sense Sasha's presence, though. He's looking at me again. I really wish he wouldn't.

"Quit looming," I say without looking up. "You're making the babies nervous."

A derisive snort. "The babies? Or their mother?"

"Don't start with me now."

He sighs. Uncle Kosti unleashes a thundering snore from the upper level, then settles back into sleep-addled mumbling. "I didn't intend for this to happen, you know. We came to protect Jasmine. Nothing more. Nothing less."

I drop the manual to the ground as I whirl on him. "And yet now, she's on the run once again, with bad men breathing down her neck. Your 'protecting' has a funny way of getting people in trouble, Sasha."

He regards me from where he's leaning against a support beam, arms folded across his chest. I wish I could resist looking him up and down, but I've failed at that since the moment we met. Even now, seething at him for what he's done, what he's brought to my doorstep, the momentary bubble of peace I'd almost convinced myself would last forever... Even now, I can't help noticing how beautiful he is.

He's taller than I remember. I think I shrunk him in my memory just so he'd be easier to ignore. If he was small, I could stick him in a mental drawer and never linger on him again. But in this reality, he's huge, with dark curls matted down with sweat and a beard that's grown thick enough to verge on wild. His nose has a crook in it that wasn't there before, but the tormented smirk underneath is the same.

It's the eyes that've changed most. There's a sadness to their depths that I definitely would've noticed. A molten, churning sadness.

Actually, on second thought, maybe that *was* always there. What I'm certain is new are the injuries. He's a patchwork quilt of ugly stitch scars and fading bruises. His skin is mottled in half a dozen different colors—blue, purple, green, yellow, red, black. A bandage looped haphazardly around his abdomen, the one I saw when he threw the canteen at me earlier, is drenched into a nauseating copper.

"You're a mess," I whisper.

He laughs. "Inside and out."

I reach out toward him. Stop myself. Reach out again. Sasha watches me the whole time, moving neither to help me nor to stop me. Eventually, I give in to the impulse.

The bandages peel away with a sickening tug. Underneath it, his wound is obscene—a jagged canyon carved through muscle, surrounded by bruises in every shade of rotten fruit. The stitches look like something from a taxidermy project. Even Frankenstein's monster would call this shoddy work.

"Who did this?" I ask. "Feliks after one too many vodka shots?"

"Dragan's parting gift." His muscles jump under my touch.

God, the mere thought of the stories underlying those three little words makes me sick to my stomach. How did Dragan get close enough to do this? Sasha is so strong, so careful and capable—so what was he doing that gave Dragan the chance?

The implied answer is obvious.

You, Ariel.

He was protecting you.

I just told him that his protection has a funny way of getting people killed. Did he almost join that club?

I accidentally graze a fingertip too close to the reopened wound and he hisses.

"Sorry," I mumble. "Sorry, I shouldn't have— Just, sorry."

He nods and touches a palm to it. It comes away smeared with blood. "It's fine. I ripped it trying to keep your sister from stabbing me through the face, actually. She'd be pleased to know she did some damage after all."

I snort. "She doesn't hate you like I do, unfortunately."

"I'd get it if she did."

"Same. And believe me, I've tried to talk her into it. No dice, though. She's a saint. We don't deserve her. Well, I don't. And actually, you definitely don't, either."

Sasha laughs, but the wince passes over his face again when the effort forces his abs to tighten and tug at the wound again.

I frown. "That's not a light graze, Sasha."

"I'm fine. It's just—"

"You're not fine," I interrupt. "You're a bullheaded man, just like the rest of them." I jab a finger at a nearby bench. "Sit down. I saw a first aid kit in the car."

I go to fetch it. When I come back in with the kit in hand, I'm half-surprised to see that he actually listened. He must really be hurting; the Sasha I know—the Sasha I *knew,* rather— would never have taken orders. He'd have been defiant for defiance's sake.

Who broke him? I wonder again.

I'm even more surprised that he lets me take off the bandages and start to dab disinfectant on the edges of the wound. I'm very, very careful not to allow myself to touch him. I know too well what happens when skin touches skin.

After all, this entire saga began when he pulled out a first aid kit and began tending to me.

"Dragan did a thorough job," I mutter.

Sasha scowls. "Not as thorough as he would've liked. I won't make that same mistake when the tables are turned."

I shake my head in disgust as I dip another cotton ball into the hydrogen peroxide. "Good to see you've learned your lesson about these stupid power squabbles." I feel like Mama, slamming kitchen cabinets and muttering about *men and their wars.* It used to seem like a grand thing she was rebelling against. Now that I'm in her shoes, though, I just feel disgusted. "Wars" aren't grand or awe-inspiring; they're just bleeding gut wounds festering in abandoned French farms. Nothing grand or awe-inspiring about that.

"Those 'squabbles' would've had you chopped up into half a dozen different pieces if I didn't intervene," he growls.

"Again with the hero act. Do you ever give it a rest?"

"Not when it's your neck on the line, Ariel." His eyes, when I glance up, are burning icy blue.

I gulp and go rummaging back in the first aid kit, just to have something to do with my hands. We're quiet for a little while.

"You should've told me you were pregnant," he says softly. It's not quite a reprimand, like I would've expected. It's too soft for that. Almost… plaintive? Like he's sad for the time he's missed.

But fuck that. He doesn't get to be sad. I didn't make any choices that he didn't force me into himself.

My hands go still. The warehouse breathes around us—wind

through broken windows, the creak of Sasha's jaw as he grinds his teeth.

"Would it have changed anything?" I ask quietly.

He doesn't answer.

I pack the wound with gauze, fingers stroking the hard planes of his stomach. His breath hitches. My own throat tightens.

Too close. Always too close.

"There." I sit back, wiping bloody hands on my dress. "Try not to make it even worse."

He catches my wrist as I stand. "Your turn."

"For what?"

"You're limping."

I rip my wrist away from him and laugh right in his face. "I'm pregnant with twins, Sasha. Everything hurts."

He stands in one fluid motion, crowding me against the wall. The splintered wood digs into my spine. His hands hover over my hips, not touching, but the heat of him seeps into my skin anyway.

"Let me help," he rasps.

"You don't get to help." My voice wavers. "You don't get to swoop in and act like some white knight after—"

"After what?" His eyes glitter. "After I loved you? After I failed you?"

The word hangs between us—*loved*, past tense—and something inside me wails in self-pity.

Jasmine's voice cuts through the dark. "Ari? You okay down there?"

"Yeah." I duck under Sasha's arm. "Peachy."

I'm starting to stride away when he speaks up again. "I didn't come back to ruin your life, you know."

That draws a derisive laugh out of me. "No? But that's your favorite game." I turn back to face him. "But yeah, sure, you didn't come back to ruin everything; that's just a fun, natural byproduct of you doing what you want all the time, and fuck what it means for anyone else, right?"

"Ariel—"

"You came back because you couldn't stand—couldn't fucking *stand*—the thought of me existing outside of your control. That's what you came back, Sasha. At least do me the courtesy of saying it to my face."

The thickening darkness hollows out his cheeks and turns his eyes to mercury. "You think this is about control?"

"With you, everything is about control."

"Not with you." He growls in his throat. "When I kissed you in that library... When I—" He cuts himself off, jaw working side to side. "That wasn't control. None of it. That was surrender."

My heart stutters. "Don't start using words like that, Sasha."

He steps closer. The farmhouse seems to hold its breath. "You asked me once why I wouldn't fall in love. Let me answer now—it's because love is the one thing my father couldn't beat out of me. The one weakness he never found. But you..." He touches my cheekbone. "You made it look so *easy*."

I knock his hand away. "You don't get to rewrite history now. You lied. You manipulated. You let me think—"

"I know what I did." His voice drops. "And if I could carve those lies out of the past, I would. But I can't. So all I can offer is this—" He presses my palm to his chest. His heartbeat thunders against my skin. "However long we have left. However you'll have me."

I wrench free and turn so I don't have to look at him anymore. With my back to him, I say, "We have until Jas and I are safe. Then you're going to walk away from us, Sasha. And I'll never see you again."

I can feel him lingering. Waiting. His breath rattles in the silence.

"You're right," he says finally. "I should walk away. That would be the noble thing to do."

I pause at the barn door, hand on the rusted handle. Outside, crickets chirp a deafening symphony.

"But I never claimed to be a noble man."

10

SASHA

The Italian border guard's flashlight rakes across the car window. Kosti breathes quietly in the seat next to me. I keep my hands loose on the wheel, bloodied bandage carefully tucked beneath the hem of my shirt, eyes straight ahead.

When he turns his attention to the back seat, the guard's gaze lingers on Ariel's swollen belly, her death grip on the door handle, the way Jasmine's arm drapes protectively around her sister's shoulders like she's twelve again and guarding her from their father's drunken rages.

Family vacation, I want to sneer. *We're the fucking Partridge Family with bullet holes.*

"*Passaporti,*" the guard barks.

Kosti leans over me and slaps a stack of euros into the man's palm. "*Amici della famiglia,* no?"

I wonder for a moment if he's gone too far. The last fucking thing we need is to spend a night in Italian jail while immigration authorities decide our fate. The thought of this underpaid country boy popping open the trunk to find a full armory and knives stained with Serbian blood is darkly funny, though.

Then the flashlight flicks off.

"Andate avanti tutti."

Ariel's exhale shudders through the car as we roll forward into the inkblot hills of Italy.

We stop to stretch our legs at a roadside chapel halfway to hell. Like the farmhouse, it's a shell of what it once was. Moonlight bleeds through shattered stained glass, painting the Virgin Mary's face in fractured blues. I lean against a pew splintered by termites and press my palm to the fresh blood seeping through my shirt once again.

Damn thing won't stay shut. There's probably a lesson in that, but I'm too stubborn to learn it.

Ariel and Jasmine settle into a pew in the back row, their heads bowed together as they whisper back and forth. I can't stop looking over at her again and again, even though her face hardens every time she catches me watching.

It's just that seeing her like this, pregnant with my children… Fucking hell.

My children. The phrase still feels foreign on my tongue, like trying to speak a language I've only heard in dreams.

Kosti spreads the map he took from the car's glove compartment out on the altar. I join him at his shoulder as we scrutinize the twisting, squiggling highways of Europe.

His finger points at where we started, just north of the Spanish Pyrenees on the western coast of France. He drags it east, zigzagging through all the back roads we took, through the pass in the Alps that spat us out into northern Italy.

"Our options are scarce," he says with a grimace. "You know where they'll be."

"At every fucking airport between here and Asia. Yes, I'm aware."

"And even if we could find a plane—"

Our eyes shift in unison to Ariel. "She can't."

Jasmine told us enough about Ariel's blood pressure and what the doctor said about not flying to alter our plans. Ariel might still want to risk it—but I sure as fuck don't. Those are *my children* in there. I intend to keep both them and their mother safe.

She's glowing blue in the gloom, caught in a ray of moonlight arcing through the stained glass. Her belly looks like a globe resting on its axis. A whole world I never knew existed.

The women see us looking at them and frown. Jasmine helps Ariel rise and they shuffle over. "We can't keep driving forever," says Jasmine. "It's not good for her."

"We won't." I glance at Kosti, who knuckles at his tired eyes. When he looks back at me, he nods slightly.

"There's a villa," I begin to explain. "Deep in the Tuscan countryside."

"It's stocked," Kosti adds. "Solar generator. Well water. Enough meat in the deep freezer to last us until Judgment Day."

Jasmine frowns. "And we stay there until…?"

"Until it's safe to do otherwise."

"What a plan that is!" Ariel's laugh couldn't be more bitter. "We're just all supposed to play house in the middle of nowhere like some happy family until what—until Dragan just gives up?"

"Until the babies come and you can make your own decisions safely," I growl.

"My due date is ten weeks away!" Ariel's hands curl protectively around her belly. "You expect me to stay trapped in some villa with you for *ten weeks*? Have you lost your mind?" She turns and gawks at Kosti and Jasmine. "He has, right? He's insane. That cannot be the plan."

"Would you prefer Dragan find you?" I snarl. "This isn't about what any of us want. It's about keeping you—all of you —alive."

"You keep acting like you're in charge, when you're literally the one who—"

Jasmine steps between us, hands raised like she's directing traffic at the gates of purgatory. "It's alright, Ari. We can—"

The chapel doors burst open as the midnight breeze picks up. Out of nowhere, wind howls through the nave, snuffing the candle Kosti lit. In the sudden dark, I see it—the way Ariel's hands instinctively cradle her stomach, the tremor she thinks she's hidden.

She's terrified.

I step into the blade of moonlight cutting through the rubble. She'll hate me for forcing her down this path, but what choice do I have? Every other road leads to ruin. So let her hate me.

At least she'll be alive to do it.

"You'll stay at the villa until the babies are born. I'll handle Dragan."

Ariel looks me up and down and snorts. "You look like you couldn't handle a grocery list right now."

Jasmine touches her arm. "He's right, Ari. With your blood pressure, and the twins... We have to think through this."

"I've had enough of men deciding what's right for me." Her face screws up into a furious scowl before smoothing out into exhausted resignation. "But fuck it, fine. I'm outnumbered on this one and I clearly don't have a choice. I'll say this, though: the second these babies are born and I'm cleared to travel, we're gone."

It's a lie. We both know it's a lie. We both feel in the marrow of our bones that, once those two little lives join our world, nothing will ever be the same.

But I don't even know how to say those words out loud. And Ariel surely has no intentions of saying them, either. With one last skewering glare at me, she storms out, sundress snapping like a battle flag in the wind.

Kosti re-lights the Virgin's candle, then ignites a cigarette off that flame. "She'll come around."

"Will she?" I watch through the broken window as Ariel paces the overgrown graveyard, muttering under her breath.

I'm not so sure.

11

SASHA

The gravel crunches beneath our tires like broken bones. I kill the engine and stare up at the villa through the dusty windshield.

It's exactly as Kosti described: a pigeon-shit-stained tomb, a stucco sarcophagus, crouching in the Tuscan hills like a stone gargoyle with its wings clipped. Vines strangle the stone walls and shutters dangle by single nails.

Under different circumstances, it might be idyllic.

Right now, it just looks like a prison.

"Home sweet home," Kosti announces, popping his door open. The smell of rosemary and damp stone invades the car.

Ariel doesn't move. Six months pregnant and she still looks like she could cut my throat with that jawline. I get the feeling she wouldn't mind trying to do exactly that.

I step out into the oppressive heat. Cicadas scream in the olive groves. My wound pulses in time with their shrieks—a fresh blossom of pain with every heartbeat. I probably ought to be in a hospital. Instead, I've been smuggling a pregnant woman and her fugitive sister across Europe in a car that smells like fear, sweat, and blood.

My father would've laughed at the weakness.

If you can stand, you're not broken, Yakov's ghost whispers through the churning heat. *And yet you waver? Pathetic.*

Ariel's car door creaks open. She moves like tectonic plates shifting—slow, inevitable, earthshaking. Her sundress strains across the curve of her belly. Our eyes meet through the dust haze. I see the twins in that look—twenty pounds of future squirming between us, binding us tighter than any ten-day vow ever could.

"Don't," she says when I reach for her bag. "I'm pregnant, not crippled."

Kosti shoulders past with two suitcases in hand. "If you two are going to stand out here and bicker, I'm going to take the best bedroom for myself."

Ariel looks at me. Scowls. Then drops her bag at my feet and stomps her way inside.

The villa's interior is rich with mildew. Sunlight slants through cracked shutters, illuminating dust motes dancing above a threadbare rug in the living room. Jasmine drifts toward the stone fireplace, trailing fingers across the mantel. Her smile fades when they come away black with soot.

"Four bedrooms upstairs." Kosti drops the luggage with a thud.

Ariel plants herself in the arched doorway. "Which one's furthest from his?"

"Ari—" Jasmine starts.

Kosti rubs his neck. "End of the hall. Rose wallpaper. Watch for hornets' nests, *koukla*, okay? It's been a while since this place had guests."

She's halfway up the crumbling staircase before he even finishes speaking. Each step makes the wood groan. We listen in silence until a door slams hard enough to shake more dust from the rafters.

Jasmine exhales through her nose. "I'll talk to her."

"Don't waste your breath." I drag a hand through sweat-damp hair. The motion pulls at my stitches with a painful twang. "Let her stew. It's what she wants."

"You're both impossible." She disappears upstairs, leaving Kosti and me standing awkwardly.

He lights a cigarette off the stove's gas burner. "Ten weeks, *neania*. Think you'll make it?"

That's the question of the year. Every protective instinct in my body screams to follow her, to ease her burden, to prepare for the arrivals that will change everything.

You just watched the mother of your children go wheezing up the stairs with a hand braced against her lower back so gravity and exhaustion didn't drag her down onto the fucking floorboards, you miserable bastard. So what if she tells you to leave her alone? So what if she despises you? Since when do you let that dictate your actions?

But the gulf between us is huge and growing, and try as I might, Ariel won't let me do the right thing. I tell myself it's better this way. She doesn't want my help—and anyway, Dragan demands my full attention. I should be plotting, scheming, preparing for war.

Instead, I find myself wondering about cribs and blankets, imagining tiny fingers wrapped around mine.

I look around to see Kosti gazing at me thoughtfully as he puffs on his cigarette.

"Will I make it?" I repeat. "It doesn't seem to me like I have a choice." Then I turn and stride toward the door.

I immerse myself in all the things that need doing—checking the perimeter, inventorying supplies, flicking the generator to life to check that it's operational.

It's a meditation of sorts. If nothing else, it's easier than dealing with Ariel. Circuitry doesn't throw temper tantrums. Wells don't look at you like you're the worst thing that ever happened to them. So long as I can focus on those things, the world takes on a manageable shape.

It's when I run out of tasks that shit takes a turn for the worse. As I sit in the kitchen late into the night and fiddle with an ancient clock that doesn't actually need repair, I start remembering things I haven't remembered in months.

Barbed wire biting into my throat as Yakov pulled tighter. "Fight, you coward! Fucking fight it! Show me you're a man!"

Would you do the same? I press two fingers to the migraine thudding in my temples. *If the twins are soft? If they cry? If they—*

A floorboard squeaks. Ariel stands in the doorway, backlit by moonglow. Her hands cradle the underside of her belly.

"Your children don't like sleeping any more than you do, apparently," she says.

I look up. Framed like this, hair loose around her shoulders, wearing a pair of faded pajamas she must've scavenged from the dresser, she looks like a fragment of a dream I don't deserve to have.

"Good," I growl, turning away. "Sleep is when your enemies catch you with your guard down."

"Oh, Jesus. Planning their induction into the Bratva already?"

I rotate a gear between my fingers. "They'll need Bratva training if they inherit your sense of direction."

"Fuck y— *Ow.*"

I'm on my feet before I even begin the intention of moving. Ariel braces herself against my arms, face screwed up with pain.

"Are you—?"

"I'm fine," she interrupts. "They just get rowdy when you're around. Rowdier than usual, I should say."

Her breath hitches, then eases as the pang goes away. My fingers twitch with the need to feel it. To catch that movement against my palm, just once.

The ache spreads into parts of me I've never felt before. "Do they… have names?"

Her arms cross over the swell. Defensive. Always defensive with me. "Jasmine keeps suggesting things. I haven't picked anything yet."

My throat tightens. "Why not?"

"I'm waiting."

"For?"

"A sign they won't inherit their father's talent for destruction, among other things."

The knife twists deeper. "Ariel, if I could—"

"Sasha, you have to stop." She steps back, shadows swallowing her whole. "I just really don't have the energy for any more serious conversations tonight."

I open my mouth to argue, then stop and let it fall slack instead. "Alright. Go get some sleep."

She stills. "Why do you even care? You're taking care of us— yes, fine, I can at least understand that. But why do you... Why do you keep trying to talk to me?"

The truth sits heavy in my mouth. *Because if you collapse, I'll use my last breath to carry you. Because these ten weeks are all I get. Because I've memorized the exact shade of green your eyes turn before you cry, and I'd like to never, ever see that shade again.*

"Enlightened self-interest," I say instead. "Can't fight Dragan if I'm stuck babysitting."

Ariel laughs miserably and shakes her head. "There's the bastard I remember." She turns, sighs, and starts the slow trek up the stairs.

I could follow her. Maybe we could have a real conversation, an honest one, one where we stop hiding our bullshit and let the real truth come out, even if it's ugly.

Or, if not that, then maybe I could get some sleep of my own. I'm running this broken body with nothing but fumes, and if I keep pushing it, sooner or later, everything will fail on me.

Instead, I make for the front door to do another lap around the perimeter. Checking for danger in every shadow.

In the darkness, I can almost convince myself that this temporary peace will be enough. That I can be content with just keeping them safe, with being a shadow at the edges of their lives.

Almost.

But as night thickens and the villa grows quiet, I hear one noise that's worse than anything my enemies could ever produce: the soft sound of Ariel crying in her room. My hands knot into fists at my sides, nails biting into palms.

Ten weeks until I have to let them go.

Ten weeks to remember why I should.

12

ARIEL

Jasmine comes in a little bit after I finish crying. She stands and looks at me for a minute, then slides into bed beside me and pulls me into her arms. I don't look at her eyes; I can't. Instead, I let my gaze settle on the wallpaper. It's got a pattern of faded roses that might've been pretty back when Julius Caesar was still in charge of these parts. Now, it's just a washed-out ruin of what it once was.

"You're an ugly crier, you know," Jas informs me after a while.

I let loose a snotty giggle. "I can always count on you for the pick-me-up."

She sighs and rubs a tear off my cheek. "I heard a bit of the argument," she admits. "You okay?"

"Define 'okay.'"

"Fair. I guess we're all a little fucked-up by now, huh?"

"We're so far beyond that, Jas."

I look out of the window and Jasmine follows my gaze in time for both of us to see a tall, black shadow passing by the fence that rings the property. I know that shadow all too well.

"He's up late," she comments.

"As he should be. No rest for the wicked."

She eyes me, amused. "That's funny, coming from someone else who's still awake way past *her* own bedtime."

Rolling my eyes, I shove a pillow in her face and turn onto my side. I can still feel her watching me, though. "He's literally just walking around in circles, as if a rogue goat is gonna come terrorize the villa," I grumble. "Who does that?"

"Someone who can't sleep because he's worried about the mother of his children?"

I shoot her a glare. "Don't start."

"I'm just saying—"

"Well, don't." I shift, trying to find a comfortable position and failing miserably. "He made his choices. I made mine. End of story."

Jasmine combs my loose hair back from my face and starts to braid it. "Is it, though? Because from where I'm sitting, it looks like you're both miserable."

"Good. He should be miserable."

But even as I say it, the image of his bandaged torso flashes through my mind. The way his hands trembled when he touched me. The darkness in his eyes when I mentioned the babies.

"And you? What should you be?"

"If you're gonna say 'happy he's back in my life,' don't bother. And if you're gonna say 'what if he's changed,' then *definitely* don't bother. People don't change."

"Bullshit." She pauses for a moment. "You did."

I open my mouth. Close it. Sasha disappears around the corner of the villa.

Grimacing, I press my palms against my eyes until I see stars. "Stop being reasonable. I need you to be on my side."

"I'm always on your side, Ari. Always." Jasmine presses her palm over mine on my belly. "Little Makris-Ozerovs. Christ, they're going to be hellions."

"Don't call them that."

"Which part? The Makris or the Ozerov?"

"Either. Both." I stare at the cracked plaster wall. "They're… Wards. Just Wards."

Outside, an owl hoots mournfully. It's funny how nights can sound so different from place to place. New York was buzzing neon liveliness; Moliets-et-Maa was the quiet shush of waves rasping on the shore. I'll have to learn the sounds out here. I have ten long weeks to do it.

"He asked about their names tonight," I whisper.

"And?"

"I told him I was waiting for a sign they wouldn't be like him." I laugh, but it comes out more like a sob. "God, the look on his face, Jas. I might as well have stabbed him."

She shifts closer, wrapping an arm around my shoulders. "You're allowed to be angry, Ari. But you're also allowed to forgive. To heal. To try again."

"What if I can't? What if I let him in and he…" I trail off, unable to voice my deepest fear.

"Becomes like our dad? Like his own?" Jasmine finishes for me. When I nod, she sighs. "That's the risk we take with love. But Sasha's not Leander. He's not Yakov. He's just a man trying to protect what matters to him, even if he's doing it badly sometimes."

Tying off the braid, she lets her hands fall to rest on my belly. "You don't have to decide anything tonight."

"There's nothing left to decide," I remind her acidly. "Ten weeks and we're gone."

"Sure." Her smile doesn't reach her eyes. "Ten weeks."

We lie back down. She starts humming an old Greek lullaby our mother used to sing, one about the moon marrying the sun. I'm scared of what I might dream about if I let myself fade off. But as I settle into a comfortable position and Jas keeps singing, I slowly feel sleep start to creep over me like a warm blanket.

Right before I drift off, I hear boots on gravel again. Still checking. Still watching. Still protecting.

The bastard.

My bastard?

I'm not ready to answer that question yet.

13

SASHA

Kosti is waiting by the fence when I finish my hundredth lap in the dark, a cigarette dangling from his laps. "You keep smoking a pack a day and you won't make it to the end of these ten weeks," I warn him as I approach, tucking my gun in the back of my pants.

"If lung cancer was going to kill me, it would've done it by now." He exhales a perfect smoke ring. "Besides, what's the worst that could happen? I die and leave you alone with your mess?"

"God fucking forbid."

"That's what I thought." He laughs. "Focus on what's trying to kill you, yeah? You've got enough problems of your own without worrying about me."

I grunt and lean against the fence beside him. The metal is still warm from the day's heat. "Problems I can handle. It's solutions that get messy."

"That's because your solutions are limited to 'shoot it, threaten it, or throw money at it until it goes away.'" He takes another long drag. "How's that working out with my niece, eh?"

I glance up at the window. A glimpse of movement—Ariel pacing, one hand pressed to her spine.

"Third time she's made that circuit," Kosti observes. "You two really are perfect for each other. Both wearing holes in the floor instead of sleeping like normal people."

"She needs rest. The doctor said—"

"Oh, please tell me you're about to march up there and order her to lie down." His eyes crinkle with unholy glee. "I could use the entertainment. Maybe she'll throw you out the window this time."

"Fuck off."

"Such gratitude. Here I am, sacrificing my peaceful retirement to help you unfuck your life—"

"I didn't ask for your help."

"Would you have preferred to die in the snow?" He stubs out his cigarette and immediately lights another.

I clench my jaw. "Do you have a point to make, old man, or are you just enjoying the sound of your own voice?"

"My point is that you're still playing *pakhan* with her. Everything's an operation. A tactical maneuver. You've got your perimeter checks, your exit strategies, your—"

"—because there are actual threats—"

"—because it's easier than admitting you're terrified." The amusement drops from his voice. "Easier than admitting that for the first time in your life, you can't strong-arm your way to what you want."

I scowl at the villa's silhouette. "She's the one treating this like a war."

"Because you keep making it a battle, you idiot." Kosti's voice takes on that irritating know-it-all tone he gets sometimes. "You're so focused on proving you can protect her that you forget to actually *care* for her."

"I do care," I growl. "Or at least, I would. If she'd fucking let me."

"Oh, she'll let you. You just have to know what to do."

"I'm supposed to—what? Serenade her? Buy chocolates?"

Kosti barks a laugh. "God, no. She'd fling them at your head." He rolls yet another cigarette between his fingers, contemplative. "When my Eleni left me—third year of our marriage, can you believe it?—I camped on her cousin's porch for a week. Brought her *koulouri* every dawn. Fixed her father's leaky roof."

"And?"

"She called me 'a cockroach who'd survive nuclear winter if he knew there was a buck in it for him.'" A grin cracks his weathered face. "Then she kissed me. Drew blood doing it, but still."

I sigh and scrub my face with a hand. The old bastard loves his fucking parables. Six months of them is starting to wear on me. "What's your point, Kosti?"

"My point is that love is a siege, not a shootout. You don't storm the gates—you starve the doubts. Outlast the anger."

He tucks the cigarette behind his ear, suddenly solemn. "Stop fighting *with* her. Start fighting *for* her."

"Fuck." I pass the hand over my face once again. "How do I even start?"

"You grovel." Kosti's laugh is rough with smoke. "You beg. You prove to her that the man she fell in love with still exists beneath all that scar tissue."

"And if he doesn't?"

"Then you become that man again." He cracks his thick neck from side to side.

My lips twitch despite myself. "You're an annoying old man, you know that?"

"And you're a stubborn young fool." He claps my shoulder. "But at least you're finally asking the right questions."

14

ARIEL

Day one in Tuscan purgatory, and I've found a new nemesis.

A rooster is crowing like it's personally offended by the concept of sleep. If I was going by volume alone, I'd guess that the feathered little bastard was parked right outside my window. Lucky for him that he's not, because otherwise, I'd be strongly considering avian homicide.

I clamp a pillow to my head like earmuffs and try to go back to sleep. I'd been in the middle of a really nice dream about floating on a sea of icing in a rowboat made out of cinnamon rolls. If I can just find my way back there, then maybe—

BOOMBOOMBOOM.

Someone's knocking on the door like a freaking SWAT team. I wonder momentarily if it's the rooster.

"What do you want, you cockadoodle-douche bag?"

"Get dressed." Sasha's voice, rougher than usual this early. "We're going out."

I squint at my phone. "It's six in the morning."

"Exactly. The best produce goes early."

"What in God's name are you talking about, Sasha?" I crack open an eye to look at him.

Big mistake. He's leaning against my door frame in a black henley. His hair is damp like he just showered, and the forearms crossed in front of his chest are brawny and beautiful.

If roosters can be offended by sleep, then I decide I'm allowed to be offended by how good-looking he is. It's not fair, dammit! He was up damn near half the night circling the property like a cotton-candy-drunk toddler buckled onto a carousel. The audacity to waltz in here like he stepped right off a *GQ* cover is insulting.

Especially because I know I look like death warmed over. My mouth is sticky with the sleep grodies and the bags beneath my eyes are puffy as hell.

He holds out a thermos. "Peppermint tea."

I blink. "Are you poisoning me?"

"If I wanted you dead, I'd use something a lot more efficient than Lipton."

I hesitate. But peppermint tea really does sound nice. So I take it from him and try one tentative sip.

"Good," Sasha approves with a nod. "Now, get up. We leave in five."

"You still haven't explained where we're going."

"There's a farmer's market in Roccastrada. You need food that doesn't come from a can."

"I need *sleep.*"

"You need folate. Iron." His gaze drops to my stomach. "Protein that isn't expired."

I roll my eyes. "Please, tell me more about what I need, since you are such an expert on all things pregnancy."

Sasha pinches the bridge of his nose like he's already getting a headache. "Don't make this hard, Ariel. Jasmine told me that your doctors said—"

"I know what they said," I interrupt with acid in my tone. "No unpasteurized cheese. No cured meats. Nothing that hasn't been rinsed in holy water blessed by the Pope himself." I jerk out of bed and plop myself in front of him. "Do you know *why* I know those things, Sasha? Because *I'm the one carrying these babies.* I'm the one who's had to go to the doctors' appointments, and watch my diet, and take all my minerals and supplements, and this and that and the other thing. *You* haven't had to do any of that. And guess what? I was fine doing it on my own. So don't act like you're the one doing me a favor. You're not."

For a moment, Sasha's face darkens, and I'm sure I'm going to get more of his usual bark.

Then it softens. Something else steals over him. "You're right," he concedes. "You have been doing this on your own. I haven't been there." His throat bobs with a swallow. "But I'm here now, and for as long as that lasts, I want to do right by you, Ariel. So let me. Let me try, at least."

Oh, this manipulative asshole. Leave it to Sasha Ozerov to pull out the pity card when my defenses are already lowered by the pre-dawn blahs. Leave it to him to know that it would work.

Because it does.

As much as I want to snark back in his face, I can't. He looks like he means what he's saying. Authenticity—the greatest con of them all.

"Fine," I mutter. "Give me ten minutes. I don't want to scare any farmers away with my morning breath."

When I get my hair into some semblance of order and make it downstairs, Sasha is waiting with a pair of bicycles leaning against the villa's stucco walls.

I pause on the top step and squint at him. "Is this supposed to be my *Eat, Pray, Love* moment?"

He looks back at me with utter blankness. "Am I supposed to know what that means?"

"*Eat, Pray, Love?* Like, the movie? Or, I mean, I guess it was a book first. But, like, Julia Roberts? She's— My God, you really have no idea what I'm talking about. You're a cyborg, I swear."

He holds out a bike handle to me. "I'll take that as a compliment. Do you know how to ride?"

"Yes, asshole, I know how to ride a bike." I snatch it from him, throw one leg over—and promptly start to tip in the wrong direction.

But Sasha is there. He lunges forward to steady me with a hand on each hip before I face-plant in the dirt. His face hangs in my vision for a moment, contemplative, calm, with just the tiniest hint of a wry smile in the corner of his mouth.

"Are you sure?" he asks, amused.

My face burns. "There was a... pothole."

He nods. "Right. Watch out for those. They come out of nowhere sometimes. In your case, quite literally."

He keeps his hands on my waist for a second longer. I forgot over the last six months how easily his fingers span me. There's more of me now to cover, as our babies grow inside me, but his palms still spread almost from hip to hip. I feel safe, nestled inside his grasp.

"You look beautiful, *ptichka,*" he murmurs.

Then he releases me. My cheeks are still hot as I watch him mount his bicycle and start to pedal. He gets maybe a hundred yards away, just beyond the fence line, before his voice floats back to where I'm still standing in place.

"Put some effort into it!" he calls. "Last one there gets the rotten eggplant."

I swear he even laughs.

Gritting my teeth, I push off and get going again.

The ride paces peacefully enough. I keep an eye out for the rooster, just in case I get an opportunity to take him out while he's crossing the road. But mostly, it's rolling hills topped with vineyards and olive tree orchards, with an endless sky overhead. Tuscany is green and brown and blue in every direction. I couldn't point us out on a map if my life depended on it, but I do know that it's beautiful.

We coast down a long, slow incline and into a village clustered together at the foot of a hill. More traffic joins us as we get closer—farmers towing carts of fruits and vegetables behind unamused donkeys, a few other locals on bikes and foot. Occasionally, a car rumbles past and kicks up little whirls of red dust.

In the center of the village—Rocka-something, Sasha called it—are rows of stalls selling all kinds of things. Bread and cheese, jarred jams, dried meat hanging from twine. Sasha parks his bike behind a trio of nonnas gossiping in flowing Italian and waits for me to do the same.

"I was just starting to get the hang of French," I say mournfully. "Back to square one, I guess."

"*Ritorno al punto di partenza,*" agrees Sasha in a flawless accent.

I whirl around to scowl at him. "Do you seriously—? No, actually, don't even tell me. My ego can't handle it if you really do speak Italian."

Face completely straight, he just shrugs. "Then I won't say a word."

He steps aside and gestures for me to lead the way. With a sigh, I do, though his hand comes to a rest on my lower back and I let it stay there.

The market erupts around us in a carnival of smells: sun-ripened tomatoes and crusty bread, lavender sachets fighting with pungent wheels of parmigiano. Old men in newsboy caps argue over artichokes while tanned women pinch peaches and talk right over one another.

We wander from tent to tent for a while. I let my cravings guide me, and Sasha is mostly content to let me pick where we go. He stays plastered to me like a shadow, but a quiet one.

Little by little, his arms fill up with the things I pick. Fresh figs. Sun-warmed tomatoes. Clusters of bright green herbs.

At a cheese stand, the vendor's wife coos over my belly. I don't understand the words, but her warm smile needs no translation. She presses samples into my hands—soft cheese, hard cheese, cheese I've never seen before.

"*Non posso*," I try to refuse, but she waves me off.

"She says it's good for the babies," Sasha translates.

I sag and accept it. "*Grazie*."

The woman beams, winks, and walks off.

"Alright, fine, I'll bite: when did you learn Italian?"

Sasha chuckles. "The Ardizzone family and I had some… disagreements over some territory in Brooklyn a few years ago. I figured it was best to meet them at their level."

"'Disagreements'? I know what that's code for."

"I was expanding market opportunities through aggressive negotiations. They objected to my tactics."

I snort and nibble at a fig. "That's what we're calling it now?"

His eyes crinkle at the corners. For a moment, he looks like *my* Sasha—the one who kissed me in library stacks and bought me an entire tabloid just to protect my reputation. Then his face smooths back into its usual mask.

"How are you feeling?" he asks as we move to the next stall. "With the pregnancy?"

I consider lying, but what's the point? "Tired. Sore. The doctor in France said my blood pressure's high, but…" I shrug. "Nothing too concerning yet."

He nods, but the frown remains in place. "It's getting warmer. Let's find somewhere to sit."

"Sasha, seriously, I'm—"

But he's already dragging me down an alley, the bag of groceries swinging at his side.

With a weary exhale, I let him.

We take a few twists and turns until the cobbled street spits us out into the courtyard of a chapel. Like the one we stopped at just over the border from France, this one is missing most of its pieces. One whole wall has collapsed, but the birds don't seem to mind at all. They twitter around the exposed wooden ribs of the structure, flitting from nest to nest and singing the whole time.

He helps me into a seat and settles down next to me. Away from the hubbub of the market, quiet is king. After a while, though, Sasha twists so we're face to face.

"Marry me."

The words don't compute at first. Then: "Have you lost your fucking mind?"

"Yes," he rumbles. "Every day since you left."

I scoot back. Rotting pew creaks under my weight. "Did Dragan hit you in the head and give you amnesia? Did you forget literally every single thing that happened?"

"I haven't forgotten a single thing, Ariel." His voice and face are scarily solemn. "I wanted to tell you. About Jasmine. Leander. All of it."

"But you didn't."

"No. I didn't. Because I'm a selfish bastard who wanted to hold onto you for longer than I deserved. I thought keeping you in the dark would let me have that. But I was wrong, Ariel. Now, the universe has gifted me a chance to fix my mistakes. I want to. I want to fix them so fucking badly." His eyes sear into me. "Can I? For us? For *them?*"

I'm dumbstruck. It wouldn't be right to say I wished for this —most of the time, I've spent my waking hours cursing Sasha's name and wishing I'd never met him at all.

But I've dreamed about it. To see his eyes again, burning not with fury but with apology. I didn't know—and I still don't— how he could ever mend the gap he tore open between us. I wanted him to try, though. I dreamed he might.

So what do I do about it now that it's here? *Forgive and forget* are three very simple words.

They're insane words, though. They're impossible.

"No, Sasha, you can't." I press my shaking hands to my belly to ground and comfort me. "These babies aren't your redemption arc."

For a heartbeat, I think he'll kiss me. Crush the arguments between our tangled tongues.

Instead, he accepts what I said with a nod. "Okay. But I won't quit on this, Ariel. I won't quit on us. I won't quit on them."

The chapel breathes with the ghosts of better people. But the silence that was so nice a minute ago is killing me now, so I stand and start the long walk back to the bicycles.

Sasha follows me, though he stays at a distance. He does the same as we ride home. Close enough for me to feel him, to know he's always with me. Far enough for him to know that some things can't be undone.

I steal glances at him whenever we round a bend. My jaw stays clenched against hope, against fear, against the devastating weight of *maybe*.

Not *yes*. Never *yes*. But…

Maybe.

15

SASHA

Ariel goes upstairs to lie down when we get home, tired from the morning's exertion. She doesn't say a word as she leaves. But I do hear her footsteps pause halfway up the stairs, like she's torn. That's what I tell myself, at least. Could be a fucking fantasy for all I know.

As I haul the groceries into the villa's kitchen, one item burns a hole in the burlap sack. The peach I swiped from the market is perfect. Overripe, velvet skin flushed red-gold and splitting at the cleft. Exactly how Ariel used to smell whenever I buried my face between her thighs.

For one second, I let myself indulge. I sink onto a wobbling stool and press the fruit to my nose. I push my thumb into its flesh to test the give. A bead of juice wells up and slides down my knuckle. Sweet, sticky, beautiful.

"Fuck."

Then I drop the peach into a cracked ceramic bowl like it scalded me.

Cooking is a tactical retreat. I dice onions, crush garlic under the flat of my knife, let the sizzle of olive oil in the pan drown out the static in my skull. The recipe itself is muscle memory—*sofrito*, tomatoes, a splash of wine from the dusty bottle Kosti unearthed in the cellar.

It's easy to let my mind mute itself. Or at least, it is for a little while—until the knife slips and nips at the meat of my hand between thumb and forefinger.

"Blyat'."

I snatch up a rag and press it to the wound. It's not deep, but the pain is bright enough to ruin the too-brief high of cooking.

I don't know what to blame. It's been a hell of a few days, end-capped with thirty-some sleepless hours since we arrived in Tuscany. I've spent longer awake in worse conditions—a week guarding Yakov's drug shipment in Vladivostok comes to mind—but my body is protesting.

Look at you, you wreck of a man. You can barely dice a fucking onion without your shoulder screaming like a banshee.

Footsteps creak on the stairs. I tense, expecting Ariel's voice. Expecting another fight.

But it's Jasmine who drifts into the kitchen, barefoot and wrapped in one of the villa's threadbare quilts. She eyes the simmering pot, then me.

"Punishing yourself?" she asks with a glance at the bloody rag in my hand.

"Just testing the knife."

She arches a brow. "And?"

"It works."

She laughs breezily and takes a seat at one of the counter stools. "I didn't know you could cook."

I look at the risotto simmering in a skillet on the stove top. The smell of butter and blooming garlic fills the kitchen with a warmth of its own. "I dabble."

"Sure you're not planning on poisoning us?"

"You and Ariel really are related; she asked me the exact same thing." I laugh and stir the arborio rice. "I didn't duck bullets with the two of you just to feed you arsenic now that we're safe."

"Ahhh, *arsenic,* that's what I'm smelling." She looks at me, a smile playing across her face. Her eyes—same green as her sister's, but frosted by fifteen years of watching over her shoulder—track every movement.

"My secret ingredient."

"That, and love, right?" Jasmine chuckles. "Ari said you kidnapped her bright and early this morning."

"She said that word? '*Kidnapped*'?"

"I may be paraphrasing." Her gaze flicks to the peach where I left it in the bowl. "You know she's allergic, right?"

I pause mid-stir. "What?"

"Oh, yeah. Big time. If she's even within the vicinity of a peach, her lips start swelling up like she got stung by bees. Guess you're not as omniscient as you think, Mr. Ozerov."

I'm already lunging for the peach and cursing under my breath, ready to launch it over the mountains, when I glance up and realize that Jasmine is laughing.

I scowl and let my hand go slack as the pieces click. "You're fucking with me."

"I wanted to see how you'd react," she confirms as she doubles over, wheezing and clutching her ribs. "You did not disappoint."

My scowl remains fixed in place as I turn back to the risotto and resume stirring. "Glad I could amuse you."

"It's cute, though. Honestly. You looked at that peach like you wanted to murder it for the sheer audacity."

I glance over again and see it lying there, orange and innocent, fuzz glowing in the afternoon light.

So what if I did want to murder it? What if it did make a unique flavor of anger rise up in my stomach, to think of this stupid fucking fruit causing Ariel so much as a millisecond of discomfort? Who the hell cares?

Jasmine reaches over to scoop it up and toss it back and forth between her hands. "She loves peaches, actually. Question for you: Is it a hair color thing? 'Cause she's really more auburn than peachy. Or is it more like a symbol? Like, she's a forbidden fruit, Garden of Eden-style?" Her nose wrinkles up. "Just don't tell me it's a sex thing. Turns out you never really outgrow the ick factor of imagining your siblings getting after it."

"It's just a fruit." I don't look up at her.

"Right. Right. Of course it is."

"Look, if you're here to rile me up—"

"Actually, I'm here because we're long overdue for a chat." She sets the peach down with a soft *thud*. "Fifteen years, Sasha Ozerov. That's how long it's been since you dumped me in Marseille with a fake passport and a *'don't look back.'* Now, you're at my door again, mucking things up, as per usual. And I once again cannot decide whether to thank you or hit you over the head with a blunt object."

The memory rises like bile—Jasmine at nineteen, trembling in a cargo container, her face swollen from tears. *Please don't let him find me. Please.* She'd clutched my sleeve like I was a saint instead of the self-serving bastard who'd profited from her pain.

"Both might be called for," I concede.

Jasmine nods. "At least you can admit that much." She pauses and toys with the corner of the quilt. "Do you know what I did that first night in Marseille? I cried like a baby, then I ate so many croissants my stomach hurt. Then I slept for two days straight. It was a confusing time, to say the least. What about you? What'd you do? Go straight to a nightclub to toast to your good fortune?"

My face darkens. "I went and talked to your father."

"You told him I was dead," she says, as if I need the reminder.

"I told him what he needed to hear."

"And what about what *Ari* needed?" Her voice sharpens. "You let her grieve."

I grip the edge of the counter until my knuckles bleach. "The choices I made kept her safe. If your father or Dragan had suspected—"

"Don't." She slashes a hand through the air. "Don't hide behind strategy. Not with me. We've come way too far for that, Sasha."

The risotto bubbles violently. I tamp down the flame, but the silence only thickens.

Jasmine sighs. "You saved my life. Gave me freedom. I'll always owe you for that. But what you're doing to Ari? It's not salvation for anyone—not you and definitely not her. It's slow, mutual suffocation."

I turn to face her fully. "What would you have me do? Walk away? Let Dragan pick her bones clean?"

"For starters, I'd have you try," she snaps. "Try being honest. Try being human. Christ, Sasha—she's carrying your *children*. If that doesn't crack your armor, what will?"

I brace against the counter, suddenly dizzy. "I am trying."

"Are you? Or are you just rearranging your obsessions?" She leans forward, eyes blazing. "Protecting her isn't love. Neither is controlling her. So what's left, huh? What's left when the bullets stop flying and all your enemies are ash stains, hm? What comes after that?"

Love is a weak spot, my father's ghost snarls. *It either betrays you or gets you killed.*

But Nataliya's voice whispers louder—her lullabies, her hands smoothing my hair after Yakov's beatings, her warm fingers slipping me honey cakes and saying, *"Shh, malysh, don't let him see you cry."*

"I don't know how to do this," I admit hoarsely. "Not one damn bit of it."

"That's honest, if nothing else." Jasmine's expression softens. "Start by apologizing. To her. To yourself, too, while you're at it."

"It's not that simple."

"It never is." She stands, quilt trailing behind her like a royal cloak. "But here's the thing about Ari—she doesn't need grand gestures. She needs *you*. The messy, flawed, terrified man behind the crown."

I stare at the peach. At the knife. At the bloodied rag I left on the counter.

"She'll never forgive me," I rasp.

Jasmine pauses in the doorway. "Maybe not. But you don't get to decide that for her."

The quilt rustles as she leaves. I'm alone again with the ghosts and the garlic.

I pick up the peach. Press it to my nose. Inhale sunlight and shame. Then I slice it open—neatly, cleanly—and arrange the pieces on a chipped plate.

A peace offering.

A prayer.

16

SASHA

After Jasmine leaves, I'm left staring at the plate of peach slices like it holds all the answers. It doesn't, of course. It's just fruit. But that doesn't stop me from looking for meaning anywhere I can find it.

The peach bleeds juice across the chipped plate. I watch it pool in the crevices of old ceramic, sticky-sweet and cloying. My reflection warps in the syrup—a gaunt ghost with too-sharp cheekbones and eyes like bullet holes.

The knife trembles in my grip. I set it down before I can slip again, though the small nick on my hand has already stopped bleeding.

But I snatch it right back up when I hear footsteps stomping through the gravel outside. I'm turning toward the door when it bursts inward—

And Kosti barges in, whistling something peppy.

"*Blyat'*, you old idiot, I almost stuck this in your throat."

Kosti turns to look at me, with one thick eyebrow raised like a caterpillar crawling toward his hairline. "Testy this morning, are we?"

Dust clings to his boots. The sharp tang of gun oil cuts through the kitchen's garlic-and-wine haze.

"Smells like my grandmother's house in here," he remarks, shrugging off his coat. "If my grandmother was a chain-smoking war criminal."

"Knowing you, she might've been." I lean against the counter, careful to keep my weight off my screaming left side. "Where were you?"

"Tending the goats."

"We don't have goats."

He grins, all yellowed teeth and secrets. "Exactly." He nods at the stove. "That supposed to be edible?"

"It's risotto, so yes."

"Looks like wet cement."

"Then don't eat it. See if I give a damn." I reach for the parmesan from the cabinet overhead. But as I do, the movement tugs at the knot of still-healing scar tissue beneath my ribs. Fire licks up my flank and my hand spasms. The block of cheese slips, cracks against the counter.

Kosti's gaze sharpens. "How's the gut?"

"Fine." I straighten my spine, refusing to let him see how the simple act of standing upright makes my shoulder ache.

"Bullshit." He crowds into my space and pokes two fingers below my sternum. I jerk back with a hiss and he nods knowingly. "Ah-ha. I thought you were fine?"

I bat his hand away. "It's nothing."

"Well, 'nothing' has you sweating like a whore in church." He squints at me. "When are you planning to go back?"

The question catches me off-guard. "What?"

"To New York. To whatever revenge fantasy you've been cooking up between your perimeter checks." His voice hardens. "Don't play dumb with me, boy. I know that look in your eyes. You can't wait to go martyr yourself."

"The sooner, the better." The paring knife winks at me from the cutting board. I press my thumb to the blade until the bite of steel grounds me. "The longer we wait—"

"The longer your bullet wound has to heal?" He barks a laugh. "Yeah, I can see how well that's going. You can barely lift a fucking pan without wincing."

"I've fought through worse."

"And that's worked out nicely for you so far?" He gestures at my bandaged torso. "Tell me, what's your brilliant plan? Hobble into battle and hope Dragan doesn't notice you're moving like an arthritic *babushka*?"

Anger flares hot in my gut. "You don't understand—"

"No, *you* don't understand." He closes the distance between us, jabbing a finger into my chest again. Right over the wound. I grit my teeth against the spike of pain. "If you go back now, you're dead. Simple as that. And then what happens to her? To those babies?"

"I can protect them—"

"You can't even protect yourself!" His voice booms, filling the kitchen. "The doctors said eight to ten weeks for full recovery. Minimum. You really want to gamble lives on your pride?"

Before I can respond, the lights flicker overhead. Once, twice, then plunge us into shadow. My body moves on pure instinct—knife already in hand as I lunge toward the door.

But the sudden movement sends agony ripping through my chest. I double over, spots dancing in my vision.

"Case in fucking point," Kosti mutters, steadying me with a grip on my good shoulder. "Sit down before you fall down, son."

The lights sputter back to life. No gunfire follows. No breaking glass. Just the whine of dilapidated wiring and the growing rumble of thunder outside.

Humiliation curdles in my throat. I shove him off.

"The generator is old and finicky," he explains. "But it's just a blip, son. Nothing needs killing."

I let the knife clatter onto the counter as I grimace. "Are you happy now?"

"Ecstatic," he responds, surprisingly gentle all of the sudden. "You've proved my point better than I ever could."

Through the window, I watch afternoon storm clouds gather over the hills. The sky darkens to the color of old bruises. In her room upstairs, Ariel is probably watching the same view, trapped by her own condition just as surely as I'm trapped by mine.

The irony would be funny if it didn't hurt so much.

Kosti busies himself at the stove, stirring the risotto I abandoned. The strong line of his shoulders betrays tension I can't quite decode. "Sometimes," he says without turning, "the bravest thing a warrior can do is wait."

"Bravery and desperation look the same in the dark."

He chuckles. "I've found them to be two sides of the same coin." He adds a splash of wine to the pan. The smell of garlic and butter intensifies. "You think I spent my morning picking daisies?"

"You still haven't said what you've spent your morning doing."

"Making sure we stay ghosts a little longer." His smile is as vague as his answer. "The less you know about that, the better."

Lightning flashes outside, painting his face in stark relief. For a moment, I see the man he must have been in his prime—the soldier, the killer, the shadow in the dark. Then he's just Kosti again, an old man stirring dinner in a decrepit kitchen.

"You're playing some kind of game," I accuse.

He shrugs. "Aren't we all?"

17

ARIEL

I don't have to wait for the rooster to irritate me this morning. My back beats him to it.

I'm sprawled across the mattress like a beached whale, clutching a pillow to my chest. I swear I've doubled in size since yesterday, and I'm feeling it. Every position is a new betrayal—left side pinches a nerve, right side makes the twins sandwich my spleen. On my back? Might as well staple my ribs to the floor.

The pregnancy books I've read call this "normal discomfort," which is downright laughable. There is nothing "normal" about any of the discomfort I'm feeling, whether we're talking about the physical or the emotional varieties.

What's "normal" about carrying the twins of a man who ruined your life?

What's "normal" about fleeing your home to shack up in a crumbling Tuscan villa?

What's "normal" about seeing Sasha pass by my window in the pouring rain, on his endless rounds yet again?

I check the clock on the wall. 4:47 A.M. The villa groans like an old man stretching as the last of the storm hurls itself against the creaky shutters. In the bathroom, a faucet drips in rhythm with the throbbing above my tailbone.

Breathe. Just breathe through it.

I've done this before. Those first months in France, when the morning sickness faded but the backaches bloomed, I used to curl around a heating pad in our apartment and whimper. Jas was working a lot, so I had no one to complain to. No one to see me crack.

A cramp claws up my right side. I bite my lip hard enough to taste copper.

"Nope," I mutter to the peeling ceiling. "Not crying today. Absolutely not."

I lie there in quiet, spasming discomfort until the clock reaches a more humane hour. Getting up sounds awful, but lying here in a puddle of my own sweat for much longer sounds even worse. So I force myself up to my feet and into a tepid shower. Then I dress in a bundle of the clothes Uncle Kosti brought back for us yesterday and waddle my way downstairs in search of coffee.

The kitchen is gloomy with the storm blotting out much of the sunrise. I'm fumbling through the cabinets, praying for coffee grounds somewhere, when a voice nearly makes me scream.

"You're awake."

I whirl around to see Sasha seated at the kitchen table. His face is drawn and weary.

I frown. He looks awful. "Did you sleep?"

He shrugs. "Not important."

"If you say so." I'm aiming for nonchalant sass, but I can't hide my worry. He's looking worse and worse with every passing day. Like he's wasting away right in front of me. There's *burning the candle at both ends* and then there's *chucking the candle into the heart of a volcano, and throwing a can of gasoline in after it for good measure.* Sasha is veering awfully close to the latter.

"Bad night?" he asks.

I scowl irritably. "I spent half of it begging my own spine to either have mercy on me or just put me out of my misery. So no, I did not sleep all that well."

His chair scrapes as he stands. "There's a hospital—"

"No!" I wince and lower my voice while looking up at the kitchen rafters, wondering if I might've woken Jasmine and Uncle Kosti by accident. "No, Sasha, it's okay. I don't need a hospital. This is all normal. Well, I mean, none of this is normal, but this part of it is. You know what I mean."

He's still squinting at me with steely eyes, though, like he'll be able to see through my lies if he looks hard enough. "Hm."

"Seriously," I insist. "I just need coffee and I'll be feeling like a million bucks."

"I thought pregnant women weren't supposed to drink caffeine."

"Take it from my cold, dead hands. I dare you." I turn back and resume rummaging through the cabinets. There are endless cans of beans and root vegetables, but I'm not seeing any coffee, until—

Sasha's hand closes around my wrist.

I wobble backward in surprise, but that motion makes my back seize up, so my palm goes shooting out for the nearest firm surface to balance myself. That surface ends up being Sasha's shoulder. Not my first choice, but it certainly meets the "firm" requirement.

The feel of his heat and brawn underneath my fingertips is like getting sucked backward into a time travel machine. Suddenly, I'm in a spa. I'm in a library. I'm in a bathroom. I'm in a penthouse, gasping and riding as the windows fog up.

Then I'm just here again. In a kitchen, scared, hurting, angry.

Sasha's blue eyes watch me take that whole mental journey without once saying a word. Then he sighs. "You're in pain."

"Lest you forget, I'm pregnant. It's a package deal."

Dawn seeps through the shutters, painting his scar silver. "How bad?"

"What difference does it make to you?" I ask. "Everyone's got scars now. It's just how things are going."

He rubs at his beard with one hand. "There are thermal springs not far from here. Twenty minutes north, give or take. It'll help if you soak for a while."

"Oh, perfect. Another fun little morning errand. Do I get—"

"Ariel." His voice drops, roughened by something that isn't anger. "Let me help you."

Those words float between us, every bit as fragile as the cobwebs in the corner. I want to snap them. Stomp them. Wrap them around his throat and see if he chokes.

But then another spasm sears through me. I hiss.

Sasha's hand twitches toward mine, though he stops just short. "Please."

"Fine," I grumble. "But if this is some ploy to get me naked—"

"*Ptichka…*" His lips quirk. "When have I ever needed an excuse for that?"

Sasha drives one-handed, the other resting on the gearshift—close, too close, to my thigh. Tuscan hills unravel outside the window, olive groves ghostly in the fog. I count crumbling farmhouses to avoid counting the number of times his gaze flicks to my reflection.

He parks where the gravel dies and kills the engine. "Here we are."

"Here" is a slash in the mountainside veiled by cypress trees. No signs. No changing rooms. Certainly no black-marble-and-champagne-tray pitfalls to avoid. Just a crescent of steaming water cupped by mossy stones, the air thick with sulfur and earth.

Sasha circles the Peugeot to open my door. I wave him off, but my body betrays me as I try to do it all myself, a whimper escaping as I lever myself out. His jaw ticks.

"I'm fine," I snap before he can speak.

"You're stubborn."

"Pot, kettle, asshole."

He huffs something that might've been a laugh in another lifetime. Then he turns and leads the way. But I can practically feel his attention radiating back down toward me, cataloging every step, every breath.

The path up is treacherous, slick with dew. Sasha walks ahead, testing each stone. I mimic his footsteps, absurdly aware of how his shoulders tense whenever my breath hitches. Halfway down, my sandal slips—

—and his hand shoots back to catch my elbow.

We freeze. His thumb taps the inside of my arm, once. "Careful," he rumbles. Then he lets go.

It's not much farther until we reach the top. We round a giant boulder and there it is.

The pool glistens below us, steam rising off its surface, calm water the color of oversteeped tea. We both stand awkwardly for a minute. I'm looking at Sasha; Sasha is looking pointedly everywhere but at me. The springs hiss like a third presence. In the corner of my eye, I see Sasha's fingers hovering at the hem of his shirt. My pulse thrums in my throat.

Then he peels the fabric off, and I'm gutted.

Old scars I've traced with my tongue. The jagged necklace of raised flesh around his neck. The newer wounds, still raw above his hip and across his shoulders. My body remembers the heat of him, the salt, the way he'd groan when I kissed that spot beneath his collarbone.

He hesitates, hand on his belt. Gray eyes lock onto mine. "You need help?"

"N-no. I'm good."

I don't feel good, though. I'm steaming up from within. Who needs hot springs when you've got repressed sex fantasies to keep you warm?

My fingers fumble with the buttons of my dress. Every brush of fabric against oversensitive skin is a betrayal.

He turns away, giving me privacy that feels a hell of a lot more like punishment. I'd do the same, but he's too quick— he shucks his pants down, revealing lean muscles clad only in a pair of black boxer briefs.

Water ripples outward as he sinks into the pool. I watch the muscles in his back flex, the droplets clinging to his shoulders. My mouth goes arid.

You've done this before, I remind myself. *You've had him roaring your name against a library wall. Compared to that, this is nothing.*

But that was before the lies. Before the blood.

Things are different now.

When the last button finally comes undone, my dress slithers down to a puddle on the grass. I step out of it in my bra and panties, ashamed by the swell of my stomach, and hurry to lower myself down into the spring so I can hide beneath the surface of the water.

But it's slow-going. Too slow. I can't see where I'm stepping, so I have to move gingerly. I can feel Sasha's eyes on me the whole time, cataloging every inch of my near-nakedness.

I fumble down, sliding from one wet rock to the next, until at last I sink up to my waist. The heat is instant relief on my lower back. I can't help letting out a whimper of gratitude.

Sasha exhales through his nose. Looks up at the mist-shrouded sky.

I sink deeper, until the water licks my chin. I'm praying it'll drown the inconvenient lust—and if not, it can just drown me.

"What?" I challenge when he stays quiet.

"Nothing."

But I catch the way his neck flushes when another involuntary moan slips out past my lips. The water's working dark magic—I can *breathe* again, the twins' weight buoyed by the water.

I can't fully unclench, though. Not with him here, barely clothed, no one else around for miles and miles. Even as the minutes bleed past and I try to tell myself that it's okay, everything's okay, my muscles stay coiled up tight.

"You should—" Sasha starts.

"If you say 'relax,' I'm drowning you in here."

He snorts. "I was going to say you should stretch your hips. The magnesium helps, and prenatal stretching improves labor outcomes."

I squint at his outline through the steam and fog. "Since when do you know about prenatal care?"

I could almost swear he blushes. "I had Feliks send me some articles."

The image is unintentionally hilarious. I want to laugh as I picture him cooped up in the villa cellar, scowling broodily at diagrams of cervical dilation.

Silence swells again. Water laps at the stretch marks branching across my stomach. I trace one with my thumb, wondering if he's looking. Wondering why I care. Lord knows there's plenty else I could be concerned about. It's been a hectic few days, to say the least. I haven't had coffee and my stomach is gurgling with hunger.

I've never felt farther from New York than I do right now. Even for the six months in France, I felt away, but not *that* far away. This, though, is like I've jumped to a different planet. Steamy fog wreathing me as I share a hot spring with this alien of a man, this enigma, this *what-the-hell-makes-you-tick* mystery who got me pregnant and ruined my life. I miss my mom. I miss my apartment. I miss Gina.

"I miss bagels," I blurt.

Sasha blinks. "What?"

"Bagels. A good, real, authentic New York bagel. I haven't had one in six months. I'd made my peace with never having one again. Or at least, I thought I did. But now... Fuck me, I'd kill for a bagel."

Sasha, to my surprise, lets out a laugh. "I've done worse for less."

But I feel like I've opened Pandora's box now, and I can't possibly keep it all contained within me. "You know what else I miss? Target. And bodega coffee. And Gina's shitty apartment with the radiator that sounds like a dying accordion." My throat tightens. "I miss *talking* to her. To Lora. To my mom. I miss so many things that I always used to take for granted, and if I don't think about them, it's fine, but if I give them even the tiniest fraction of a thought, my heart starts to hurt so bad that I feel like I'm gonna die."

Sasha's quiet for three heartbeats. Four. Five. Then he reaches for his discarded pants on the rocks.

I tense as he pulls out his phone—black, encrypted, almost certainly bulletproof. He powers it on, taps through menus, then extends it toward me.

"Call them."

The device glints in the mist. I eye it like it might bite me. "You're joking."

"You think I'd joke about this?"

"They could trace—"

"Not this line." His jaw flexes. "Five minutes. That's all I can risk."

My fingers tremble as I take it. I'm still waiting for the other shoe to drop, but Sasha climbs out before I can retort. Water sluices off him in sheets, those black briefs clinging obscenely to curves I swore off six months ago. I look away just in time to miss the worst of it—but not before my body stirs.

He wanders over to a boulder a few yards away. Just out of earshot, but close enough to be here in a second if I need him. He just sits silently, gazing over the fog-crowned hills in the distance.

So I dial.

One ring. Two. I'm just about to give up hope when—

"Hello?" Gina's voice crackles through, sleep-rough and absolutely glorious.

A sob tears up my throat. "Hi, Gee. It's me."

18

ARIEL

The dial tone buzzes in my ear long after Gina's laughter fades.

Five minutes wasn't enough.

Five lifetimes wouldn't be enough. There was just so much to catch up on.

Feliks bought this stupid loft in Tribeca—can you believe it? Says he wants us to have space for you when you visit. Which better be soon, Ward. I'm not hauling twin strollers up five flights by myself.

Mist coils around the phone clutched in my white-knuckled grip. I sink deeper until the water kisses my chin, trying to drown the way Gina's voice cracked when she mentioned how thin Mom's gotten.

I've been checking in on her as often as I can. She keeps saying it's acid reflux, even when I found her crying over a box of your old baby clothes.

A fat raindrop plinks against the phone screen—wait, no. That's a tear. God. When did I start crying?

The stone beneath me grinds into my tailbone. I don't care. I can barely feel it over the vise crushing my heart. All those weeks rationalizing my exile—*they're safer this way; this is temporary; I can always go back*—crumble like wet newspaper.

My old life isn't paused. It's rotting without me.

Cool rivulets streak down my cheeks. Rain, fog, or tears? Who cares? It all tastes salty and sad.

Every bit of news was like another drop in a storm. Gina's moving in with Feliks. Mom is unraveling. Lora has actually stayed in a relationship for longer than a few weeks, and she thinks this might really be the one.

Gee put a brave face on for all of my news, because that's just what she does. *Babies or no babies, Sasha or no Sasha, there's still a happy ending in this for you, Ari. I'm gonna make sure of that. What else are best friends for?*

Another sob breaks free. I slap a hand over my mouth, but it's no use. The sound reverberates off the rocks—a wounded animal howl that startles birds from the cypress trees. Water sloshes as I fold into myself, thumbing at the swell of our babies. *My* babies. The only bright spots left in this dark, endless freefall.

Through the blur, I see Sasha's silhouette tense on the boulder. He doesn't turn. Doesn't speak. Just sits there, carved from the same stone as the mountains, while I fracture into a thousand jagged pieces.

My shoulders shake. Tears drip hot onto the water's surface. I don't know what exactly I'm crying for. Is it for Gina's empty apartment, where we used to split cheap wine and cheaper gossip? For Mom's hollow eyes, touching baby clothes I outgrew a long time ago? Or is it for the version of me who thought running meant freedom instead of this slow drowning in dark waters?

I feel him approach. Closer. Closer.

I don't look up. Don't breathe. Just press my forehead to my knees and let the springs swallow what's left of me.

Sasha's touch lands like a lightning strike—electric and inevitable. Warm palm curving over my bare shoulder. The calluses I know so well, dragging against water-slick skin.

I freeze. Every cell sings, *Danger.*

"Look at me, *ptichka.*" His voice gravels through the mist. *Little bird.* The old endearment almost breaks me.

I don't look up. Can't. If I turn now, the last of my walls will crumble.

His finger strokes the nape of my neck. Spasms ripple through me—not pain this time, but something else, something highly off-limits. "Ariel."

The single word cracks the dam. I spin in the water, sending waves against the rocks, and shove at his chest. "You don't get to—"

He catches my wrist. Pulls it to his lips. Presses a kiss to my racing pulse.

"I know." Another kiss to my palm. My ragged breath hitches. "I know."

His other hand skims my waist beneath the water. Heat blazes where his fingers graze the swell of my stomach. Not dominance. Not demand. A question.

What if?

My thighs graze his ribs as I shift. They remember what I've tried so, so hard to forget: the way we used to move together, greedy and gasping.

Three things happen at once:

Rain patters against the surface where our bodies don't touch.

The twins kick—a frantic flutter beneath his palm.

Sasha's breath gusts hot against my ear. "I thought… Christ, I thought I'd never get to…"

And then his mouth is on mine.

Slow. So fucking slow. Like we've got all the time in the world, not a lie or bullet or an ocean between us. His tongue traces the seam of my lips, gentle where he was once rough, coaxing where he used to take. When I groan, he swallows the sound like communion. Urgent fingers tangle in my hair, tilting my head back as he deepens the kiss.

I surrender. I let myself melt into the solid heat of him, into the dizzying familiarity. His taste brings back a dozen nights just like this. Bathrooms and dressing rooms and his penthouse sheets. He'd bite my neck to tether me to him when I got too close, the growl of *mine mine mine* as I came…

Then I tear my mouth away. "Stop."

He doesn't. His lips chart a desperate path down my throat. Teeth scrape the hollow.

I shove hard against his shoulders. "I said *stop!*"

That does the trick. His grip loosens instantly. We stare at each other, panting. Spring water laps at the fresh bruises we've carved into each other's skin.

He looks wrecked. Hair wild from my fingers. Scar flushed crimson. "Ari—"

"No. This is… this is bad, Sasha. You lost the right to touch me when you lied."

His throat bobs. I watch the apology die before it's born.

Rain sheets down in earnest now, sluicing over his scarred torso. Over the ghosts of us twined together in the steam.

Without another word, he turns and climbs from the pool. I watch him dress, every movement tight with restraint.

I sink until sulfur fills my nostrils. The heat burns away the salt of his kiss on my cheeks.

The crunch of his receding footsteps fades into the storm. I know he hasn't gone far, but at least he's out of sight for now.

Only then can I let myself sob.

For the man I kissed.

For the man he became.

For all the shattered pieces of us still littering the four thousand miles between here and a place called home.

19

SASHA

The path has turned to soup beneath our feet. Each step threatens to slide out from under us as rain lashes sideways, turning the world into goopy smears of gray and green. My bullet wound pounds with every movement, but I can't focus on that. Not when she's storming ahead in that fucking sundress, hair plastered to her neck

I watch her slip on the muddy path again, my hands twitching with the need to steady her. But I can't. Won't. Not after what just happened in the springs.

The kiss haunts me with each step. Because it was so easy to do. She melted against me, her lips soft and yielding, and for as long as it lasted, I fooled myself into thinking that maybe it wouldn't ever stop.

But it did. Of course it did.

You lost the right to touch me when you lied.

She's right. But that doesn't stop me from wanting to try

again. To explain. To make her understand that everything I did—every lie, every manipulation—was to keep her safe.

The rain whips harder, and I see her stumble once more. Before I can stop myself, the words tear free:

"Marry me."

Ariel freezes mid-step, her back going rigid. The storm howls around us, but all I can hear is my own pulse thundering in my ears.

"Marry me," I say again.

Ariel whirls, eyes volcanic. "Are you *insane?*" Lightning cracks the sky. I reach for her elbow; she jerks free. "I don't need your fucking proposals, Sasha. I need—"

"What?" I bare my teeth. "Penance? Blood? Say it and it's yours, Ariel."

A gust nearly knocks her sideways. She scrambles for balance. "I need you to stop lying! To stop pretending this is about anything but your own ego!"

"Then take the deal!" My roar startles birds from the trees. "Let me keep you safe, provide for the children—"

"I don't want your kind of safety!" Her scream shreds the downpour.

Thunder groans. Her sandal slips. I grab her waist before the mud claims her.

"Don't touch me," she hisses.

But I can't release her. Not when her pulse races under my palm. Not when the pink flush from the springs still paints her collarbones so prettily.

"You don't get to force me into exile, then waltz back in like some savior." She shoves hard enough to stagger us both. "You don't get to play house now that the world's on fire."

"No one is playing anything. This isn't a game." I snap her against me, noses nearly touching. "Every hour we waste fighting, Dragan's sniffing closer."

Her lips part—God, those lips—but I don't kiss her again. Can't.

"So marry me, Ariel," I rasp again. Begging. *Pathetic.* "Let me fix this."

"You can't fix *you*." Her breath hitches. Raindrops cling to her lashes like diamonds. "You're still that scared boy choking on his father's lies. You think a ring changes that?"

I don't answer. She wrenches free.

"Watch your step," I snarl at her retreating back.

"Or what? You'll ship me off for fifteen years, too? You'll tell Jas I'm dead? You'll—"

It happens in fragments.

Her foot hits a slick patch of stone. Her ankle rolls. A gasp tears from her throat as her arms windmill outward.

My body moves before the scream even leaves her lips. Mud sucks at my boots as I lunge, arm outstretched. Stupid. *Stupid.* It all hurts so fucking bad. My ribs scream like rusted hinges, muscles tearing where bullets tried to carve me open months ago.

I swear I catch her. For one tortured second, her scent floods me—peaches and panic. Then momentum betrays us both. What started as an attempt to save her turns into me knocking her further off-balance. White fireworks explode behind my eyes as catch becomes shove. She goes down hard and slams into the mud with a wet *crunch*.

"Ariel!"

The sound she makes when she hits the ground will haunt me forever. A sharp cry of pain that cuts through the rain and goes straight to my core.

She curls into herself immediately, both hands clutching her stomach. Rain sheets down her pallid face. Her sundress rides up, streaked with filth and something dark. Blood? Mud? I can't tell. My vision tunnels. Every scar on my body burns.

"No, no, no..." The words spill from me like a prayer as I drop to my knees beside her. Mud soaks through my pants, but I barely notice. All I can see is her face contorted in pain, the way her fingers dig into the swell of our children. "Ariel, look at me. Where does it hurt?"

She flinches when I reach for her. Her free hand fists in my soaked shirt. "They— I felt them kick. *Hard.* Sasha—"

I freeze. I'm twelve years old again, crouching over Mama's body on the pavement, wondering how to put her back together. History isn't repeating—it's rhyming, vicious and mocking.

"I'm taking you to the hospital," I tell her, already shifting to gather her in my arms. "Hold onto me."

This time, she doesn't argue.

∿

The steering wheel creaks under my grip. Rain hammers the Peugeot's roof like gunfire. I floor the accelerator, tires hydroplaning through a curve, as Ariel's whimper grates at my ears.

"Almost there," I lie.

Her knees press against the dashboard, hands splayed over her stomach. Every ragged breath kills me. I should've carried her down the hill. Should've let her rip my eyes out rather than risk this.

Stupid. Reckless. Weak.

"They're moving. I think—maybe it's okay?"

I glance over. Rainwater streaks through the mascara pooling beneath her eyes. Her sundress clings to the curve where our children grow. Alive.

For now.

The next bend comes too fast. We skid. Ariel's head snaps toward me—green eyes wide, lips parted in a silent scream. My healing ribs scream as I wrench the wheel. Gravel pings against the undercarriage, but we straighten back out and keep charging down the road.

A contraction? Spasm? Whatever it is, her body seizes.

No. No no no.

I stomp the gas. The engine wails. Ariel's fingers dig into her thighs, blunt nails tearing holes in soaked cotton.

"Talk to them." The words rip free before I can choke them back. "They know your voice."

Her sob shreds what's left of my composure. "I can't—I don't know what to—"

"Anything." I swerve around a lumbering tractor. "Please."

A shaky inhale. Then, barely audible over the storm: "Hey, little loves. It's Mama."

My throat clots. She's never called herself that before.

"You're giving me gray hairs already, you know that?" Her palm circles slowly. "But that's okay. We're okay. Just… hold on, yeah? Just a little longer."

A guttural noise escapes me. Ariel's gaze flicks up, tracking the tear I don't bother to hide.

The hospital materializes through the downpour—a concrete monstrosity crowned with flickering red letters: ***Pronto Soccorso***.

I mount the curb beside ambulances, doors flying open before the car fully stops.

She tries saying something, but I'm already lifting her. Her arms loop around my neck, forehead pressed to my jugular. Blood smears my collar. Hers? Mine? Doesn't matter.

The automatic doors hiss open. A nurse shouts in rapid-fire Italian. I follow the gurney they shove under us, refusing to release her hand even when they try to pry me away.

Until, finally, we reach the exam room. I can't go any farther. I can't save her now; only they can.

"Ariel."

She turns her head on the sterile pillow. Tears carve paths through the dirt on her cheeks. "Don't you dare leave me, Sasha Ozerov."

"I won't," I vow to her. "I never will again."

The doors swing shut in my face.

My reflection in the glass shows a wild-eyed stranger—hair matted with rain and blood, shirt clinging to half-healed scars. I press my palm to the cool surface. Somewhere beyond it, my heart beats in three bodies.

Just like that, the waiting begins.

20

SASHA

I've never hated anything more than these fluorescent lights.

It's not the first time I've had that thought. Nor is it the first time I've squinted at lights just like these and wondered what fucking demon manufactures them. They have to be the product of some lower level of hell. The buzz, the glare, the intermittent flicker—it's designed to drive a man mad.

It's working.

I pace back and forth this cramped, overheated hallway, growling under my breath. Back and forth. Back and forth. A caged tiger in a bloodstained shirt.

An elderly woman clutches her rosary tighter as I stalk past her chair for the hundredth time. One look at her and I can guess her whole life story. Born here, raised here, will die here, in this barren patch of dirt. She's never seen anything like me and she never will again.

So what the fuck do I care if she's frightened? *Guess what, babushka? I'm frightened, too. I'm fucking terrified—not only of what might be happening on the other side of those stubbornly closed doors, but also of what I myself might do if the news that passes through them is anything less than,* "Mr. Ozerov, your family is perfectly okay."

Family. That's a fucking word. For a long time now, it's been meaningless to me. Since I buried my mother and broke my father's neck, "family" has been Feliks and no one else.

Like everything else in my world, that has now changed.

A nurse approaches warily. She's holding a clipboard between us like it would protect her from me if push came to shove. In Italian, she says, "*Signore,* you're bleeding."

I pause and look behind me. I can see the muddy path I've been treading up and down the linoleum. I can also see the red slash of smeared blood dripping next to every footprint. When I check my bandages, I notice that I've once again ripped stitches wide open.

I'm hyper-aware of everything going on around me. The old nonna whispering *Ave Maria* under her breath. Mud caked beneath my fingernails. Paper rustling, wheels squeaking, and the lights, the damned lights, shrieking endlessly overhead.

Most of all, somewhere deep in my head, I hear the echoing scream.

Ariel's scream.

The crunch of impact, skull on stone.

My hands, always fucking useless when it counts.

Pathetic.

I look at the nurse. *"Non puoi aiutarmi in nessun modo che conti davvero."*

You cannot help me in any way that matters.

She backs away, making the sign of the cross over herself. Smart woman. I'm in no mood for their concern, their procedures, their fucking paperwork. My body can wait. Everything can wait.

I resume pacing. Another lap. The mud is starting to dry, flaking off my boots with each turn. I count the steps—seventeen from end to end.

The memory of Ariel's face twisted in pain haunts me. I did this. I grabbed her. I caused her to fall. If anything happens to her or our children because of my stupidity, my impatience…

My fist connects with the wall before I realize I've thrown the punch. Plaster cracks; the old woman shrieks. More stares. A security guard shifts in his chair, hand drifting uncertainly toward the radio on his belt.

I almost wish he'd call for backup. *Try and move me, motherfucker. I dare you to try.*

But the doors I wish would open remain closed. I strain to hear something, anything, but there's nothing.

A janitor slides past me, mopping down the hall. The scent of the antiseptic he's using sears my nostrils. Citrusy. Mama's perfume used to smell like that. Like lemons.

Right up until it didn't.

Her body splayed on the sidewalk. My hands, too small to stem the bleeding. Eyes blank…

My wounds pulse in time with my heartbeat. Blood trickles warm down my side, but the pain is almost welcome. It's something to focus on besides the crushing weight of helplessness.

I've killed men with my bare hands. I've built an empire from blood and bullets and sheer fucking bravado. But here, in this sterile hallway with its buzzing lights and judging eyes, I'm nothing. Less than nothing. Just a man who couldn't protect what matters most.

Another lap. Another seventeen steps. The mud continues to flake away, leaving pieces of me scattered across the floor like breadcrumbs leading from nowhere to nowhere.

I stop my pacing halfway through a lap and rest my forehead against the cold glass of the door, willing it to open. On the other side, Ariel fights for three lives. On this side, I can only wait and pray to a God I stopped believing in long ago.

Don't you dare leave me, Sasha Ozerov, she'd said.

But I'm the one left behind, pacing these seventeen steps in a loop I can't escape.

Through gritted teeth, I pull out my phone. The screen is still damp from the springs, but it works. Kosti picks up on the first ring.

"Don't talk; just listen. Ariel fell. We're at—" I look around me until I find the name of the hospital printed above the door. Then I read it off in clipped, emotionless syllables. "Get here. Now."

He doesn't waste time with questions, just grunts his acknowledgment before hanging up. Good man.

But when the call ends, my thumb lingers over the screen. It's strange to be so distant from a man I've always called my brother. Since our days in the slums of Moscow together, causing chaos and evading my father's tyranny, Feliks has been at my side for everything of importance. Now, I'm half a world away from him, and it's like missing a limb.

Fucking hell. I'm getting sappy. God forbid he ever learns about these thoughts; he'd never let me hear the end of it.

I hesitate for a moment longer. It's not assistance I need; there's precious little he can do from America. There's nothing to coordinate, nothing to torture, nothing to kill.

Nothing but the demons in my head.

I press call.

"Well, well." His voice is hazy with sleep, but the sardonic edge is there. "The ghost speaks. Speaketh. Whatever."

"Shut up." But there's no real heat in it. The cadence of his voice smacks me harder than I expected, like homesickness for a place I didn't know I'd missed.

"Your social skills haven't improved in exile, I see. "

"Ariel's in the hospital. I'm not in the mood for jokes."

The humor drains from his voice instantly. "How bad?"

"I don't know yet. She fell. There was blood. That's all I've got."

A sharp intake of breath. Then: "What do you need?"

"Nothing. I just…" I trail off, unsure why I really called. To hear a friendly voice? To confess my failures to the one person who's seen me at my worst? "I fucked up, brother."

"You're there with her?"

"Yes."

"Then you haven't fucked up completely." A pause. "What about the babies?"

"No word yet." My voice stumbles on the last word. Feliks is kind enough to pretend not to notice.

"Want me to fly out?"

"No. Stay in New York. Keep building." *Keep the empire standing for when I return.*

If not for me, then for my children.

He hadn't said much when I texted him about the pregnancy. Just a classic **I'll be damned. More Sasha Ozerovs soon? The world shudders.** Maybe he knew that I wasn't ready to assess the meaning of it all yet, and so it was easy to hide behind the usual jokes and bullshitting.

I start to say, "I—" But then the doors swing open and a man emerges.

He's a doctor, by the looks of him, if white coats mean anything out here. He scans the room and sees me and his eyes widen.

"I have to go. The doctors—"

"Call me when you know more," he cuts in. "And Sasha… I'm here for you, brother. Always."

He hangs up before I can give him shit for being so in touch with his feelings.

The doctor shifts his weight back and forth as I charge up to him. He's got shadows under his eyes that say he's been here for a while. With a gulp, he launches into rapid Italian, medical terms flying past faster than I can track. I catch fragments: monitoring, scans, *distacco della placenta*— placental something. My jaw clenches as it all washes over me in an incomprehensible wave.

I can't deal with this shit. I need simple, direct.

"English," I growl.

He switches over, though his accent remains thick and halting. "Placenta." He mimes tearing. "*Distacco?* Bleeding, maybe. We watch. One hour, no more."

My fists clench at my sides. "The babies?"

"Strong. Both, yes."

"And she's okay?"

If he's intimidated, he hides it well. He nods. "She asks for you." The doctor touches my arm—brave of him—and adds quietly, "Let us do our work. Soon. Soon, you see her."

Then he turns and the doors swallow him whole. Behind me, the janitor mops my blood from the floor. Swirls of pink vanishing down the drain. Overhead, the fluorescents seem to increase in volume, like angry cicadas. I'm suddenly overwhelmed by a desire to be anywhere but here.

I see a sign over a nearby door: ***Obitorio.***

I know that word. *Morgue.* That'll work.

I push through and descend the stairs. The first thing that hits me is the smell: antiseptic masking decay, the same in every hospital across the world. My boots echo against linoleum floors that have seen too much death.

It might've been optimistic to hope for escape. The morgue's fluorescent buzz matches the one upstairs—different circle of hell, but the same devils in charge.

And those devils seem determined to make me remember things I'd much rather forget.

I'm twelve again, sitting on a metal bench while technicians wheel my mother past in a black bag. Father's hand clamps down on my shoulder, fingers digging into muscle and bone.

"Stop crying," he hisses. "Ozerov men don't cry."

I'd bitten his wrist. A feral thing. As was he—he'd slammed my face against the corpse fridge. I swore into the metal, through bloodied lips: *Never again. I'll burn the world before I let someone I love die scared and cold and far from home.*

Now, the morgue hums its old hymn.

Never again, you said.

Ariel's blood streaks my palm.

Never again, you vowed.

So much for keeping my promises.

The morgue door creaks open. I don't look up—don't care if it's the security guard, a meddling nurse, or even an animated corpse coming down here to awaken its brethren. But then a voice slices through the rot.

"I think all the security guys are too scared to tell you you aren't supposed to be down here."

Jasmine's flats click against the tile stairs. She joins me sitting on the floor with my back against the wall, skirts pooling around her like ink. For fifteen years, I've only seen her in flickers of daydreams. I told myself she was happy, whole, free, because my conscience needed to know I'd done the right thing. Now, here she is: in a fucking morgue while her sister meets God knows what kind of fate upstairs.

How's your conscience feel about that one, eh, Sashenka?

Her fingers wrap around my crimson-smeared hand. The gesture is so pure, so unthinking. It floors me. "What do we know?"

"Not much. They're gonna be okay, I think." The words rasp my throat raw. "For now. Alive, if nothing else."

The scent of her steams between us. "And you?" She squeezes until I meet her gaze. "Are you alive, Sasha Ozerov?"

The refrigerating motors hum. Twelve-year-old me screams into the blank steel doors.

"I love her, you know."

She brushes my knuckles. "I know."

"I love her so much it fucking terrifies me. She makes me want to be... better. Different. More than just Yakov Ozerov's son with his hands full of blood." I swallow hard. "But look what I've done to her. To both of you. Look how close I came to—"

"Stop." Jasmine's voice carries iron I've never heard before. "You are not him. You will never be him."

"No?" I gesture at our surroundings: the morgue, the shadows, the guilt heavy as a coffin lid. "I put her here, just like he put my mother in the ground. The same violence. The same legacy."

"The difference," she says quietly, "is that you're sitting here hating yourself for it. Where is he?"

"Burning in hell, if there's any justice in this universe."

"Hell is a place in your mind," she murmurs, with the quiet of someone reciting something they've dwelled over for too many long nights. "You can walk out of it any time you like. All you have to do is—"

The door bangs open. We both look up the stairs to see a timid nurse. "*Signore? Tua moglie...*"

Jasmine's grip on my hand tightens as I bound to my feet. "Sasha."

I pause. The freezer at my back exhales frost. Jasmine is looking up at me. Her face is so like Ariel's and yet so different, like someone drew one from the memory of the other.

"It's going to be okay," she tells me.

I wish I had her confidence.

I cover her hand with mine for a moment, unable to speak. Then I let go and follow the nurse up towards the light, leaving the ghosts of my father's legacy behind in the morgue where they belong.

Upstairs, Ariel is waiting.

21

SASHA

I pause outside the door. I'm half-tempted to go back to the waiting room and borrow that old woman's rosary. If there were ever a time for prayers, this would be it.

Then I remember who the fuck I am, and I walk inside.

The beeping hits me first. Three distinct rhythms merging into a symphony that makes my knees weak: two rapid flutters accompanied by a slower, steadier pulse.

Our children.

Their mother.

All still breathing.

Proof I haven't destroyed everything. Not yet, at least.

Ariel looks impossibly small in the hospital bed, swallowed by starched white sheets and medical equipment. Her skin is nearly as pale as the linens, except for the dark circles carved beneath her eyes. Tubes snake from her arms, and electrode pads peek out from the neckline of her hospital gown. The mud and rain are gone, but somehow, that only makes her seem more fragile.

A different doctor stands at the foot of her bed. He looks at me and begins to speak in Italian. I have an easier time understanding him. *The fall caused some minor placental disruption. Not a complete abruption, but enough to warrant concern.*

I grip the metal railing of her bed until my knuckles go white. Ariel's hand twitches toward mine but stops short.

"The twins are stable," the doctor continues. "Heart rates normal, good movement. But…" He pauses, looking between us. "Complete bed rest. Minimum one week. No stress, no physical activity. The risk of preterm labor is very high if—"

"She won't lift a finger." My voice sounds strange to my own ears. Raw, like I've been screaming. Maybe I have been, inside my head.

"I'll have the nurse bring in the paperwork," the doctor says, backing toward the door. "Call if anything changes."

When we're alone, the beeping fills the silence between us. I watch the monitors, memorizing the patterns of those three precious heartbeats like they're coordinates leading home.

"I'm sorry," I whisper. "I never meant to—"

"It's my fault. Not yours." She reaches out to touch my knuckles. "Just an accident. Nothing more."

I kneel at her bedside and press my forehead to her hand. Yakov started with "accidents," too. A push here, a shove there. Always with an excuse, always with regret afterwards. Until the day came when he stopped bothering with those things.

The excuses and regret disappeared.

The bruises stayed.

I can't stop seeing Ariel's face as she fell. The terror in her eyes. But even as she tumbled down, her hands went not to break her fall but to cradle our children.

I'm glad I'm kneeling already, because otherwise, I'd collapse. Her fingers are warmer now, but too delicate. Everything about her seems so utterly fucking breakable.

"I pushed you. I grabbed you. I tried to—"

Fuck me. These words are impossible to say. How do I tell her that my greatest fear isn't Dragan or losing my empire, but becoming the monster who gave me this scar? That every time I close my eyes, I see myself morphing into my father's reflection?

"I'm the one who ran down a muddy hill." Her nails bite my scalp, forcing my gaze up. "Like a fucking idiot in flip-flops."

"But I said—"

"We both said things we shouldn't have. We keep doing that. You'd think, eventually, we'd learn." Ariel cups my face tenderly. "We both have amends to make, Sasha. You're not the only one who's been running scared."

The monitor beeps steadily, a metronome counting the seconds between who I was and who I need to become. I turn my face into her palm, letting her touch anchor me to this moment. Not to the ghosts of my past or the shadows of what might be, but to here and now. To her.

"I won't let him win," I whisper against her skin. "I won't become him."

Her fingers tighten in my hair. "I know."

We stay like that for a while—me kneeling at her side, her stroking through my hair again and again. On second thought, who needs rosary beads? I have this woman to pray with. To pray for.

After a while, though, my body begins to ache. I haul myself upright and start for the door.

But Ariel catches my wrist. "Don't go," she says when I look back at her. "Not yet." Then she wriggles to the side and pats the space on the bed next to her.

I look at it and laugh. "I'm a little bigger than that, *ptichka.*"

She rolls her eyes. "Yes, yes, you're huge and strong and we are all pitiful in comparison. Now, shut up and come cuddle me. I'm cold."

With a tortured laugh, I obey. The bed creaks under our combined weight. I brace one arm above her head, terrified of crushing her, but Ariel yanks my collar hard enough to pop a button. "Stop hovering. Lie down."

"You'll fall off the edge."

"Then catch me." There's a ghost of her old teasing in her voice. "You're good at that, when you're not the one pushing me."

She's all sharp angles under the thin gown—hip bone jutting into my thigh, IV cord tangled between us. I settle on my side, hand hovering over her stomach. The bed wasn't built for someone my size, let alone two people, but we manage.

Her head finds the hollow of my shoulder, breath warm against my throat. My palm stays pressed to the swell of her stomach, protective and possessive. Through the thin hospital gown, I can feel the flutter of movement—our children, safe and alive despite my mistakes.

"They always settle down when you touch them," Ariel murmurs, already heavy with exhaustion. "Like they know their papa is keeping watch."

Papa. Two syllables shouldn't be that heavy. I'm going to be a father.

Not a father like him, though. Never like him. These children will never know the taste of fear or the sting of betrayal or how it feels when barbed wire tears your throat in two. They'll never have to learn how to hide bruises or hold their breath when footsteps approach their door.

After a while, Ariel's breathing evens out into sleep. I press my lips to the crown of her head, breathing her in. Memorizing the weight of her leg hooked over mine, the prickle of her lashes against my pulse. This—us—is a shooting star I'm cupping in bleeding palms.

Please. Let me keep it. Just this once.

"Marry me," I whisper to her.

She won't say yes. She can't. But that doesn't mean I'll stop asking. I'm going to keep asking, again and again, until she believes that I mean what I say.

I can wait.

22

ARIEL

ONE WEEK LATER

How many hours of staring at the same ceiling does it take for a person to go insane?

Asking for a friend.

I'm lying on my back because that's all I do these days, looking up at shadows dancing across the stucco as another storm rolls in. The ceiling has exactly one hundred and forty-three cracks, in case anyone was wondering. I've counted each and every one of them. The particularly interesting little fellas get names.

Crack Johnson.

President Andrew Crackson.

Snap, Crackle, and Pop.

The lights flicker again. Storm number four this week wails against the window. It feels like they're getting worse. Each storm inevitably knocks out the power for a minute or two, dropping us into a breathless dark until the generators perk back to life.

Not that it changes much for me. I'm stuck here whether we have power or not.

Sasha took the doctor's orders to heart. He wasn't kidding about not letting me lift so much as a finger. Since we got back to the villa after one night's stay at the hospital, the man who once ordered hits without blinking now fusses if I so much as reach for a glass of water. Yesterday, I caught him arguing with Jasmine about the proper way to fluff my pillows. It would be funny if it wasn't so surreal.

Almost as surreal as him being here at all. I'd wondered for six months how it would feel for the husband chair in every exam room to be filled.

It's filled now.

Sasha shows no signs of vacating it.

I, surprisingly... don't hate it? It's hard to hate something you find yourself longing for in idle moments. Sure, I tried to replace Sasha's face with someone else's in my fantasies, but I dunno—Chris Hemsworth's jawline just never quite looked right when I superimposed it onto Sasha's body.

I guess I'm just scared of letting myself start to rely on it. On him. On that chair being filled, every time I look.

You emotional little dreamer, I tell myself when the monitors sync with his snoring. *You're pathetic.*

Right on cue, there's a knock at the door. "Lunch," Sasha announces.

I take a look at the tray he's holding and grimace. "I'd rather chew the bedpan than eat another salad."

"Unfortunately for you, while the bedpan is high in iron, it severely lacks in B-complex vitamins." He sets the tray on my bedside table and settles into the chair where he's taken up residence these days.

"I'm gonna turn into a huge 'B-complex' if you keep force-feeding me rabbit food."

"Eat," he growls, "or I'll strap you to the bed."

"That would change literally nothing. I'm here anyways, aren't I?"

Sasha grins. "Now, you're starting to understand."

He spears some greens with a fork and holds it out to me. His face says, *I dare you to say no.*

"I can hold a damn fork, you know."

"Prove it." His smirk sharpens. "Move your arm without wincing."

Bastard. The muscle strain from the fall still burns, but I'd rather swallow live bees than admit it. So, with no other choice, I part my lips. The fork's edge presses against my tongue.

His eyes never leave mine.

"Happy?" I ask around the tang of radishes and carrots.

"Getting there." The room dims as thunder rattles the villa. Sasha's head snaps toward the window, shoulders tensing.

"It's just a storm," I remind him.

But he doesn't relax. Shadows carve his profile into something feral, beautiful. A guard dog waiting to lunge.

The lights die.

I feel his weight shift before I see it—his body curving over mine, one arm braced against the headboard. The generators hum to life seconds later, revealing his knuckles white on the fork.

Only when his eyes meet mine again does he ease back into his chair.

He thrusts the next bite at me. I take it, defiant, even as heat pools low in my belly. Teacup steam fogs his scar when he offers it. Our fingers tangle on the porcelain. He strokes my wrist—once, fleeting—before retreating.

"I really am fine, you know. It's basically been a week. I could get up and—"

"You're fine when I say you're fine," he snarls.

The words would sound tyrannical from anyone else. But I've learned to read the undertones of fear in Sasha's voice, the way his growl roughens when he's worried. It makes me want to simultaneously soothe him and smother him with a pillow.

"Sasha. Seriously. I'm okay. Let me at least feed myself."

He glares at me for a second. But then he sighs. "Fine. But when I come back to get that tray, it better be gone."

I throw him a sloppy salute. "Sir, yes, sir. And when you say, 'Jump,' I'll say, 'How high?'"

He returns my salute with a one-fingered salute of his own. Then he turns to leave, though not without a last, meaningful glance at the salad.

When the door clicks shut behind him, though, I immediately abandon the tasteless shrubbery and pick up the journal from underneath my pillow. Page one has a list I've been working on all week.

Pros of Letting Sasha Ozerov Back Into My Life:

1. *Obnoxiously good-looking.*
2. *Very tall.*
3. *Like, very tall.*

My pen hovers. The page blurs. All the things I can't bring myself to write down go spiraling through my mind's eye.

His forehead pressed to my hospital bed rail as he prayed. Desperate mutters in Russian. A palm spanning my entire belly and the two worlds contained within it when he climbed in beside me, all restrained strength, like he could shield us from the world with just his ragged breath.

I shiver and redirect my attention to the other half of the page.

Cons:

1. *Lied about Jasmine.*
2. *Violent.*
3. *Like, very violent.*

It's a stalemate.

Outside, warm rain slaps the courtyard tiles. Sasha's voice slices through the storm, arguing with Kosti about how to repair the sputtering generator. He leans against the villa's crumbling fountain, one hand pressed to his ribs. Even from here, I see the tension in his jaw, the damp sheen on his temple.

Stubborn protectiveness, I write in the **Pros** column, then immediately scratch it out. That's not necessarily a good thing—his overcautious hovering drives me crazy half the time. The sad little salad at my side is proof of that.

Sasha's voice raises up over the wind. "—said 'generator for everything we could ever need.' Does that not include *actual fucking power*, Kost—"

"—told you I haven't been here in years! I'm not a damn electrician, son. I barely know how to dial—"

Jasmine tugs Kosti's sleeve to pull him away from his rant. "Let Sasha play handyman. We need groceries before the roads flood anyway. You and I can take the trip into town."

The engine of the Peugeot coughs to life. Sasha starts to head inside. But just before he disappears from sight, he pauses and looks up at my window. He stands there, silhouetted, soaked shirt clinging to the hard lines of his back.

The pen squeaks in my hand.

I should resent this. The performative martyrdom. The way he's grafting himself into the infrastructure of my survival, one repaired fuse and forced beet salad at a time.

But all I taste is hope as he limps down into the cellar.

I make a few half-hearted attempts at the salad before I give up, lean over toward the open window, and scrape the whole thing out into the courtyard. Maybe that asshole rooster will choke on a beet.

The empty plate comes back wet as the storm rages on. I'm fishing for my journal again when suddenly, with a mournful wheeze, the power goes out. And when the lights die this time, they don't come back.

I count sixty-three heartbeats before I decide, *Screw this.*

My legs wobble when I swing them over the mattress. An oversized robe hangs from the bedpost. I cinch it around my belly, fabric straining over the growing swell. The floorboards creak as I shuffle toward the door with one hand braced against the wall for support.

Darkness clusters in the hallway. I know these turns by now —right at the crack in the plaster, left where the grandfather clock ticks. Thunder snarls as I reach the stairs from the second story to the ground floor.

A faint, guttural Russian curse rolls up from the shadows.

"Sasha?"

No answer. Just the rasp of labored breathing.

I descend step by step, palm slick on the railing. When I reach the ground floor, I pause and listen. For a moment, there's nothing. Then I hear it again.

"Motherfuckinggoddamnblyat'blyat'blyat."

I suppress a smile. I take it that generator repair is not going so well.

Shuffling my way blindly over to the cellar door, I start the hike downstairs. It's slow-going in the dark and the stairs are old, so I'm extra careful. But when I reach the bottom, there's some light.

A flashlight lies propped up in one corner. Its beam catches Sasha crouched against the wall, shirt abandoned to reveal fresh blood seeping through his bandages.

The generator's guts spill across the floor like it's just as broken as he is—wires severed, parts scattered. Sasha's knuckles drip onto a wrench.

"I didn't know they made handymen so foul-mouthed out here," I remark.

There's a clank and another curse as Sasha extracts his head from the mess. "Someone has to do it."

I can't help giggling. "Hero complex acting up again?"

He scowls at me. "It's more useful than your martyr fetish."

"Says the man who'd rather bleed out than ask for help."

"This generator is going to be the one bleeding out if it doesn't start fucking cooperating," he spits, like he can intimidate the thing into proper working order.

"It takes a big man to insult an inanimate object to its face like that," I say, suppressing another laugh.

Sasha remains unamused. "You're supposed to be in bed, not down here antagonizing me from the fucking peanut gallery."

"Bed is a lot less fun."

A lot less visually interesting, too. Sasha's shirtless body may be a wreck, but it's a beautiful one. His muscles flex as he wrestles a rusted bolt. Sweat glazes the scarred planes of his back, tattoos shifting with every motion.

"And yet, for at least—" He checks his watch by the glow of the flashlight. "—sixteen more hours, it's the only place you're allowed to be. Besides," he adds with a devilish gleam in his eye, "I can think of plenty of ways to have fun in bed."

That rasping edge in his voice makes my insides squirm in a way I haven't felt in six long months.

"Stay over there," I warn him. "The generator is a lot more likely to let you stick your hands in it than I am."

Sasha laughs. "You weren't all that hard to convince, if I remember correctly."

My jaw falls open. "Asshole!" I look around for something to weaponize. Finding a bundle of wires by my feet, I chuck them at his head.

He ducks and keeps laughing. Then it fades into something more serious. "I mean it, though, Ariel. This isn't me being a control freak; I just want you and the babies to be safe."

Dammit. Unfair tactics win yet again. It's criminal that he keeps getting away with this.

"But if you insist on disobeying," he says, "I'll carry you upstairs myself."

Again, something low in my belly quivers in a way that's not at all unpleasant.

"Fine." I turn and start the slow trek back to the stairs. That nice heat stays simmering the whole way. It occurs to me how easy it would be to let bygones be bygones. Kosti and Jasmine will be gone for a while yet—maybe hours, if the rain keeps them stranded in town. I could stay down here and take what I want from Sasha. A quick, breathless romp in the dark. No one would have to know. I could pretend it never happened. My hormones, if nothing else, would be extremely pleased.

But I can't do that. Some bridges can't be uncrossed, and that's one of them. I need to remember where the lines are and why I put them there.

It's for the best this way, I tell myself. Just go back upstairs and climb into bed. Hell, maybe even take Sasha's suggestion to heart. A little fun in bed all by your lonesome and you can kick that horny can down the road for a little while longer.

That sounds like a much better idea. Once I'm upstairs, I can let myself be transported somewhere else entirely. I'll dissipate all these unwanted feelings and get back to my grim, unwavering focus on the nine weeks left until the rest of my life begins.

As I reach the top of the stairs, I find that there's only one problem with that plan.

The door won't open.

The handle doesn't budge when I twist it. "This cannot be real." I try again, but it's even more stuck than it was before. "Fuck. Fuckity fuck. Uh… Sasha? Can you help me, please?"

The wrench clanks. Sasha's boots thud up the stairs behind me. His heat presses close as he reaches over my shoulder to try the knob.

"Move," he growls.

"Wow, so helpful—"

The door groans but doesn't budge. Sasha curses again. The flashlight wobbles underneath his face.

He steps back, fingers flexing like he might try to punch through solid oak. I grab his wrist. "Don't you dare," I snap as he prepares to turn himself into a battering ram. "If you hurt yourself again, we'd be stuck here until Kosti and Jasmine get home, and who knows how long that'll be?"

"Goddammit. Fine." Darkness swallows his smirk. "I guess the fun stays down here for now."

23

ARIEL

My nipples could cut glass.

We've been down here for an hour and I'm already wishing I'd never rebelled against Sasha's bedrest instructions in the first place. "Under my covers" sounds like a really nice place to be right now.

If nothing else, it'd be less tense. Sasha and I are sitting in the pool of light from his flashlight—which, conveniently enough, is growing dimmer and dimmer with every minute that passes.

"Kosti is supposed to get new batteries," he explains with a grimace.

"Perfect," I chirped back. "What wonderful timing for them to die."

It is actually nice in one sense, which is that darkness is gradually swallowing up his face. The less of him I can see, the better, seeing as how the Hungry Hungry Hormones I'd been so eager to work out upstairs seem intent on sticking around.

And they sense prey.

Or predator, rather. Because Sasha Ozerov, shirtless in the dark, is the kind of thing that does hunting all on its own.

"You're shivering," he notes suddenly.

I cup my hands over my chest so he can't see proof that he's one hundred percent on the money. "Am not."

His shirt hits my lap before I can protest—still warm from his body. We're on the mountain all over again, but this time around, there's way less glitter to amuse myself with.

"Don't," he says when I try to hand it back. "The babies need you warm."

"I said I'm fine."

"You're stubborn, is what you are."

"Takes one to know one."

But I still shift uncomfortably. Turns out a thin, silk bathrobe is not ideal attire for crouching in dank cellars. Who knew? I've never felt more exposed.

Well, that's not entirely true. I once wore a basically invisible bikini to drive a man I knew a little bit crazy. That involved a pretty fair amount of exposure in its own right.

The memories crop up, bit by bit, and my internal heat goes up a degree for each one. On the plus side, I'm no longer quite so cold. On the downside, I'm now much, much more turned on than I was before.

Problematic.

"Okay, new pastime for our indefinite imprisonment." I clap once, the sound swallowed by musty air. "Let's play Two Truths and a Lie."

"Are we on an elementary school playground?" he drawls.

"Actually, we're stuck in a cellar, in case you hadn't noticed. And if I have to sit here and listen to you breathe for the next six hours, I might go cuckoo. Just indulge me. Please."

Sasha sighs. His flashlight-cast shadow rears against the opposite wall. "You've lost your mind."

"And you've lost the ability to say no. I'll start." I shift on the cold concrete, the robe riding up my thighs. "One: I set my seventh grade science fair project on fire to avoid presenting. Two: My first kiss was in a jump castle. Three: I used to steal my mom's *Vogue* magazines to sketch wedding dresses in the margins."

"The science fair," Sasha decides immediately.

"Wrong." I bite my lip to keep from smirking. "Mrs. Townsend's classroom probably still smells like burnt poster board."

His eyes narrow. "The wedding dresses, then?"

"Not that, either. Mom thought the pages were haunted," I admit. "Dozens of disembodied gowns floating in her perfume ads."

"A jump castle, then." Sasha's scoff warms my neck. "How romantic."

"'Stupid' is a better word. Your turn, tough guy."

He leans back, muscles flexing. "One: I killed my first man at fifteen. Two: I once nursed a stray puppy back to health.

Three: When I was fourteen, I stole my father's vintage Lada and drove it into the Neva River."

I study his face for a minute. "The puppy's a lie."

His smirk glints in the dying flashlight beam. "What gave it away?"

"The part where you're not secretly a Disney princess."

"Pity. I'd look good in a ballgown."

My turn again. I tuck hair behind my ear, pulse thrumming where my thigh touches his. "One: My college boyfriend proposed with a Ring Pop at a Waffle House. Two: I tried dating other men while I was pregnant, just to prove I could move on. Three: I've never been in love before you."

Sasha's flashlight sputters. His voice is a strained croak. "The Ring Pop."

"No," I say sadly, confirming what he already knew. "French guys just don't do it for me."

"Is that the only reason, Ariel?"

We're working with the barest of gleams now. It's just enough to see his outline in this windowless cellar and no more than that. "No. It's not. I couldn't move on because, even when I hated you, even when I cursed your name... I still missed you, Sasha."

He swallows and nods. "My turn again, right?"

My throat feels too tight to answer, so I just nod right back.

"One." His breath flutters against my collarbone. "I've dreamed of you every night since you left." Closer now, lips skating my temple. "Two. I read every article you ever published." Closer still, teeth at my earlobe, heat blanketing every inch of me. "Three. I've slept outside your door every night this week."

The flashlight gives one final whine and dies, submerging us in complete darkness. I feel Sasha shift beside me, his breath warm against my cheek.

"The second one's a lie," I mumble. "You don't care about my writing."

Sasha's finger comes up to graze my chin. "I care about every fucking word that comes out of your mouth, Ariel. Even the ones that gut me. Maybe even especially those ones."

Then his mouth finds mine in the darkness. It's a messy kiss, fumbling like it's the first time we've ever done it. When he pulls away, he stays close enough for our breaths to mingle.

"The others were true, too. I watch you sleep," he rasps. "Count every breath. Memorize the way your lips part when you dream." His thumb smears my ruined lipstick. "I missed you in my bones, *ptichka.* In the hollow places Yakov carved out."

"I missed you, too," I whisper. "Every damn day."

His exhale shudders through me. "Then stop running from me."

I feel trembly and insane all over. My fingers won't stop shaking, not from cold, but from something else entirely. A chill that doesn't have anything to do with temperature.

"Here's three more," I mumble. "I want you. I don't want you. I don't know how to be without you."

I hear Sasha's breath catch. "Maybe not everything is so easily divided into lies and truths. Maybe we're just always meant to be messy and conflicted. Maybe... maybe we can make it work anyway."

"Yeah," I whisper back, fueled by stupid hope and midnight dreams and the romanticism that my mama carved into my bones, the same way Sasha's father carved hate into his. "Maybe we can."

This time, it's me who kisses him.

He drags me into his lap, the two of us fused at the mouth, with my belly as a surprising new presence between us. "*Moya lyubimaya*," he growls between kisses. His hands shove the robe up my thighs. "So fucking perfect."

"Sasha, I—"

"Shh." He nips my jaw. "Just let me..."

His mouth closes over my nipple through the flimsy silk. I arch with a whimper. The rational part of my brain—the one that makes pro/con lists and swore to keep boundaries— drowns in a flood of oxytocin and poor decisions.

His hardness at my inner thigh is huge and impossible to ignore. I reach down to palm him, loving it, hating myself for it, wanting it all too badly to care about the difference between those things.

Sasha is right—truths and lies are all so jumbled up; how could people who were raised the way we were ever hope to figure it out? We just do the best we can with what we have and try to let our better sides win.

My better side wants this so fucking badly that I can't tell it no. As a matter of fact, as Sasha's hands slip up my thighs to cup my ass and grind me against him... as his kisses flare hot like streaking comets from one breast to the other... as he drags a finger across my aching pussy...

All I can say is *"yes."*

I fumble to free him from his pants. He's huge and thick in my hand, velvety soft but rock-hard. He groans as I wrap my fingers around his base.

I raise myself up and line him against me. I shouldn't—*we* shouldn't—but I want to so, so, so—

Then the cellar door opens.

"Ariel? Sasha?" Jasmine's voice slices through the haze. "Why is there salad in the front—"

Flashlight beams blind us.

We freeze—me half-naked on the shelves, Sasha's hand shoved down between my legs, his lips glistening. Jasmine's choked laugh echoes down the stairs.

"Well." She clears her throat. "Glad to see you're... bonding."

Then she turns and shuffles away.

Sasha's chest heaves against mine. Slowly, so slowly, he helps me to my feet. The robe slithers back into place. My dignity, however, remains in tatters on the cellar floor.

He tucks a lock of hair behind my ear. His hands shake. "Ariel..."

"Let's just say, *That happened,* and then move on as if it didn't." I step back, hugging myself. The cold rushes in where his heat had been. "It's better that way, I think."

He watches me climb the stairs, each step heavier than the last. He makes no move to follow.

In the kitchen, Jasmine pretends to be extremely occupied with sorting groceries. Kosti whistles off-key as he takes another trip to the car to retrieve the rest. I beeline for the bedroom. Lock the door. Slump against it.

My lips still tingle. His taste lingers—coffee and guilt and want. Down the hall, the shower kicks on. I imagine him under the spray, one fist braced against the tile and the other wrapped around himself, water sluicing over the wounds we've given each other as he does what I should've done: burned away the lust before it got out of control.

The journal waits under my pillow. I pick up my pen and add to it.

Pros of Letting Sasha Ozerov Back Into My Life:

1. ***Kissing him feels like home, even when it shouldn't.***

When the floorboards creak hours later, I pretend to be asleep. Sasha's shadow pauses at the foot of my bed. Then he turns and retreats back into the hallway.

I can tell by his footsteps, though: He doesn't go far.

24

ARIEL

The Moka pot is growling at me. I'm inclined to growl back.

After... whatever the hell we're calling last night, I woke up in the foulest mood known to womankind. My back is hurting like I never went to the hot springs in the first place, my head feels like a donkey kicked it in two, and I barely slept at all, tossing and turning between dreams of Sasha and a rooster I'm really learning to despise.

All of which means, of course, that Jasmine and Kosti come thumping downstairs singing fucking *showtunes*.

"Five hundred twenty-five thousand six hundred miiinuuuuutes..." they wail. They're somehow in perfect unison and yet wildly off-key at the same time. It's honestly kind of impressive.

They stop when they see me eyeing the Moka pot with my back steadfastly turned to Sasha. For his part, Sasha shows the exact same amount of interest in talking to me. He's been pushing a pile of scrambled eggs around his plate since the minute I came downstairs. Both of us are perfectly happy to ignore the hickey blooming on my collarbone.

I see Kosti and Jas look at each other. Jas speaks first. "... Everything alright down here, love?"

"Oh, we're doing fucking *grand*," I mutter. "For fuck's sake, why won't this fucking coffee boil? My God. I'm being divinely punished."

"Right. Grand. Well... open the hatch! It's medicine time." Jas, still humming, reaches above me to the cabinet where we've been keeping the prenatal vitamins. She plucks down the orange bottle containing my blood pressure meds, unscrews the top, and starts counting pills out into my upturned palm. "One... Two... Ope. Well, that's not so grand."

Sasha looks up, brow furrowed. "We're out?"

Jasmine shakes the empty pill bottle. "Lock, stock, and barrel."

"Fuck," he says.

"Fuck," I say.

"Road trip!" chirps Jasmine.

That immediately sets off a massive storm of arguing and cross-talking. The four of us keep raising our voices until we're all shouting over each other. The Moka pot keeps growling louder and louder, too, like it doesn't want to be left out.

"—supposed to refill them—"

"—not my fucking job to babysit—"

"—if I'm not allowed to lift a finger, then how could it possibly be—"

What it boils down to is this: I need those meds. They're the only thing keeping my blood pressure from flying up to join the comma club. But the *farmacia* in Roccastrada has a limited supply. Same with the local hospital. A proper refill will require a trip all the way to the city of Siena. Given how bad the roads have been with all the storms lately, that means at least a ninety-minute drive each way. And Sasha seems to think that that's just beyond the pale.

He is in my face, snarling, "You're not cleared for—"

"—sitting in a car?" I snap. "Wow, what a *strenuous* activity. However will I manage? It's almost like you—"

Jasmine snorts. "Ariel, you should really consider—"

Kosti chimes in, "The girl is not a prisoner. Let's all be reasonable and—"

It all comes to a sudden and abrupt end when Sasha pulls out his snarliest snarl. "That's fucking enough."

All of us finally fall quiet. I look at him. Kosti and Jasmine have been cowed into submission.

Me? Not so much.

"No," I say. "Not 'enough.' I've been on bedrest for a week and I'm going to go absolutely fucking Looney Tunes if I have to stay here for a minute longer. Also, as of four hours ago, I'm officially free as a bird. And anyway, it doesn't make sense for it to happen any other way. Jasmine doesn't speak Italian, Kosti can't drive for shit, and you don't know enough about my medical conditions to answer questions. So you and I are going to play nice. We're going to get in that car and drive to Siena. And you know what? I might even roll the window down and enjoy the trip a little bit. That's what's happening, Sasha Ozerov. I dare you to tell me otherwise."

His nostrils flare as he stares down at me. Blue eyes churn. Then: "Fine. The car leaves in five, whether or not you're in it."

Sasha drives like he has a personal vendetta against every sharp corner. He doesn't seem super thrilled with me, either.

I roll down the window. He reaches across me and rolls it up.

I turn on the radio. He turns it off.

I start to hum. He presses a finger to my lips and says, "Don't even fucking think about it."

Two Truths and a Lie. What a stupid game. If I never play it again, it'll still be too soon.

But even though the tension between us is disgustingly thick after the cellar shenanigans, I really am happy to be outdoors again. Most of the storms have gone to bother someone else, so through the windshield, sunlit Tuscany blurs into daubs of cypress and terracotta.

When we reach Siena, Sasha parallel parks with a jerk of the wheel that makes my teeth clack. "Let's make this quick."

He's already out, circling to my door. When he yanks it open, his palm splays against the small of my back. Heat seeps through the shirt. He grazes the lowest bump of spine as I shuffle out, breath hitching.

"Watch the curb." His warning rumbles through his chest into mine.

I stumble anyway. His arm bands around my waist, hauling me flush against him. Our reflection warps in a shop window

—a grotesque parody of domesticity. His scarred throat. My swollen belly. The violet bruise on my collarbone where his mouth fused to my pulse in the dark.

He releases me so abruptly I sway.

Inside the pharmacy, I do my best impression of a mime while explaining my prescription to the elderly clerk. Sasha looms at my shoulder, offering blunt grunts to clarify one point or another.

"*Aspetta*," the clerk murmurs when we're done, vanishing into the back. He returns a moment later with the pharmacist in tow, carrying a white paper bag, his smile crinkling behind wire-framed glasses.

"*Una bella famiglia!*" the pharmacists crows. He switches to English. "Twins are a blessing. You and your husband must be so happy."

Sasha's hand flexes against my lower back. I open my mouth to correct him—*we're not together; he's just the sperm donor*—but Sasha cuts in first.

"Couldn't be happier," he grits out.

The pharmacist just nods, oblivious to the tension radiating through Sasha's hand and into my spine. He taps the prescription label. "Blood pressure is high, yes?"

"Only when I'm around," Sasha mutters.

I elbow him. "I'm fine. The human barnacle here is the problem, but not for that much longer, praise be."

The pharmacist blinks, my sarcasm lost in translation. Sasha's lips twitch. "She says thank you."

The man shuffles through more questions—due date, ultrasounds, any complications. Each answer tightens the invisible wire between us. Sasha answers in clipped Italian when I falter, his palm a brand through my shirt.

Finally, the chatty pharmacist bids us farewell. Sasha's fingers brush against mine as he takes the bag from me. He starts for the door, but I pause. "Actually, my bladder is about to burst." I turn to the pharmacist. "Can I use the, uh... *il bagno?*"

The man chuckles, probably because I just made an absolute mockery of his native tongue. "*Si, si.* Right this way."

I follow him and pee quickly. When I'm done, I step back out of the shop and into the mid-morning glow. The pharmacy door jingles shut behind me. Sunlight stabs my eyes as I scan the sidewalk.

Which is... empty.

My pulse jackhammers, worst case scenarios immediately cropping up like weeds. *He left. He actually fucking left me.*

Or what if it's worse? What if Dragan found us? What if—

Then I spot him. Half a block down, Sasha stands frozen in front of a window display. When I catch up to him and see what's captured his attention, my heart stills.

It's a baby boutique. Cribs, onesies, little leather shoes small enough to fit in my palm. His throat bobs as he traces the outline of one sole against the glass—a gesture so tender it wrenches something loose behind my ribs.

Don't let this sway you, cold logic whispers. *Leaving is survival. Fool me once, right?*

But the man in the reflection—jaw slack, fingers hovering over ghost-children he'll never know—isn't the Bratva king who broke me. He's just a boy who grew up harder than he should have, tossing wishful coins toward a future he still thinks he doesn't deserve.

"Sasha…?"

He startles. When he sees it's me, his mask slams down. "Let's go."

Yet as we walk away, he keeps glancing back—at the shoes, at my belly, at roadkill happy endings littering the cobblestones between us.

I watch the Peugeot's taillights disappear down the drive, taking Sasha with them. He didn't even look at me when he dropped me off at the villa—just waited until I was safely up the steps, then reversed like the devil himself was riding shotgun.

Jasmine materializes beside me, two gelato cups in hand. Pistachio drips down her wrist as she hands me one. "Where's he off to in such a hurry?"

"He mumbled something about needing a drink."

She scoffs. "No man ever has 'a' drink. Ten or twelve, maybe. However many it takes before he accepts his own bullshit."

"There isn't enough alcohol in all of Italy for that," I mumble. I take a bite of gelato and sink to my butt on the stone stairs.

Jasmine joins me. "So. How many times did you bone in the car?"

"Jas! We didn't—"

"Relax, kiddo. I'm joking. Although it did look like I interrupted something below the belt in the cellar last night. Wanna talk about it?"

"Not really."

"Well, I do. So let's talk about it."

My face is burning. "It really wasn't a big deal."

Her eyebrow goes vertically skeptical. "That hickey suggests otherwise."

I clamp a hand over my collarbone and curse myself for forgetting to cover it up. "Fine. It was more than 'not a big deal,' but still less than a big deal. It was… a moment of weakness."

"Mhmm," she hums. "And how many more 'moments of weakness' will it take before you two stop beating around the bush?"

I turn away from her, but the image of Sasha's face pressed against that baby shop display follows me. The raw vulnerability in his expression as he traced those tiny shoes. For a moment, he wasn't a wolf or a liar—he was just… Sasha. My Sasha.

"It's not that simple," I whisper.

"No?" Jasmine's voice softens. "Because from where I'm standing, it looks pretty clear. He loves you. You love him. And those babies deserve to grow up better than we did."

I'm shaking my head before she even finishes talking. "You're saying I should love him back, but… How am I supposed to do that? I can't just forget, Jas."

"No," she agrees. "Maybe not. But what's the next step between here and forgiveness? Maybe try that out for a while." She kisses me on the forehead, then rises. "Anyway, that's just my two cents. Do with it what you will."

I sit there for a while after she's gone. My gelato has melted into ice cream soup, but the sun is beautiful as it descends behind the hills.

The next step between here and forgiveness—what does that look like? The cellar felt like some kind of middle ground. It wasn't love; we all know that can never happen again. But it was... something. Feasible, maybe. That part of things has always been easy for us.

If I find a way to separate what *can* be from what *can't* be, then maybe Sasha and I can make something work. At least for the next ten weeks.

Sex isn't love. Love isn't sex.

One can exist without the other...

Right?

I stand up. The bag of pills is still in my hand, I realize. I look down at it and sigh. As if I needed another reminder of what Sasha has done to me, I've got his babies and the meds I need to keep them alive right here with me.

The bottle label is in Italian, but I don't need to speak it to know what it reads. Or at least, what it might as well read.

For chronic delusional syndrome. Take twice daily until reality sets in.

I throw back a pair of them and go to get the bicycle.

25

SASHA

The first glass of grappa goes down easy. The second, too. By the third, I'm almost starting to breathe again.

The taverna owner pours more amber poison into my glass without asking. Wise choice on his part. He obviously knows better than to interrupt a wolf chewing off its own leg.

The universe today seems intent on filing my fangs and telling me to have at it, though. *Devour yourself. Why not? You've spent your whole life training to do exactly that.* Between the debacle in the cellar, that cursed baby clothes boutique in Siena, and the sight I saw when I first walked into this little bar, I've got plenty of appetite for self-destruction.

I was barely a step inside the door when I felt a presence sweep past me from behind, scarcely knee-high. Looking down, I saw a little girl in a white cotton dress, dirty and grass-stained at the hem from playing outside. She beelined straight for a man in a corner booth who was laughing with his friends.

As soon as the man saw the little girl, he set down his drink and dropped to one knee. She hit his open arms with a delighted squeal as he peppered her with kiss after kiss.

A woman slipped in in the wake of the little girl, laughing just like them, carrying a rosy-cheeked babe in her arms. She went over to kiss her husband and daughter.

It was the light in their eyes that did me in. They were just so fucking happy to see each other. The husband was suntanned and sweaty from a long day's work and the wife smelled like flour and laundry. I could see their entire life at a glance, in a single whiff.

Simple. Full. Satisfied.

They're gone now. But across the room, the ghost of that family still lingers—the father's booming laugh, the toddler's sticky fingers smearing gelato on the checkered tablecloth, the little girl shyly asking her daddy for a sip of his wine.

The light in their eyes. The light in their *fucking* eyes.

I tip my glass back until the last drop hits my tongue. It tastes like kerosene. "*Yob tvoyu mat,*" I snarl at the empty chair beside me. The wood creaks like it's judging.

The owner raises a bushy eyebrow. "*Problemi con l'amore?*"

I snort. *L'amore?* No, this is not *l'amore*. *L'amore* is for men who don't have blood under their fingernails.

I hold my glass out and grunt for him to refill.

I look up as he does. The mirror behind the bar shows every fucking mistake I've ever made. Unshaven jaw. Bloodshot eyes. The scar at my throat puckered and raw—Yakov's final gift. And it just keeps on giving, doesn't it?

I throw back most of the refill, then turn my eyes down to the dregs of the blonde liquid swirling in my cup. Is this cup four? Five? I've lost count. Numbers go blurry at the edges while I sit here and pity myself.

But when I glance up in the mirror again, it's not just my own miserable face I see.

It's hers, too.

Ariel stands framed in dying light, her hair an auburn wildfire against dusty glass. My fist tightens around the cup. *Blink. She'll disappear. Another grappa-fueled hallucination. If you don't blink, you know what's going to make you happy. She's going to slide onto the stool next to yours, all fire and fury and that infuriating vanilla-peach shampoo. She'll make you say it out loud —that you* want *the happy lie. The domestic farce. The right to come home to someone who doesn't flinch when you touch them.*

I blink.

I blink hard.

She doesn't disappear.

"You shouldn't be here," I tell her without turning around.

"And you shouldn't drink alone." The stool beside me groans as she sits. Her knee bumps mine. Every muscle in my body tightens.

"Go back to the villa, Ariel."

"Or what? You'll brood harder? Keep this up and you're gonna pull a muscle. And honestly, you're in rough enough shape as it is."

She isn't wrong. Not by a long shot. It's hard to believe that there was a time when this marriage was just about power, about securing Leander's alliance. Now, look at me—getting drunk in an Italian taverna because I can't handle seeing tiny fucking baby shoes in a window display.

She shifts on the stool, trying to get comfortable. Her elbow bumps the bar as she overbalances. My hand twitches with the instinct to steady her, but I force it to stay flat against the wooden counter. She doesn't want my help. She made that much perfectly clear when she suggested we pretend the cellar never happened.

The dress she's wearing is new. Something flowing and cream-colored that makes her look softer than she truly is. More vulnerable. The neckline dips just low enough to show the mark I left on her collarbone last night, and beneath that, the fabric stretches taut over her belly. My fingers ache with the memory of her skin.

Feeling her pregnant between us... Fuck, that changed things. That changed so many things that I'm trying to find answers at the bottom of a glass now.

"*Qualcosa da bere?*" the owner asks her.

"Just water," she answers. Then, catching my sideways glance: "Though I'd kill for one of what he's having."

I snort. "You're not a killer."

"Oh, I don't know about that." Ariel bites back a smile. "I killed your liver's hopes and dreams just by showing up here, didn't I?"

"You want my liver?" I rasp, tracing the glass rim. "Take it. Take whatever the fuck you want."

She doesn't. Of course she doesn't. The mirror behind the bar shows a gruesome little trio—her haloed in taverna lamplight and pitying me; me hunched like a gargoyle and pitying myself; and, inside of her, a pair of lives that'll be glad to have me as their father.

Call *that t*wo truths and a lie.

"Maybe not that," she says. "I get the feeling you're putting that poor organ through its paces tonight." She pauses, then says, "I really am jealous, though. It'd be nice to have a sip of something. Just to take the edge off. Quiet things down."

"If only it worked like that. I'm five deep and the shit in my head is louder than ever."

"Well," she sighs as the bartender slides a bottle of sparkling water to her, "maybe this will do the trick then."

"You want a medal?" I mutter. "A plaque? *'Here Lies Ariel Ward's Self-Restraint'?*"

Her laugh is a brittle thing. "You're such an asshole."

"Yes." I swirl the grappa. "Thus the drinking."

The silence stretches, strained as barbed wire. I don't look at her. Can't. If I do, I'll see the dress, the swell of our children beneath it, the way her throat moves when she swallows. I'll break all over again.

Her fingers drag through the damp ring my glass left on the bar. "You left before I could say—"

"Don't."

"—thank you."

I freeze.

"For taking me to Siena," she says softly. "And also, for… caring enough to fight me on it."

I throw back more of the drink. "It's not care; it's logistics. Healthy mother, healthy heirs. Simple math."

"Oh, don't give me that shit, Sasha." Her eye-roll is scathing. But then she sighs and some of the tension goes whistling out of her. "There is some math to it, though. I've been... thinking."

"Dangerous habit."

"About our situation."

I arch a brow, though I still refuse to turn to face her. Her knee presses into my thigh, warm and deliberate. I don't move. Don't breathe. The grappa turns to acid in my gut as her fingers come to rest on my forearm.

"We're adults," she continues, voice pitched low. "We want each other. Why complicate it with feelings? That's math, right? Subtract out the feelings. Add in the sex."

Maybe I've had too much to drink after all. "You think *fucking* will fix us?"

"I think it'll make the next ten weeks bearable, if nothing else."

"What happened to hating me and everything I've ever done?"

"Hate's a strong word," she demurs.

"So is love. But we've already proven how well that one works out." Her hand is still touching my arm. Five little points of contact that feel like fishhooks in my skin. I shake my head and pull away. "You're either delusional or fucking with me. This can only end in disaster, Ariel. It can't be what you want."

"I want release." Her eyes burn, bright and level. "You want a distraction. Seems fair."

My scar tingles. "And the babies?"

"—are currently the size of eggplants and very uninterested in our sex lives." She leans in, peach-vanilla shampoo drowning out the grappa stench.

Ariel has one thing down cold: The math is simple. Ten weeks of fucking versus fifty years of longing for what once was. Ten weeks of her nails down my back versus a lifetime of cold sheets and colder what-ifs.

I drain the glass and turn to seize her by the wrist, just shy of bruising, so she knows this isn't a joke.

"If we're going to play with fire, we need rules," I growl. "No feelings. No sleeping over. No…" My thumb passes over the hickey I left last night. "… *marks.*"

She doesn't hesitate. "Deal."

"And when it's done…"

"We're done." She nods. "Scout's honor. It's a hate-fuck for convenience's sake. It'll never be anything more than that."

The owner chooses that exact moment to shuffle back in from his smoke break outside, clearing his throat. "*Signori,* we are—"

A wad of my euros smacks his chest. He fumbles the catch, blinking at the bills fluttering down to his sawdust floors.

"Get out," I bark.

It does not require translation.

He scurries away, still clutching my money. The door's rusted bolt screeches when I slam it home behind him. Windows next—every latch twisted until my palm bleeds. Behind me, Ariel's breath stutters.

When the outside world is barred away from us, I pivot to face her.

She's all soft edges wrapped in cream silk, the dress clinging to every cursed curve I've tried to evict from my mind. Lamplight gilds the mane of her hair, loose curls spilling over her shoulders. That swollen belly mocks me. Her lips part on a frantic breath, glossy and bitten-red, and Christ, I want to ruin them all over again.

Every line of her screams *mine*—the way her hips tilt toward me, the flush creeping below her neckline. She's a loaded gun in a lace-trimmed holster, safety off, and I'm done pretending I wasn't born to pull the trigger.

I cross to her in three huge strides.

Her back hits the bar hard enough to rattle glasses. I cage her in, forearms braced on polished oak. The wood presses rigid lines into her thighs where my hips slot against hers.

Through thin cotton, her heart hammers like drums against my chest. Mine answers in kind. Her throat bobs when I drag my nose along her jaw.

It's permission.

Collapse.

Surrender.

The first button pops easy. Two, three, and four reveal inches of skin at a time as I remember just how much I fucking missed this.

She gasps. Rolls her hips. "Sasha—"

"Say it." My thumb rasps over her nipple. "Why we're here."

Her head thunks against a liquor shelf. "Sex. Just… sex."

"Just sex," I echo, biting the lie into her mouth.

Through the streaked window, Tuscan night falls. My hand skims her belly—our shared little sin—as I hike her leg around my waist.

No feelings. Just friction. Just the chokehold of her thighs. Just the sob she swallows when I finally—*finally*—sheathe myself in her heat.

26

ARIEL

The grappa burns my tongue when he kisses me. It's not gentle—nothing about Sasha Ozerov ever has been—but I don't want gentle. I want the bite of his teeth, the sting of his stubble.

If it doesn't leave me sore tomorrow, I don't want it.

He lifts me onto the bar with a growl. A bottle of limoncello shatters on the floor, sharp citrus flooding the air. I don't care. All I care about is the heat of him between my thighs, the way his cock parts to the deepest point in me.

He rips my dress down by the neckline and up by the hem, so that it puddles around my waist. There's no preamble, no patience—just Sasha burying himself to the hilt in one brutal stroke.

"*Bozhe moi,*" he rasps, hips stuttering. "Still so fucking tight."

"Still so fucking big," I shoot back, nails raking his scalp.

My back arches off the bar. He doesn't let me adjust, doesn't let me think. Just sets a punishing rhythm that rattles my teeth.

"Look at me," he demands, fingers tangling in my hair. "Look at me when I'm inside you."

I force my eyes open. His gaze burns through every lie I've told myself. That this is just physical. That I don't still love him. That I won't break when he walks away again.

He reads it all. Of course he does.

But I see it in him, too. As his teeth nip at my neck, giving birth to the hickey he just swore not to leave, I see how flimsy his hold on himself really is.

He's as wrecked as you are. He's every bit as fucked.

"No," he growls, slamming into me harder. "Don't retreat into your head. Stay here. With me."

I bite his shoulder to muffle a sob. He tastes like salt and sin. The bar digs into my spine, the pain sharp and grounding. I need it—need the ache to counter the pleasure mounting low in my belly.

"Sasha—"

"Say it." He finds my clit and strokes rough circles that steal my words. "Say you want this."

"I want—" The orgasm hits like a freight train, tearing through me with a violence that borders on cruel. He drinks my scream with a kiss, swallowing every shattered syllable.

He doesn't stop or slow. Just fucks me through the aftershocks until I'm raw and shaking, until pleasure tips back into pain.

"This is just sex," he growls again against my collarbone. Does he need the reminder, or do I?

"Right. Just… *ngh…*" His tongue swipes the hollow of my throat, and I forget how words work. *Just sex*, I scream internally as his palm slides up my thigh. *No feelings. Just… friction. Yeah, friction. Simple. Clean. Clinical.*

But there's nothing clean about the way he fucks me. It's merciless. We're making a mess, breaking bottles, stools tipping over, but I just can't find it in me to care.

"Again," he orders, dragging me to the edge of the bar. My legs hook around his waist as he pins me against the wall. Plaster crumbles under my shoulders. "Come for me again."

"I can't—"

He sinks his teeth into my neck. "Yes, you fucking can."

We're a tangle of desperate angles—his hips snapping brutally, my legs clamping his waist, the bar's edge leaving welts on my ass. My back arches as he hits a spot that liquefies my spine. "Sasha, I—!"

He smothers the admission with his palm. "Don't. Don't say it." His thrusts turn punishing. "Just take what you need."

The second climax is slower, hotter, a molten spill that leaves me boneless. He holds me up with an arm under my ass, the other hand fisted in my hair. His thrusts turn erratic, ragged breaths flaring hot against my skin.

"Ariel…"

He spills inside me with a groan that sounds like surrender. For one heartbeat, for two, we're fused—foreheads pressed together, lungs heaving, his cock still pulsing deep within me.

Then he pulls back, looks at me, and with his cock still inside me, he says, "This means nothing."

I almost believe him.

But then he pulls out and it hurts too badly to be "nothing." Cold air replaces the heat of him. I slump against the bar, dress bunched around my waist, thighs sticky with sweat and cum. He tucks himself away, every movement sharp, controlled.

No feelings. No sleeping over. No marks.

Well, two outta three ain't bad.

"Well." I swipe a trembling hand across my mouth. "That was…"

"Math."

"Yeah." I hop off the bar, wincing at the ache between my legs. "Just math."

But my pulse is going bananas in my throat. *Liar,* it whispers.

Liar, liar, liar.

27

SASHA

The clothes hit me in the face before I even open my eyes the next morning.

I crack one eye open to find Kosti looming over my bed with the smugness of a man who's been awake for hours. "Rise and shine, *neania*. We're going shooting."

"Go fuck yourself."

I grunt and roll over, burying my face in the pillow. Every muscle protests the movement. Not surprising, given how I spent last night. And the night before that. And the night before that.

For the last week since the taverna negotiation, every midnight has been the exact same. It's simple math: Ariel plus darkness equals release. I sneak into her room to fuck. There are no feelings, no marks, and no sleeping over. Just friction and need. Just her nails down my back as she bites her lip to keep quiet. Just my hand over her mouth when she forgets herself.

Just math.

"I said *up.*" A balled-up pair of socks hits my ribs. "Up, up, up. Your aim's gone to shit and we both know it."

This is how men like us say *I worry you'll get yourself killed*, because fuck knows we could never say those words straight up.

"My aim is fine," I snarl. "You, on the other hand, are starting to sound like the dementia is catching up."

Kosti clucks his tongue. "You won't sass your way out of this one, son. You think Dragan is going to wait until you get your feet back under you? Until you're back in tippy-top shape? Fuck no, he won't." He yanks the pillow away from me. "Get your ass up, boy. You've been avoiding this long enough."

He's right. Of course he's right. But that doesn't mean I have to like it.

I lever myself upright, wincing. The bullet wound in my side pulls tight, a constant reminder of how far I've fallen. Used to be that I could take three rounds to the chest and still wake up swinging. Now, look at me—hiding in the Tuscan countryside, sneaking into Ariel's room every night like a teenager because I'm too weak to do anything else.

I peel myself off sweat-damp sheets, exhausted and depleted.

"Anyhow," Kosti says as I rise, "I'm sick of you moping. You and Ariel not looking at each other—it's exhausting."

No, *exhausting* is spending every night buried inside of her. When I'm there, I think of nothing. When I'm not there, I think of being there. My whole day is spent dreaming of the stolen hours we can fuck and forget.

Fuck *to* forget, rather. The sex is a way of keeping heavier things at bay.

So far, it's working.

Yakov would have words about this. None of them kind.

"I don't mope."

"No. You *brood*. It's worse." His gaze lingers on the fresh scratches down my back, but he says nothing. "I'll be in the car."

When he's gone, I dress mechanically in the predawn darkness. Tactical pants, boots. My hands only shake a little as I do up the laces. Progress, I suppose.

I linger for a second by Ariel's closed door, thinking of how nice it would be to slip in there and greet the morning with her in my arms. Then, with a sigh, I turn and keep going.

The drive to the abandoned quarry is mostly quiet. Kosti hums along to Italian pop songs while I stare at the sunrise bleeding over the hills. Ariel's scent still clings to my palms.

The case with my favorite Glock sits heavy in my lap. I've barely touched it since we got here. Another thing Yakov would've had words about.

The quarry is exactly what you'd expect: a massive bite taken out of the mountainside, leaving behind tiered walls of craggy, exposed limestone. At the bottom, weathered targets dot the gravel and empty brass casings glint in the dirt—evidence of Kosti's solo practice sessions.

"Nervous?" Kosti asks, slinging his AK over one shoulder as we leave the car and walk to where we'll set up.

I slam the magazine home harder than necessary. "Don't be ridiculous."

I check the Glock with movements that should be automatic but aren't. Muscle memory fights with injury as I load the magazine. The familiar weight feels wrong in my palms, like reuniting with an old friend only to find they've changed.

Or maybe I'm the one who's different.

I line up with the beer can resting on a rock about fifty yards out. No matter what my body has gone through, this part never leaves me.

Exhale.

Steady.

Gentle squeeze, and…

I miss by a fucking mile.

I frown as I see just how badly wide my shot veered. "Cross-wind," I mutter. "Gotta adjust." I crack my neck from side to side, then start the process all over again.

Exhale.

Steady.

Gentle squeeze.

And…

Worse. Much worse.

"*Chtob u tebya hui vo lbu vyros,*" I curse.

Kosti watches, lighting a cigarette. The crack of the match is louder than my missed shots. "Was that the wind again?" he asks. "Or did the gun let you down?"

"Fuck you."

"The answer is neither, Sasha." He exhales a plume of smoke. "It's your head that's the problem."

I raise the Glock again, teeth gritted. Fuck the can; the next target over appears in my sights—a paper outline of a man, black and white.

Simple. Math.

Boom.

Ten yards in the wrong direction. The target remains pristine.

I, on the other hand, am a mess. I'm sweating out of nowhere, even though the morning is relatively cool. Pain lances up my side, bright and hot. "The fucking sights are off."

"The sights are fine and you know it." He exhales a smoke ring. *"You're off."*

Another shot. Another miss. The gun recoils in my grip like a spooked horse. What to blame now? Sleepless nights? Months cut off from my men, my money, my empire? *Oh, poor fucking me—my mattress wasn't TempurPedic, so I can't kill anymore?*

I fire again.

Again, I miss.

"You're anticipating the recoil," Kosti observes. "Flinching before you even pull the trigger. Like you're afraid of the pain."

I turn on him with a snarl. "I'm not afraid of anything."

"No?" His eyebrow climbs. "Then why are you still here?"

We both know he's not talking about the quarry anymore.

I empty the rest of the magazine into the target. The shots are sloppy, scattered. None of them would have killed a man. Some wouldn't even have slowed him down.

My hands are shaking so badly now that I can barely reload. Sweat trickles down my spine, cold sweat, ice-cold fucking sweat.

"Let me see it." Kosti reaches for the Glock.

I twist away. "Fuck off."

"Sasha—"

I load a fresh clip and start over. In my head, I'm seventeen again, in a basement, wire around my throat. *Ssyklo.* Boom. *Ssyklo.* Boom. *Ssyk—*

Kosti steps into my eyeline and forces me to lower the gun. "Enough."

"Move."

"I'm not moving, and if you try to pull the trigger, you'll blow your goddamn foot off. Let go of the gun, Sasha."

I sigh and let him pry the gun from my slack fingers. He turns, cigarette still stashed in the corner of his mouth. With half a dozen quick, efficient shots, he obliterates the target.

Head. Head. Torso. Torso. Head. Groin.

Dead.

The truth molders between us, another corpse rotting in the Tuscan sun. I can't outshoot a crippled octogenarian right now. Can't protect Ariel. Can't even protect myself.

He doesn't have to say anything. I know what he's thinking.

I'm not ready. Not even close.

Dragan's out there somewhere, gathering his forces, encroaching on everything I've ever conquered. And here I am, missing paper targets and fucking Ariel in the dark like it's going to fix anything.

"I left something in the car," I lie. I don't look at Kosti's face—I just turn and march back up the hill.

When I reach the Peugeot, I slump into the passenger seat. The upholstery reeks of Kosti's cigarettes. Through the windshield, he paces the quarry's edge, phone pressed to his ear. Arguing with someone.

A memory surfaces—Zoya dabbing vodka on the knife wound I'd earned at sixteen, her hands steady as scalpels. *You're lucky it didn't hit bone*, she'd scolded. *Next time, maybe you'll think before picking fights with grown men.*

Next time. Always *next* time that I'll be better, smarter, stronger, faster.

Except now there are no *next times* left. Just this—broken promises, a quarry full of spent casings, a villa full of bad choices.

Maybe I can make a good one for a fucking change.

Zoya answers on the second ring. "*Solnyshko?*" Her voice is warm honey and home. "I've been worried."

I close my eyes and let her voice transport me somewhere else. I'm not in a sunbaked quarry anymore—I'm in her kitchen as she feeds me and Ariel honey cakes. "I wanted to keep you out of this," I rasp to her. "I thought that was best. But… fuck. Maybe I was wrong about doing it all myself."

Kitchen clatter dies down as Zoya stops whatever she was doing. "Tell me what you need from me, Sashenka."

I tell her.

Then I hang up. March back down the hill. Line up my sights. Exhale. Steady. Gentle squeeze…

Bang.

The bullet hits dead center. Right through the paper heart.

28

ARIEL

The sheets still smell like him.

I shove my face into the pillow and breathe deep. It's humiliating how that paints a stupid smile on my face. If I press my ear to it, I swear I can almost hear his murmured grunts still echoing, like how the inside of a seashell sounds like the ocean.

Just sex. Just sex. That's the mantra. He says it, I say it, and we both pretend to believe it's still true.

But I knew from the first thrust in the taverna that I messed up. You can't keep sex out of love or love out of sex. They're two peas in one fucked-up pod.

My thighs still ache, even though it's been hours since he left. Another night of slipping in, fucking me silently with his palm over my mouth, then slipping right back out.

No puns intended.

A knock startles me upright in bed. "You alive in here, o sister of mine?"

I yank the duvet up to my chin like Jasmine will see the evidence written on my skin. "Awake, yes. Alive, less so."

Jasmine nudges the door open with her hip, two steaming mugs of tea in hand. Her gaze flicks to the mangled sheets, my underwear on the floor, all the things that of course she would instantly catalog and understand. "Rough night?"

"Bite me."

"Looks like someone already did." She sets a mug on the nightstand. The ginger fumes make my nose wrinkle. "Really, though—you doing okay, Ari?"

I blow on my tea. "Shouldn't I be asking you that?"

"Don't deflect."

"I'm not."

"Are, too."

"Fine." The ceramic scalds my palms. "I'm just, like... Ish."

"Ish," she echoes, lips pursed thoughtfully. "What kind of 'ish' are we talking here?"

"Unsettled-ish, maybe."

"Ah. The technical term." She tucks a wild curl behind my ear, her touch lingering like Mama's used to. "Want to unpack that?"

I look at my reflection in the black puddle of the tea. "It's nothing. Just... hormones. Sasha being Sasha. The usual."

Her gaze flicks to the rumpled sheets. "The usual involving midnight calisthenics, I see."

"Jas—"

"You don't have to tell me." She squeezes my knee through the duvet. "But you can't outrun it forever, you know. Whatever *it* is. Ish or not-ish."

"Oh, I beg to differ. I'm the queen of outrunning. Olympic gold champion."

Jas flicks me in the ear. "Outrunning your feelings, maybe. Outrunning me? You wish, Miss Ish." She stands, sunlight catching the silver streaks in her hair. "I need help with something out back. Get dressed."

"What kind of something?"

"The kind that involves sunlight and not brooding in your stank-smelling cave all day long." She tosses a pair of Kosti's old overalls at me. They land with a *thwap*. "Wear these. You'll thank me when the rat snakes show up."

The "something" turns out to be a quarter-acre of weeds behind the villa that Jasmine has decided, in her infinite optimism, will become a vegetable garden. Does it matter to her that we'll be gone in ten weeks and therefore will not be here when these things bear fruit? No, it does not. Does she care that yardwork sounds miserable? Not one bit.

"This is hell," I say, hacking at a thistle with more violence than strictly necessary.

"This is character-building." Jas yanks a root ball free with a grunt. "And also, free childcare prep. Twin toddlers will make this look like a spa day. You will long for fields of weeds and the silence in which you once tended to them."

The sun crests the villa's clay-tiled roof, baking the sweat down my spine. I'm ankle-deep in topsoil and actually, dare I say, maybe even starting to enjoy myself, when boots crunch gravel behind us.

"Where's the fire?" I ask without turning.

Sasha's shadow stretches long over my shovel. "Elsewhere."

I swipe sweat from my brow. "Care to elaborate?"

Kosti shoulders past with a rifle case. "Care to mind your business, *koukla?*"

I frown. "Really, though. Where are you two gallivanting off to?"

Kosti and Sasha look at each other, then both shrug in unison. "Elsewhere," they chorus together.

With perfect comedic timing, Jas and I roll our eyes in unison, too. "You guys are spending too much time together," I mutter with a scowl. "It's… unsettling."

"Ish," adds Jas.

"We'll be back soon, my lovely nieces," Uncle Kosti chirps. "Have no fear."

Then, whistling, he turns and saunters toward the rental car. Sasha follows him, though not with one long, hard look back at me.

"What's gotten into them?" I ponder when the car disappears down the drive. The former rosebush—now more of a thorn-bush—that I'm murdering takes another hit. "They're being weird."

Jas tosses me a canteen. "Stop being dramatic. Drink some water and pass the shears."

I take a long chug as I watch dust settle where the Peugeot vanished.

By sunset, blisters outnumber regrets. We stand and admire our battlefield—rows of turned earth, the skeletal remains of an old trellis we dug up, and the distinct absence of the rat snakes about which I was warned.

Jasmine inspects a blistered palm. "Not bad for day one."

"Day one of *what,* precisely?" I ask.

"It's been a dream of mine since I was a little girl to have a garden," she explains fondly. "New life pushing up through the earth, fresh produce. Sounds dreamy, right? Have you ever had a carrot right out of the ground?"

"How poetic," I say with a laugh. "And no, I have not. Nor have you. We grew up in Brighton Beach, Jas."

"Exactly. I bet it tastes like candy."

"I bet it tastes like carrot."

She splashes me with the last of the lukewarm backwash in the canteen. I laugh in outrage, then throw a clot of dirt that explodes in spectacular fashion against her turned back. From there, things dissolve into dirt flying back and forth until we're both cackling and absolutely filthy from head to toe.

Eventually, the sweat overcomes the giggles. But it doesn't stop Jasmine from pulling me into a hug and planting a sloppy kiss on top of my head. "I love you, Ari. Never forget that. Whatever you're going through is what I'm going through, too."

"I love you, too."

We both look up when the sound of a distant engine starts to grow louder. A minute later, the Peugeot crests the hill and comes to a sighing stop in front of the villa.

"Ah, the conquering heroes return," I tease as Sasha and Uncle Kosti clamber out of the vehicle. "All hail. Has the world been saved? Have the secrets been buried?"

My sarcasm dies mid-bite when he yanks open the backseat.

Sunlight catches on pearls first—the double strand Mama never takes off. Then the sundress, butter-yellow and rumpled from travel. Her chignon is flawless.

When she's out, she pauses and looks at us. "My girls," Mama breathes, hands fluttering over her mouth.

My shovel clatters to the gravel.

While I'm still mid-processing, Zoya unfolds herself from the other side, all no-nonsense linen and shrewd eyes. "Try not to faint, Belle. You already cried the whole flight."

"You—" I'm six years old again, skinned knees and messy braids, as I gaze stupidly at my mother, then at Sasha. "You brought her *here?*"

Sasha leans against the Peugeot, arms crossed. He shrugs and says nothing.

I run toward her. Mama's perfume envelops me—gardenias and home. Her palm cradles my cheek, trembling. "Oh, baby girl," she murmurs over and over again. "Look at you. *Look* at you. I can't stop looking at you."

The twins kick.

Or maybe it's my heart, swollen and raw between us.

Then I step aside. Mama looks over my shoulder and I follow her gaze. Jasmine is still standing where I left her in the garden. Both she and Mama have a hand to their mouth.

Slowly, slowly, Jasmine starts to move toward us. She picks up speed as she goes. Walking and then jogging and then sprinting until she's flying over the ground and into Mama's arms.

Their collision is somehow gentle despite its speed. Like two clouds melting together. Mama cradles Jasmine's head to her shoulder as if she's afraid she might disappear if she clings too tight.

Same, Mama. Same.

I hang back, one hand cradling my belly as I watch them cry and laugh and touch each other's faces. The scene feels surreal to me, so I can only imagine what she's feeling. My mother finding out about both her long-lost daughter and her impending grandchildren in the same breath.

Belle's palm cups Jasmine's cheek. "My girl. My brave, beautiful girl."

Jasmine's shoulders shake. "I'm sorry. I'm so sorry I left you—"

"Hush now. I'm the one who owes you all the sorries in the world. But we're here now. We're here, baby. That's all that matters."

Jas chokes out a laugh through her tears, her knuckles white where they clutch Mama's cardigan. Fifteen years apart, and now this. My chest throbs, an ache unfurling that has nothing to do with pregnancy heartburn.

Mama's pearls catch sunlight when she turns toward me, her smile wobbling. "Ari, sunshine, come here." She holds my hand and Jasmine's together as the three of us knit a circle of arms together. Mama grazes my belly with the backs of her knuckles. The touch breaks something loose inside me.

"I'm sorry I didn't tell you sooner," I whisper as tears spill down my cheeks.

"Don't you dare apologize to me, princess. You don't owe me a single sorry, either. I just want to sit here for a minute with my babies and breathe. Can we do that? Is that okay?"

"Yeah, Mama," I say through a choked throat.

Jas nods, too.

As she pulls us into a tangled hug, I glance over her shoulder and look at Sasha. He's leaning against the hood of the car as Zoya pokes and prods his ribs, muttering in Russian. He swats her away, but there's no heat in it.

Our eyes meet.

He smiles.

~

Dinner is a time capsule.

Spanakopita crust flakes onto my plate as Kosti serves dish after dish under Belle's direction, his tattoos absurd against her floral apron. "Remember when you used to burn the *tyropita*?" Jasmine grins, licking feta off her thumb.

Belle swats her with an oven mitt. "Remember when you set the toaster on fire trying to make Pop-Tarts?"

"That was *one time*—"

Zoya laughs into her wine. Sasha sits back in his chair, face blank but calm. He hasn't eaten much, but some of the usual storm clouds that live over his head 24/7 seem to have dissipated.

It's like we've all come to an unspoken agreement to keep things light, for tonight at least. Maybe it's just that there's been so much heartbreak and suffering over the last six months that it's crazy to bring it to this dinner table. Even if it's sticking our head in the sand, even if we're purposefully being oblivious, it's nice.

Family dinner. Like we've always done it.

The air is dense with oregano, lemon, garlic. Kosti produces a record player out of nowhere and spins Mama around the room as she laughs. When Sasha asks Zoya if she wants to dance, she playfully whacks him in the shins with her cane and tells him to stay the hell away from her.

Nothing is fixed, of course. Dragan is still out there, we're still stuck here, and the world is as broken as it's ever been. The weight of Mama's unasked questions hangs heavy in the air. *What happened with Leander? How did I end up pregnant? Why am I here with the man who was supposed to be my husband?* But she doesn't voice any of them. just passes the spanakopita and smiles when I take seconds. For tonight, in this house, at this table…

We're okay.

I'll take it.

"Let me help you get ready for bed," Mama says once the dishes have been cleaned, in that tone that means it's not really a request. It's so achingly familiar that I can't refuse.

We go upstairs, arm in arm. She sits me at the vanity, just like when I was little, and begins brushing my hair. The repetitive strokes are soothing, almost hypnotic. Each stroke of the silver brush pulls me backward—toward princess braids before school plays, to nights just like this one. All the tiny little moments of normality woven in between the darker chapters.

"You used to yelp when I hit a snarl," she murmurs, working through a knot at my nape. Her reflection smiles in the vanity mirror. "Remember?"

"I don't miss those detangler tears," I laugh. The scent of her almond oil makes my throat ache. You don't realize how much you've missed a thing until you get to have it again, however briefly.

That almond oil scent lingers even after she sets the brush down. But when her hands go still on my shoulders, I catch her watching me meaningfully in the mirror. She touches a fading bruise beneath my collarbone. "What kind of tears are we crying these days, sweetheart?"

My knuckles whiten in my lap. "Can we not—"

"You love him." Not a question.

I focus on the vanity's nicked wood. "What I feel doesn't matter. This... arrangement... It's temporary."

Her sigh ribbons through the silence. "Oh, Ariel. When have you ever been good at temporary?" The brush resumes its path, gentler now. My scalp prickles where her gaze lingers. "Hearts want what they want, dear. Even when our heads scream *no*."

"What if my heart's an idiot?"

Her laugh is warm, familiar. "Then you'll be in excellent company." The brush glides through a final snarl. "We're all fools for love in one way or another. The trick is deciding whether to fight it, or let it make you brave." She kisses my head. "I know what you are. Sleep well, my brave girl. I'll see you in the morning."

She shuffles off down the hall. I hear Jasmine's door open and their two voices start to flow together. They keep going, a comforting melody layered on top of the croaks and groans of the old villa.

The sheets are cool against my sunburnt shoulders as I slip into bed. Mama laughs at something Jasmine says—that deep belly laugh I haven't heard in so long.

Through the window, more sounds float in. Zoya and Sasha, out in the courtyard, murmuring in Russian, like a bass line to the song of all my loved ones being here.

I press a palm to the swell beneath my ribcage. The twins kick in stereo—left side, then right—as if they're as warm and fuzzy as I am.

What if my heart's an idiot?

Maybe it is. Maybe it isn't. Right now, though, it's hard to be anything but happy as sleep lowers me down into dreams that don't feel awfully different from how reality went today.

29

SASHA

The cracked sundial in the villa's garden is off by exactly eighteen minutes. I've been timing it against my watch since dawn.

I've been timing other things, too.

Three hours since I left her bed.

Seven weeks until the babies come.

Time used to move like bullets—straight, precise, predictable. Now, it's all chaos, stretching and compressing around Ariel's smile, her laugh, the soft sigh as she comes in my arms, while the villa, full of life, does a sigh of its own all around us.

Just sex, we keep saying.

It's getting harder and harder to believe.

The tap of Zoya's cane against stone announces her arrival. She's dressed for war in gardening clothes, her silver hair tied back with what looks suspiciously like one of Kosti's old bandanas. *Oh, fucking Christ.* If she and him start shacking up, I'll nuke the planet and tell God to start over.

"These silly girls," she mutters in Russian, jabbing her cane at various spots in the turned earth. "No sense of proper spacing. No understanding of drainage. Who taught them to plant like this—wolves?"

"They seemed enthusiastic."

"Enthusiasm without knowledge is how you get root rot." She prods a particularly suspicious patch of soil. "Speaking of rot…"

"Zoya—"

"Don't 'Zoya' me. You look awful. Come here and take off that shirt so I can get a proper look at you."

There's no point arguing. I submit to her examination, wincing as her fingers find tender spots along my ribs. She clicks her tongue at each flinch, each half-healed bruise.

"You're not sleeping," she accuses.

"I sleep fine."

"Liar." Her hands are gentle despite her sharp tone. "You think I don't recognize restless eyes when I see them? I raised you, *solnyshko*."

I grunt noncommittally, but she's already launching into a story about her rooftop garden in Brighton Beach, how she spent years coaxing stubborn plants to life in that salt-stained soil.

"Everything worth having takes time," she concludes, finally stepping back from her inspection. "I learned that watching my first tomatoes grow. Such fragile things at first. But with patience, with care…" She trails off, squinting at me. "That's not what I really meant, though."

"Then please," I drawl, "enlighten us on what you really meant."

"Don't be smart with me." She smacks me in the back of the head with her cane, then gestures in a sweeping arc across the half-started garden, taking in the uneven rows, the ambitious scope of it. "Some things need *roots* to grow." The knowing look she gives me could pierce armor. "Like families."

"We're not—"

"If you try to tell me this isn't a family," she cuts me off, "I will hit you again, and this time, I won't be gentle about it."

The scent of coffee saves me from having to respond. Belle emerges from the villa, carrying three steaming mugs with practiced grace.

"I thought I heard voices," she says, distributing the coffee. Her smile wrinkles when she surveys the garden. "Oh, dear. Why do I get the feeling one of my girls was responsible for this?"

Zoya accepts one of the mugs with a nod. "I was just telling Sasha how these girls need proper instruction. In my day, every woman knew how to tend a proper garden."

"Oh, I tried teaching them. But ask me if those little hellions ever wanted to listen." Belle settles onto a stone bench, tucking her feet beneath her. "I had the tiniest herb garden on our fire escape in New York. Just a few terracotta pots, but the basil…" She inhales, like she can still smell it. "Leander used to say he could follow the scent home from three blocks away."

Something in her voice—a soft, bruised note—brings a memory of my own mother's window box flooding back. Six geraniums in chipped pots. Defiant spots of red against the city's gray. The only beautiful thing Yakov never managed to destroy, though not for lack of trying. My mother would sing to those flowers in the morning, her voice as bright as their petals.

I catch Zoya watching me, her eyes knowing. She remembers those flowers, too—she's the one who helped my mother plant them.

Belle and Zoya fall into easy chatter about compost ratios, and just like that, the ghosts retreat. But the memory of those geraniums lingers, red as hope against concrete.

Then the villa's back door creaks open.

And my throat goes dry.

Ariel stands in the doorway wearing one of my shirts, the white cotton gone nearly translucent in the morning light. Her hair tumbles wild over one shoulder, still mussed from my fingers three hours ago. From this distance, I can see the shadow of a mark I left on her collarbone, barely hidden by the collar.

The collar slips off one shoulder as she stretches, fabric riding up. That fucking swell of belly peeking through when she twists to tie her hair back...

She freezes mid-yawn, caught. Our eyes lock.

Just sex.

Just lies.

Zoya clears her throat pointedly. Only then do I realize I've been staring.

Belle, oblivious to the XXX-rated path my thoughts just took, smiles at her youngest daughter. "Good morning, sweetheart! Come join us. We were just admiring your... handiwork."

Ariel blushes as she pads over to us. She stoops down to pluck a weed from the dirt and scowls at it lying limply in her hand. When her shirt inches higher, I catch the dark lace of panties peeking above her sweatpants waistband. My cock stirs.

I drain my coffee, even though it's hot enough to scald my throat raw.

"Well," I cough, "I need to go check on—"

"Nonsense," Belle interrupts. "You can't let two old ladies and a pregnant woman tend to this garden all alone! We need a big, strong man like you to help us with the heavy lifting. Isn't that right, girls?"

Zoya nods. Ariel blushes. Belle just smiles brightly.

Emotional terrorists, the lot of them.

I sigh. "No, of course not. How may I be of service?"

That's how I end up toiling away in the hot sun. As hours pass, I cuff my pants above the ankle and strip my sweat-drenched shirt off to cast it aside. Where is a storm when you need it? For three weeks now, it's rained and knocked out the power damn near every day. But when it's time for me to dig miles of neat rows while Zoya barks orders at me like a drill sergeant, suddenly, the sun wants to hang out.

Zoya meanders by every few minutes to criticize my technique. "Deeper," she instructs, jabbing at the soil. "The roots need room to spread."

Men used to piss themselves in fear when I walked into a room. Now, I'm kneeling in a garden bed, taking orders from two grandmothers, while doing my damndest to avoid gawking at the woman I fucked into oblivion last night.

The whole time, that woman is crouched at my side. I tried to tell her early on to go easy, to rest often for the babies' sakes, but she told me that there was a sharp-edged hoe in the shed that I could go fuck myself with, and I decided it was best to not offer any additional advice.

There's enough danger percolating between us anyhow. Our fingers touch as she passes me another seedling. "Is that good enough?" she asks, poking at the hole she's been digging.

I have to clear my throat before I can answer. "Deeper."

She looks at me. I look at her. We both then shift our gazes elsewhere.

It's best that way.

Gravel crunches behind us. "Well, isn't this domestic?" Kosti's voice carries more amusement than any man should be capable of before noon. He settles onto a stone bench, lighting a cigarette with theatrical slowness. "Never thought I'd see the day—Sasha Ozerov, getting his hands dirty with actual dirt instead of blood."

"Shut up and help," I growl.

"Can't, I'm afraid. Doctor's orders. Bad back." He grins around his cigarette. "I'm here in a strictly advisory capacity."

Jasmine follows him out and joins us, and little by little, the rest of the day passes in a blaze of Italian sun. The earth is raw and black as we turn it over, as little green things take up residence.

In a year, it'll be green.

In a decade, it'll be greener still.

Part of me wants to remind these women that none of us will be here to see it. There's a ticking time bomb waiting to blow up this happy little bubble we're planting. An expiration date that's coming sooner rather than later.

But I won't be the one to bring it up. Hell, I'm doing my best to forget it myself.

Because, as I stand and dust my hands, I'm smacked sideways by a feeling that this is how it ought to be. Zoya is lecturing Jasmine on fertilizing methods while Kosti teaches Belle how to roll a cigarette. At my feet, Ariel is kneeling as she tucks the last of our seedlings into its new bed.

She belongs here. She belongs in this garden, in these clothes —*my* clothes—and in this makeshift family we're piecing together out of broken parts and borrowed time.

When Ariel struggles to rise, I steady her with both hands. She's left a perfect handprint in the dirt—five fingers pressed into the soil. Without thinking, I stoop down to press my own hand beside hers. Her print is smaller, but somehow, it makes mine look less threatening. Less like the marks I usually leave behind.

She notices. Her eyes meet mine, and this time, neither of us looks away.

30

ARIEL

"I have a surprise!" Jasmine sing-songs as she flounces into the kitchen, brandishing her phone like it's made of gold.

I look up from my daily cup of ginger tea, immediately suspicious. She scowls at me. "Oh, don't give me that sourpuss face."

"Your last 'surprise' ended up with me kneeling in the dirt for a week straight."

"And now, look at the beauty we get to feast our eyes on every single day!" she crows, throwing a hand to the window. Through it, I see a wide field of tilled dirt, with little green leaves sticking up like pubes.

"Truly a sight to see," I mumble. "As tempted as I am by today's offer, though, I'll pass."

She comes over and tweaks my nose. "No, little missy, you shall *not* pass," she says in her best Gandalf impression. "This surprise is unpassable. Impassable? No, unpassable. Final answer."

"You're scaring me, Jazzy."

"Don't be scared! Be *excited!*" She rubs my shoulders, probably to butter me up. Unfortunately, it's a highly effective negotiation tactic, because they've been aching.

"What kind of surprise are we talking about, specifically?" I ask.

She dances around me, eyes lighting up. "The kind that involves you doing your best Tyra Banks smizing while looking absolutely gorgeous with that pwecious widdle baby bump of yours!"

The piece of toast I'm holding freezes halfway to my mouth. "*What?*"

"A maternity shoot!" She's practically vibrating with excitement. "I hired a guy named Giovanni that I met in the village last week. He's the best photographer in the region. He's done work for *Vogue Italia!*"

I'm not sure which word summoned Sasha from the cellar, where he's been working on the generator again. I'm guessing it was "guy," not "*Vogue Italia*," but then again, the man is full of surprises.

Whichever the case, he looks unpleased.

"Absolutely not," he thunders. "Cancel it."

"No can do," trills Jasmine. "The deposit has already been paid."

"Then unpay it. I'm not having an outsider here. Much less an outsider taking pictures of us."

"Oh, relax." Jasmine waves him off. "Kosti recommended him. Right, Uncle?"

Kosti looks up from his newspaper, cigarette dangling from the corner of his mouth. "Giovanni's good people. Done work for me before. Very discreet."

"See? It's all coming together." Jasmine turns those pleading eyes on me. "Plus, he's kinda, sorta on his way here. ETA one hour, tops."

"An *hour?*" I splutter. "Jas, I'm wearing Kosti's old overalls and haven't washed my hair in two days!"

"That's why I'm telling you now." She grins. "Plenty of time to make yourself presentable."

"I said no." Sasha's jaw is clenched. "It's not happening."

"Oh, let them have this." Mama materializes behind him with fresh coffee. "When was the last time I saw my daughter photographed, hm? And now, with the babies coming…" She trails off meaningfully.

I watch Sasha's resolve crumble under the combined weight of Jasmine's puppy eyes and Mama's guilt trip. It's kind of impressive, actually. They've got him completely unraveled.

"Fine," he growls finally. "But I'm running a background check first."

"Already did," Kosti pipes up helpfully. "Clean as a whistle."

Sasha glowers at him. "Whose side are you on?"

"The side of preserving precious memories." Kosti folds his paper with a flourish. "Now, shall we discuss wardrobe options for our lovely mother-to-be?"

I groan and drop my head into my hands. "I hate all of you."

But Jasmine is already dragging me toward the stairs, chattering about lighting and angles and the importance of capturing this magical time in my life. Behind us, I hear Sasha muttering darkly in Russian.

He can grumble all he wants. We both know he's powerless here. As am I. We're just collateral damage in a well-meaning conspiracy.

Though I have to admit, as Jasmine pulls various flowing dresses from her suitcase... It might be nice to have some photos that don't involve me looking like a sweaty gardener in borrowed overalls.

What's the harm, right?

"Beautiful, *bellissima*! Now, Signore Ozerov—hands lower on her belly. Yes, cradle the life you created together. Perfect."

Sasha's palms burn through the thin cotton of my dress. I count his breaths against my neck—five, six, seven—each one tighter and hotter than the last.

I'm starting to think that this was maybe unwise. Yes, I'm sure that one day, I'll treasure these photos more than life itself, as proof that motherhood has its beautiful moments. Right now, though, I'm mostly concerned by the fact that Sasha's palms on my waist are getting more and more possessive and he's starting to breathe like an angry bull.

My best guess is that it has something to do with how Giovanni is... shall we say, *touchy-feely*. He has combed my hair countless times, smushed my boobs together twice to emphasize my cleavage, and in one particularly shocking move, reached up my dress to adjust my panty line.

It's not that he's a sexual threat to Sasha—after all, Giovanni's husband is the one who dropped him off at the villa. Nice guy. Very thick mustache.

But Sasha's eyes are narrowing into the thin slits that I know precede violence.

"Relax your jaw, *signore*," Giovanni calls from behind his lens. "You look like you're posing for a mugshot, not your first family portrait. Yes, yes, there! Beautiful! Now, look at each other like you cannot wait to make more babies!"

"Jesus Christ," Sasha growls under his breath, and I have to bite my lip to keep from laughing. But when I turn my head to meet his gaze, the humor dies in my throat. His eyes are storm-dark, pupils blown wide, and I'm suddenly, vividly reminded of how those hands felt pinning my wrists to the mattress at 3 A.M. last night.

Lately, it's started to get out of hand. We're fucking like absolute rabbits, multiple rounds, with Sasha spending hours going down on me in between. I didn't know it was possible to come a dozen times in a row. You learn something new every day, I suppose. Even now, I'm still wet and wobbly, though it's been hours since Sasha pulled out of me and slunk mournfully back to his side of the villa.

The fact that he has his hands plastered to my hips and that I can feel his dick hardening against the curve of my ass is not helping matters whatsoever.

This is just pretend, I tell myself. *Like playing dress-up.*

Except the heat pooling low in my belly feels pretty fucking real.

Giovanni lowers his camera and grins at us. "Perfect! But the light, she changes too fast." Giovanni squints at the treeline.

"We must move to the forest. The rays through the leaves will make Mama here glow like an angel."

Sasha goes still. "The forest."

"*Si, si!* Most romantic!" Giovanni's already shoving equipment into his bag, because apparently, he's incapable of doing anything at less than a hundred miles per hour. "The trees, they frame the love story!"

I glance up at Sasha. His jaw is clenched so tight I'm worried he'll crack a tooth. "We can just—"

"It's fine. The sooner we get this over, the better."

We follow Giovanni into the forest, leaving Mama, Kosti, and Jasmine behind, the three of them tittering like schoolgirls from the front steps of the villa.

The air under the trees hums with golden hour magic—or maybe that's just the adrenaline buzzing in my ears as Giovanni flutters around me, adjusting the diaphanous silk draped over my shoulders until he reveals a bit more skin than I'm entirely comfortable with.

"No, no—ah, *yesss*," he croons, fingers lingering on my hip. "Now, let the fabric fall just so... yes, yes, the curve of the belly, the shadow of the breast—perfection!"

Sasha's boot crunches a twig behind the photographer. I don't have to look to know he's coiled tighter than a spring, that muscle in his jaw doing its angry little dance.

"Sway for me, Ariel. Like water, like air."

I'm not sure how to move like either of those things while seven months pregnant with twins, but I give it my best shot. The resulting shimmy makes the fabric slip dangerously low across my breasts.

From his position against an oak tree, Sasha's entire body goes rigid. He's been getting progressively more murderous-looking with each of Giovanni's "adjustments" to my poses. The last time Giovanni's fingers grazed my hip to angle me toward the light, I swear I heard Sasha growl like a bear.

"Now, perhaps we lose a layer, yes?" Giovanni's hand drifts toward the knot securing the silk cups of the gown behind my neck. "*Naturale.* Just a hint of the maternal form. Very tasteful. We must capture the rawness, the vulnerability of motherhood—"

"Touch that," Sasha growls, "and I remove your hand."

I roll my eyes. "Relax, Rambo. It's called art."

"*Art.*" The word drips venom.

The photographer chuckles nervously. "Signore, perhaps if you stand just over there, by the birch—"

"No."

"Sasha—"

He steps into the dappled light, all pent-up menace in a black shirt that clings to every lethal line. My traitorous pulse kicks. Giovanni pales, clutching his camera like a shield.

"We're done here," rumbles Sasha.

"But the golden hour approaches! The light will be—"

Sasha plucks the camera from Giovanni's hands and replaces it with a thick envelope. "This is more than adequate compensation for your time. And your camera."

"I… but…" Then Giovanni opens the envelope, and his eyes go wide. "Ah. *Si, si,* of course." He starts gathering his equipment even faster than the first time around and disappears without a word.

I wait until Giovanni practically jogs away down the drive before turning to Sasha. "That was a bit dramatic, don't you think?"

"He was going to undress you." His jaw works. "In the middle of the fucking forest."

"It's called artistic nudity, darling." I adjust the slipping fabric. "Very tasteful. Very *naturale*."

"There's nothing tasteful about another man's hands on what's mine."

The words churn between us, heavy as thunder. We both know this crosses about a dozen different lines in our "just sex" agreement, but I'm finding it hard to care when he's looking at me like that.

"Yours, huh?" I arch an eyebrow. "Funny, I don't recall signing any property deeds."

His hands find my hips, yanking me closer. "No? Then why are you still wearing my marks from last night?"

Well, shit. He's got me there.

"The twins are yours," I concede. "The rest is still up for debate."

His fingers slide up to the knot Giovanni was reaching for. "Want to debate it right now?"

"I think you don't know what 'debate' means."

"I know what 'mine,' means," Sasha replies, hedging closer to me until our hips are flush. "And I know that no one photographs my wife but me."

'Wife' stops me cold. It's not a term we use. Ever. It belongs to that nebulous future we both pretend doesn't exist, along with 'marriage' and 'forever' and all those other dangerous words that cannot, should not, will not happen.

"I'm not your—"

The camera shutter cuts me off. *Click.*

Sasha lowers the Nikon, gaze dark over the lens. "Smile, *ptichka.*"

"You're insane." I hitch the slipping silk higher. "And I'm not posing for some mafia maternity pinup."

Click.

"There." His mouth curves. "That scowl is perfect."

I lunge for the camera strap. He spins me against a tree, bark rough through the flimsy gown. His breath scorches my ear. "You want art? I'll give you art. *Real* art."

The next hour bleeds gold.

He doesn't tell me to arch or pout. Just circles with the camera, murmuring Russian filth that makes my nipples peak. *Click.* The silk slithers off one shoulder. *Click.* My laugh as wind tangles my hair. *Click.* The raw hunger in my eyes when his thumb scorches over my hip.

"Good girl," he murmurs when I finally give up the fight against the last tie keeping the dress fastened to me. It begins to slide down my body. "Now, touch yourself where you want my hands to be. Look at me like you did in the library," he rasps, backing me against a sun-warmed boulder. "Like you want me to ruin you."

His knee nudges mine apart. "Sasha—"

Click.

"Beautiful," he breathes. But unlike Giovanni's constant stream of praise, this single word feels like it's been ripped from somewhere deep inside him. "You're so fucking beautiful, Ariel."

His fingers trace where the camera lens just traveled, and all my clever words evaporate. The silk puddles around my feet as Sasha pulls me down with him onto the soft earth.

This is different from our usual midnight collisions. No angry biting, no bruising grips. His touch is reverent, almost careful, like I'm something precious instead of just convenient.

I should stop it. I have to. I will.

But as I open my mouth to tell him no, he presses two fingers inside of me, and all the protest dies with a single choked breath.

The Nikon slips from his fingers, landing in moss with a soft thud. Sasha's hands replace the camera lens—calloused palms framing my face, thumbs tracing the swell of my bottom lip. Sunlight paints gold streaks across his scar as he leans in, achingly slow, until our breaths tangle.

He doesn't kiss me.

Not yet.

His mouth ghosts along my jaw, my throat, the flutter of my pulse. The forest holds its breath. When his teeth graze my nipple, I arch into him with a gasp.

"Easy, *ptichka*," he murmurs against my skin. Moss cushions my spine as he strips bare, each movement deliberate. My belly rises between us like a full moon. He pauses, hand splayed beneath it.

Something cracks in his gaze.

Then he's everywhere—lips mapping constellations across my collarbones, fingers threading through mine, pinning them above my head. The forest spins as he enters me, our rhythm easy and deep. No teeth, no fury. Just sunlight and sweat and his groan vibrating through my ribs when I clench around him.

Coming feels like flying.

I expect him to bury the moment in sarcasm afterward. A crude joke. A reminder that this is nothing. But when it's done, neither of us speaks. Speaking would mean acknowledging whatever just happened here—how different it felt, how much closer to making love than fucking.

So we stay silent, listening to the forest's music, pretending we're still just two people scratching an itch instead of whatever we're becoming.

That night, I'm in my bathroom on my hands and knees, desperately trying to scrub dirt stains and grass stains and, well, *other* stains from the dress Jasmine lent me.

But a whisper of paper from behind draws my attention.

I turn, frowning, until I see it.

A photograph, slipped under my door like a love letter.

My hands shake as I pick it up. The shot is perfect—me, caught in a shaft of sunlight, head thrown back in genuine

laughter as my hands cradle my swollen belly. I look...
powerful. Soft. *Real.*

Not the artificial poses Giovanni wanted. Not the sultry
shots that followed. Just me, unguarded and alive, captured
through Sasha's lens in a moment of pure joy.

I should throw it away. That's what our arrangement
demands—no mementos, no feelings, no evidence that could
be used against our hearts later.

Instead, I open my journal and carefully tuck the photo
between its pages. *Just this once*, I tell myself. Just this one
small piece of proof that for a moment in a sunlit forest, I
was more than just a convenient body. I was *his.*

Even if we'll both pretend to forget it tomorrow.

31

SASHA

It's storming again.

Lightning flickers through the villa's warped windows as Zoya's fingers dig into the knot beneath my shoulder blade. My jaw clenches, but I don't make a sound.

She'd love that. I can just picture how wide she'd grin if she made me grunt in agony. But I'm as stubborn as she says I am. Won't give her the satisfaction.

The massage table creaks as she shifts her weight, moving to a particularly tender spot where Dragan's bullet tore through muscle. Rain starts to patter against the glass, marking time with each stab of pain.

The room reeks of her homemade liniment, all camphor stinging my nostrils. "Christ, *malchik*. You're even more of a mess than I thought you were."

Her fingers find the bullet wound and test it. Puckered flesh remembers how it felt—steel chewing through meat, concrete rising up to kiss my skull. Fuck, that alley was so cold.

I grind my molars as her palm presses down, checking the give.

"Still favors the left," she tsks. "Gonna walk crooked if you don't—"

"Enough, Zoya."

"*Ebat'*, you always were a shit patient." But her hands gentles on the next pass. We both stare at the window where rain blurs the forest into green smears.

The back door creaks open downstairs—Ariel's laughter tangling with Jasmine's as they both run in from where they've been gardening in the rain. My pulse jumps. Zoya's smirk digs fresh furrows into her face.

"There," she says finally, patting my unmarked shoulder. "That should help with the stiffness. Though God knows you'll just undo all my work the next time you sneak into that girl's room at night."

"I don't know what you're talking about."

"*Ach,* liar, liar, Sashenka. The whole villa has ears, you know." Zoya sits on the foot of the makeshift massage tables. "These old walls, they talk. Especially at three in the morning."

I focus on the rain against the window and say nothing.

"Not that it matters to an old woman like me. You're the one doing the walk of shame every sunrise." She taps a wrinkled finger at her lips. "Though I suppose shame requires actually feeling something."

"Is there anything else you'd like to discuss?" I grit out. "Weather? Taxes? Nothing at all?"

She slaps my foot. "You're worse than your father at talking about feelings."

"I am nothing like him."

"No? I see a few similarities. He also thought feelings made him weak. That love was a luxury he couldn't afford."

Pain lances through me, but it's not from the wound. "This isn't about—"

"Everything is about that. Every wall you build, every heart you push away." Her voice softens. "You think I don't see how you look at her? At her belly?"

The storm crashes closer, thunder shaking the villa's bones. Or maybe that's just me.

"What if I become him?" The Russian slips out before I can stop it, barely louder than the rain. "What if I hurt them like he hurt us?"

Zoya's hands are still on my back. For a long moment, there's only the sound of the storm and my ragged breathing. "The fact that you're asking that question," she says finally, "means you never will."

Quarter to four in the morning finds me doing the same walk I've done every night for weeks now. I know all the creaking spots in the floorboards, how to jump from side to side to avoid making a peep. Ariel's door swings inward silently. I'm halfway to her bed, already hard, when—

The lamp clicks on.

Golden light spills across Ariel's face, catching the sheen of tears before she can wipe them away.

I freeze halfway there. "I'll go."

"No!" Her hand darts out, fingers hooking into my belt loop. "Stay. Please."

Please. She's never said *please.*

I study the anchoring grip on my jeans. Smell her shampoo clinging to the bedsheets. Hear the hum of the villa settling around us—Jasmine's soft snores down the hall, Belle's wind chime clinking in the storm.

Traitorous things, all of them. Witnesses to this unraveling.

"I know what you're afraid of," she whispers. "I heard you talking to Zoya."

My first thought is to get the fuck out. My second and third thoughts are more of the same.

But the longer I stay there and look at Ariel's face—open, honest, completely free of judgment—the more I feel little clock gears in my face winding down. A cuckoo bird of the heart chirping that now is the time for this kind of thing.

She sits up, sheets pooling around her waist. The swell of her belly catches the lamplight.

"How do you do it?" I ask hoarsely. "How do you stay... good, after everything your father did to you?"

She lets out a shaky breath. "I don't know if I am good. Sometimes, I wake up terrified that I'll look in the mirror and see him looking back." Her free hand curves over her stomach. "That these babies will grow up seeing the same monster in me that I saw in him."

"You could never be—"

"That's my point, Sasha. Neither could you."

The silence stretches between us, filled with all the things we never say. All the fears we pretend don't exist in the dark.

"I'm just as scared as you are, you know," she says. "They already look like us. Your nose. My chin. What if they get your eyes, too? Or my stubbornness? Or our stupid, reckless grief?" She turns her face up to me. "Or worst of all... What if they're perfect, Sasha? What if they're so utterly, completely perfect that it takes your breath away just to look at them— and then we ruin them anyway?"

The lamp flickers as power dies from the storm outside. Shadows dance across the ultrasound taped to Ariel's mirror —two blurry shapes curled like commas.

Our mistakes. Our miracles.

"Ariel—"

"It's okay." She presses a finger to my lips. "I'm not really asking. I know you don't have the answers. Just... stay tonight. No sex. No jokes. Just... stay."

Her breath steadies first. Soft. Even. Trusting.

Idiot woman. You don't know what you're asking me.

But when she tugs me toward the bed, I follow.

32

ARIEL

The heat is unbearable. I've never been more miserable in my life, which is saying something considering my track record. Sweat drips down my spine as I fan myself with an old magazine, watching Sasha and Kosti fiddle with the ancient air conditioning unit for what feels like the hundredth time today.

"Try it now!" Kosti calls out. Mama flips the switch, and the unit makes a noise like a dying cat before sputtering into silence again.

"For God's sake," I groan, shifting uncomfortably on the couch. The twins are particularly active today, probably unhappy about being trapped in their own personal sauna. "I'm going to melt."

Jasmine appears with another glass of ice water, but the ice has already started to melt before she can even hand it to me. "This is ridiculous." She wipes her forehead with the back of her hand. "We're all going to die of heatstroke. They'll find puddles where we once stood. Human soup."

Kosti abandons the A/C unit and lights a fresh cigarette, seemingly unbothered by adding more heat to the atmosphere. "When I was young, during particularly hot summers in Greece, we would sleep outside. The stone terrace should be much cooler than in here."

Sleeping outside sounds shitty. On the other hand, I'll take anything that's not another night of tossing and turning in my sweat-soaked sheets.

The last week has been unrelentingly brutal. No storms have rolled through to break up the monotony, so it's just wall-to-wall heat without pause or respite. We're all going a little stir-crazy. So Kosti's suggestion finds more receptive ears than it would have otherwise.

Before I know it, we're all dragging loungers and blankets outside. The sun is setting in a tangerine sky, and—I'll be damned—there's finally a hint of a breeze.

The stars wink to life one by one as darkness settles over our makeshift bedroom. Jasmine and Mama are huddled together on their loungers, their soft murmurs mixing with the chorus of crickets. The occasional click of chess pieces punctuates the night as Zoya and Kosti face off by lantern light, their by-now-familiar bickering carried away on the breeze.

I shift again, trying to find a position that doesn't make my back scream or put too much pressure on my belly. But I'm afraid we're rapidly approaching the stage of pregnancy where *comfort* is nothing but a pretty lie.

At last week's checkup, the doctor's eyes bulged when she saw how big I'd gotten. That's usually not the kind of thing a woman wants to see, but I'm beyond caring. Even growing life inside of you loses its allure after a while, it turns out.

With five weeks left until these little gremlins vacate the premises, it's safe to say I'm ready for the next adventure.

I roll over again, nestle in, and sigh. "This is it," I mumble to myself. "This is the one. The world's most comfortable, undeniably perfect sleeping position. No one has ever been so cozy or so— *Ow*, goddammit, my back."

Without a word, Sasha reaches over from his lounger and hands me one of his pillows. I hesitate for a moment before accepting it, tucking it behind my lower back. The relief is immediate.

"Thanks," I mumble.

He grunts in response, but I catch his eyes lingering on my stomach. He's been doing a lot of that lately. Well, more than before, which was already a lot. Now, it's like he can't bear to look at anything else.

Like always, I wonder what he's thinking. He's been so good about being open with me since I heard him talking to Zoya. It still all takes place under cover of darkness, but now, between rounds of making my eyes roll back in my head, we whisper back and forth to each other. It's easier when we can't see. Safer that way.

"Hey, Jas," I call out. "Remember when you used to take me out on the roof and make up constellations?"

Jasmine giggles. "Duh. Do you remember when Dad caught us out there? I thought he was gonna lose his freaking mind."

I shudder at the memory. It was funny then, back when we didn't know as much, although a little bit less so now. "He had the shotgun in his hand and everything."

"You peed your pants when the flashlight hit us."

"Because you said he fed trespassers to the geese in the park!"

Mama laughs, too. "You girls were always finding your way onto that roof," she chimes in. "Just like when you were tiny and would climb out of your cribs. Jasmine, you used to help Ariel escape even before she could walk."

"That's because she'd cry if I didn't," Jasmine defends. "Cry Baby Ari."

"You were both rather… vocal," says Mama. "You both came out screaming. Jasmine was loud enough to crack the nursery window. When Ariel was born, I thought I had a silent one—then *boom*, lungs like a foghorn."

Jasmine lobs a pistachio shell at her. "You're making that up."

"Am not! Ask Kosti. He was there."

Kosti guffaws as he takes another of Zoya's pawns. "I thought I had banshees for nieces, both times. Who knew I'd be so right?"

Jasmine and I both throw things at him. He ducks, laughing.

The laughter fades as everyone settles back into their chairs. I yawn and Sasha reaches out to stroke the hair back from my face. I look over at him.

"What are you thinking about?" I whisper.

He's quiet for so long I think he might not answer. Then: "Which constellations I want to teach our children."

Our children. We don't usually say it quite like that. More often than not, it's "the babies" or "the twins."

"Yeah? Which ones?"

"The North Star, of course. That way, they can always find their way home."

I reach out to lace my fingers through his. That's too tender —I should counterbalance it with something else. I should say something cutting. Make a joke. Remind us both of the lines we've drawn.

Instead, I find myself lifting the edge of the blanket in silent invitation. "Keep me warm?"

He hesitates, and for a moment, I think he'll refuse. Then he moves, careful and quiet, until we're sharing not just the blanket or the lounger, but the narrow space between waking and dreaming.

When I risk a glance up, he's staring at where his fingers linger against my skin. There's no smirk, no leer—just raw, unguarded want that mirrors the ache low in my belly.

The others snore on, oblivious. Jasmine mutters something about tax brackets in her sleep. A bird trills its first tentative song. Normal sounds. Safe sounds. Anything to anchor me against the dangerous truth taking root—that I want his hands everywhere now, but not for the reasons we agreed upon.

I want them for *more.*

~

I wake to sunlight warming my face and the distant sound of birds. The others must have already gone inside. Their loungers are empty, pillows and blankets abandoned. Only Sasha's thick blanket remains, still wrapped around me like an embrace.

Something crinkles when I shift. A piece of paper, folded beside my pillow. When I open it, my breath catches.

The paper contains a rough sketch of stars connected by careful lines. It's not a real constellation—I recognize enough from Jasmine's childhood lessons to know that. Instead, it forms the shape of two tiny figures nestled together, like the ultrasound image taped to my mirror. Beneath it, in Sasha's precise handwriting:

For our children.

I don't need a North Star to tell me what's become blindingly obvious now: We're well past the point of no feelings.

There's no going back from here.

33

ARIEL

The birthing center looks nothing like I imagined. No sterile white walls or harsh fluorescent lights—just warm terracotta and climbing vines, like someone's nonna decided to turn her villa into a medical facility.

Which, according to the plaque by the door, is exactly what happened.

Sasha's hand rests at the small of my back as we follow the receptionist down a sunlit hallway. The contrast between this and our last Lamaze "class" couldn't be more stark. This place is conspicuously absent of Gina in a ridiculous wig pretending to be a New Age guru. There will be no exaggerated breathing exercises or jokes about chakra alignment.

Today feels like serious business.

The woman up front looks the part, too. She's short and fierce, with steel-gray hair twisted into a severe bun. Her name tag reads **Signora Rossi** in precise handwriting. *"Benvenuti!"* she cries as we approach. "You are the Ozerovs?"

I hesitate, but Sasha nods for both of us.

Signora Rossi beams. "*Perfetto!* Come, come." She ushers us into a room filled with birth balls and yoga mats. "First baby, *si?*"

"First two, actually," I say, patting my belly. "Twins."

Her eyes light up. "*Gemelli!* Double blessing. Then we have much to cover."

The birthing class room fills up with other couples, all of them looking as apprehensive as I feel. The vinyl mat sticks to my thighs as Sasha and I lower ourselves between a pair of German tourists and a local couple holding hands. I'm already bracing myself for Sasha's inevitable complaints about this whole thing being a waste of time.

But they never come.

Instead, he's pulling out a small notebook, scribbling notes in his precise handwriting as Signora Rossi begins explaining different labor positions. When she demonstrates a particular breathing pattern, he actually raises his hand to ask a question about the timing.

His focus terrifies me more than any intentionally scary thing he's ever done. This is the same intensity he uses for interrogations, for dismantling rivals. Now, it's being directed at… memorizing pelvic tilt for optimal dilation?

I stare at him, wondering if he's been replaced by some kind of parallel universe version of himself. This is nothing like the last time we did this. He looks… invested. Determined.

He looks like he fucking *cares*.

Signora Rossi begins explaining perineal massage. Sasha's

brow furrows as he raises his hand and asks, "How often should we practice this?"

I immediately choke on my water. "You cannot be serious."

But he doesn't blink or seem to notice that it's an absurd question. His hand does reach out to find my thigh and rest there. Gentle. Reassuring. I don't think he even realizes he's doing it.

So what do I do?

I go along with it, duh. What else can I do besides that?

Even as things get more intense, all I can do is sit back and enjoy the ride. We're supposed to be partners in mutual destruction, not... this. His calloused palm spans the stretch marks he kissed raw last night. He mouths *Vydokh* against my temple during the exhale drills—*breathe out*—like it's a prayer.

The Italian couple beside us coo over his dedication. I want to scream that it's a trick, a front, a facade. But when the instructor praises his form, Sasha's touch caresses the nape of my neck—a fleeting, tender thing that smashes my resolve wide open.

During a break, I press my forehead to my knees. *Just hormones*, I lie to us both. *Just biology. Just math.*

His pen scratches on.

Signora Rossi claps her hands. "Now, partners—time to practice supporting through contractions. *Andiamo!*"

Sasha's already moving behind me, his thighs bracing behind mine as I sit on the stupid purple yoga mat. His palms slide up my sides, just shy of ticklish. The class fades—there's just the mint-and-cedar scent of him, the warmth of his breath fanning over the back of my neck.

"Breathe, *ptichka*," he murmurs against my ear. His fingers dig into a knot I didn't know I had, coaxing a moan from my throat that has the German tourists chuckling.

I elbow him, red-faced. "Less happy ending, more labor support."

His chuckle vibrates through me. "You want textbook? I can do textbook." His hands shift, palms cradling the curve of my belly as he leans us both forward into a closer semblance of the "comfort position" from Rossi's diagram. "Better?"

No! Worse! Much worse! I'm a mess, inside and out, sexually, emotionally, orgasmically, karmically. This was all a very bad idea.

"Forty seconds," Rossi calls. "Hold the pose!"

Sasha's lips hover over my temple. "You're doing good."

The praise shouldn't matter. We've fucked in dressing rooms, against printing presses, on forest floors—a million places more exposed than this.

So why do I feel like I'm melting into him?

"Time!" Rossi trills.

I scramble upright too fast, knees popping like mini fireworks. "Great. Nice work, team. Looks like we're done."

Sasha catches my elbow, steadying me. "Ariel—"

"I'm great!" I blurt, though he didn't ask. I yank free of him and gesture at the exit. "I do need some air, though. Or a Xanax. Either one."

I stride out, but I don't get far. In the hallway, I find the coziest looking patch of floor and sink to a seat, rehearsing breathing techniques until my heart stops palpitating.

My laugh comes out jagged and delirious. Of course. Of fucking course this would be the thing to finally soften him —not guns or gangs or my smart mouth, but the clinical horror of childbirth prep.

The classroom door creaks open. Sasha looms in the threshold, backlit by the birthing class's salt lamp glow.

He arches a brow. He doesn't really need to ask the question.

I press the heels of my hands to my eyes. "Just realizing I'd rather birth these kids in a Denny's parking lot than spend one more minute—"

His fingers curl around my wrists, gentle but firm. "Look at me, Ariel."

The hallway spins. Or maybe that's just me.

"Whatever this is," he says quietly, "we're in it together. For good."

The words, too kind to be coming from a man like him, slip under my skin the way they always do. I want to claw them out. Or wrap myself in them. Can't decide which.

"You don't get to promise that."

"Don't I?" His palm settles over my belly as he kneels next to me. "They're mine. You're mine. That makes every fucking breath I take yours, too."

I open my mouth—to laugh, to scream, to agree—but Rossi's voice cuts through the tension.

"*Signori!* Back to class, *per favore!* We practice breathing through nipple stimulation now!"

Sasha's mouth twitches. "Still time for that Denny's, if you want."

I laugh and he helps me up. Together, hand in hand, we walk back in.

Somehow, the nipple stimulation is less invasive than it seemed. We make it through the rest of class mostly without incident. Sasha has filled pages of his notebook, but now, between scribbles, he looks over at me and flashes a reassuring smile.

It'd be easy to blame all my nerves on the biological Everest that's waiting for me to climb it in four short weeks. Delivering one baby, much less two, is no joke. And to be sure, that's definitely part of it.

But it's also delivering *his* babies, in *this* place, under *these* circumstances. Thank God I have my mom and Jas here to hold my hands through it. And though I never thought I'd say it, thank God I have Sasha here, too.

After today, if my perineum needs massaging, he'll know exactly what to do.

Signora Rossi thanks us all for coming and the other couples begin to shuffle out. I join the back of the pack, but Sasha says, "Wait here," and goes to whisper with the teacher.

I frown when he passes a thick stack of euro bills to her. Rossi's eyes widen, but she nods and hurries out after the rest of the students with a cryptic smile in my direction.

Sasha follows behind her and locks the door.

When he turns back to me, the predatory gleam in his eyes makes my breath catch. I back up until I bump into one of the birthing balls, steadying myself against it.

"More practicing?" I ask, aiming for sarcasm but my voice comes out breathy.

"I take my homework very seriously." He stalks toward me with lethal grace. "Don't you want to be prepared?"

My laugh is shaky. "I don't think this was what Signora Rossi had in mind for the equipment."

"No?" His hands find my hips, steadying me as I wobble on the ball. "I think we're being good students."

There's something different about this. About us. The playfulness mixed with intensity, the way his hands cup my face… It terrifies me how right it feels.

"Sasha…" I whisper, not sure if I'm warning him or pleading.

His forehead presses against mine. "I know, Ariel. I know. But here's the thing." He draws in a tense, shuddering breath. "I came here for the babies. To learn how to keep them—and you—safe. We did that. But now, I need something in return."

"What's that?" I whisper.

"I need *you.* Because if I don't put you on your back and make an absolute mess of your pussy right now, I think I might fucking die."

Sir!

I let out an insane, giddy laugh. "This is the problem," I whisper as heat leaches up to my face.

"What is?"

"That I don't know how to say no when you say things like that to me."

My heart is pounding in my chest. I'm not sure if it's from the fear or the anticipation. Maybe both.

He pushes me back onto the ball, then raises my legs up against his chest, calves hooked over his shoulders. He presses a kiss to the inside of each ankle. Gentle, like a butterfly landing. Then, tucking two fingers inside the waistband of my leggings, he peels them down and tosses them aside without a care.

Sinking to his knees, he spreads my thighs wide and starts to nibble his way up from my knee. I go from nearly giggling with ticklishness to a breathy *Oh* when his mouth passes over my center.

His eyes stay absolutely fixated on me as he pulls the seat of my panties aside and presses one teasing kiss to my clit. He never blinks. Never looks away.

I'm exposed, vulnerable, and I fucking love it. I love the way he looks at me, like I'm the only thing that matters in this world.

He leans down, his tongue finding my clit, and I gasp, my hands gripping his hair. He chuckles, the sound vibrating through me. "You're so wet, Ari. So fucking wet for me."

I moan, my hips bucking against his mouth. He's right. I'm so fucking wet. I'm so fucking ready.

He licks slow rings around me. Every pass brings him closer and closer, gets me wetter and wetter, so that when he finally slides a finger inside me, it goes in without the tiniest bit of resistance. He crooks it up toward his face and I see stars.

His tongue descends on my clit. Two fingers. Three. The ball is squishy and wobbly beneath me as I buck and writhe while Sasha licks me to a drooling orgasm.

I'm still pinwheeling when he stands up, his cock hard and ready. He grabs a support rope and wraps it around my wrists, securing me to him like a leash.

I'm at his mercy now.

He bumps the ball back and forth so I bounce and flail around. I laugh, the sound coming out breathy and needy. He smiles, eyes dark. "You want more, Ari?"

I nod. He leans down, his cock rubbing against my entrance. I want to touch him so fucking badly, but he's got my wrists bound with the rope.

"St-stop... teasing..."

"Who, me?" he asks innocently. His face goes dark as he starts to slowly drag the tip of his dick up and down my pussy. Never entering, just a taunt graze. "No, Ariel, I won't stop teasing. I'm going to do this... and this... and this... until you're dripping and pleading for me to finally go in. You can moan all you want, but it won't make me go one second faster. In fact, that sound is music to my ears—so I might just go a little slower, and a little slower than that. You'll be half-crazed by the time I'm done, won't you? You'll have eyes rolling back in your hand and you'll bite your lip raw. And then I'm going to tease you one... more... time... That'll be the one that breaks you. But it's only then that I'll finally slide into you, Ariel. It's only when you're truly about to lose your mind that I'll give you everything you want."

It's like he's casting a spell on me. Every sentence is underscored with that delicious, unbearable friction as he toys with my clit. I'm everything he swore I would be: dripping, pleading, needy, desperate. There's no limit to the things I would do to have him all the way inside me.

I look up at him, tears filling my eyes. "Sasha… please."

He smirks, hair falling over his forehead. He's the devil I always thought he was. But he's *my* devil now.

"I knew you were a good girl, Ariel. Show me just how good."

Then he pushes inside me, filling me completely, and as always, that first stroke steals every last bit of my breath away.

I cry out. He muffles it with a heavy kiss.

He starts to move, his hips thrusting against mine. The rope chafes at my wrists, but I'm grateful for it, because it tethers me to reality, when everything else feels like it's melting into oblivion. The ball rolls back and forth, squishing and rocking and squeaking, and I'm moaning, he's panting, we're fucking like this is the first time or the last time, I can't tell which.

But then his smile fades. His eyes blacken. He leans down, his mouth finding mine again with more intent than ever before, as he says the only thing that could possibly bring me any higher than he's already brought me:

"I love you, Ariel Ward. I fucking love you."

I'd say it back if I could, but then he fucks into me so hard that it doesn't matter what I say, because my body is saying it for me with every clench and squeeze and wordless moan.

I come.

He comes.

We both fall into each other, boundaries blurring, breath mingling, worlds colliding.

He helps me dress afterward, rolling my leggings back on and hiking them up over my swelling hips. His touch is gentle, littered with kisses everywhere—my neck, my shoulder blades, the curve of my spine.

I don't return the favor—I'm too greedy for that, and watching Sasha dress is one of my guilty pleasures. So I just sit back and enjoy the show.

He drags his pants back up over his toned butt and fastens his belt. His abs disappear, one row at a time, as he hikes his shirt back on and buttons it. He's always so precise about his appearance. Cuffs get rolled perfectly, hair smoothed down. As if anyone who sees us walking out of here won't know exactly what we've been doing.

I let out a mournful sigh when his body is hidden from view again. It's almost a shame that he's not required to stand on a pedestal in a busy intersection all day long. People should get to look at him. He's an international treasure.

On the other hand, I don't mind that he's all mine.

We're almost out the door when he says, "Almost forgot this." I stand and watch as he jogs back to retrieve the journal he filled with notes today.

"Gonna add to that now?" I tease. "'*Ariel likes the three-fingers plus clit combo. Note for next time: consider optimal perineum involvement.'*"

But instead of laughing or joking back, his face goes serious. "I want to be ready," he says quietly. "To help you. When the time comes."

That steals my breath more effectively than any of his kisses. In that moment, it's so easy to glimpse the future stretching out before us: Sasha beside me in the delivery room, those strong hands that deal death so easily now cradling new life instead. A pair of glistening pink babies resting on his bare chest.

It's too much. Too real. Too close to everything I've been trying not to want.

I look away first, focusing on retying my shoelaces. "Well, at least one of us was paying attention."

Finally, the darkness passes and he grins at me. "We can always do some more homework back at the villa, if you missed something important."

"They do say practice makes perfect…"

But even as we fall back into our familiar rhythm of banter, I feel the weight of his words settling into my bones.

When the time comes.

Not if.

When.

34

SASHA

Late nights are when the past rears its ugly head. The familiar jitter in my feet that drives me to walk, pace, plan, patrol. I steal a cigarette from Kosti, with every intention of smoking and brooding while I did my usual laps of the perimeter, searching for threats.

But the jitter fades before I even begin. It's not the first time they've faltered—lately, those instincts aren't as urgent as they once were. The voices in my head—one voice, really, just Yakov's, a broken record of *Pathetic-Ssyklo-Pathetic-Ssyklo* —aren't as loud.

I've got new voices keeping me company now. These are far more pleasant. They sound like Ariel's breathless moans, her laugh, the delighted *Ahh* when I finally find the itch on her back that she can't reach herself anymore. The images with it are pleasant, too: her belly pressing through a sheer white gown. green leaves poking up through rich, black earth.

I don't mind the change as much as I thought I might.

Perhaps that's why I'm halfway to the door, gun in hand, ready to patrol, when I decide that maybe it's okay to rest for a night. I set the gun back where it lives and retreat to my study. The unlit cigarette in my hand gets tucked back into Kosti's pack.

That doesn't mean I have to be useless. I could still work for a while. Feliks sent me a packet of documents tracking Dragan's movements, and it needs attention. All signs say he's circling something big; it's best for everyone involved if I figure out what that something might be before it's too late.

But when I slip in my study, it's not my laptop I see open on my desk.

It's Ariel's. She must've left it in here when she was borrowing the room for a bit of privacy earlier. The screen pours out in a sea of blue light.

I step around to close it—then stop. My own name catches my eye.

Dear Sasha,

They have your nose.

I should close it. Walk away. This is her space, not mine, and I have no right to invade it. I'm halfway to the door when I growl and turn back around. I drop into the chair and start to read.

Dear Sasha,

They have your nose. I keep staring at the ultrasound, trying to convince myself if I'm imagining it. I wish I was. We left you behind, after all. You're an ocean away now, and I'd like for you to stay there forever.

Because there's no telling what else of yours they've inherited, and we can't outrun it all. I'll give them fire; that's a certainty. But will you give them ice? I wonder if you know how frigid it is to be near you sometimes. I feel my fingers and toes slipping away from me, like they're dissolving. It's frostbite of the heart.

And the heart is too wild of a thing to live locked up in a cage of ice.

The cursor blinks like a dare. I know I shouldn't be reading this. I'm a thief in her mind, stealing thoughts she'd never give me freely.

But even though I'm a changed bastard, I'm still as greedy as I ever was.

And when it comes to Ariel Ward, all I want is *more*.

So I read on.

Lately, your tenderness terrifies me more than your cruelty ever did. When you rub my swollen feet, I forget what else those hands have done. When you whisper lullabies to my belly, I don't hear the same tongue that ordered a murder before we'd ever said hello.

The screen blurs. I grip the desk until the wood creaks.

I want to believe the man who kisses my stretch marks is real. But which version of you gets to claim him? The killer or the caregiver? The monster or the—

The sentence dies mid-thought. Unfinished.

Guilt curdles in my throat as I sit back in my chair. This is worse than catching her naked—this is like sawing her open and turning her inside-out. She sees the rot in me, the same decay that hollowed out Yakov. She's asking the same questions I've spent weeks asking myself.

What infections do I carry?

What will she catch? What will our children catch?

She's wrong about one thing, though: *Frostbite of the heart* is no death sentence. Cold preserves. Ice keeps things intact. Cold is *necessary,* goddammit.

But when I press my forehead to the desk, I feel the phantom heat of her burning through.

A gasp jerks me back upright. I raise my head to find Ariel framed in the doorway, one hand clutching her belly, the other white-knuckling the doorframe. Her eyes dart between me and the laptop I'm still touching, horror dawning like a slow bleed.

"How much did you read?" When I don't answer fast enough, she repeats it louder. "How *much*, Sasha?"

I sigh. "Enough."

She crosses the room in a few quick strides and snatches the laptop, clutching it to her chest. "Those were my private thoughts. My journal. You had no right—"

"Your thoughts—about me. About our children." I rise from the desk, hands spread. "I think that gives me some right."

"Wrong." She backs away, shaking her head. "If you wanted to know how I felt, you could have asked me. Like a normal person. Instead of—of *sneaking*."

"Would you have been this honest if I had?"

"We'll never know now, will we?" She bares her teeth. "Because you couldn't resist playing spymaster. Always watching, always calculating. God forbid you just talk to me."

"I'm talking now."

"No. You're justifying." She shifts the laptop to one hip, using her free hand to stab a finger at my chest. "There's a difference."

I straighten up and clench my jaw. "Words are words, Ariel. Even if you think they're true, they never tell the whole story. It's actions that say it all. Because the man you describe there?" I point at the laptop. "You fucking *hate* that man. But the man you fucked in that classroom today—you loved him, didn't you? So which is real? The words or the moans?" I advance on her, hemming her back against the closed door. "You think I don't see you flinch when I touch you? That I don't hear the 'what-ifs' in every silence? Tell me I'm wrong. Look me in the eye and say it."

She trembles—not from fear, but from fury. From the same desperate hunger that keeps drawing us back to this same desperate precipice time and time again.

"I don't know if I love you or hate you," she whispers. "That's the problem."

"If you love me, then love me. If you hate me, then hate me." I lean down until our breaths tangle. "But do it out loud."

"What's the point?" she asks, her breath trembling as she hides her face from me. "This might be news to you, Sasha, but you're not exactly the easiest man to talk to. You... you hide. You lie. You don't know how hard it is to look at you and not know what you're thinking. I just want to know what's going on in your head. That's all I've ever wanted."

I open my mouth to argue—then I think better of it.

Frostbite of the heart. It'd be easy to be insulted by that, wouldn't it? Pride is one of my many faults, and Ariel's always known where to stick that particular knife. *You're a cold fucking bastard,* she's saying. I could let that anger me.

Or I could do what she's telling me to do: step outside of my own skin for one fucking second and look through her eyes instead.

So I do. What do I see?

I see a tall, dark-eyed, miserable son of a bitch who's clenched his jaw for so long that every smile feels like cracks skittering in the frost, dangerous cracks, the kind that come right before the iceberg sinks underwater, never to be seen again.

Giving up my rage and my past is a kind of death, yes.

But it's the only way to make room for life to come in from underneath.

"You're right," I rasp.

Ariel freezes mid-tirade, her fury stuttering. "What?"

"I said you're right." I step back, hands raised in surrender. "I took what wasn't mine. Again. Old habits. I'm sorry, Ariel. Not just for the man I am. But for… this. For all of it."

She blinks. "I almost think you mean that."

I laugh humorlessly. "I want to. Fuck, I want to so badly, Ariel. I just have to convince myself that it's okay to love something I might one day lose."

Surprised tears stud her eyes. "Why are you so sure you'll lose me?"

"How can I not be?" I grit out. "One minute, you're under my hands, screaming my name. The next, you're halfway out the door, taking my unborn children with you. I needed—"

"A cheat sheet?" Her laugh cracks. "Some secret code to tame me?"

"To understand you."

Silence thickens. Owls hoot from the treetops outside.

"Writing... helps," she says finally, tracing the laptop's logo. "Sorting the mess in my head. What's real. What's fear. What's just... you."

I crouch before her, eye level with the swell of our children. "And what am I?"

Her fingertip grazes my scar. "That's a question I'm still learning how to ask."

I press my forehead to her knuckles. "Let me know when you figure it out. Maybe by then, I'll know how to answer."

Ariel laughs, though the sound is stained with unshed tears. Then she bends down to kiss my forehead. "You're insane, Sasha Ozerov."

"Utterly and irrevocably," I agree. "I can't promise that'll change. But I can promise that I won't look again where I shouldn't. You have my word."

A ghost of a smile touches her lips. "The great Sasha Ozerov, making promises about boundaries? Who are you and what have you done with my brooding Russian mobster?"

"I took the good bits of him and buried the rest in the garden. Though I do still wonder whether you'll run when you put them all together and see what kind of picture it forms."

Ariel tilts her head to the side. "What if I don't hate it as much as you think I will? What if I'm starting to like the view, hm?" She laughs softly and touches my cheek. "Even the jagged parts."

I move her palm to my scar. "Even this?"

"Especially this." Her breath hitches as my lips touch her fingertips. "It's where you end that matters to me, Sasha. Not where you begin."

The leather chair creaks as we both settle onto it, Ariel nestled in my lap. The laptop's glow illuminates her face in the predawn darkness as she opens it and scrolls back to the document.

"You don't have to," I tell her, but she shakes her head.

"I want to. Just… some of it. The parts I choose."

I nod, and she begins to read. Her voice is soft but steady as she shares fragments of our story through her eyes—the first meeting in the Met bathroom. The night on the mountain. The moment in Paris when she realized she was falling for me despite herself, when Jasmine played violin for us long before Ariel knew just how close we were to perfection.

She falls asleep eventually, trailing off in the midst of a sentence, the laptop still lying open.

I could keep reading. Or I could do what I do instead:

Close it, leave it behind, and carry her to bed, where I hold her until the dawn comes. Right when it's breaking through the windows, I whisper into her ear, "Marry me, Ariel."

She's asleep, so she doesn't hear me and doesn't answer.

That's okay. She'll answer soon enough.

35

ARIEL

The garden path has never seemed longer than it does tonight. My swollen feet shuffle uncertainly over the uneven stones, but Sasha's arm around my waist keeps me steady. He's been hovering closer lately as the pregnancy progresses, as four weeks has shrunk to three, treating me like I might shatter. Usually, it annoys me, but right now, I'm grateful for the support.

It's a strange day.

Ever since Mama arrived, we knew that we'd have to deal with the elephant in the room at some point. Or rather, the elephant who's pointedly *not* in the room.

After all, Leander's death meant Jas and I lost a father. That Kosti lost a brother. I don't know what Mama would call him these days, but I'm sure it's still hard to bear such a sudden and violent end to someone to whom you gave such an essential part of your life.

The sun soaks the garden warm and bright as it sets behind the hilltops. Sasha and I follow the trail of stone pavers that

Jasmine spent all week settling into place. She, Uncle Kosti, and Mama are waiting at the end, next to the spiral of river pebbles sparkling clean in the light.

Such a Jasmine thing to do, washing each one by hand. I guess, as the only one of us who's been alive for their own funeral, she had some thoughts on how these things are supposed to be done.

Sasha passes my hand to Jasmine, who clutches it tight. I catch his eye and mouth, *Thank you* before he retreats to the shadow of the villa, giving us the privacy we need for this moment.

I stand in silence while Mama scatters rosemary around the stones, an old ritual that none of us can recall the reason for. This is the place where Leander Makris will be remembered. Not his body—that's lost to us now—but his memory. The good parts, at least. The father who taught me to ride a bike. The husband who danced with Mama in their tiny kitchen. The brother who made Kosti laugh until wine came out his nose.

It's strange to mourn someone you spent so long running from. But as the four of us huddle together in the fading light, I realize that's exactly what we're doing. Mourning not just the man he was, but the man he could have been. *Should* have been.

Mama's fingers find mine in the growing dark. She smells like that fancy French hand cream she's used since I was little. When I was young, I used to sneak into her vanity and steal it, just so I could smell like her. Some part of me is still that child, wanting to crawl into her lap and let her smooth my hair until the world makes sense again.

Instead, I pick up a stone. It's cool and heavy in my palm, water droplets catching the last rays of sun. I add it to Jasmine's spiral, completing the pattern that marks where we'll remember Leander Makris.

Not Leander the mob boss. Not Leander the arranged marriage broker.

Just… *Baba.*

"Well." Kosti clears his throat. "I suppose we ought to say something." He's been so quiet I almost forgot he was there, a shadow among shadows. "I'd like to remember nice times, though. Do… do you girls remember the cigarette boat? You might not—you were so young. That stupid thing cost more than our first house in Astoria. Leander showed up at the dock wearing this ridiculous captain's hat." He shakes his head, chuckling. "Crashed it into the pier within ten minutes. Scratched the hell out of the paint job. But he just laughed and said, 'That's what insurance is for, little brother.'"

I'd forgotten that story. Forgotten how Dad used to actually laugh. It feels jarringly at odds with the man I knew, who smiled either sadly or not at all.

Mama goes next, her voice soft as wind through the olive leaves. "Before all the money, before you girls, before… everything, we had this tiny apartment in Queens. The stove only worked half the time. So, every Sunday, he'd wake up early to buy fresh bread from the bakery down the street. Always came back with chocolate croissants, too, even though we couldn't afford them. He said a man who couldn't spoil his wife a little didn't deserve to have one." She swallows hard. "That's who he was, before everything else. A bright-eyed boy with flour on his shirt, bringing me breakfast in a paper bag. I want to remember him like that."

Jasmine plucks a sprig of thyme, rolling it between her fingers. "Remember his chess set? The one with the marble pieces?" She smiles, but it trembles. "He'd let me arrange the board however I wanted, break every rule. Said creativity was more important than winning. Until it wasn't."

My turn. They look at me expectantly. I open my mouth, but the memories stick like thorns in my throat.

Then it hits me: chlorine, summer heat, the scratch of concrete pool deck against my pruned toes. "The Hamilton Hotel pool," I mumble. "I was terrified of the deep end. He spent hours in that water, holding me up by my belly while I flailed around and cried." I can still feel his hands, steady and sure, promising I wouldn't sink. "He kept saying, 'Trust me, *neraïdoula mou*. Baba's got you.'"

Even that memory has a shadow. All those swimming lessons, and he still let me drown in waters far deeper than any hotel pool.

But that's not the story we're telling tonight. Tonight, we're remembering the father who wore a captain's hat and smelled like flour and lost at chess and held his daughter up until she learned how to float.

"He loved you both," Mama says, voice cracking. "In his way."

Jasmine's laugh is pure scorn. "His way sucked."

"His way was not always the right way," Kosti agrees.

The cicadas swell their song as the sun dips below the hills. Behind us, Sasha lights a cigarette—the flare of his lighter, the faintest plume of smoke. Not intruding. Just… present.

With trembling fingers, Mama pulls something out of her pocket: a gold wedding ring that she took off the day she left home. I haven't seen her wear it in fifteen years. As we all watch, she bends down to give it a final home. The gold catches the last ray of sunlight as she nestles it between two river stones.

Jasmine reaches into her pocket and withdraws something that clicks against her nails: a chess piece crudely whittled from wood. The king. She sets it next to Mama's ring.

My contribution burns in my pocket where I've kept it folded all day. The paper is soft from nervous handling, its edges worn. I've spent weeks working on it in secret, sketching out the branches of our tangled family tree. From Baba's own grandparents in Athens, to him and Mama, Jas and me. The Ozerovs are on there, too. I couldn't stop myself from looping them in; they're as much a part of our story as anyone now. Yakov, Nataliya, Sasha… they grow and intertwine with us. At the highest branch lies the twins' empty spaces, waiting to be filled.

I tuck the sheet beneath a rock and step back. The paper shifts in the wind. Our family names blur together, Makris flowing into Ozerov like watercolors bleeding across a page.

Kosti withdraws an old maritime compass, a brass antique. "You always did have a terrible sense of direction, brother," he murmurs, placing it among the stones. "Maybe this will help." The needle spins lazily, settling on a bearing that doesn't quite point north.

Then we're done, and I don't want to think about Baba anymore. He did what he did and he had his reasons, even if they weren't very good in the end. He didn't break us. Not fully. We're all chipped and scarred and battered, but here.

I look up at Sasha, who's just a smear of shadow and the

orange ember of a cigarette beneath the awning of the villa. He nods and holds out his hand.

I go toward him.

My future is that way.

36

SASHA

The temperature gauge in Marco's vineyard reads forty-two degrees Celsius, which explains why my linen shirt is already plastered to my back. But the locals don't seem to mind the heat. They're all chuckling as they join the throngs meeting up in front of the cantina, awaiting today's marching orders.

How we even ended up here remains a bit of a mystery. A neighbor came calling, though "neighbor" is stretching it to its maximum, seeing as how the villa is situated two miles from the next closest inhabitable structure.

But I was out repairing a fence on the southern border of the property and Marco came bearing gifts of Italian coffee beans and bottles of wine, and the women were easily swayed.

So before I knew it, they'd volunteered Kosti and me—mostly me—to help with the grape harvest at Marco's vineyard.

I tried to fight. But Ariel is... highly persuasive. Particularly with her clothes off.

In the end, I conceded. Several times.

Now, I'm sweating my ass off and the day has barely begun. I keep one eye on Ariel as she waddles toward the wooden vats where all of Marco's many victims are gathering for his instructions. She's wearing a loose cotton dress that makes her look deceptively delicate, though I know better. Just this morning, she threw a shoe at my head for suggesting she might want to skip today's festivities.

"*Benvenuti, amici!*" Marco's voice booms across the yard. He stands in one of the massive oak vats, fingers already stained purple from picking grapes. The man has the enthusiasm of a circus ringmaster and hands that never stop moving when he talks.

He starts waxing poetic about the history of the vineyard and the value of neighborly love. Silver hair, sun-leathered skin, eyes crinkled from decades of squinting into Tuscan light. A widower, according to village gossip. Even I can admit that the man has charisma in abundance.

Belle, apparently, couldn't agree more.

She gravitates to the front of our little crowd, transfixed. When Marco mimes face-planting into a vat during his first harvest, she doesn't just laugh—she *giggles*. I've never heard that sound from her before. It transforms her entire face, erasing fifteen years of careful composure.

"Looks like someone's got a crush," Ariel whispers, elbowing me in the ribs.

"Your mother? Never." But I'm smirking as I say it, watching Belle tuck a loose strand of hair behind her ear. Marco notices the gesture and winks at her, which sets off another round of giggles.

"Come, come!" Marco waves Belle forward to illustrate how, once all the grapes are gathered, we'll stomp them into juice. "It is simple! Like dancing, *sì?*"

He extends his hand to help her up onto the platform. Innocent touch, lingering just a half-second too long. Belle's cheeks flush pink.

"Five bucks says he asks her to dinner by sunset," Ariel murmurs.

I snort. "Ten says she beats him to it."

"So weird," she mumbles, cheeks heated.

"Does it bother you? If it does, I'll—"

"Don't you dare do anything, Mr. Intrusive," she snaps, yanking me by the wrist before I can go waterboard Marco with grape juice. "I'm just wondering what the proper etiquette is when you witness your mom's midlife sexual awakening."

All around us, the crowd is laughing as they get ready for the day's work. Marco is draped over Belle now, demonstrating how to swirl stems into a crown. I hear him teasingly call her *vedova nera,* a black widow, and she laughs and smacks him playfully in the chest.

Ariel watches, equal parts amused and horrified.

I've seen this look before. The reporter cataloguing details: sunlight caught in wine-dark splashes, kids chasing each other with stolen clusters, Belle's fingers grazing Marco's stubble. I know what she'll write tonight: *There's life here, real and unfiltered, pulsing through the veins of the vines.*

"Don't," she says suddenly, back stiffening.

"Don't what?"

"Don't start with the—" She waves a hand. "The smoldering eyes. The 'careful, Ariel, you almost look happy' routine."

I duck to steal a kiss on her cheek. "I can smolder. This isn't quite that. But if you'd like…" My fingers slip beneath her sundress.

"Hands to self," she says, shoving me away. But she's laughing, I'm laughing, and the sun no longer seems quite so brutal.

Soon, we're assigned to a crew and we get to work. The muscles in my back still protest as I hoist another basket, but the burn feels good. Like waking up and stretching after a long sleep. Two months ago, this would have torn my stitches and left me twitching in pain. Now, there's just a dull ache where Dragan's bullet carved its path.

"I can manage that one," Ariel insists, reaching for a basket.

"Not a chance." I shoulder past her, adding it to my stack. "Your job is to look pretty and supervise."

She rolls her eyes but doesn't argue. Instead, she falls into step beside me as we work our way down the row. The sun beats against my neck while my boots sink into earth softened by last night's rain. It should feel like labor, but there's something meditative about it—the repetitive motion, the whisper of leaves, Ariel's quiet humming.

Her hands never stay idle long. She plucks grapes with surprising dexterity, adding them to my baskets whenever I set them down. When she stretches up to reach a higher cluster, I steady her with a palm against her lower back.

"Missed a spot," I murmur, reaching around to swipe a bead of sweat from her temple. My fingers trail down her neck, lingering at her pulse point.

"You're supposed to be working, not feeling me up," she scolds.

"I'm excellent at multitasking."

The better part of the morning passes with an easy rhythm. I'm surprised every time I reach just an inch beyond where I've allowed myself to go these last six months, and I find that there's no pain waiting for me there.

I can bend.

I can stretch.

I can *move.*

Kosti, wherever he's wandered off to with Zoya, would tell me I'm pushing my body too hard, too fast. But for the first time since that bullet tore through me, I feel whole. Strong. Ready.

It's not perfect, of course. But I'm not biting my teeth and sweating bullets from agony. No, it's just the Tuscan summer that has me sweating the normal kind of bullets. I'm inwardly relieved when Marco hops up onto the wooden platform and claps his hands.

"Attenzione!" he cries out. All of the crews gather close.

With a flourish, he gestures to the half a dozen vats filled to the brim with grapes. "Any volunteers to begin?"

I have to bite the inside of my cheek to hide a smirk when Belle steps up.

She's grinning shyly and batting her eyelashes. Ariel and Jasmine exchange glances that make me glad I never had a sister to conspire with.

"Verdict's in," Jasmine murmurs. "Mama's smitten."

For his part, Marco looks like he just won the fucking lottery.

He helps her up, her sundress hiked above her knees, and they immediately forget that the rest of the world exists. Laughing, I turn to Ariel. "I guess we'll have to find our own way."

"I don't know…" She eyes the wooden rim of the nearest vat dubiously. "These ankles aren't exactly Olympic-ready. More like bratwurst-ready."

But I'm already moving behind her. "Would I let you fall?"

My hands find her waist and I lift her like she weighs nothing—a trick that gets harder each week as the twins grow. She squeaks in surprise, then giggles as I set her carefully into the vat. The sound echoes off the wooden walls.

"This is disgusting," she announces, grimacing as purple mush oozes between her toes. Then her expression shifts. "Actually… wait. This feels amazing."

I hop in beside her, and immediately understand. The crushed grapes are cool and slick. Strange at first, but once I get used to it, it's a welcome relief from the heat.

"Marco says we need to keep moving," I tell her, taking her hands. "Otherwise, the juice won't flow properly."

"Well, if *Marco* says so…" She waggles her brows. "Are you as smitten with him as Mama is?"

Growling, I bend down and flick a jet of purple juice at her. She squeals, a sound that hits my dick and my heart in unison, as she kicks back at me.

We have to rein in the fight when the clapping of the crowd rises into a beat, though. *Stomp, clap, stomp, clap.* I steady Ariel with my hands spanning her hips, just in case she falters.

I think she's playing me like a fool, though. She leans back, pressing her ass against me, and speeds up. We're a mess of tangled limbs, crushing fruit, laughing, laughing, *laughing.* Each movement brings us closer until we're sharing the same breath, purple-stained and sun-drunk.

Eventually, all the grapes have been groped, the juice is flowing, and the sun begins to fade. Workers start to trickle home in twos and threes, calling *"Ciao, ciao"* back over the shoulders, chatter trailing them long after they've disappeared over the hills.

Kosti takes Zoya home in the car, promising to come back and fetch us, though we all know he's full of shit. Jasmine winks and says she'll walk with a new group of friends who live on the way. With Belle distracted by Marco giving her a private tour of the wine cellar, that just leaves me and Ariel with the last remaining batch of grapes.

Ariel eyes me innocently. "We should probably finish this last set off, right?"

"Of course," I say, as solemn as I can.

I help her back into the final vat. It's quieter now. More shadows clustered in the corners. I can't decide if the air is fermenting or if I'm just high on the way she keeps darting teasing little looks in my direction, her skirts raised high to reveal glimpses of thigh and ass.

She picks up a foot and plops it down. An errant drop flies up and hits me square in the middle of the forehead.

"Careful," I scold. "You're making a mess."

"I thought you liked it when I got messy?" She bites at her lip, then grabs my hands, pulling me into an impromptu dance. The crushed grapes underfoot make everything slippery, forcing us to hold each other closer for balance.

I watch a droplet slide down her cheek and get hung up on the Cupid's bow of her lips, so I bend down and lick it off.

Ariel's eyebrow raises. "There's a droplet on my hip, too," she informs me. "Wanna give it the same treatment?"

I grin wickedly. "Thought you'd never ask."

Then I grab her, pick her up, and pin her to the wall of the vat so her pussy is at face-level, her legs draped over my shoulders. She shrieks and clings to my hair as I lick exactly where she told me I should.

"S-Sasha! Sa— *Fuck*."

She tastes like grapes and lust. If I wasn't drunk on her before, I am now. I'm merciless and she comes fast, hard, quivering on my face.

Ariel can barely stand upright by the time I put her back down on her own two feet. "*Now*," I brag, "you are properly messy."

She looks the way I want her to always look: hair wild, sex-mussed, lips swollen from chewing on them. Her eyes are gleaming and the pink spots on her cheeks stand bright. Purple streaks mark her from head to toe, as the dress clings to every curve that I've worshipped again and again, though it's never enough to satisfy me for long. Even now, I'm dying to taste her again, though it's only been a few seconds since I last had her taste on my tongue.

"You're insatiable," she accuses.

I bow. "Thank you."

"Who said that was a compliment?"

I point between her legs. "*She* did, for one."

Laughing, Ariel headbutts me in the chest like a puppy. Then she slides one arm around my waist and one hand down the front of my pants. "She's got some more things she'd like to tell you," she whispers to me.

Fucking hell, no one has ever been hotter.

The vat creaks as I lower her into the muck. Sun-baked pulp seeps through my knees. She gasps when I yank her dress up, when I bury my cock inside of her.

I don't let her breathe as I'm fucking her deep into the mash. She claws my back, chanting broken syllables between bitten-off moans. We're animals, rutting in the ruins of harvest, staining each other beyond recognition.

Afterward, we pant in the wreckage. Ariel traces a purple handprint on my chest. I idly wonder what it would look like to ink that there permanently.

"I'd say that's a thorough mess," she concludes, looking around us. "Does it ruin the wine? I hope not."

I laugh and kiss her again, with her taste and the wine's still mingling on my tongue. "Baby, I'd pay every dollar I have for a single bottle of this."

We haul ourselves out under cover of darkness. Cleaning up is a laughable concept—we'll have to do the two-mile walk of grape-stained shame, though the prospect of showering together at the end of it makes it seem not so bad.

But as we're fumbling for the path in the twilight, we hear laughter. Both Ariel and I look up to see Belle and Marco sharing a bottle of wine on the porch of the winery. He whispers something into her ear and she tosses her head back to laugh.

"Look at them," Ariel murmurs, settling back against my chest. "I haven't seen her smile like that since— since ever, really."

Belle's laugh drifts down to us on the evening breeze. Marco has produced a block of parmesan from somewhere, and he's cutting it with exaggerated ceremony that has Belle covering her mouth to stifle her giggles.

"Think he knows she hates parmesan?" Ariel asks.

"Better question: think she'll tell him?"

"Not a chance." She tilts her head back against my shoulder. "She's too busy pretending to be charmed by his terrible jokes."

"Those aren't pretend laughs."

"I know." Her voice goes soft. "That's what makes it perfect."

We should probably hurry home. The sun is setting and we're both sticky from sugar and sex. Our shadows stretch long and tangled across the trampled earth. Two more happy wrecks in a vineyard full of them.

But for now, I'm content to hold her like this, watching the sun paint the sky in shades of purple that match our skin, while across the vineyard, her mother remembers how to fall in love.

37

ARIEL

Just when I thought the generator was on our side, it goes and betrays us again. I've taken to calling it Judas.

It's the third time this week that Judas has stabbed us in the back, and it's barely Wednesday. I wiggle my toes against the footstool, watching candlelight flicker across the kitchen's exposed beams. My "throne," as Sasha calls it—this absurdly plushy wingback that he hauled down from the library—creaks as I shift my weight.

A tooth-rattling peal of thunder cracks just as Kosti lights the last candle. "Well," he says, "that's about as good as that's going to get."

"*Nu vot*," Zoya sighs, her hands deep in a bowl of *pelmeni* dough. "At least the storm waited until after I taught Jasmine the proper pleating technique."

The gas stove's blue flame casts weird shadows as Mama and Jas work side by side, their fingers quick and sure as they fold perfect little dumplings under Zoya's stern eye.

Lightning strobes through the windows. I start to count under my breath: "One Mississippi, two Mississippi—"

CRACK.

The thunder is getting closer.

Mama looks up from her batch of dumplings. She's gotten awfully proud of her handiwork these days. Zoya even gave her a "Not bad" last week, which is about as effusive as the old woman's praise ever gets. "Did I ever tell you girls about the blackout during the '03 heatwave? Leander tried—"

Rap-rap-rap.

I frown. Thunder with no lightning? That's strange. But then—

Rap-rap-rap.

That's not thunder.

That's someone knocking on the door.

"Knocking" is a pretty polite way to put it, actually. It's less a knock and more a full-body slam against our heavy wooden door. My heart jumps into my throat—because I only know one person in the world who knocks like that.

We all freeze. Sasha's hand drips olive oil from the bruschetta he's assembling as he moves toward the door. I see him pluck the cleaver from the cutting board as he goes.

My heart is freaking out. It can't be. It can't be. It can't…

"Surprise, bitch!"

As soon as Sasha rips the door open, Gina comes barreling in, as if dropping in unannounced on a mob boss in hiding who's literally holding a red-stained knife—red from tomatoes, not blood, but still—is something she does every day.

She hits me in a blaze of wet, magenta bangs and a squeal that's more deafening than any summer thunder could ever hope to be.

I wrap my arms around her and squeeze until the squeal hits octaves never before heard by man or womankind.

"Oh, don't worry about me," comes another familiar, sarcastic drawl. Feliks thumps through the door with an obscene amount of luggage in his hand. "I'll just carry *allthefuckingbagsmyself.*"

I swing my feet off the footstool and stand, still hugging Gina. Feliks shuffles inside and plops the soaking wet bags on the ground. After him, Pavel and Lora come slinking in. They all look like they tried to swim here rather than drive, but the smiles are irrepressible.

Gina grins at me. "What?" she says when she catches my dumbstruck expression. "You didn't think we'd let you have these babies without your emotional support team, did you?"

I'm a sopping mess in my own right, but unlike them, I can't blame the rain. It's just pure, unchecked tears of joy pouring down my face.

I hug them all in turn. Gina, Feliks, Lora, Pavel—then I start from the top and do it all again.

Feliks chuckles as he loops an arm over my shoulders. "There's more of you to hug these days, darling," he remarks.

Gina hits him over the head. "Never say that to a woman, idiot!" Then she laughs and kisses him on the cheek.

I step back as Feliks and Sasha lock eyes. Suddenly, the temperature in the room plummets.

The men shuffle awkwardly in place. Two schoolboys, I swear. Deathly allergic to feelings. The prospect of displaying emotions gives them both verbal constipation.

"We woulda been here sooner," mumbles Feliks. "But you really picked the goddamn middle of nowhere to hide out. Anyway, thought it was time for a little vacation."

"Were you followed?" Sasha grits out.

Feliks rolls his eyes. "Don't disrespect me like that, you son of a bitch."

Sasha's face is ice. Iron. Steel. Marble. Then—

It cracks.

It splits right down the middle into the biggest, goofiest smile I've ever seen on him, as he strides forward and grabs his best friend into a tight hug. They pound each other on the back and cackle like only boneheaded alpha males can do.

A few more drops of water hit the ground at my feet. I pretend it's rain.

Zoya ends the moment when she comes clomping in, clicking her tongue, thrusting towels at everyone. "Dry off before you catch death! Idiots, idiots, all of you!"

The storm howls outside. It's not letting up anytime soon. But inside, there's laughter.

Soon, the kitchen transforms into a war zone of delicious chaos. Zoya barks orders like a drill sergeant, Kosti pours shots of grappa far more often than is wise or necessary,

Jasmine teases Mama, Mama teases me, I tease Jasmine. Gina and Lora stay stuck to my side, while Sasha and Feliks stare into each other's eyes like they're doing their own rendition of Lady and the Tramp.

It's all just so damn happy that I can't stop smiling. My face hurts.

After we eat until everyone is bursting, we commandeer the dining room table for what might be the world's most ridiculous poker game. Sasha insists it's called "Moscow Hold 'Em," though I swear he's making that up. Whatever it's called, since we're short on supplies, dried penne stands in for chips, though Feliks keeps stealing from his own pile to snack on.

"*Sem, vosem, devyat,*" Sasha murmurs in my ear, his breath warm against my neck as he teaches me to count cards in Russian. His hand rests on my belly. "Good. Now, show me how to bet fifty."

I fumble through the words, mangling the pronunciation so badly that Feliks nearly chokes on his contraband pasta.

"Your accent is terrible," Sasha tells me fondly, kissing my temple. "Try again."

Gina throws a penne at his head. "Stop helping her cheat!"

"It's not cheating," I protest. "It's… expanding my cultural horizons."

"'*Cultural horizons,*' my ass," Pavel grumbles as I sweep another pot my way. "That's the third hand in a row she's won."

Lora pats his arm consolingly. "Don't worry, babe. You can have some of my pasta; I'm not even hungry."

My gaze drifts around the candlelit table, taking in all these little love stories unfolding. Feliks can't seem to go more than thirty seconds without finding some excuse to touch Gina—plucking imaginary lint from her shirt, tucking her newly-magenta hair behind her ear, or just letting his fingers trail across her shoulders as he pretends to peek at her cards. She pretends not to notice, but her secret smiles give her away.

"That's not how you're supposed to play that hand," Pavel insists, reaching for Lora's cards.

She swats his hand away. "Well, maybe if you weren't such a control freak about everything—"

"I am not a control freak!"

"You alphabetized my shoes last week!"

"They look better that way!"

Their bickering dissolves into laughter and kisses, and I have to look away to hide my grin. Who would have thought my ditzy former coworker would end up perfectly matched with Sasha's most uptight lieutenant?

Even Mama seems to be caught up in the romance of the evening. Marco showed up at our door an hour ago, drenched from the storm and bearing bottles of his best wine. Now, he's teaching her Italian cooking terms, standing close enough that their arms rub with every gesture. I've never seen her blush so much.

The weight of someone's stare draws my attention. I turn to find Sasha watching me. His eyes are dark in the candlelight, filled with an intensity that makes my skin prickle with awareness. He doesn't look away when I catch him—if anything, his gaze grows heavier, more deliberate.

Heat blooms in my chest and spreads lower. It should be illegal, the way he can undress me with a look even in a room full of people.

Even after everything we've been through.

Even with my belly swollen with his twins and my ankles puffy and my back aching.

I lift my cards higher to hide my flushed cheeks. He just winks.

Eventually, I get too tired to keep my eyes open. The excitement of the unexpected arrival has gotten to me. I mumble goodnight to everyone, then start the trek to my bedroom. But I pause at the top of the stairs, one hand braced against the wall. The villa's wooden beams creak and settle around us, no longer strange and foreign but familiar. A silly question bubbles up in my head.

When did this place start feeling like home?

Sasha's hand finds the small of my back, steadying me. "Tired?"

"A little." I lean into his touch without thinking. Another habit I've developed here—reaching for him, trusting him to be there. "It's been a night."

"Couldn't agree more. Gina threatened to feed my testicles to wild boars if I ever hurt you again."

I perk up with a bright smile. "Didn't you miss her? I sure did."

We should move. Go to bed. Maintain those careful boundaries we've drawn. But I'm rooted to this spot, caught in the strange magic of the storm-dark hall and the sound of our family's voices filtering in from all sides as they find their way to their bedrooms for the night.

"This wasn't supposed to happen, you know," I whisper, more to myself than him. "I wasn't supposed to…"

His fingers tilt my chin up. In the shadows, his eyes are impossibly soft. "Wasn't supposed to what?"

"Build a life here. With you. With them. All of it."

Instead of answering, he bends down and kisses me. Not the desperate, hungry kisses we usually share in darkness. This is something else entirely—tender, achingly gentle, like he's trying to tell me something his words can't quite reach.

I should pull away. Should remind him of our rules.

Instead, I wind my arms around his neck and kiss him back, pouring all my complicated truths into the space between our hearts.

Downstairs, someone starts singing. The storm rages on. And in this quiet hallway, I let myself fall a little deeper into the life I never meant to build.

38

SASHA

I stay for as long as I can.

Cuddling Ariel to sleep in my arms is as close as it gets to salvation for a man like me. I can't keep myself from touching the swell of her pregnant belly again and again. She's soft, warm, and fragrant. Everything my life is not.

But eventually, I have to rise.

There is business waiting for me downstairs.

Even after I extract myself and get to my feet, though, careful not to wake her, I feel torn in two. I don't want to leave this room. This moment.

So I linger in the doorway, watching the gentle rise and fall of Ariel's chest. She's curled on her side, one hand splayed over her belly even in sleep. The sight does something to my chest that I'm still not used to—a sharp twist followed by an expanding warmth. Like I'm growing into a dimension I didn't know existed.

It's quieter than it was when we first slunk up here. The storm has finally passed, leaving behind that particular stillness that follows summer rain. In the silence, I can almost pretend this is just another peaceful night. That I'm just a man watching his pregnant wife sleep.

But I know better.

My fingers trace the familiar shape of my gun, tucked into the waistband at my back. The weight of it grounds me, reminds me who I really am.

I am still Sasha Ozerov. *Pakhan* in exile, but *pakhan* nonetheless. I am still the man who will do whatever it takes to protect what's his.

Ariel shifts in her sleep, mumbling something that might be my name. The movement makes her dress ride up to reveal the curve of her hip. Even now, after all these months, the sight of her fucking floors me.

My beautiful little bird. No longer so broken.

I force myself to turn away. Feliks is waiting downstairs. But as I pull the door closed behind me, I allow myself one final glance at the life I never expected to want: my woman, my children, safe in our bed.

Whatever comes next, I'll make damn sure they stay that way.

I find the men hunched over the kitchen table like vultures over carrion. Maps and documents cast long shadows in the candlelight, since Judas the generator is still refusing to cooperate. Feliks's fingers drum an uneven rhythm against a stack of surveillance photos while Kosti and Pavel exchange glances loaded with meaning I don't like.

"Tell me," I say, settling into the chair across from them.

Feliks slides a photo across the table. "Let's start with the damage. This is our Chinatown warehouse. Three days ago."

I study the image. The loading dock where we used to move product into Queens is a blackened husk. Scorch marks climb the brick walls like vines. "Casualties?"

"Mikhail. Dmitri. The new kid—what was his name? The one with the stutter."

"Yuri," Pavel supplies quietly.

I grimace. I remember teaching Yuri to field strip a Makarov last spring. His hands shook so bad he dropped the slide pin twice. But he had potential.

Had.

"That's not the worst of it." Feliks produces another photo. This one shows Wei Huan, the Bratva's liaison to China, emerging from a dim sum restaurant with Dragan four blocks away from the smoldering ruins of my warehouse. They're both smiling. "The Serbs have been making moves on our Asian connections. Three meetings in the past week. Wei Huan is just the tip of the iceberg."

"Fucking snake," I mutter, but there's no real heat in it. Huan is a businessman. We all knew he'd jump ship the moment someone offered him a better deal. "The Taiwanese routes?"

Kosti shakes his head. "Gone. Along with the gambling dens in Flushing and the protection racket on Canal Street."

My jaw tightens. Those operations took years to build. Thousands of hours' worth of carefully cultivated relationships, all gone because I've been playing house in Tuscany instead of—

No. I shut that thought down hard.

I've made my choices. I won't regret them now.

"What about the docks?" I ask.

"Still holding, but barely." Pavel unfolds a detailed map of the Port Authority terminals. Red X's mark the spots we've lost. There are more of them than I'd like. "But Dragan's offering the longshoremen triple what we pay. It's only a matter of time before they all start slipping away."

I trace the familiar geography with my fingertip. Every X represents dead men, lost revenue, shifting loyalties. A decade of power being methodically dismantled while I heal and hide and fall deeper in love.

"He's being smart about it," Feliks summarizes, respect and disgust mingling in his tone. "Taking us apart piece by piece. No big moves that would draw attention. Just death by a thousand cuts."

I lean back, processing. *Problems I can handle. It's solutions that get messy.* I once told Kosti that. His response was, *That's because your solutions are limited to 'shoot it, threaten it, or throw money at it until it goes away.'*

What do I do now, though? This is a war I was raised to fight, trained to fight. Who do I shoot? Who do I threaten?

"What are our options?"

The silence that follows tells me everything I need to know. But I wait for them to say it anyway.

Feliks meets my eyes. "We go back. Now. Before there's nothing left to go back to."

An unexpected spasm rips through my shoulder as I lean over the maps, and I can't quite suppress the grunt of pain. *Fuck.* The bullet wound is singing its favorite song tonight.

I'd hoped we were past that.

Kosti's eyes track every tremor, every aborted movement. The old bastard doesn't miss anything. "You're not ready yet, son," he says quietly. "Another few weeks of healing could mean the difference between victory and death."

I bare my teeth at him. "I've fought with worse."

"And look how well that worked out for you last time." His voice is mild, but the rebuke lands. "The twins aren't due for three more weeks. Use that time. Build your strength back. If you go rushing into it, then—"

My fist slams into the table, rattling the glasses. "Three weeks is too long. You heard Feliks—we're hemorrhaging territory. By the time the babies come, there might not be anything left to fight for."

"There are other ways," Pavel interjects. He spreads his hands over the map, indicating key points. "Look—we hit them here, here, and here simultaneously. Coordinated strikes. You direct from a secure location while our crews do the heavy lifting. Minimal physical risk to you."

I study the marks he's made. The strategy is sound. But...

"That's not how this works." I flex my shoulder, testing the limits of the pain. "The men need to see me. Need to know I'm willing to bleed alongside them. Leadership from behind a desk is no leadership at all."

"Better a living leader than a dead hero," Kosti mutters.

He's right. I know he's right. But the thought of hiding while my men fight my battles makes bile rise in my throat.

"What about a compromise?" Feliks suggests. "We spend two weeks gathering intel, moving pieces into position. Then you come back for the final push, once you're stronger."

I close my eyes. Above us, floorboards creak as someone—probably Ariel—shifts in their sleep. The sound twists something in my chest.

I made her a promise. No more lies. No more choosing power over love.

But what kind of love can I offer if I'm too weak to protect her? What kind of father will I be if I let Dragan strip away everything I've built?

My shoulder throbs, a steady reminder of my limitations. Of how close I came to dying last time.

Problems I can handle. It's solutions that get messy.

"Two weeks," I say finally. "Not a day more. And I want daily reports on every movement Dragan makes."

Kosti nods, satisfied. But I notice he doesn't quite meet my eyes.

A muffled cry pierces the night. My body moves before my brain can catch up. *Ariel. Moaning in fear.*

I'm halfway out of my chair when Feliks's hand catches my wrist. "Boss." His voice is gentle but firm. "We need to finish this."

The maps spread across the table swim in my vision. Territory lines blur into meaningless shapes as another whimper filters through the ceiling. I know these nightmares. I've held her through enough of them to recognize the cadence of her fear.

My shoulder throbs as I force myself to sit back down. The bullet wound seems to pulse in time with her distress.

Feliks watches me with too much understanding in his eyes. He's seen me gut men without flinching, seen me take bullets without breaking stride. But this—this helpless tension as I listen to Ariel struggle alone—is this what finally breaks me?

"She'll be fine," he says quietly. "The sooner we finish this, the sooner you can go to her."

I grunt in acknowledgment, but my eyes keep drifting to the ceiling. Each sound is like a hook in my chest, pulling me in two directions at once. When did I become this man? This person who can be unmade by a woman's nightmare?

"Focus," I growl, more to myself than the others. But even as I bend over the maps again, my ears strain for any sign that her dreams have eased. *Just a little longer,* I promise silently. *Hold on,* ptichka. *I'll be there soon.*

We talk strategy, trying to find a way to break down Serbian defenses and reclaim the key patches of the city. Eventually, the others shuffle out, their footsteps heavy with the weight of everything we've discussed. Only Feliks remains.

"You didn't answer my question earlier," he says as he gathers the surveillance photos into a neat stack.

"Which one?"

"About being ready." He taps the stack of photos against the table, squaring the edges. "And I don't mean physically."

I scowl at him. "Did I wander into a confessional booth by mistake?"

He sighs, running a hand through his hair. "Look, I've known you since we were kids smashing windows in Moscow. I've seen you make impossible choices. But this..." He gestures vaguely upward, toward Ariel. "This is different."

"How?"

"Because for the first time in your life, you actually have something to lose." His voice drops lower. "Something that matters more than power."

I want to deny it. Want to tell him that nothing matters more than maintaining control, that love is still the weakness I've always believed it to be.

But the words stick in my throat. I know they're untrue. He does, too.

Feliks watches my internal struggle with knowing eyes. "Just... think about it, okay? Really think about what you're willing to sacrifice. Because once we start this, there's no going back."

He leaves before I can respond. Maybe that's for the best— I'm not sure what the fuck I would say anyway.

I sit in the dark kitchen for a long time, surrounded by maps of a kingdom I may have to choose between keeping or deserving. When I finally go upstairs, moonlight catches a pair of open eyes, glowing like silver coins. Ariel doesn't ask where I've been or what kept me. She doesn't need to.

The mattress dips as I slide in beside her. Her body instinctively curves toward mine. My hand finds its home on her hip.

"Whatever you're planning..." she whispers into the darkness, her voice barely a breath, "just come back to us."

I pull her closer and inhale her scent. She trusts me to return. After everything, she still believes I'll choose her—choose us —over the darkness that's always defined me.

I press my lips to her temple and make a silent vow to prove her right.

39

ARIEL

No one told me the third trimester came with superpowers.

As we approach the two-week mark until the twins make their debut, I feel like I'm hyper-aware of everyone's movements. Maybe it's some primitive maternal instinct kicking in, this constant tracking of where bodies are in space.

Right now, I can't stop watching how Jasmine keeps drifting backward whenever someone steps closer to her, maintaining this precise bubble around her that no one else seems to notice. She's been weird all night—quiet, shy, face drawn and shadowed. The longer we all hang out after dinner, the more she keeps turning in toward herself.

I frown and file it away to ask about later.

The garden smells incredible tonight. The day's heat is dissipating as the sun sets. I breathe in deep, letting the mingled scents of oregano and mint wash over me as I waddle around with the wine bottle.

"More?" I offer, holding up the Chianti that Marco brought over.

Lora accepts with a smile, but Gina waves me off. "None for me, thanks."

My brain takes a second to process what I'm seeing: Gina's hand protectively curved over her still-flat stomach, that telltale glow in her cheeks that I recognize from my own mirror.

I almost drop the bottle.

"Oh my God." The words come out as a *Calvin & the Chipmunks* squeak. "Gee, are you…?"

Her face splits into the biggest grin I've ever seen. "Eight weeks!"

I wrap her up like an anaconda and squeeze as hard as I can. "Why didn't you tell me the second you got here, you jerk?!"

"I wanted to wait for the right moment!" She hugs me back, careful of my belly. "Plus, you know, there was the whole dramatic rainstorm entrance to coordinate. You know me. I never shirk on drama."

"Details," I demand, grabbing her hands. "I want every single detail."

As Gina launches into the story of how she found out, I catch Jasmine shifting further into the shadows of the herb garden. The movement is so subtle that I doubt anyone else notices.

But I do.

I want to go to her, to pull her into our circle of joy. But something in her face says to let her be for now.

"—and then Feliks actually fainted," Gina is saying, dissolving into giggles. "Like, full-on passed out on the bathroom floor when I showed him the test."

"That tracks," I snort. "Big, bad mobster, brought down by a plastic stick with two lines on it."

"Our men are ridiculous," she agrees, then sobers slightly. "But... they're ours."

I clutch her hand, understanding everything she's not saying. Complicated men are not all sunshine and rainbows. But they are ours, aren't they?

"Our babies are going to be best friends," I tell her, my voice thick with hormones and happiness. "Just like their mamas."

"But enough about me," Lora interjects dreamily, propping her chin on her hands.

We all laugh. "Don't make jokes!" I chide her. "I'm dying to know about you, too. How's it going with Mr. Musclehead in there?"

"Ugh, 'fabulous' doesn't even begin to cover it." She fans herself and does another soap opera sigh of delight. "He's just an angel. I know that's not always easy with me. I can be... tough."

Gina fake-gasps. "You? 'Tough'? Never!"

"But," continues Lora with a teasing scowl, "you just gotta find the one who likes your brand of spice, you know? When I showed Pav the portrait I painted of him after our first date, he hung it up on his wall then and there. He's my kind of crazy."

I smile at Lora's lovey-dovey eyes, but my attention keeps

drifting to the shadowy edges of the garden where Jasmine lurks.

"Now," I say, "I just need you two lovebugs to infect my sister. Right, Jas? What's your preferred kind of crazy these days?"

My sister startles at being addressed directly, like a deer caught in headlights. For a moment, I think she might bolt entirely. Then she laughs. But it's light, practiced. Perfect. Too perfect. "Oh, you know me—married to my music. The only man in my life is Johann Sebastian Bach."

But I see the way her fingers clench around the wine stem until her knuckles bleach white. The way her shoulders tighten imperceptibly under her flowing dress.

My frown deepens. But prodding in front of everyone is a recipe for disaster. So I just watch as she takes another measured sip of wine, her smile never wavering.

It'll be fine, though. She's just thrown off by the sudden company. We'll find our groove; everyone will settle in; life will be okay.

I notice the exact moment that proves wrong.

"... just so paranoid lately," Gina is saying, rolling her eyes fondly. "He won't let me go anywhere without three bodyguards. Says Dragan's men could be anywhere, watching, waiting..."

The wine glass slips from Jasmine's fingers.

She catches it before it can shatter, but not before deep red splashes across the flagstones like blood. Her eyes are staring at something in the distance that no one but her can see.

I know that look. God, how could I ever forget it? It's the same vacant stare she wore at fourteen, when Papa came home with blood on his shoes. At sixteen, when his "business associates" would linger too long at dinner, their eyes crawling over her like insects. At nineteen, when... When everything happened.

My hand instinctively covers my stomach as nausea rises that has nothing to do with pregnancy. I thought I'd buried those memories deep enough that they couldn't touch us anymore.

"Jas?" I keep my voice soft, gentle, like how she used to speak to me when I was little and scared. "You okay?"

"Fine!" Her laugh is brittle. "Just clumsy. Two left feet and two left thumbs to match!"

But she's angled her body away from us, creating distance. Her eyes keep darting to the villa's doors and windows, like she's wondering how hard it would be to run for cover.

Gina and Lora exchange confused glances, but they don't understand. They didn't grow up learning to read the silent language of fear.

I try to steer the conversation somewhere safer. "Hey, Jas, tell Gina about the—"

But Jasmine is already on her feet, moving awkwardly, too sharp and too fumbling at the same time. "I just remembered," she mumbles, her voice pitched too high. "I need to... water the herbs. And check on the... The basil needs pruning."

It's been raining for weeks. The herbs are drowning, not thirsty. But I don't point that out. I just watch her walk away, my heart clenching at how wrong it looks. My sister used to move like music. But right now, she might as well be made of sugar glass and chicken wire.

Gina leans toward me. "Is she okay? That was kind of…"

"Weird," Lora finishes, twirling her wine glass nervously.

They don't get it. How could they? They weren't there when Dragan's name first entered our lives. They didn't see what his "courtship" did to her. They didn't hear her crying herself to sleep every night, didn't watch her slowly fade away until she was nothing but a shadow wearing my sister's face.

"She's fine," I tell them. "Probably just tired."

I sit with Gina and Lora until they finish their wine. Then I pin blame on the babies and slink upstairs for an early bedtime.

I don't go straight to my room, though. I hear music, and I know even before I go to Jasmine what I'll find.

Sure enough, when I peek through the crack in her door, she's got the secondhand violin she bought from a shop in the village tucked underneath her chin. Her face is screwed up with concentration and she's sawing at the strings like the bow is a blade held to Dragan's throat instead.

It's Tchaikovsky, I think, though that's her area of expertise, not mine. But I've never heard her play it quite like this before.

Every note bleeds raw emotion—anger, fear, grief, defiance. All the darkness she keeps locked away behind her perfect smile and carefully measured movements comes pouring out through her fingers.

I feel so stupid. How long has she been hiding this? How much haven't I seen? How much weight is the music carrying for her, and how much more can it take until both she and it collapse? Every perfectly executed phrase contains echoes of old screams. Every crescendo carries the weight of tears she never let fall.

When she's done, the final notes hang in the air like bonfire smoke. Jasmine's bow arm drops, and her shoulders slump. For a moment, neither of us moves.

Then I cross the room and wrap my arms around her from behind, as best I can with my belly between us. She lets out a shuddering breath and leans back against me.

We don't speak. We don't need to.

I just hold her and say with my touch that she's loved.

40

SASHA

I can't sleep.

My mind churns with maps and markers—New York, splayed out in my head like a buffet. I know every fucking block of my city. I know where the money comes from and where it goes. I know who gets to take a nibble of it as it passes through their hands and who doesn't. I know which plate it all ends up on.

For fifteen years, the answer to that has been "mine." *My* plate is where the feast ends up. Ever since I snatched Jasmine from Dragan's maw and set her free, it's all been mine, mine, *mine*.

Shit has changed now.

Dragan flipped the buffet table when he slaughtered Leander in front of us and pumped his bullets into my body. It's been a fucking mess ever since, and I've been too weak to storm back in and clean it up. That hasn't stopped me from dreaming of it—almost every night for eight months now, between dreams of Ariel, I've dreamed of him. Of rubbing that bastard's face in the disaster he created until he suffocates in it, drowns in it. But I've been too powerless to make it happen. A dead man walking. A broken puppet.

Now, though, my body is almost ready. But Dragan isn't going to just give me back my seat at the table. I'm going to have to take it. It's going to cost me blood and a pound of flesh, maybe more.

I know all that.

So explain to me why I'm wondering, for the first time in my life… *am I willing to pay that price?*

I know what Yakov would answer. He'd call me a fucking coward, a pussy, a disgrace to the Ozerov name. Hell, he might be right.

But on the other hand, Yakov is food for the worms in half a dozen different unmarked graves right now. So who gives a damn what he'd say? I care more about a different opinion these days.

And she's sleeping right next to me.

Dragan's smirking face fades from memory as I open my eyes and look down at Ariel's shadow in the darkness. She's all curves these days. The curve of her hip, her belly, her cheek, her lip. If it was up to me, I'd keep her in bed for the rest of our lives so I could memorize every single one of them.

She might let me. She's got my hand clutched in hers, even though she's mid-slumber, and it doesn't look like she has any intention of letting go. If I woke her up right now and told her I'd give up everything, every last square inch of my kingdom, what would she call me?

Like she can hear the question throbbing in my head, she moans, stirs, and tucks herself into me. That's an answer. It's enough for her that I'm here right now. When I wrote notes in that Lamaze class, it was enough for her. When I carry her up the stairs, that's enough for her. If we're fucking or cuddling, stargazing or smashing grapes in a sun-soaked vineyard, so long as I'm by her side, that's enough.

But what if it's *not* enough? What if I want more—not for me, never for me, but for her? For our children?

What if I want to give them the whole fucking world on a silver platter? What if I have to die to keep them safe?

What does "enough" mean then?

There are no answers in the darkness. There are only cracks in the ceiling, summer breeze kissing the roof, and owls outside flitting from tree to tree.

Then, out of nowhere, there's something else.

A creak.

Something shifting in the darkness.

Most people wouldn't notice it. Just another groan in an old house's nightly symphony of settling wood and aging stone. But I've spent eight long weeks learning the language of this place. I know damn fucking well that this sound doesn't belong.

So I extricate myself from her embrace and slide out from under the covers as slowly as I can. I'm wearing only boxer briefs, so the moonlight streaming through the window lights up my whole body, every last scar and tattoo.

I retrieve a gun from the dresser. Then I stand still and wait, ear cocked.

Silence.

Silence.

… *Ctchk.*

This one was closer.

I ghost toward the bedroom door, my bare feet silent as I pad over the floorboards. The villa's layout unfolds in my mind. Seven entry points on the ground floor. Three sets of stairs. Two viable escape routes from the second story if things go sideways.

But they won't. Because whatever threat has breached our sanctuary will stop breathing as soon as I put a bullet in its skull.

I look back one final time at Ariel.

Sleep well, ptichka. *Let me handle the darkness.*

I float down the stairs, avoiding the ones that squeak. Two steps shy of the ground floor, I pause. There it is again—the squeak of a rubber sole on the kitchen tile.

When I stoop low enough to stick my head out without drawing attention, I catch a glimpse of a shadow prowling toward the living room. He's backlit by the garden lights, the fucking fool. Only an amateur would let his silhouette precede him.

But amateur bullets kill just as fast as a professional's do. I have no intention of letting that happen.

A second shadow springs up to join the first. So the motherfucker brought a friend. That's fine—I brought a whole clip of ammunition. Plenty to spare for both of them. I crouch on the bottom stair with my breath suppressed as I wait for the intruders to step into the line of fire.

As I wait, eight weeks of playing house flash through my mind. Eight weeks of gardening and cooking and rubbing Ariel's swollen feet. Eight weeks of pretending I'm not what I am.

But I know what I am. I'm the man who will paint these walls red to keep her safe.

The intruder's boot appears. In the shadows above him, I adjust my grip on the Glock. The weight feels good. My hand knows what shape to take, how hard to squeeze the trigger. It's not anger flooding my system now—it's the calm, cold certainty of knowing what I was born to do.

The only thing that's changed is the reason why.

I think of Ariel sleeping upstairs, belly round with my children. Think of how vulnerable she'd be if these fuckers got past me.

This is the old, familiar ice, yes.

But this ice is colder than it's ever been.

I sight down the barrel. The first one straightens up, reaching back to help his partner. His throat is exposed. Perfect.

I move.

Two silent steps down. One more. The old stairs don't dare whine under my feet. I am shadow. I am death.

I am what Yakov made me.

The second man's head appears in the window. His eyes widen as he spots me.

Too late.

My first shot takes him in the throat. The sound is muffled by the suppressor—just a wet *thwip* that ends in a bloody gurgle. He flops back into the garden, leaving his partner alone.

The survivor spins, blade already drawn. Fast. But not nearly fast enough.

I grab his knife hand and slam it into the counter's edge. Bone crunches and the blade clatters to the floor. His mouth opens to scream. I shove my gun between his teeth.

His eyes are liquid with the purest kind of animal fear. There's not a man present in this mind anymore—there is only a frightened beast realizing just how many mistakes paved the path that brought him to me tonight.

"I agree," I snarl at him. "You fucked up."

Then I pull the trigger.

Thwip.

The man goes slithering to the floor. I stand over his cooling corpse, watching crimson pool beneath what remains of his shattered skull. The blood spreads in a perfect circle across the Italian tile, like a dark halo.

But when I bend down and rip the ski mask off, it's not the grizzled Serbian face I expected to see. This boy—because that's what he is, a fucking boy, scarcely old enough for his beard to fill in—is still wide-eyed in death. He can't be more than twenty-five at most. Local, by the looks of him.

I frown.

There has to be something here—a phone, a note, some scrap of evidence linking this back to Dragan. The Serbs must have hired local muscle to do their dirty work.

But as I turn out his pockets, my certainty begins to waver. No burner phone. No orders written in Serbian. Just a cheap leather wallet containing thirty euros and a crumpled photo of some local girl. Even the gun in his hand is laughably cheap.

There's only one conclusion to be drawn: This wasn't some calculated strike against me. This was just a stupid kid who picked the wrong house to rob, who had no idea what kind of monster was waiting in the darkness.

I sit back on my heels, suddenly tired. All this death. All this blood. The familiar ice in my veins feels heavy now. Unnecessary. Like using a sledgehammer to kill a fly.

But what choice did I have? Even a petty thief could have hurt Ariel. Even a local thug's bullet could have found her heart.

I straighten back upright and remind myself not to mourn for him. Who gives a fuck if he's young? If he's stupider than he was cruel? He ventured where he shouldn't have and he paid the price.

I cannot and will not apologize for that.

As I stand there and look down at his face, I wait for the pain to come. My legs should wobble. My gut should sting. All the things Dragan did to me in that frigid back alley should be agonizing, the way they've been for eight long months now.

But the pain never arrives. More importantly, my hands didn't shake. Not once. Not when I pulled the trigger, not when I crushed his knife hand, not even now as I holster my weapon.

There's only one conclusion to be drawn from that, too: I am ready.

These past eight weeks of playing house in Tuscany, they were necessary. So was my time in Kosti's safehouse in Vermont before that. The physical therapy, the rest, the careful rebuilding of damaged muscle and tissue—it all served its purpose. But that chapter is over now.

It's time to go home. Time to take back what's mine.

Because this is not the first wave of men who will come for what's mine. Thug or not, there will be more after that, and more after those, until these hills are crawling with parasites who think they can steal from my plate.

No.

Fucking.

More.

No. I'm going back to my home, and when I set foot on that shore, I will be what I've always been: Sasha fucking Ozerov, the man who brought the Serbian empire to its knees fifteen years ago. The man who will do it again—but permanently this time.

I wipe blood from my hands with mechanical efficiency. Upstairs, Ariel sleeps peacefully, unaware of how close danger crept to our door tonight. She'll never know—I'll have the bodies disposed of before sunrise.

But this is the wake-up call I needed. We can't stay here forever, playing at normal life while Dragan consolidates his power. The time for healing is over.

The time for war has begun.

I pull out my phone and text Feliks: ***Pack your bags. We leave for New York in 24 hours.***

Then I get a rag and start to mop up the blood.

41

ARIEL

I wake to cold sheets where Sasha should be. The space beside me still holds the indent of his body, but it's been empty long enough for the heat to fade.

My heart knows what that means long before my head does.

But it's early in the morning, when things and thoughts are fuzzy and dreamy, so I let myself pretend for a little while that I don't know what my bones are telling me has already begun.

When I make my way downstairs, though, each step feels heavier than the last. Down here, I won't be able to pretend anymore. The twins are restless, turning and kicking like they're every bit as uneasy as I am. I pause on the final stair, one hand pressed against the swell of my belly, trying to soothe them.

Or maybe trying to soothe myself.

The sound of a zipper is what draws me down the last few steps. I round the corner to see Sasha in the entryway, methodically folding clothes into a black duffel bag. His movements are precise, practiced—the routine of a man who's packed for war before. His gun rests in a holster on the kitchen counter. I could swear I see a fleck of blood gleaming on the nozzle.

He doesn't look up, but his shoulders tense. He knows I'm here.

"You're leaving, aren't you?" I croak. "You're going back."

He keeps packing. "We knew we'd get here eventually, Ariel. This isn't a surprise."

"What happened to 'not until the babies come'?"

He's half-turned away, but the muscle cording in his jaw is all the answer I need. "Things changed."

"What kinds of things?"

"The kinds of things that don't concern you."

"Be more fucking vague, I dare you," I snap.

He pauses, a shirt folded in his hands, before sighing and setting it down. "I thought you trusted me to make the right choices for us. For this family."

I want to laugh in his face. Or maybe kiss it. Or maybe claw it to ribbons, I'm not sure. This is the ice I was talking about in my journal entries. I feel myself shivering from it, like little pieces of me are numbing with every passing second. "And I thought you trusted me enough to tell me when you were planning on going to do something stupid."

"Is it 'stupid' to keep you safe?" he asks as he picks up the gun and pops out the clip. This time, there's no mistaking what I see—there are two fewer bullets in there than there ought to be.

"It's stupid if it costs *you* to make that happen!" I cry out. "Sasha, what don't you understand: A safe world that doesn't have you in it is not the world I want to live in!"

He rams the clip back into the gun with a *clack* that makes my heart ache. Then he looks up at me. "Two men broke in last night, Ariel. They're buried in the garden now." He advances on me, and I step back instinctively, almost screaming when my heel strikes the wall at my back. "They were idiots. But what happens when two more come after that? And two after that? And two after that? And what happens if those next men *aren't* idiots, hm? What happens if there are trained killers slipping through our windows and rappelling down our roof? What the fuck do you think happens if I don't put myself between you and them? I'll tell you what happens." He points two fingers in the shape of a gun at my forehead and whispers, *"Bang."* Then he lowers them to the crest of my belly. *"Bang. Bang."*

My face is hot and streaked with tears as I slap his hand aside. He says something, but I don't hear, nor do I want to. Right now, I just want to be far the fuck away from Sasha Ozerov.

I storm outside, needing air, needing space, needing anything that isn't the sight of a duffel bag in the doorway with a half-empty gun resting on top.

But I only get about two steps into the garden before I freeze in place.

It's an absolute disaster. Jagged basil stems, leaves ripped clean. Torn oregano roots dangle like exposed nerves. The dirt is churned everywhere, all of our neat rows completely wrecked. I'm ready to blame Sasha—didn't he just say what he did to my garden? But it's not so easy to blame him. It never really is, is it?

Because standing in the middle of it all is the true culprit.

A goat.

A fucking *goat*.

The creature lifts its head, jaw working side to side, green flecks caught in its beard. It blinks at me with rectangular pupils, thoroughly unrepentant.

"Hey," I say. Weak. Like I'm the intruder here.

It stomps a hoof into the rosemary. Crushed needles release their pine-sharp stink.

My hands flutter uselessly. Eight weeks of Jasmine and me coaxing life from this stubborn Tuscan soil. Eight weeks of pressing seeds into dirt, whispering, "Grow, grow, please just grow" as my own body swelled.

Now, it's all mud and teeth-marks. Ruined.

The goat bleats.

"Get—" I swipe at my cheeks. "Get *out*."

It doesn't. Just lowers its head and takes a deliberate bite of my last surviving lavender. Purple petals vanish between yellowed molars.

Something in me snaps.

I lurch forward, waving arms made clumsy by thirty-four weeks of twins. "I said *go*! Shoo! *Vaffanculo*, you—you *bastard*!"

It trots three steps left. Stops. Chews. Stares.

My bare feet get sucked into the hungry mud as I give chase. The goat dodges with infuriating ease, dancing a few yards out of reach to take another bite.

"Why won't you just listen?!"

The words rip loose from somewhere deep inside me, raw and shrill. The goat freezes. For one glorious second, I think I've won.

Then it pisses on the chamomile.

A sound escapes me—half-laugh, half-sob. Of course. Of course! Why would the goat do what I want it to? Why would Sasha? Why would *anyone?* I feel like I've spent my whole life being shunted from one manipulator to the next. Baba, Sasha—now, I've got a fucking goat bossing me around, wrecking the last things left that I care about and pissing on the remains.

I sink to my knees, the hem of my nightgown soaking up the dirty water from last night's rain, and let the tears come. I cry like I haven't since I was a little girl. It's not about the garden, not really. It's about Sasha leaving without warning, about the blood on his gun that I have to lie to myself and pretend I didn't see, about the two fresh graves somewhere in this very soil that I'm kneeling in.

The goat chomps away, unconcerned with my breakdown. Through my tears, I watch it demolish the last of my mint.

"I hate you," I tell it wetly. "I hate you so fucking much."

It just bleats again, mouth full of my hard work, my careful planning, my desperate attempt at creating something permanent in a world that keeps shifting under my feet.

Mud squelches from behind. Sasha's shadow falls across the wreckage of the herbs, long and lethal. I don't look back, but in front of me, the goat glances up, bleats softly, then turns and scampers away into the hills.

"Ari—"

"Don't." I shove aside the hand offering to help me up. Instead, I get up on my own, even though it's harder than ever these days. My knees peel from the mud with a sound like tearing skin.

That doesn't stop him from trying to touch me again. This time, when I smack his hand away, I do it with a purpose. "I said *don't*, Sasha."

His eyes are sad and patient. "Just wait and—"

"Wait for what? The next disaster? The next time you vanish to play mobster while I—"

"This is why I'm going." His scar glows white with tension. "To *end* the disasters. To keep you safe."

"Safe?" A hysterical laugh escapes. I gesture at the garden. "You can't even protect basil!"

He steps into my space, mint and cedar and misery all flowing together. "You think I want this? To leave you pregnant with my children in some—"

"*Our* children." My voice cracks. "And yes, I do think that. Because you're good at leaving. It's what you do best."

Something flickers in his eyes—a wound, swiftly buried. Good. Let him feel it.

He reaches for me. "*Ptichka*—"

I slap his hand away for the third time. "Don't. Don't soothe. Don't lie. You'll march off to die nobly, and I'll be here—" My palm taps my belly. "—alone with them, explaining why the dirt stays empty. Why nothing ever grows."

His jaw knots. "We'll replant."

"It's not about the plants, goddammit!" I say. "It's about… about building something that lasts. Something the world can't just eat." I sweep my arm around to encompass the garden. "You want to know what this is really about? Look at this. Really look at it. Eight weeks of work destroyed in, what, twenty minutes? That's our life right there. Everything we build gets trampled. Everything we plant gets fucking devoured. And now, you're leaving, and I'm supposed to just sit here and twiddle my fucking thumbs while I hope you come back? While I hope you don't end up buried in some unmarked grave while I'm changing diapers alone?"

A breeze riffles the remaining seedlings. He follows my gaze to the goat's hoofprint sinking into soft soil.

"I'm coming back," he says.

"You don't know that."

"I do."

"Bullshit." My laugh tastes like brine. "You're rushing into war half-healed because you'd rather die a king than live as a man who—"

"Who what?" He crowds me against the villa wall, hands caging my hips. "A man who stays? Who tends gardens? You think that's who I am?"

Tears in my eyes blur his face. "I think you're terrified to find out."

The silence is devastating. His eyes search mine like he keeps hoping I'll take mercy on him. But I'm not the one doing the torturing here—he is. I can't even be mad, because I'm the one who handed my heart to a killer and told him to do with it as he pleased.

I have only myself to blame for where we've ended up.

"I don't even know if I can do this without you," I croak. "These babies… God, Sasha, what if I'm terrible at this? What if something goes wrong during the birth and you're not here? What if—" He reaches for me again, but I step back, wrapping my arms around my belly. "No. You don't get to comfort me right now. You're choosing to go. You're choosing to leave us here alone. So you have to live with seeing exactly what that does to me."

"Ariel—"

"Just go," I whisper. "Go back to New York. Go fight your war. But don't expect me to pretend I'm okay with it. Because I'm not. I'm really, really not."

For one heartbeat, I let myself believe he might stay. His eyes soften at the corners, his fingers twitch toward me, and hope blooms like a dangerous flower in my chest.

But then he turns and walks away.

My knees give out and I slide down the villa wall, unable to hold back the sobs anymore. They tear out of me like living things, these fears I've been carrying. Fear of being alone. Fear of raising our babies without him. Fear of him dying out there in the cold streets of New York while I'm trapped here in the sun-drenched hills of Tuscany, miserable in paradise, powerless to save him.

The burglars died first this morning.

The garden died second.

My hope is the last thing to go.

42

SASHA

The Hudson smells like diesel and dead fish when we slip off the cargo ship. New York's breath hasn't changed. But her face…

Feliks whistles through his teeth as we cruise down Brighton Beach Avenue. "Looks like Dragan redecorated."

Eight months gone, and already, New York feels both achingly familiar and jarringly wrong, like coming home to find all your furniture rearranged by a stranger's hands.

I lean forward between the seats as Feliks drives, drinking in every detail. The streets are still mine in my head—every corner, every alley mapped out in perfect clarity. But what fills those spaces has shifted.

"Serbian flag," I mutter as we pass Dmitri's old bar. The red-blue-and-white stripes mock me from where they hang, limp and damp in the autumn air. "Dmitri would rather die than fly that."

"He did," Feliks says quietly. "Two months ago. Dragan's men made an example."

My fingers curl into fists. Dmitri was no saint, but he poured me my first shot of vodka when I was sixteen. He deserved better than dying for a fucking flag.

We turn onto Coney Island Avenue, and the wrongness only deepens. Where Nikolai's bakery used to fill the street with the smell of fresh bread, there's now a Serbian butcher shop. The neon sign is garish, bloody red reflecting off puddles in the street. Three young thugs lounge outside. They track our car with predatory eyes.

"Keep driving," I tell Feliks when his foot twitches toward the brake. "Not yet."

He obliges, but I can feel the tension radiating off him. Pavel shifts in the backseat, his hand never far from his weapon.

Block after block reveals more changes. More Serbian businesses. More of my people's livelihoods destroyed or corrupted. The boarded-up storefronts tell their own stories —Misha's pawn shop sealed behind corrugated metal, Oleg's garage stripped down to its concrete bones. Even the fucking bodega on the corner of Ocean View and 7th sports new Serbian ownership, if the crates of Jelen Pivo stacked outside are any indication.

"Like cockroaches," I growl. "Everywhere I fucking look." My knuckles ache around the Glock in my lap.

"Boss?" Feliks glances at me in the rearview. "Where to?"

I consider our options. The warehouses will be watched. The docks are no doubt compromised. But there's one place Dragan won't expect me to go.

"Take us to Babushka's Lap."

As we drive, the anger builds, slow and cold, familiar as breathing. This is my city. My streets. My people. And this fucking Serbian dog thinks he can just waltz in and take it all?

I think of Ariel back in Italy, crying in our ruined garden. Of the twins growing in her belly. All the things I left behind to come fight this war.

She's wrong about what she said: I didn't come here to die. I came here to take back what's mine—not just for me anymore, but for them. For the family I never thought I'd have.

And Dragan? He's about to learn exactly what happens when you wake a sleeping bear.

The kitchen at Zoya's restaurant is full of my men. Bratva captains crowd around the scarred steel prep table, their faces drawn tight with eight months of barely-contained rage. They all look worse for the wear. Ilya's tailored suit hangs loose from too many skipped meals. Roza's lacquered nails click against a tablet, the only sign she'll ever show of the anxiety bubbling beneath her surface. Viktor's knuckles gleam raw pink and ooze blood.

Roza spreads out a map of New York, and as a group, we run again through what Feliks told me the night he arrived in Italy. Brighton Beach. Coney Island. The docks. Little Odessa —everything that used to be mine, it's all Dragan's now.

Ilya fills in the legal side of the thorns in our side: unannounced IRS audits hampering our businesses, union disputes hamstringing our workforces, permitting issues suddenly cropping up everywhere we've tried to build or expand. It's all Dragan, pulling strings, fucking with us in every way he knows how.

As they talk, I trace the familiar streets with my fingertip. My territory has been reduced to a few scattered blocks. But what catches my attention isn't the map—it's my own hand.

Rock steady. Not a tremor in sight.

I toy with my Glock, checking the action. The weight settles into my palm like it never left. My shoulder doesn't scream when I sight down the barrel. My fingers don't shake on the trigger. The rest and rehabilitation have done their work. The weakness Dragan carved into my body is gone.

"That's enough," I say, cutting off their litany of losses. "We're not here to count wounds. We're here to inflict them."

My captains straighten, hunger gleaming in their eyes. They've been waiting for this—for me to come back, to give them purpose again.

I'm ready to deliver.

The map is already bleeding red push pins, but I stab a fresh one into Red Hook. "Dragan's Achilles' heel isn't his army— it's his reflection." Case in point: I flick a photo of Dragan's new Midtown penthouse across the table—floor-to-ceiling mirrors in every room. "He's Narcissus. Pure fucking ego. He'll chase every threat personally. So, to tempt a narcissist out of his cave… we give him threats everywhere."

Viktor leans in. "Hit the gambling dens and diamond district same night?"

"Same *hour*." My finger traces circles around key points on the map. "Here. Here. Here. And here. We hit them all at once. Make him dance." I tap the central Brighton Beach warehouse. "Roza, clone his burner phones. I want his men getting conflicting orders from a dozen different numbers."

She grins, shark-like. "I'll make his comms scream."

"Viktor, check our old protection network. See who's still breathing, who might be willing to flip back if properly motivated. Then give them that motivation, however you deem necessary."

I slide my gaze to Ilya. "And you—I want everything on his legitimate businesses. Tax records, health code violations, union complaints. Find me pressure points, then poke them."

"What about the docks?" Feliks asks.

"That's where you come in." I trace the shoreline. "Watch his shipments. I want to know exactly what comes in, what goes out, and most importantly—what he handles personally."

My captains lean forward, hungry for more.

"We have twenty-four hours to line it all up," I tell them. "That's a tight window, so it means the work must be clean. No mistakes. No assumptions. When we move, we move with perfect intel or not at all."

I study the map again. Dragan's empire looks vast on paper. But paper burns. And every empire has its weak points—you just have to know where to shove the knife.

Feliks's phone buzzes against the steel prep table. He answers with a grunt, then his face darkens. "Boss. Serbian scouts, three blocks away. Moving this direction."

Roza's taser clicks on. Viktor's chair screeches back. I catch Ilya's eye across the table—he's already reaching under the counter for the sawed-off shotgun that Zoya keeps taped there.

"How many?" My thumb strokes the Glock's grip. Steady. Always, always steady now.

"Three, maybe four." Feliks peers through the blinds. "Snapping pictures of the storefront."

"Shit." Ilya adjusts his tie with trembling fingers. "They found us."

"No." I rise, rolling tension from my shoulders. The old bullet wound beneath my ribs stays silent. "If Dragan knew I was here, he'd send forty. Not photographers."

"So what do you wanna do?" asks Viktor.

A grin spreads across my face. "Educate him on his mistake."

We pour out into the night. August wind razors between brick tenements, carrying the reek of Serbian cigarettes from the alley.

"There," Feliks whispers, jerking his chin toward movement at the far end of the alley. "Three targets. On foot."

I assess them through narrowed eyes. Young. Cocky. The kind of muscle Dragan sends when he wants roving eyes but doesn't expect serious trouble.

Perfect.

"Circle around behind," I murmur to Pavel. "Feliks, take the fire escape. I want them boxed in when they reach the middle of the alley."

My men melt away into the shadows. I stay where I am, counting heartbeats. One. Two. Three…

The Serbians saunter closer, talking quietly among themselves. They haven't spotted us yet. Good. Let them come to me. Right up to my fucking doorstep.

When the first Serbian draws even with the dumpster, I step out of the shadows. "*Dobro veče, gospodo,*" I say softly.

Good evening, gentlemen. Spoken in their own tongue.

Their eyes go wide with recognition. But before they can reach for their weapons, Feliks and Pavel materialize behind them. The trap snaps shut with beautiful precision.

What follows is quick, brutal, and deeply satisfying. My body moves like it was never broken, muscle memory taking over as I slam the first man's head into the brick wall. It pops like a fucking watermelon. His friend tries to draw, but my elbow finds his throat before the gun clears leather. The third manages to get off a single, wild shot that goes harmlessly wide before Pavel takes him down with a bullet to the leg.

When it's over, I'm barely breathing hard. No pain anywhere —nothing but the rush of victory singing in my blood.

I look down at the two remaining Serbians lying groaning at my feet. "I'd ask you to tell Dragan his time is coming," I say in Serbian. "But you won't be around to see it."

Three shots echo in the alley. Three bodies cool in the late summer air.

I'm ready.

The penthouse feels wrong. Dust sheets shroud furniture like corpses in white body bags. I rip them off couches where Ariel once pinned me with her thighs, sending particulate ghosts dancing in dawn's gray light.

I move through the space like a ghost, touching things that shouldn't matter. A pink elastic band on the bathroom counter catches my eye. Ariel's. I pick it up, hold it gingerly in the palm of my hand. I look at it for a long, long time.

If it weren't for my phone buzzing, I might've stood there for even longer. But when I pull it out, I see her name lighting up the screen.

ARIEL: *Just checking you made it back okay.*

Five words. Careful. Distant.

Ice.

Before I can talk myself out of it, I hit *Call*.

She picks up on the first ring. "Hey."

"Hey."

Silence stretches between us, rife with all the things we're not saying. I want to tell her about the hair tie, about how seeing it made my chest ache. Want to ask if she's sleeping okay without me there to rub her back.

Instead, I say, "You're up late."

"Braxton Hicks. Practice contractions." A pause. "False alarm, though."

"You're okay?"

"Fine."

More silence. I hear her breathing on the other end of the line, tense and measured. Like she's choosing her words as carefully as I am.

"Well," she says finally. "I'm glad you made it back safe."

"Yeah."

"And you're... okay?"

I think of the three bodies cooling in the alley behind Zoya's. Of how steady my hands were when I pulled the trigger. "Getting there."

"Good. That's… good."

The conversation dies again. We used to be able to talk for hours about nothing. Now, we can barely string together three sentences.

"I should let you sleep," I say.

"Probably."

Neither of us hangs up.

"Sasha?"

"Yeah?"

She takes a breath like she's about to say something important. Then: "Never mind. Goodnight."

The line goes dead before I can respond.

I stare at the phone for a long moment, then set it face-down on the nightstand. Dawn is starting to creep through the windows. I should sleep. Should focus on the war ahead.

Instead, I pick up her hair tie and twist it between my fingers until the sun comes up.

43

ARIEL

Judas is acting up again. It's dark and sticky, with not a breath of breeze or A/C to break up the hot monotony of summer in Italy.

And yet I still wish I had Sasha's heat next to me. I'm lying in bed, drowning in the oversized fabric of his shirt that I couldn't bring myself to wash after he left. His cedar-and-mint scent still clings to the collar, though it's starting to fade.

The twins are restless tonight, turning and kicking like they know something's wrong. I press my palm against the spot where Thing 1 is doing somersaults. "Shh," I whisper. "I miss him, too."

The call earlier left a sour taste in my mouth. All those stilted words and silences that said too much and not enough.

I roll onto my side, the mattress groaning under my weight, and stare at the wall. Moonlight pierces through the shutters, painting jagged lines across the plaster. I'm so tired—of the pregnancy, of the distance, of feeling like I'm losing him all over again. I'm so tired of being tired, and I feel like I've been exactly this tired for a long, long time.

My phone screen suddenly blazes to life on the nightstand. Sasha's name appears above the FaceTime icon. My heart lurches. We just talked—well, attempted to talk—less than an hour ago. What could he possibly...?

I almost let it ring out. Almost.

But my finger slides across the screen before I can stop it.

Sasha's face fills my screen, and the sight of him knocks the air from my lungs. His hair is mussed, like he's been running his hands through it. The usual pristine dress shirt is wrinkled, top buttons undone. There are shadows under his eyes that weren't there when he left Italy.

"Sasha, is everything—"

"I couldn't sleep. Not after— Fuck, I can't stop thinking about you." He drags a hand through his hair, and I catch the flicker of a pink hair tie on his wrist—mine, from months and months ago. "I'm tearing myself apart here. This city, this war... it's eating me alive, but I need you to know that I'm doing it for you. For them."

His gaze drops to my belly, and I shift, suddenly aware of how the shirt rides up, exposing the swell.

"Sasha—"

"No, listen." He leans closer, the screen trembling in his grip. "I'm a bastard, I know that. I've fucked up more times than I can count. But every move I make, every bullet I fire—it's to keep you safe. To give our kids a world where they don't have to run." His voice breaks on *run*, and I see it: the boy beneath the scar, the one Yakov tried to choke out of him.

"I'm not good at this. Staying soft, staying open—it terrifies me. But losing you… that's worse."

Something hot and painful expands in my chest. "You think I care about that? About territory and power? All I want is—"

"Me," he finishes. "I know. But don't you see? That's what I'm fighting for. The chance to be that man. The one who stays. The one who tends gardens instead of burying bodies beneath them." His eyes bore into mine through the screen. "I'm not running away from that future. I'm trying to secure it."

I press my fingers against my lips, fighting back tears. "And what if securing it kills you?"

"It won't." The familiar steel enters his voice. "Because I have something worth coming back for now. Something worth living for."

A tiny foot kicks against my ribs, as if in agreement. Despite everything, I find myself smiling. "Three somethings, actually."

His answering smile is soft and fierce and everything I've been aching for since he left.

The cicadas outside reach a fever pitch. Sasha's pixelated face waits, suspended in the blue-lit dark. My thumb brushes the screen before I can stop it, smearing his jawline into a watercolor wound.

"I'm not—" My voice splinters. I try again. "I'm not angry you left, you know. Well, it's not *just* that."

He doesn't interrupt. Just gives me the space I need to unfold everything that's been swelling up inside of me.

"It's that I'm *terrified*." I swallow and keep going. "That I'll spend the rest of my life explaining to our children why the city mattered more than they did. That you chose New York over—"

He stands abruptly, camera jostling as he strides to the penthouse balcony. Night wind snarls his hair. For one heart-stopping second, I think he'll hang up.

Instead, he flips the camera.

New York sprawls below—a beast made of light and skyscraper fangs. His voice comes rough through the speakers. "I want you to look at this, Ariel. Look at all of it very, very carefully." His finger comes into the screen. "You see the green glow? That's the Met. Over there, at the foot of that building, is the restaurant where we had our first dinner. The spa is to the east. If you squint, you can see Central Park, where we sat on a bench and had hot dogs. This city is filled with the places that made us *us*, Ariel."

Sasha flips the camera back on his face. The expression there makes my breath seize up in my throat. Eyes black with intensity, jaw clenched tight. "And you know what? If it was going to cost me you or our children, I'd strike the match to burn it all down myself."

I touch my quivering lips. "Sasha…"

"I used to think that the past was what mattered. There are alleys I've bled in out there, courtesy of my father's hand. Stretches of asphalt that held my mother until she died. Do those get to hold the same sway over me that the places we first kissed do? No. Fuck no. The city isn't a kingdom, *ptichka*. It's a grave."

Wind whips the microphone. Far below him, a lonely siren wails.

"But you—" He brings the phone close until his scar fills the screen, until I can count each stitch mark Yakov left. "You're the resurrection."

The twins kick hard enough to ripple the shirt of his I'm wearing. His gaze drops, transfixed.

"I'm coming home," he rasps. "Not for power. Not for pride." Callused fingers brush the camera in a ghost caress. "But for the first sunrise you wake in my arms with our children between us."

Manhattan's heartbeat thrums through the speakers— subway growls, taxi horns, the million chaotic rhythms that built him. But underneath, steady as a pulse:

"Because I love you, Ariel Ward."

I shift position, trying to find a comfortable angle despite my heavily pregnant belly. His shirt, swaddled around me, rides up again as I move. Through the phone, I hear Sasha's sharp intake of breath.

"I miss you," I whisper into the darkness.

"I miss you, too," he growls back. "Every part of you."

"Which part of me, specifically? The hormonal crying? The peeing every ten minutes? Or the—"

"All of it." His knuckle whitens where it grips the phone. "Every impossible, infuriating inch."

I can feel the energy shifting. From the dark, swirling angst to something... hotter. My skin is flushing, nipples hardening, as he bites his lip and lets out a barely restrained snarl that unlocks something inside me.

"Which inches do you miss the most?" I tease. I let my hand trail down and tease up the hem of his shirt. "Like... this one?"

He gulps. "That one," he agrees. "One of my favorites."

I hike the shirt higher, up to the bottoms of my breasts, though I keep my hips turned so that, even though I'm not wearing any underwear, all he can see of my lower half is my outer thigh.

"How about this one?"

"That one might be even better."

His breath is haggard over the phone. Even though he's half a world away, mine is, too. I can practically feel his imaginary fingertips replacing mine, peeling my shirt higher, until one aching nipple comes free.

"You're such a pretty fucking angel for me, Ariel. Fuck, I want to watch you devour yourself."

I gnaw at the inside of my cheek. "It'd be better if you were here to do it for me."

"Oh, but I am," he snarls. "All you have to do is close your eyes and let me take over."

I do what he says. His voice starts to come through in a savage rumble, dripping with wet heat.

"I'd tweak each nipple into a peak. You'd feel that little zing of shock ripping through you. You'd gasp so fucking pretty for me, wouldn't you? And I'd pass my tongue right between those parted lips so I could kiss the gasp right out of your mouth."

I'm doing everything he says as he says it. My nipples zing, my lips part, the gasp flies free. I can hear the smile in Sasha's voice as I obey.

"I'd take my time crawling back down you. I'd push that shirt up and off. I'd worship every fucking inch of your body."

I groan and let my hands slide down in time with his instructions. Past stretch marks that branch like lightning forks, the dark line bisecting my belly, the thatch of auburn curls between my legs.

"By the time I got that low, you'd be so ready for me. But I'd wait just a minute longer. Not too much longer, because I'm so fucking ready for you, too, Ariel. But one minute. Because nothing is better than watching you squirm."

"I want you, Sasha."

"Have me then. Let me lap you up while I clench your thighs in my hands. Let me slide two fingers into you and twist them in that way that makes you fall the fuck apart. Let me hear you moan while I do it, because nothing in the world can ever make me harder than you telling me you want me as bad as I want you."

I'm touching myself now, rubbing my clit in a blur as my back arches up off the bed.

"By the time I finally push inside you," he purrs, "we're both so close to coming, aren't we? We're both right on that edge. It won't take much. I'll pin your face against my chest so your moans are for me and me alone. And I'll fuck you so slow and sweet that you don't know where one stroke stops and the next begins. You'll come for me once, right on my cock, because you're a perfect filthy angel. Maybe I'll even let you come a second time. And then right when I can't possibly hold back anymore, I'll come, too."

"I'll take it," I gasp. "I'll take it all. I want you so, so badly, Sasha."

He grins. "Good girl. Show me how you fall apart. And Ariel… you'd better look at me when you come."

The pressure builds cruel and sweet—ripe peaches splitting their skins. His choked groan as I crest syncs perfectly with the pulse between my legs. White light fractures the screen when I start to convulse, his shirt damp with sweat and other things.

"I— I— I— I love you, Sasha Ozerov."

Post-climax tremors make the phone wobble in my grip.

When I finally still, he's breathing like he ran here from Manhattan. We stare at each other through the pixelated wreckage—naked in ways that have nothing to do with skin.

I gulp, my mouth suddenly dry. "Did you…?"

Sasha shakes his head. "No, and I don't want to. I'm saving myself for you, *ptichka*. When I get back—that's *when* I fucking get back, not 'if'—I'm going to give you every single part of me. Head to toe, heart to soul. And then I'm going to give you more babies, once we have these ones in our arms. And more, and more. Do you hear me, Ariel? Do you believe me?"

"Yes," I whisper through tears and aftershocks and heartache and love. "Yes, Sasha, I believe you."

Neither of us wants to hang up. I lie down, but I prop my phone on the pillow beside me, adjusting the angle so I can still see Sasha's face through my heavy-lidded eyes. The tender way he's looking at me makes my heart squeeze in my chest.

"You should sleep," he murmurs.

"So should you." I nestle deeper into the pillow, pulling his shirt tighter around me. "Big day of mobster stuff tomorrow."

His lips quirk. "Something like that."

"You know what I mean." I yawn, unable to fight the post-orgasmic drowsiness anymore. "Just… be careful, okay?"

The twins shift inside me, settling down for the night. I place my palm over the spot where Thing 2 just kicked. Through the screen, I see Sasha's eyes track the movement.

"I wish you could feel them," I whisper. "They're so active tonight."

"Soon." His voice is rough, strangled. "I'll be home soon."

The word *home* catches in my chest. I don't have to ask where exactly *home* is anymore. I know what he's say: *It's wherever we are together.*

My eyelids grow heavier with each blink. Sasha's face blurs at the edges, but I fight to keep looking at him. I'm afraid that, if I close my eyes, he'll disappear forever, washed away like chalk drawings in the rain.

"Sleep," he says again, softer this time. "I'll stay on until you do."

"Promise?"

"I swear it."

His face is the last thing I see as consciousness starts to slip away—those blue eyes watching over me, protective even through thousands of miles of digital distance.

Just before sleep claims me completely, I hear him whisper something. The words float through my mind like dandelion seeds, too delicate to grasp fully.

"Marry me, *ptichka.*"

But I'm already drifting off, unable to tell if it's real or just another dream about the future I want so desperately with him.

That's okay. If he means it, he'll ask me again when he's home.

44

SASHA

The Glock's slide snicks in place. Full metal symphony.

Feliks peers through the nicotine-yellow blinds of the office we're squatting in, looking for anything abnormal in the streets below. "I hope it's true what they say about God loving drunks and idiots," he mumbles. "Because this plan is crazy."

I toss him a flask of bourbon from the desk. "Just in case, take a sip. Check off both boxes."

He laughs and throws back a nip of the liquor, then passes it around. Viktor, Roza, and Ilya all follow suit. When it gets back to me, I cap it and set it aside. I don't need liquor. Not for bravery or luck.

I have all the things that matter going for me already.

Ariel's hair tie sits pink around my wrist. It's hilariously out of place with my black tactical gear and the many weapons littering the surface of the desk, but somehow, it's the piece that ties it all together.

I told her I'd come back to her.

I fucking meant it.

Today is how we make that happen.

The old leather chair creaks as I lean back, watching Roza's pirated surveillance feeds flicker across my monitors. Dragan's men scurry like ants between Red Hook warehouses and Midtown penthouses glittering like diamond-encrusted tumors. They're predictable in their patterns. Stupid in their confidence.

"Alright. Last checks time. Timeline's set," Feliks announces, spreading a map across my desk. Red dots mark our targets: gambling dens, warehouses, front businesses. All the pillars holding up Dragan's empire. "Viktor's men are in position at the docks, with the Albanians in place as extra muscle. Roza's ready to scramble their communications. I've got the Triad on the casinos, two Bratva teams on the drug packaging facilities, and two more groups of the meanest Russian bastards you've ever met ready to bust up every weapons storage depot Dragan has to his name. Plus, thanks to your boy Kosti, every remaining loyal Greek is armed to the teeth and waiting to be rerouted to wherever we need them. All ready to move at the stroke of midnight."

I holster the Glock, leather creaking. "And the main event?"

Feliks grins, all teeth. "Truck's loaded. Enough C4 to redecorate Dragan's skull across six boroughs."

Pavel fidgets and sighs from his seat in the corner. "The Greeks..." He hesitates. "You sure about trusting them? After Leander?"

"They hate Dragan more than they hate us," I say. "And Kosti promised they're good for it. That's enough for now."

The monitors flicker. Grainy footage shows Dragan barking orders at the docks, that fucking lupine strut of his. I flex my healed hand. Every joint moves smoothly. Not a hitch or tremor to be found.

Feliks tosses me a Kevlar vest. "Zoya made me swear you'd wear this. She also said, *'Don't die, idiot.'* Her words, not mine. I would've called you a *fucking* idiot."

I chuckle as I strap it on. My reflection catches in the window—dark clothes, darker eyes, scar white against my throat. I look exactly like the monster Ariel first ran from. But now, that same darkness serves a better purpose: protecting what's mine. Keeping my family safe.

I touch the hair tie again. My skin is still prickling with the aftermath of the FaceTime call as dawn rose. How she smiled at me through the phone screen last night, belly swollen with our children.

Everything I am, everything I've built—it all comes down to this moment. This chance to carve out a future where my kids never know their father's kind of pain.

Ilya checks his watch. "It's 11:47."

I nod, feeling the old familiar battle-calm settle over me. "Let's go remind these fuckers whose city this is."

God help anyone who stands in my way.

The warehouse clock tower chimes midnight.

My boot heel crushes a spent cigarette, the first I've had in days. Above us, spotlights swing like drunken pendulums.

The hair tie bites into my wrist as I look at Feliks where he stands to my left.

I nod. He nods back.

Then the dogs come pouring out of hell.

Every Bratva man at my back takes aim and fires. Shrapnel peppers the loading bay. A Serbian's half-eaten gyro hangs suspended in midair before splattering against a forklift, followed by the bloody remains of the man who was eating it. I put two in another's chest before the first boot even hits ground.

Then we run barking from the shadows. My whole Bratva, down to the last loyal man, descends on Dragan's main warehouse, preceded by a hail of gunfire. Serbian soldiers and scouts are cut down like the harvest. Some scream as they go. Most don't get the chance.

"Flank left!" Pavel's voice crunches through comms. I vault over a pallet of counterfeit vodka, the Glock's rhythm syncopating with my pulse.

Crack-crack. Two more shadows drop.

It's smoke and gunfire everywhere, laced with the wails of these drowning rats. My phone vibrates once in my tactical vest—Roza's signal that their communications are officially scrambled. Right on schedule. I can hear the confusion in their shouts as conflicting orders and white noise surge through their earpieces.

A meaty hand grabs my ankle. I stomp down hard—nasal cartilage crunches—then silence the offender with a knee to the trachea. A throwing knife finds his neighbor's eye before the body finishes sliding down the shelves.

I check my watch. 12:11 A.M.

"Status?" I growl into the mic.

Feliks's laughter crackles in response. "The Albanians took the docks easy as pie. As we speak, the Triad guys are roasting Serbs in the Golden Dragon's woks. We might've set some new land speed records on this one, boss."

A grin splits my face in two. I perk up when I hear a man screaming in Serbian, because my bloodlust has not quite been fully sated yet. When I round the corner of the warehouse, I see him: one of Dragan's lieutenants, backing into a freezer unit, AK-47 trembling.

His eyes dart to the hair tie, then up at me.

I smirk at him. "My fiancée sends her regards."

One shot in each kneecap brings him to the floor. He collapses, bawling, as I stride up to him, pluck the rifle from his grip, and cast it aside.

"Look at me." I press the Glock's warm barrel under his chin. "Where's Dragan?"

He points one quivering finger down an adjacent hallway. I nod in grim thanks. Then I end his miserable life.

Leaving the dead lieutenant behind, I stride down the hall like the Grim Reaper, stepping over bodies and adding others to the piles.

My boots leave bloody prints on the concrete. Each shot I fire is precise, economical.

Another Serbian breaks cover, screaming as he charges me with a knife. Poor bastard must have run out of ammo. I sidestep his wild swing and put him down with a double tap to the chest. Textbook.

In the warehouse beyond me, the gunfire is already starting to die down. It's been less than fifteen minutes since we breached, but the warehouse floor is littered with Serbian corpses. A few survivors have thrown down their weapons, hands raised in surrender. They won't last long.

I key my radio. "Building secure. Phase one complete."

Feliks's voice returns: "All the rest of the secondary targets all went down simultaneously. They never knew what hit them, Sasha. Clean fuckin' sweep."

I allow myself a small smile as I reload. Dragan's empire is crumbling, and he doesn't even know it yet.

But he will.

Very, very soon.

I kick open the door at the end of the hall down which the Serbian lieutenant pointed. It's an empty office, unremarkable. But the leather of Dragan's office chair still holds his body heat.

I run my fingers over the mahogany desk, imagining him sitting here not ten minutes ago, thinking he was untouchable. I wonder what he's thinking now.

The wall safe hangs open, its contents scattered. I'm sure they're nothing important—Dragan is an arrogant motherfucker, but not a stupid one. Sure enough, all I find are useless passports, ledgers, a Glock 19 with serial numbers acid-scorched.

I'm slamming the drawer shut when tires crunch outside.

I stride to the window and look out. Three stories below, a black Mercedes pulls up at the curb, its armored bulk gleaming under sodium lights.

And there he is.

Dragan emerges from a side door, flanked by what's left of his security detail. Even from here, I can see the tension in his shoulders, the way his head whips back and forth as he surveys the street. He knows he's fucked. The silence from his outposts must be deafening. As deafening as this C4 is about to be when it blows this warehouse to the fucking sky.

Just before he ducks into the car, some instinct makes him look up.

Our eyes lock through the glass.

His face goes slack with shock as recognition hits. The great Dragan Vukovic, seeing a ghost. Seeing the man he thought he'd killed, standing in his office like Death himself has come calling.

I bare my teeth in what might charitably be called a smile. I want him to see me. I hope he understands exactly what's coming for him.

His bodyguard yanks the car door open, breaking the spell. Dragan practically dives inside.

I watch the Mercedes peel away, leaving rubber on asphalt.

"Run, run, little rabbit," I murmur, tapping the tip of my gun on the window glass. "It won't be much longer now."

45

ARIEL

I'm hovering in that hazy space between sleep and waking, where everything feels soft and uncertain. The twins are tumbling and kicking like they sense my unease. I shift position for the hundredth time, trying to get comfortable. It doesn't happen.

Four days since he left. Four very long days. Still, there's cedar and mint clinging to the sheets if I look hard enough, the ghost of him haunting our bed. I press my face into his pillow and inhale deeply. I'm only torturing myself, but how can I stop?

Just as I'm finally starting to drift off again, something changes in the air.

A presence.

A weight.

My eyes flutter open, adjusting to the darkness. Moonlight spills through the shutters in silver ribbons, and there—outlined in that ethereal glow—stands Sasha.

I must be dreaming. "You're supposed to be in New York," I croak, still wondering how much of this is real.

"And you're supposed to be asleep."

He's watching me with those intense eyes, still dressed in black tactical gear, looking deadly and beautiful. My breath catches in my throat as our gazes lock across the moonlit room.

He crosses.

Three steps. Two. One.

Then he's on me—no, actually, he's kneeling next to me, cupping my hand between his.

"I have something for you."

From his pocket, he produces a small, wooden box, patinated green with age. The hinges creak as he opens it, revealing a delicate gold ring nestled in faded velvet.

"This was my mother's," he says quietly. "The only thing of hers I managed to save. After... after what Yakov did to her, I buried it with her. Couldn't stand the thought of wearing it or selling it. But I couldn't let myself melt it, either." His throat works. "But today, after everything was finished with Dragan, I went to her grave. Dug it up myself."

"Sasha..."

"She would have loved you," he whispers, turning the ring so it catches the moonlight. "She would have loved what you've done to me. Who you've made me." His eyes meet mine. "Will you wear it? Not because some arrangement demands it, but because you choose to be mine?"

"Say it properly," I rasp.

He stills. "Marry me, Ariel Ward." Not a question—a raw-throated plea. "Not for politics. Not for peace. Not for profit." His thumb swipes my tears, smearing salt and iron. "But only because I'm yours. Always was. Always will be."

I close my eyes. It's not because I need this time to think it over; truth be told, I've known my answer for many, many weeks now. But it's just because everything with us has always happened so fast, such a blur of moments and places and two truths and many more lies woven in between. So when it comes to this moment, this perfect moment, I want it to last just a bit longer than the others.

Just one extra breath, to seal it in amber. I'll want to come back to it, I think. I'll want to hold this moment in my hands again and feel exactly what I'm feeling right now.

"Yes," I whisper. "Yes, Sasha Ozerov, I'll marry you."

46

ARIEL

Things 1 and 2 are not pleased with Gina's driving.

As she whips yet another hairpin turn way too fast, with complete disregard for the capabilities of this poor little rented Peugeot that's been through hell and back, both babies start stomping their feet on my bladder.

"Gee! The brake is the one on the left! Goddammit!"

But she's singing way too loudly to Italian pop radio to even hear what I'm saying. That's confirmed when she whips around, hair flying like Medusa's in the wind screeching through the open window, and flashes me the biggest smile I've ever seen from her.

"I know, right?!" she says. "It's the best day ever!"

I cover my face. "Eyes on the road! Hands at ten and two! Ahhh!"

It's hard to be too mad at her. Well, that's not completely true —if we die in a fiery car crash on the way to get my wedding dress, I will in fact be pretty pissed in the afterlife.

But aside from the questionable driving, she really has been an absolute angel from the second she saw me coming down the stairs at breakfast with Sasha's ring on my finger. She made me feel like the most special girl in the world when she damn near tackled me into the stairs, screaming with pure joy.

Everything's been mostly a blur from there. Gee cried, Mama cried, Jasmine cried, Lora cried enough for all of us put together. Even Zoya shed one solitary tear. Then they all demanded a play-by-play down to the exact word, and *then* they all scolded Sasha for proposing to me when I had morning breath, and only after that did they all hug him and make him feel uncomfortable in the only way Sasha Ozerov ever feels uncomfortable: by expressing genuine emotions in his presence.

Okay, fine, he's a work-in-progress.

But he's *my* work-in-progress now. Officially.

Once the tears had been teared and the hugs had been hugged, they immediately launched into planning mode. I had a whole committee of wedding planners before my own sobbing had even eased up.

Item #1 on their agenda? Wedding dress shopping.

Thus the crazy car ride.

I'm squished between Jasmine and Mama in the backseat, trying to find a comfortable position for my massive belly. Every bump in the road makes the twins protest, but I can't bring myself to care. Not today.

My fingers keep finding their way to Sasha's ring. The gold is warm now from how much I've been touching it, twisting it, looking at it every chance I can get. His mother wore this ring. The mere thought makes my chest tight.

"You're going to wear it smooth if you keep fondling it like that," Jasmine teases, nudging my shoulder with hers.

I stick my tongue out at her. "Let me have this moment."

"Oh, you'll have plenty of moments," Gina calls from the driver's seat. She catches my eye in the rearview mirror. "And every single one is going to be better than that first disaster of an almost-wedding."

"Gee…" I start, but she's on a roll.

"I mean it! No stuffy Met gala this time. No Greek mobsters breathing down our necks, and sure as hell no arranged marriage bullshit." She ticks off each point on her fingers, somehow still managing to navigate the winding road, albeit barely. "Just you, your hot Russian hunk, and everyone who actually loves you."

Mama's hand finds mine, squeezing gently. When I look at her, there are tears in her eyes. "I never thought I'd get to do this," she whispers. "Shopping for my baby's wedding dress. With both my girls."

"Mama, don't," I warn, feeling my own eyes start to well up. "If you cry, I'll cry, and then my makeup will run, and then—"

"And then you'll look exactly like you did that evening in the Met bathroom," Gina interrupts cheerfully. "Which, by the way, is where this whole beautiful love story started. So maybe some running mascara would be appropriate."

"That is *not* where the story started," I protest, but I'm laughing too hard to elaborate.

The car hits another pothole and the twins kick in protest. I rub my belly, trying to soothe them. "Sorry, babies. Aunt Gina thinks she's in *Fast and Furious.*"

"Hey! I'm driving perfectly normally for Italy!"

"That's what worries me," Jasmine mutters, making Mama laugh.

The sound of all of us together—laughing, teasing, *alive*—fills the tiny car like sunshine. For so long, I thought I'd lost this. Lost them. But here we are, squeezed into a Peugeot that's seen better days, heading to find the dress I'll wear when I marry the man I love.

Not because anyone's forcing us.

Just because we chose each other.

The village appears ahead—ochre walls draped in bougainvillea, cobblestones worn smooth by centuries of feet. Gina parallel parks so badly that some poor driving instructor back in New York probably just woke up in a cold sweat with dubious guilt clawing at their stomach. A Vespa tumbles over after she kisses it with the bumper. She looks at it, shrugs, then looks at me.

"Alright, Ward." She kills the engine, sunglasses sliding down her nose. "Ground rules. No chiffon. No big, droopy veils that make you look like a discount nun. And if anyone mentions how 'ivory symbolizes purity,' I'm keying their car."

Jasmine helps me unfold from the backseat, her grip firm under my elbow. "You realize she's seven months pregnant with twins, yes? We're aiming for 'glowing fertility goddess,' not 'virginal blushing bride.'"

Heat crawls up my neck. "Can we not—"

The little bell above the door chimes as we enter *Atelier Sposa Maria.* Compared to the glaring Mediterranean sun outside, the boutique's interior feels cool and dim, like stepping into a secret garden made of tulle and lace instead of flowers.

Maria herself emerges from behind a rack of dresses, and her lined face breaks into a smile that makes me instantly feel at home. Her eyes drop to my belly, then light up like Christmas morning. "Ah, *bellissima!*" She claps her hands together. "*Due bambini!* What joy!"

Before I can respond, she's already circling me like a friendly hurricane, muttering rapid-fire Italian mixed with the few English words she knows. Her hands flutter around me, measuring without touching, assessing angles and curves I didn't even know I had.

Gina slings an arm around my shoulders. "What my friend needs is something that says, 'I'm carrying the heir to a crime empire, but make it fashion.'"

"You come, come," she insists, beckoning us deeper into her shop. "*Perfetto timing.* The babies make you glow like Madonna."

The boutique is nothing like I imagined when I used to daydream about dress shopping in New York. No stark white walls or intimidating mirrors. Completely devoid of rail-thin attendants giving judgmental side-eye to my expanding waistline. Instead, the space feels lived-in, loved. Vintage photographs cover the walls—brides from decades past, their joy preserved in sepia tones. Dried flowers hang from exposed wooden beams.

Maria disappears behind a heavy velvet curtain, still talking to herself in Italian. I catch maybe one word in twenty, but her enthusiasm needs no translation.

"This is perfect," Mama whispers, squeezing my hand. Her eyes are already glistening again. She's a leaky faucet today. It's contagious.

Before I can agree, Maria bursts back through the curtain with an armful of ivory silk. "For you, for you! Special dresses for a special mama bride."

She lays them out one by one on a worn chaise lounge, handling each gown like it's made of spun sugar. These aren't the restrictive meringues I feared—they're fluid things, designed to celebrate my body, not constrain it.

"See?" Maria points out the clever panels and elegant draping. "We make you feel like a queen, not a penguin."

I laugh. The fabric feels like water between my fingers. "They're beautiful."

"*Si, si*! Beauty for beauty!" She pats my cheek like a doting grandmother. "Now, we try. Show these *bambini* how Mama sparkles, *no?*"

Looking around this cozy shop, at these perfectly imperfect dresses, at the women I love most gathered close, I feel tears threatening again.

But this time, they're the good kind.

This is exactly how finding my wedding dress should feel. Not in some sterile Manhattan showroom, but here, in this little slice of Italian heaven, surrounded by love and history and the smell of dried roses.

As I start to try them on, everyone plays exactly the role I would've expected from them.

Lora on Dress #1: "Oh my gawd, you're like a beautiful marshmallow!"

Mama on Dress #2: "Perhaps a bit... old-fashioned, sweetheart. But still gorgeous!"

Gina on Dress #3: "Your curves are *curving*, lady!"

I frown at Gee. "In a Dolly Parton kind of way, or are we talking more like the Michelin Man?"

Her lack of an answer tells me everything I need to know.

When I emerge from behind the velvet curtain in Dress #4, Gina immediately whips out her phone, circling me like a fashion photographer on speed. "Work it, girl! Give me angles! No, wait—that's your bad side. Other way. Yesss, perfect!"

"Every side is my bad side right now," I laugh, trying to twist despite my belly. "I'm the size of a planet."

"Nonsense!" Lora is already dabbing at her eyes with a tissue. "You look like an angel. A glowing, pregnant angel."

"You said that about the last two dresses," Gina points out, not unkindly.

"Because they were all beautiful!" Lora sniffles harder.

Mama flutters around me, adjusting the fall of silk across my shoulders, smoothing invisible wrinkles. Her hands are gentle but insistent as she fusses with the train. "Maybe if we pinned this part here..." she murmurs, more to herself than to me. "Yes, yes, yes."

I'm about to turn to look at my reflection—when I notice Jasmine.

She's been quiet through the whole process, watching from her perch on the vintage settee. Unlike the others, she doesn't rush to comment on each dress. She waits, observes, only speaking when she has something real to say.

But now…

Now, she's staring at me with tears in her eyes.

"Jas?" I whisper.

She stands slowly, one hand pressed to her mouth. For a moment, I think she won't speak at all. Then her voice comes out rough, like she's fighting past something stuck in her throat.

"You look like Mama on her wedding day."

The boutique goes silent. Even Gina lowers her phone.

Mama makes a small sound and reaches for Jasmine's hand. "You remember those photos?"

Jasmine nods, wiping quickly at her eyes. "I used to sneak into your closet to look at them. You were so happy in that picture, Mama. And now…" She gestures at me, a watery grin breaking through. "Now, my baby sister's wearing the exact same smile."

I have to blink hard to keep from ruining my makeup. It's been so long since I've seen Jasmine let her guard down like this, let herself feel something pure and uncomplicated.

"So," Maria asks from somewhere behind me, "this is the one, *si?*"

For the first time since I emerged in this one, I look at my reflection. It's… everything. White as snow, flowing, simple. It cradles my baby bump without shame. It makes me feel like exactly who I want to be when I marry Sasha: strong, beautiful, and completely, gloriously free.

"Yes," I decide. "This is the one."

Once the seamstress has taken measurements, I settle onto the velvet couch, carefully arranging my regular clothes around my belly. Maria insists we can't leave without celebrating properly, so she bustles around with a tray of delicate cookies dusted with powdered sugar and glasses filled with prosecco and sparkling water.

"For good luck!" she declares, pressing a crystal flute of bubbling water into my hands in place of the alcohol. "*Salute!*"

Everyone raises their glasses. Mama and Lora are still wiping away tears, while Gina keeps sneaking glances at her phone, probably texting updates to Feliks.

I'm about to take a sip when Jasmine touches my arm. "Can we…?" She gestures toward a quiet corner near the window.

I follow her to two carved wooden chairs tucked between racks of veils and vintage accessories. Jasmine's fingers twist in her lap. "What's on your mind, Jas?"

She takes a deep breath. "I need to tell you something. About Sasha."

My heart skips, but I stay deathly quiet.

"It's okay. It's not a bad thing. You don't have to look terrified." She laughs and cups my cheek in her warm palm before tucking her hands back in her lap. "When he helped me escape... he didn't just save my life. He gave me a choice. Agency. The thing Dragan and Baba and everyone else tried to take away." She looks down at her hands. "I was so angry for so long, Ari. At everyone who tried to control me."

"I know," I whisper. "I was angry, too."

"But Sasha..." Her voice catches. "The man who helped me wasn't the cold monster everyone thought he was. He risked everything to help a terrified girl he barely knew." Finally, she meets my eyes. "And watching him with you... he's grown into someone even better. Someone worthy of my little sister's heart."

Tears blur my vision. "Jas..."

"I know what it's like to be trapped in an arranged marriage to a monster," she continues. "If I thought for one second that's what was happening to you, I would have kidnapped you out of there myself. But this?" She gestures to my ring, my belly, my face glowing with happiness. "This is real. And you have my blessing, for whatever that's worth."

I grab her hand, squeezing tight. "It's worth everything."

The ride home is as chaotic as the first, but this time, I can't stop smiling. ABBA's "Dancing Queen" blasts through the tinny speakers.

"YOUNG AND SWEET, ONLY SEVENTEEN!" Gina belts out, completely off-key.

Jasmine joins in from my left, while Mama claps along from my right. Even Lora is swaying in the front passenger seat.

I close my eyes and let the warmth of the moment wash over me. The late afternoon sun paints the inside of my eyelids gold, like honey dripping, slow and sweet. My mother's perfume mingles with the breeze coming through the open windows. The ring on my finger catches the light every time I move.

"Come on, Ari!" Gina calls over her shoulder. "You know you want to sing!"

And you know what? I do.

So I join in, not caring that my voice cracks on the high notes or that the twins are using my bladder as a dance floor. The five of us—sisters by blood and choice—screech our way through the chorus like teenagers at a slumber party.

"God," I wheeze when the song finally ends, wiping tears from my eyes. "I never thought I'd have this."

Jasmine squeezes my hand. "Have what?"

"This." I gesture vaguely at all of them, all of *this*. "Family. Love. Choice." My voice catches. "Freedom."

Mama's arms wrap around me from the side, and she presses a kiss to my temple. "You were always meant for this kind of happiness, baby. Even when you were small, your heart was too big for the cage they tried to put you in."

The twins kick, as if agreeing with their grandmother. I spread my palm over the spot where Thing 1—definitely the more dramatic of the two—is showing off.

"Your babies are going to be so loved," Lora sighs dreamily. "Like, the most loved babies ever."

"The most *spoiled* babies ever," Gina corrects, starting the car again. "Between all of us aunties, plus Zoya, plus whatever poor soul has to tell Sasha 'no' when he wants to buy them ponies..."

I laugh, but my heart swells at the thought. My children will never know what it's like to feel trapped or afraid. They'll grow up surrounded by fierce protectors, gentle teachers, and so much love it'll overflow.

As we wind our way back toward the villa—toward home— Whitney Houston's voice soars through the speakers, and we all join in again, singing about a love that lifts us up where we belong.

47

ARIEL

Tradition is bullshit.

It's my wedding morning and yes, yes, I know that it's bad luck to sleep with your groom the night before you're married. But as I wake up and instinctively stick my cold feet toward where he should to warm them up, it's bullshit that I find the bed empty instead.

I'm sure Sasha is equally grumpy. He had to bunk on a couch in Feliks and Gina's room for the night, and I bet he's doing the same thing I'm doing right now: reaching out and wishing he could touch me.

Besides—bad luck? For *us?* Who cares?! What could possibly go wrong that hasn't already gone wrong multiple times in our love story?

I get up and waddle to the window. The sun is so yellow and beautiful that it makes the whole world look like it's been dipped in cake batter. Below the horizon, my sisters-in-spirit are already hard at work. Gina balances precariously on a ladder, draping fairy lights between crooked olive trees while

Lora spots her from below. Jasmine weaves between wooden chairs, positioning them in neat rows and tying bundles of wildflowers to the end seats.

Just love. Just family. Just choice.

I press my palm against the window glass, my other hand cradling my swollen belly. The babies shift beneath my touch, as if they're taking in the scene below just like I am.

"I know," I whisper to them. "I can't wait, either."

My thumb finds the scar on my left palm, the one Sasha bandaged in that bathroom a lifetime ago. That night tasted like panic and champagne. Today smells like jasmine and fresh-baked *koulourakia* drifting from the kitchen. What a world of difference.

A gentle breeze rustles the olive leaves, making the fairy lights dance. Jasmine pauses in her work to lift her face to the morning sun.

When she opens her eyes, she sees me batting my eyelashes at her from my window, ruining her Disney princess moment. She laughs and throws a swatch of flowers up at me. She misses by a mile, though, and hits Gina instead, who then drops a fairy light on Lora's head, who shrieks and flails like she just got hit by a sniper. Their laughter floats up to my window, and I find myself laughing right along with them.

This is exactly how a wedding morning should feel. Soft light, beloved faces, and the quiet certainty that I'm exactly where I'm meant to be.

When the decorations are done, the women all pour into my room to help me start getting ready. They're like nervous butterflies, all of them, flitting around and landing on me and taking off again. Only Mama's hands are steady as she helps me into my dress.

"Hold still, *solnyshko*," Zoya scolds, wielding a hairpin like a sword. "Your curls, they fight me like angry snakes."

"They've always had a mind of their own," Mama laughs, smoothing the fabric over my belly. " Not unlike their owner."

From her perch on my bed, Jasmine clears her throat dramatically. She's been "practicing" her speech all morning and my cheeks hurt from laughing. "'Dearly beloved,'" she intones in a voice that sounds more like a chain-smoking Batman than an officiant. "'We are gathered here today…'"

"Oh God, stop," I giggle, earning another scolding tap from Zoya. "You sound terrible."

"What? This isn't authoritative enough?" Jasmine drops her voice even lower. "'DO YOU, SASHA OZEROV…'"

"I'm going to pee myself if you keep that up," I warn, which sets everyone off laughing again.

Gina circles us like a documentarian, her phone perpetually raised. "This is gold. Pure gold. The making-of documentary is going to be better than the actual wedding."

"Less talking, more holding still," Zoya mutters. But I catch even her smiling in the mirror.

She works for a few more minutes before she steps back, claps her hands, and declares me finished. Everyone clusters around to see for themselves. They ooh and aww, and I can't decide whose face makes me smile the biggest. Gina's beam? Lora's cartoon-heart eyes? Zoya's scowl?

But when I slide my gaze to Mama, she's frowning.

"Mama? Everything okay?" I ask.

She touches a finger to her lower lip. "You're missing something."

I start touching myself from head to toe, trying to figure out what's wrong. "Is it my— I mean, the neckline was supposed to—"

But before I can fully descend into panic, she reaches out and grabs my wrist. "No, no, dear, nothing like that. It's just that you need something borrowed. I've got just the thing."

My hand flies to my throat as Mama unclasps her signature pearl necklace—the one she's worn every day since I was fifteen years old. The very first thing she bought for herself after she walked out on the man she once thought she loved.

"Mama, no…" I protest weakly, but she's already moving behind me.

"Hush," she tuts, draping the strand around my neck. The pearls are warm from her skin. "Every bride needs something old. These pearls have seen love die and love be reborn. They've witnessed both darkness and light." Her fingers tremble as she fastens the clasp. "Now, they'll see you choose your own path—the one thing I always wanted for my girls."

In the mirror, I watch tears slip down her cheeks as she adjusts the necklace. The pearls gleam softly against my skin, like they've been waiting all this time to rest here, on this day.

"Mama…" I try again, but she shakes her head.

"No crying," she says firmly. "You'll ruin Zoya's hard work."

Uncle Kosti's arm is steady beneath my hand as we pause at the top of the aisle. "Ready, *koukla*?"

I can't speak past the lump in my throat. I don't know if I'm really ready, anyway. How could I be? Every second is the most perfect second I've ever had. I want to memorize every detail.

The warm August breeze tousles the curls framing my face. In the seats are the people I love most in this world. Over their heads hang lights like the stars came down low just for us, while flickering candles mark the path from where I stand up to the altar. I want to remember how it smells in the air, how the silk of my dress feels on my skin, how the stirring trees are the soundtrack I never knew I wanted for my wedding.

But most of all, I want to remember Sasha's face.

He stands beneath an arch woven with white wildflowers, hands clasped behind his back. He's wearing a dark navy suit with an ivory shirt, open at the throat. On his feet are oxblood leather loafers, so perfectly chosen that I want to laugh out loud. His beard has been shaved close to the skin, so it's just dark, rough stubble coating his cheeks. His eyes have never been bluer as they drink me in, every bit of me, from the flowers woven into my hair to my bare toes, because "heels" and "nine months pregnant with twins" were never, ever gonna mix.

I've seen Sasha in so many states—angry, passionate, tender, fierce. But I've never seen him look quite like this. Like he can't quite believe what he's seeing.

Neither can I.

Feliks stands beside him as best man, practically vibrating with barely-contained joy. Jasmine waits at their side, ready to officiate, looking celestial in a lavender slip dress.

"Yeah," I tell Uncle Kosti. "Ready."

And so the march begins. With each step down the aisle, I feel like I'm reliving some part of the past that brought me here. We started as strangers in a bathroom, became enemies by arrangement, then lovers by choice. Every twist in our path has led us to this place, this garden, this moment.

Back to each other, time and time again.

As Kosti and I reach the flower arch, Sasha extends his hand. I release my uncle and take my fiancé.

When I'm in position, Jasmine clears her throat. "We're gathered here today to witness something extraordinary," she begins. "Not just the union of two people, but the triumph of choice over fate. Of love over fear." Her eyes meet mine, then his. "Sasha... Ariel... I've watched both of you fight your way here. Through darkness, through pain, through all the reasons you had to give up. But you chose each other every step of the way. Well, almost every step."

My vision goes fuzzy. Sasha's hands tighten around mine.

"I could say a lot about what each of you means to me. Sister. Savior. But it's not my words that matter. It's yours. So I'll step aside and let you share the vows you've written."

I gulp. I'm up first. I insisted on that, because if I go second, I'll be a blubbering mess at the end of Sasha's vows and there's no chance I'll get through my own words.

Here goes nothing.

"Sasha Ozerov," I say, reading off the page torn from my journal. "I wrote once—in a journal you peeked in; shame on you—that love is war waged softly. Honestly, pretty good line, not to pat myself on the back too much. But it's not true, as it turns out." I peek up at him. *Blue,* so blue, cornflower blue, sky-blue, the most undeniably perfect blue that has ever been painted on this earth. "Love can be waged hard. It can be waged loudly. It can be waged silently. It can be waged when you're a breath apart or a world apart. But love doesn't reach its truest form until you realize that it's not a war at all. I tried to fight against you from the moment I met you. Now that I'm standing here before you, ready to be your wife, my vow is this: I'm not here to fight against you anymore. I'm here to fight *with* you. I am here to be your soldier, your avenging angel, your reason, your why. I'm here to stitch your wounds and kiss your bruises. I'm here to be soft so you can be hard. I'm here to be gentle so you can be cruel. I love you, Sasha, and I vow to keep doing that long after all the wars have ended."

I don't risk a second glance up until I'm done. When I do, I see something I didn't think possible: a single tear sluicing down Sasha's cheek.

His turn. He clears his throat. "Ariel... You were on the other side of a door when I met you," he rumbles. "A bathroom stall door. A *men's* bathroom stall door, actually." A laugh ripples through our friends and family. "But do you know why that's so perfect, Ariel? Funny enough, you do know the answer. You read it from a book for me once."

I close my eyes, because I can picture the moment: me pinned against a shelf in the New York Public Library, Sasha huge in my field of vision as he plucked a book from over my head and thrust it into my hands. Long before love was ever a concept in our heads, he knew that there was more to this than we knew how to face. So he borrowed someone else's words to say what we refused to.

Under my breath, I recite the words from *Anna Karenina* in unison with him. *"He stepped down, trying not to look long at her, as if she were the sun. But he saw her, like the sun, even without looking."*

When we finish, he smiles. That lone tear glistens untouched on his cheekbone. "You are my sun, Ariel. You are the bird that flies above it. You are the light I cannot be—so let me be the shadow that keeps you pure. Let my hands be dirty so yours can be clean. Let my sleep be broken so yours can be whole. I'm not your nightmare; I'm the nightmare of anyone who would ever think of dimming one second of your shine. So this is my vow: I vow to keep you flying, *ptichka*. For as long as we both shall live."

48

SASHA

There are kisses, and then there are *kisses.*

This is the latter.

But then again, this part has always been so easy for us. As I pull Ariel into my arms, lower her halfway to the floor, and press my lips to hers, it's not that it feels so different than any kiss before.

It's that it feels *exactly* the same as the very first time.

The same tremor, low in my stomach.

The same certainty. The same fear.

The same nuclear, undeniable, blasphemous, holy fucking heat ripping through from me into her, from her into me, scorching us both and then remaking us from the ashes, over and over again, a million lifetimes passing with every second.

It felt like this when I kissed Ariel in a bathroom, before I ever knew her name. It feels like that now. And then in so many places in between: libraries and forests, bathhouses and mountains, New York and Paris, day and night, in love and in hate, in lust and in longing. The world has changed shape around us a thousand times. But this—the feeling of her mouth searing against mine—has always, always been here.

Coming back up to standing feels like bobbing back to the surface of an ocean in the middle of a hurricane. It's wild up here. Everyone is losing their minds.

Feliks learned how to fucking *whistle,* apparently, and Gina must be to blame, because the two of them are like goddamn tea kettles as they blast off repeatedly.

Zoya found what appears to be an unlimited supply of dry rice. She and Kosti are hurling it at us with matching wicked grins. For a pair of old fogeys, their aim and velocity are both surprising. It's like getting hit with shrapnel.

Belle is clapping along as Marco starts up on an accordion, which, safe to say, is not my preferred brand of music.

At least Pavel and Lora aren't actively assaulting us. That's probably because no one has ever cried as hard as Lora is crying without needing an emergency IV to rehydrate. There is a literal puddle in her lap, and it's all Pavel can do to keep her upright. Happy tears—I think—but lots of them.

"*Bozhe moy,*" I mutter against Ariel's mouth. "Can we not have one moment of peace?"

She laughs, the sound pure sunshine. "Peace was never really our style anyway."

At some point, the hooligans ease up and let us walk down the aisle without an excessive number of projectiles aimed at our heads and eardrums. Laughing, they pour in behind us as we all go to the banquet table set up for the reception.

The tables themselves are as at-risk as my wife and I are. They're sagging beneath the weight of metric tons of Zoya's pierogis and bottle after bottle of Marco's reds.

I nudge Ariel. "Which one of those bottles do you think is our 'special blend'?"

Her cheeks go scarlet as she elbows me hard in the ribs. "If you breathe a word about that to anybody, I will kill you. Husband or not, you will not be safe from my wrath."

I laugh as I drape my arm over her shoulders and pull her into my embrace. "You should've put that in your vows."

We settle into our seats in the midst of all our loved ones. Fairy lights shiver in the warm breath of night—fireflies trapped in glass. I count them and shake my head in amazement.

One of them for each time I almost lost this.

I've never been one for parties. Too many variables, too many opportunities for things to go wrong. But watching my wife—*my wife;* hell, I'll never tire of saying that—glow in the candlelight as she listens to Gina tell a story, I find myself enjoying it in a way I never knew was possible.

I'm *at ease.* Not at arms, but at ease. Completely unconcerned.

We eat and drink and drink and eat—sparkling water for Ariel, though I think she's drunk enough on the moment that the lack of alcohol doesn't bother her in the least. Zoya truly outdid herself, and on a ridiculous lack of prep time, too. In the middle of the long table is the crowning glory: a sturgeon that could feed ten times the number of guests, flesh decorated with paper-thin cucumber slices and fresh herbs. Around it, mounds of black caviar glitter like bullet casings, cradled in delicate blini that release wisps of steam into the perfumed air. Greek dolmades surround the centerpiece in concentric circles, stuffed with herb-scented rice and pine nuts. Belle swears that she'll take the recipe to her grave. Spanakopita and moussaka, beef stroganoff with mushrooms and sour cream, gleaming buttered noodles, crimson borscht —it's endless. Obscene. When Zoya dips into the kitchen and comes back with platters of dessert, everyone lets out a horrified groan.

The whole time, Ariel sits beside me, one hand resting on her belly while the other stays linked with mine under the table. She hasn't stopped smiling since we said our vows.

When not a single person is capable of putting down a single calorie more, Jasmine stands. She's got her violin in hand. We all fall silent. "Ariel asked me to make something for their first dance. Just... I don't know," she mumbles. "It doesn't have a name. It's just... well, it's just the best I could do."

I rise and help Ariel to her feet. She comes with me, lips parted in the softest smile. "I'm too huge for this," she protests weakly. "Even if I wasn't a billion months pregnant, I just had enough food to stuff an elephant."

"You look beautiful to me," I murmur.

She blushes and rolls her eyes. "You're the one who has to watch me waddle in place."

"Then let's make it a first waddle to remember." I kiss her neck, the sensitive spot just below the cliff of her jaw that she pretends not to love. She squirms, laughs, butts her head into my shoulder.

She is everything to me.

When I nod to Jasmine, she begins to play.

The first notes pierce the night air like silver arrows. I recognize the melody immediately—an old Russian lullaby my mother used to hum.

But then, as Ariel and I sway on the grass, it shifts, weaving into something else. A Greek folk song, maybe. Then the lullaby again. Russian, Greek, back and forth, melting into something altogether new.

Beside me, Ariel's breath catches. Tears spill down her cheeks as she listens to her sister play. Jasmine's eyes are closed, her body swaying with the rhythm.

I spin Ariel out, then reel her back in, pressing my lips to her temple. "I love you, Ariel Ozerova," I whisper into her hair.

She melts against me, and I feel her tears dampen my shirt. But these aren't the tears of fear or grief I've seen her shed before. These are the tears of a woman who has everything she ever wanted.

The song arcs into a crescendo. Melancholy transformed into something else. Alchemized. From grief to gratitude and then to something beyond.

One last note. It lingers, echoes, triples, fades... Then the cicadas begin to sing along.

Nothing has ever been more perfect.

From there, the dance floor fills in. Gina connects to a speaker and starts blasting music, and I've had enough wine to let Ariel keep me out there. Feliks twirls Gina, Marco has Belle dizzy with affection, and even Pavel is taking awkward with Lora, shuffling steps from side to side, somewhat in tune with the beat.

Ariel's laugh warms the hollow of my throat as we dance—her hips cradled in my palms, my chin hooked over her shoulder.

But when I glance over at the table, I frown.

Because Zoya is sitting by herself.

I scan the garden as I sway with Ariel, keeping my movements smooth so she doesn't notice my sudden tension. A quick headcount reveals one missing.

Where is Kosti?

My arms tighten fractionally around Ariel's waist. She hums contentedly and nestles closer, completely unaware that anything might be amiss. Her pearls catch the fairy lights as she moves.

"Happy?" she murmurs against my chest.

"More than I deserve to be," I answer honestly, even as my eyes continue their sweep of the perimeter.

Twenty minutes ago, Kosti was right there by the wine station, trading war stories with Feliks. It could be anything. He could've been sent to the kitchen to replenish the water pitchers. Hell, he could've stepped inside to take a piss.

But the space where he should be is glaringly wrong. Like a face savagely ripped out of a family photograph.

I press a kiss to Ariel's temple, breathe in the familiar peach scent of her hair, and catch Feliks's eye over her head. *Kosti?* I mouth.

His brow furrows. He does the same sweep I just did, then meets my eyes again.

Both our frowns tilt further downward.

A slight tilt of my chin is all it takes. He passes Gina to Lora and immediately makes his way toward the villa, whistling happily, casual enough not to draw attention.

"What are you thinking about?" Ariel asks, pulling back to study my face.

I school my features into perfect contentment. "How beautiful you look in candlelight."

She laughs and swats my chest. "Smooth talker. Do you think you're getting lucky tonight or something?"

"I did have plans for you."

"Oh, yeah?" She grins seductively. "What kind of plans?"

We turn another slow circle. Through the windows, I track Feliks's progress through the villa's ground floor. No sign of alarm yet, but the knot in my gut won't ease.

Not tonight, I think fiercely. *Whatever this is, it can't happen tonight.*

But then Feliks appears at an upstairs window. Kosti's room. Even from here, I can see his face is stricken and pale.

He crooks his finger at me.

Come here.

49

SASHA

I bend down and press a kiss to Ariel's temple. "Gonna go find the bathroom, *moya zhena,*" I murmur in her ear. "Don't have too much fun without me."

She laughs and pulls me down for one more kiss on the lips. "No promises."

But the smile dies on my face when I start the trek into the villa.

Feliks meets me by the foot of the stairs. From the dance floor, his face was bad; up close, it's far, far worse.

"You look like you've seen a ghost," I tell him.

He just shakes his head. "Wait until you see."

I don't know what I'm bracing myself for as we mount the staircase and go down the hall to Kosti's bedroom. A heart attack? Did the old man slip and fall? Did the cigarettes finally catch up and exact their vengeance?

It occurs to me, perhaps for the first time, what a debt I owe Kosti. I feel like a selfish bastard for waiting this long to see it. He dragged me from that alley and saved my life. Why? Was it loyalty for Leander? Hatred for Dragan? Love for Jasmine, or simply balancing the scales?

He did so much more than simply pull me out of harm's way, though. For six months, he stood over me. Stood by me. Kept me breathing. Kept me sane. And if he did it by irritating the fuck out of me sometimes—well, we each have our own methods.

Never once did he ask for thanks or repayment. No matter how many times I offered it, he'd simply shrug it off and light another cigarette. "You owe me nothing, *neania*," he'd say. "Not one red cent."

So my teeth are clenched as I round the corner to his room, ready for blood or an old man on death's doorstep.

What I find instead is…

Nothing.

The closets are stripped bare. His go-bag, always packed and ready by the door, is missing. His bed has been neatly made, sheets drawn taut. It's like he was never fucking here.

Actually, that's not entirely true. The desk is the only item of furniture that still shows some signs of life. I see a black, rubberized phone. A notepad. And a laptop with a stark red screen.

"Feliks," I growl, pointing at the computer screen, "what the fuck is that?"

In the center of the screen is a skull and crossbones. Beneath that, two words: ***DELETION COMPLETE.***

"It's wiped," he explains. "Roza's showed me something like this before—it's like taking a nuke to the hard drive. There's nothing left to salvage, no matter how good you are."

He passes me the phone and the notepad. The inbox contains a single text, with a string of coordinates. On the top page of the notepad…

I'M SORRY, **NEANIA.**

I drop them both. Standing in the middle of the room, I look around. The evidence is staring me in the face, but I don't want to see it. I refuse to see it. I won't fucking allow it to take shape in my head.

Feliks fidgets at my side. He can see what I'm denying. He knows it as well as I do.

Through the window, we can hear the music and laughter from my wedding reception. My wife's joy, pure and perfect, floating on the night air.

All I can think is, *It's not fucking fair.* The world is not a fair place; I've known that since the day I was born. No one earns what they get, or gets what they deserve. It just *is.* Everything simply *is.*

And what this is is betrayal.

I feel sick to my stomach. But I force myself to paste on a smile when I hear a knock at the door and I turn to see Jasmine appearing in the doorway.

"Hey, goofs!" she says brightly. "Ariel's starting to open presents downstairs. She's looking for you."

I step in front of the laptop so she doesn't get the chance to see. The burner phone and notepad get tucked into my pockets. Still grinning, I nod. "Perfect. We're right behind you."

But Jasmine isn't stupid. Her eyes narrow as she takes in the stripped room, the tense set of my shoulders. "What's wrong?"

"Nothing," I say roughly. "Tell Ariel I'll be there in a minute."

She doesn't move right away. "I'll keep her distracted," she warns. "But hurry. You know how perceptive she is."

I nod once, sharply. "Thank you."

As Jasmine's footsteps fade down the hall, I turn to Feliks. "Get Pavel. Search the grounds. He can't have gone far. And call Roza. I want to know exactly what kind of deletion program that is."

"And you?"

I straighten my jacket, already moving toward the door. "I'm going to go watch my wife open presents and pretend this is still the happiest day of my life."

Everything that was so perfect earlier is now cloying and wrong. The garden's scent is overwhelming; the fairy lights are tacky, fake, fucking ridiculous. I look around at the rice still scattering the grass and wonder how we ever convinced ourselves that it was okay to be normal for a little while.

But I can't show her that. I vowed to be darkness so she can be light, and I'll defend that vow with my last fucking breath. Tonight, that means contorting my face into a smile as I step out of the villa.

Ariel's laughter rings out—bright, trusting, *wrong*—and my teeth grind together. She's perched on a wrought-iron chair, swollen belly brushing the edge of the gift table.

"Sasha, look!" She holds up a ridiculous lace lingerie set, laughing hysterically. "Gina knew exactly what size you'd be!"

I want to laugh. Fuck me, wouldn't it be nice if I could laugh? But there will be no lingerie tonight. All of the plans I had for Ariel are gone now. Dust in the wind. If we're lucky, we'll survive. If we're unlucky...

I won't dwell on that yet.

Still chuckling, she sets the lingerie in her lap and picks up a small envelope. "From Uncle Kosti!" she announces, holding it aloft. She looks around for him and frowns. "Is he still peeing? My God, old man bladders are even worse than pregnant ladies'. Oh, well. I'm sure he'll be back in a sec."

No. My pulse jackhammers in my throat, but I can't speak. *Don't open it. Don't—*

Too late. The seal cracks under her thumbnail. The letter inside comes rustling out.

Ariel's smile dies mid-sentence.

I see the exact moment the words sink in—the blood draining from her face, her knuckles whitening around the paper. Her lips move soundlessly, tracing some fresh horror.

Then she stands. The lingerie slides from her lap and lands with a plop in a patch of mud. Black earth staining the white. Sucking up the muck, the filth, the ugly reminder that nothing in my world can ever remain pure for long. Not even for one night.

The letter goes next. It flutters out of her hand like a dying bird and lands at her feet. I'm close enough to see the same handwriting on it as the words written on Kosti's notepad.

No. Not like this. Not again.

Ariel's eyes find mine. "Not again," she whispers. "Not again."

Then her horrified face gets hit with a lightning bolt of pain. She plummets to her knees with a hand pressed to her womb.

The scream she lets out shatters my world.

50

ARIEL

Koukla,

You're reading this because I'm already gone. Don't look for me. By the time your tears dry on this page, I'll be halfway to a place where men like me don't get to die old.

I've told you this before, but I was there the day you were born. I held you, pink and squalling, in my arms. As I did, I promised I would keep you safe. I swore it on the saints, even though we both know I stopped believing in anything but the weight of a gun years ago.

So you must believe me on this point: I tried.

Koukla, *I swear to you I tried.*

When Leander betrothed Jasmine to that Serbian dog, I thought, This is how it starts. The rot. The slow bleed. *But I was a coward. Told myself it wasn't my place to interfere. That the Makris girls were born to be bargaining chips, and who was I to question the currency of our world?*

But it didn't take long to show me how wrong the rules of our world truly are.

Your sister came to me once, in those ugly first weeks. Eyes bruised like overripe plums. I cleaned the blood from her split lip and thought, This is where loyalty gets us. This is the cost of silence. *I tried to stop it. I told Leander that Dragan had a taste for cutting up girls who talked back.*

Your father merely shrugged. "Jasmine knows her duty."

Then he sent her back to the beast.

It was Sasha who came to tell us that Jasmine was dead. He said the Serbian brute had done what brutes like him do—gone too far. Put her in a grave she did not deserve. I beat myself senseless and I swore that, next time, if there was a next time, I would not sit by idly. I would act.

But, as you know, your sister wasn't dead. For fifteen years, we thought she was. We were wrong.

Everything changed the night of your engagement party.

I'd been digging, Ariel—digging and hunting and searching, because something in my heart said the story did not add up. I was right! You cannot imagine how good it felt to learn that I was right. When I heard Jasmine's voice... It was like she was born again. That she, like you, was once again a pink and happy baby in my arms.

She told me what Sasha had done. How he learned of her suffering and offered her a way out. How he snatched her from Dragan in the dead of the night, framed him for a "murder," and gave her a new lease on life.

You might still think that's what happened. You might still believe he saved her. My God, what a story it is! The noble Bratva prince, smuggling Jasmine to Marseille like some fairytale knight!

But then I learned otherwise.

You see, koukla, *some knights raise the dragons they slay. Sasha didn't merely discover Dragan's cruelty—he* cultivated *it. He fed the man's worst impulses during long nights playing chess and sipping rakija. Laughed when Dragan bragged about breaking his last woman's ribs. "A man who can't control his woman is no man at all," Dragan would say, and Sasha would raise his glass. "To control."*

He needed the alliance to fracture. Needed your father desperate enough to hand you *over next—because he knew that, when the time came, Sasha would be the one who received the Greek's alliance. So he made sure Dragan's hands were around Jasmine's throat before he ever laid eyes on her.*

Sasha did not save Jasmine from her marriage.

He condemned *her to it.*

At first, I wanted to kill him. To toy with the lives of innocents like that... it is beyond the pale. But as I sat with the thought, it occurred to me that killing Sasha would not be enough. As long as men like him exist—men like Dragan, men like your father—they will keep using the people around them as pawns. The only way to truly protect you both was to bring down the whole game. To set the kingpins at each other's throats.

That is what I've done.

I know the price of what I've done is measured in blood. Perhaps I'm no better than them now. But I couldn't watch another generation of Makris women be sacrificed on the altar of men's ambitions.

The only thing that gave me pause was you, my darling. I know you think you love him. I've watched you twist yourself into knots trying to reconcile the monster with the man. But some stains don't come out, no matter how hard you scrub. When I saw you glowing at that altar tonight, I knew I had to make my choice.

Either I burn this whole fucking world down, or I let him poison you, too.

I couldn't do that. I made a promise the day you were born. This is what that promise looks like.

So forgive me. Or don't. But above all, I beg of you this: don't let him spin this into another pretty lie. The man you married didn't change. He simply learned to hide his knife better.

Your uncle,

Kosti

I look up. Sasha stands a dozen yards away from me, looking back.

He took off his jacket while we were dancing. Now, the first raindrops of a storm that snuck over the horizon splatter against his shoulders. Every single one leaves its mark.

"Not again," I whisper. "Not again."

The letter slips from my fingers. It touches the dirt at my feet. As it does, something rips through me. Lightning, but not lightning in the sky. This is lightning from *within*.

With it comes a fear. I wish I had a word, but it's unlike any fear I've ever felt before. Even if I did know how to describe it, the pain it brings muzzles me. All I can do is let out an inhuman wail as the lightning forks and branches and burns parts of me that only my babies' dancing feet have ever touched.

I crash to my hands and knees. It's as if decades pass as I crouch there, on all fours like an animal, screaming wordlessly. I'm being burned alive, squeezed by a cruel god's giant fist.

Finally, slowly, it relents. I can feel it preparing to strike again, though. Like it's merely inhaling between efforts.

I look up again at Sasha. He's blurred and refracted by my tears. Torn between coming to my rescue and knowing that he's the last person alive I ever want to touch me again.

Not again.

Not again.

"You... you knew," I choke out. "You let him hurt her. You orchestrated it."

His eyes frost over. "It wasn't like that."

Thunder rumbles over the horizon. As I watch, distant lightning—the real kind—breaks on top of the hills. They look like teeth chewing the sky. Jagged, broken, rotting teeth.

I hate this place. I hate this place so fucking much. I want out of here and away from him.

But as the next bolt of lightning in my womb cracks, I'm pinned on hands and knees to the earth.

I bite down my cheek so I don't scream this time. But the skin doesn't last long—when it gives way, I taste and feel the hot trickle of blood.

I spit the blood on the soil between my hands and look up again. The rain is thickening now, coming down harder. Soon, Sasha's white shirt is drenched and ruined.

"You told me you saved her. *Saved* her, Sasha? Do you even know what that means? Are you even capable of doing something selfless?"

In the corner of my eye, I see Jasmine bend down next to me and pick up the letter. Her hand flies to her mouth as she reads. A horrified gasp stills on her lips, halfway between swallowed and screamed.

"I was wrong," Sasha whispers. "I am not the man I was then."

I bark out a laugh at that. "How can you not be? No, better question: how the *fuck* am I supposed to believe that? You're just such a pretty liar, Sasha Ozerov. You make the world look however you want it to look. And I'm stupid enough to fall for it, every single time."

I plant a hand on the chair I was in moments ago and use it to leverage myself up. Mama comes rushing to help me, but I wave her off. I want to do this alone.

Next to me, Jasmine is slowly sinking into a chair of her own. She's eggshell white, that hand still covering her mouth like it'll stop the screams from coming just as long as she keeps it there.

"You married me," he rasps. "Some part of you at least has to believe I'm telling you the truth. I am not what I was then, Ariel. You looked into my eyes an hour ago and I know you saw that I'm changed."

The rain turns his shirt translucent. I want to claw it off him. I want to claw *him* off the earth.

"You think a vow fixes it?" My voice fragments into a thousand shards. "You think marrying me erases what you did to my sister?"

Lightning again, overhead and within at the same time. I grit my teeth against the agony as the rain pours, pours, pours.

"It wasn't like that." His hands flex like he wants to reach for me. Like he still has the right.

"Bullshit." I press a palm to the molten, churning ache in my belly. "You fed her to him. You sat there while he—"

"I kept her *alive!*" The roar bursts out of him, raw and ragged. "One way or another, Leander was going to do what he wanted. He would've killed her for refusing the match. Dragan would've skinned her alive if she'd fled without my help. So yes—I let him think cruelty was our common language. I let Dragan carve his initials into the world so I could carve mine into his throat when it mattered."

Another contraction. White-hot supernova, pressure like the earth crushing me in its jaws.

Sasha takes a step forward. "Ariel—"

"Don't." I spit blood and rainwater at his feet. "Don't you dare make this sound noble. You didn't save her. You used her. Used me. You needed Leander's empire. Jas and me... we're nothing more than the shiny keys."

Thunder drowns out his curse. When it passes, he's closer— close enough that I smell the storm on his skin. "You really believe that? After everything?"

"I believe *this.*" I fumble the letter from Jasmine's slack grip and shove it against his chest. "You let him hurt her. You laughed."

He doesn't look at the paper. His eyes stay locked on mine, blue going black at the edges. "You want the truth? Fine. The first time Dragan cracked her rib, I drank with him until dawn. When he bragged about making her beg, I refilled his glass. And every second—" His voice breaks. "Every fucking second, I told myself it was the price of keeping her breathing."

I'm distantly aware that the rain has become torrential. Damn near biblical. We'll have to go in soon, or we'll be swept away.

But no one moves. My mother, Zoya, Marco, Gina, Lora, Pavel, Feliks—all of them watch in mute, dumbfounded shock as Sasha, Jasmine, and I stand still in this fucked-up triangle that none of us can escape.

"But the real truth," Sasha snarls, "the only one I know you'll believe, is this: I would do it all again."

Mama gasps.

Feliks's jaw drops.

My eyes stay fixated on Sasha. Only on Sasha.

"I would do it all again," he repeats as he advances toward me where I stand, clinging to the iron chair like a crutch. "I would mold Dragan to be violent. I would arrange his marriage to Jasmine. I would help her fake her death. I would send her across the ocean. I would tell you and your father and your mother that she'd died. I would plan with Leander to make you my bride. I'd let you keep mourning your sister, thinking she was dead. I would redo every lie, every betrayal, every cruel, calculating deception… because it brought me to you."

It hurts. What he's saying hurts and what's happening inside me hurts. All around us, the storm moans as if the world itself is hurting, too.

I close my eyes as tears become rain, and both of them soak through my wedding dress. "I thought I knew you," I whisper. "I thought I saw the real man beneath the monster. But there is no beneath, is there? The monster is all there is."

Lightning flashes. In the strobe, I see it: the exact moment his heart fractures.

I don't have long to linger on him, though. Because the next contraction that comes is the most undeniable yet. Then pain blots out everything: his face, the storm, the lies. Just fire and pressure and the terrible, tearing sense of *split*.

Mama rushes to my side, her hands cool on my face. "The babies," she gasps. "Something's wrong."

"We need to get her to a hospital," Gina says, already pulling out her phone. But after a moment, she curses. "No signal."

Zoya starts barking orders; Lora quivers; Feliks and Pavel stand with fists clench, caught between love and loyalty. Marco, poor bastard, doesn't know what the hell he's wandered into.

But I barely have eyes for any of them. My world is shrinking down to a one-inch wide pinpoint, focused on Sasha's face. It's all I can see.

Feliks appears at Sasha's shoulder. "The storm's knocked out the power lines. The roads will be flooding soon."

Sasha says nothing.

Feliks again, rain plastering his hair to his forehead: "Boss. Kosti's trail is still fresh. If we move now, we might catch him before he vanishes completely."

Sasha says nothing.

"Sasha, goddammit, you have to decide! Do something, for fuck's sake! Choose!"

51

SASHA

I thought I would've been better prepared for this. How many times have I watched men die at my feet, cursing my name with their last breaths? How much blood have I seen oozing into the ground right in front of me?

I've seen death. Hatred. God knows I've seen blood.

Nothing made me ready for this, though.

The storm howls like a living thing. In front of me, lying prostrate in the dirt, Ariel screams like the exact opposite: like something unholy and wrong. Through the curtain of rain, I watch as her face—my wife's face, my fucking *wife*— contorts in pain. Every bolt of lightning illuminates it whiter and whiter, worse and worse.

Another contraction hits. Ariel's fingers dig into the ground. Blood trickles from the corner of her mouth where she's bitten through her cheek to keep from screaming.

My feet won't move. I'm caught between the magnetic poles of duty and love, paralyzed by the choice before me.

Feliks's phone buzzes. He answers, listens, then curses violently in Russian. *"Blyat'.* Boss—"

"Not now." My voice sounds strange, distant.

"You need to hear this." He grabs my shoulder, forces me to look at him. "Roza just called. Dragan's men are hitting us everywhere at once. The warehouse on 49th. The clubs in Brighton Beach. The shipping terminal. Even the old safehouse in Queens. They knew exactly where to strike."

The implications sink in slowly, like poison spreading through my veins. "Kosti."

"He must have been feeding them intel for weeks. Maybe months." Feliks runs a hand through his rain-soaked hair. "Everything we rebuilt after the last attack—it's all burning, boss. Right fucking now."

My empire is crumbling. Again. But this time, the betrayal cuts deeper because it comes from within.

From *family*.

Another bolt of lightning splits the sky. In its flash, I see Ariel's jaw open wide, but no sound comes out.

"The contractions are too close together," Zoya says, her voice tight with worry. "The babies are coming."

The old me wouldn't have hesitated. The old me would already be in a car, racing toward the coordinates on Kosti's burner, leaving a trail of blood and bodies in my wake. The old me would've chosen power over love every single time.

But I'm not that man anymore.

… Am I?

I close my eyes. Everything I've built, everything I've killed for, is slipping through my fingers like water. One word from me could save it all. One choice.

Another scream tears through the storm. This one isn't thunder—it's Ariel.

My eyes snap open. "Tell Roza to get everyone out. Save what they can."

"And Kosti?"

"Let him run."

His eyebrows shoot up. "Sasha—"

"I said let him fucking run." I'm already moving toward Ariel. "My wife needs me."

But before I can reach her, something catches my eye. Jasmine, who's been silent since reading Kosti's letter, suddenly stands. Her face is a mask of cold fury I've never seen before.

Feliks doesn't see it coming. None of us do. One moment, Jasmine's a statue, carved from marble and old scars. The next—

She lunges forward and snatches the gun from his hand, along with the burner phone. Growling, he lunges right back at her—but he freezes when she levels the gun at his chest.

Everyone goes deathly still. "Jasm—"

"Not another fucking word, Sasha." Her voice doesn't shake. It's the steady hum of high-tension wires carrying too much load.

Behind me, Ariel's scream crests and breaks against the storm. I don't turn. Can't. Every muscle coils, ready to intervene—but the gun's safety switches off with a click that drowns out thunder.

Feliks leans toward her, hand outstretched. "Jasmine, if you just give me the—"

"Try it," she dares. "See what happens."

He takes a half-step forward. "Jasmine, goddammit, put that down before—"

The gun swings his way. "Back. The. Fuck. Up."

Rain soaks through my shirt, my skin, my bones. I taste iron. Everything's rusted through.

"Jasmine," I say carefully, "you don't want to do this."

"Really?" Her laugh is bitter, sharp-edged. "You think you know what I want? You've always thought that, haven't you? That you know best. That we should all dance to your song."

"Jas—"

"Fifteen years," she whispers. "For fifteen years, I've been grateful to you. Thanked you in my prayers. Called you my *savior*." She spits the last word like it tastes foul. "But you weren't saving me at all, were you? You were just… trading up. A better deal. A fresher pawn."

"It wasn't like that," I say. The same thing I told Ariel. But the words sound hollow even to my own ears the second time around.

"Oh, yes, it was." She sighs. "But as much as I might want to, I won't kill you. Not because my sister loved you, though the devil knows you don't deserve a drop of her goodness. I'm only letting you live because of those children. You won't ever see them, if I have my way. You'll never lay a fucking finger on them. But they will know that somewhere out in the world, you exist. That's for *them.* Not for you."

Jasmine's eyes—*her* eyes, Ariel's eyes, Makris eyes—glint in the lightning. "Now, answer me this: Is he with Dragan?"

"You should—"

She jabs the gun into my chest. "Where is Kosti going?" The gun doesn't waver. "Tell me the truth. You think he's with Dragan, don't you?"

I hesitate. Behind me, thunder crashes.

The safety clicks off.

"Don't lie to me," Jasmine snarls. "Not again. Never again. Where. Is. He. Going?"

I close my eyes briefly. "Yes. The coordinates on that phone —my best guess is that they lead to Dragan."

"Good." She starts backing away, the gun still trained on my heart. "That's where I'm going, then."

"*Ti mou,*" Belle cries, "please—"

"Don't follow me." Jasmine's voice lashes out. "Any of you. I mean it. I'm done being pushed around. Done being someone's piece. From now on, I move myself."

"You'll die," I tell her roughly.

Her smile is terrible to behold. "Maybe. But at least it will be my choice. My move. For once in my life, I get to decide what happens to Jasmine Makris."

She retreats. A step at a time. The rain pounds harder. Through sheets of it, I watch her fade into shadow.

Then she's gone.

I stand frozen, staring into the darkness where she disappeared. The coordinates on that phone will lead her straight to Dragan. To certain death.

But when I turn back to Ariel, I know I cannot follow. She's curled on her side in the mud, face contorted in agony as another contraction rips through her.

My wife needs me.

My children need me.

Even as my sister-in-law runs headlong into death's arms, I know there's only one choice I can make.

I drop to my knees beside Ariel and gather her into my arms. "I've got you, *ptichka*," I whisper. "I'm here. I'm not going anywhere."

She sobs and clutches my shirt. Whether from pain or grief or if she simply wants to drag me into the pain with her, I'll never know.

But I do know this: sometimes, the most brutal choice is staying still while the world burns around you.

So here I stay.

As thunder shakes the sky, here I stay.

As Jasmine races toward death, here I stay.

As Kosti spins his webs, as Dragan laughs, as my empire is reduced to rubble and ash…

Here I stay. Here I stay. Here I *stay*.

52

SASHA

"We need to get her inside," Feliks bellows over the storm. "It's fucking Armageddon out here, man!"

I shake my head and roar back, "It's too late to move her!"

Together, we rip the tablecloth free, sending dishes and food clattering to the ground. The wind fights us, but we manage to create a crude shelter, anchoring it to chairs and tables with anything we can find: our belts, a string of the fairy lights, Pavel's shoelaces. It's not much, but it keeps the worst of the rain off Ariel's face.

But I don't even know if she notices. She's beyond us now. Elsewhere. Delirious from pain as the contractions cluster closer and closer together.

Zoya thrusts a phone flashlight into my free hand. The beam judders across Ariel's face—sweat-slick, pallid, pupils blown wide. Her lips move soundlessly around words that might be my name or a curse or both.

Her dress and hair are plastered to her. Black tears run down her cheeks. Her mouth is a bottomless O, ringed with red.

Worse, though, is the red slicking her thighs. Zoya is crouched low as Belle cradles Ariel's head in her lap. Gina and Lora sit on either side, stunned into ashen silence.

Lightning comes. Thunder follows. The villa's lit windows flicker once, twice, then die completely. Darkness swallows us whole as the power gives up and the fairy lights are extinguished.

"*Blyat',*" Feliks curses, fumbling with his phone's flashlight. The beam catches Ariel's face at an awful angle, highlighting the agony etched into every line.

Ariel's fingers dig into my forearm. "Sasha…" she moans, eyelids fluttering, eyes unseeing.

"I'm here." I brush wet hair from her face. "I've got you."

"J-J-Jasmine," she whispers. "Where's Jasmine?"

"Breathe, Ariel. Save your strength."

But she thrashes against me. "Have to… have to find her…"

"Hush now." I tighten my grip as another contraction hits. Her back arches, a sound like breaking glass tearing from her throat.

Zoya snarls at Lora, who runs inside and returns with an armful of towels and the villa's first aid supplies. It's not much, but it's all we have. Belle follows with a pot of water that's nowhere near as hot as we need, but it'll have to do.

The storm rages. Thunder cracks overhead like artillery fire. And through it all, Ariel burns in my arms, caught between consciousness and delirium, calling for a sister I let slip away into the night.

I've never felt more powerless in my life. Not even when my father had barbed wire around my throat. At least then, I knew how to fight back.

But this? This is a different kind of helplessness entirely. All I can do is hold on and pray to a God I stopped believing in long ago that He'll keep her safe through this night.

In the strobe of Feliks's phone and the intermittent lightning, I count the seconds between Ariel's pulses. They're rabbit-quick under my palm. Too fast. The medical kit lies gutted at our feet: gauze, scissors, a half-roll of surgical tape. Useless tools for this wet, screaming dark.

Zoya's hands disappear between Ariel's legs. "Head's crowning."

Ariel's breath hitches. "No—no, it's too soon—"

"Breathe," I order, thumbs digging into the base of Ariel's spine. She'd mocked these positions weeks ago—*Who needs a birthing ball when you've got a Bratva boss?*—but now, her body arches instinctively into the pressure.

"Fuck your—*ah!*—breathing techniques." Her fingers dig into the wet earth. "God, it hurts."

"I know, *ptichka*." I keep my hands steady on her back, kneading the muscles there. "But you're doing so well."

She barks out another laugh, this one edged with hysteria. "Remember our first Lamaze class? When Gina was pretending to be the teacher?" Her words break off in a gasp as the contraction peaks. "Bet you... wish you'd paid more attention now."

"Inhale for four counts," I say calmly, demonstrating. "Hold for seven. Exhale for eight."

Her eyes narrow even through the pain. "Y-you... actually remember?"

"Of course I do." I stroke her back as she tries to match my breathing. "I remember everything about that day. The ridiculous exercises. The way you kept almost breaking character to laugh. How beautiful you looked, even when you were trying your hardest to push me away." I lean close to her ear. "Now breathe with me, Ariel. Just like we practiced. In... hold... out..."

She follows my lead, our breaths syncing as the contraction slowly ebbs. For a moment, we're back in that silly class, before everything went wrong.

Before truth became lies and love became ash in our mouths.

But then thunder crashes overhead, and reality crashes back with it. My wife is in labor too early, my sister-in-law is hunting a monster in the dark, and my world is burning down around me.

"Push!" Zoya urges, hands frantic near Ariel's knees.

Ariel's skull cracks against my collarbone. "I can't—"

"You can." My palm splays across her heaving stomach. "You will."

But then I see Zoya's face tighten with concern. "The first one is breech," she mutters to me in clipped Russian. "*Blyat.* We need to turn the baby."

Ariel's eyes roll wildly. "What? What's wrong?"

"Nothing's wrong." I keep my voice steady even as fear claws at my throat. "The baby's just coming feet-first. We're going to help them turn."

Her fingers dig into my forearm hard enough to draw blood. "Don't lie to me. Not now. Not about this."

"Never about this." I meet her gaze. "Trust me one last time. Just for this moment."

Thunder crashes. In its echo, I hear her whisper, "I don't know if I can."

But she has no choice. None of us do.

"On the next contraction," Zoya instructs, "you'll need to help me guide the baby. Your hands are bigger, stronger."

I nod, shifting position. Ariel's thighs tremble against my palms as I brace her legs wider. The intimacy of it strikes me —how many times have I touched her like this in passion?

But never in pain. Never in fear.

"Ready?" Zoya asks as Ariel's body tenses. She grabs my wrist, shoving it into the wet heat. "Find the heel. Gently."

My fingers brush something—knobbed ankle, petal-soft skin. Ariel jerks, a wounded sound tearing from her throat.

"Hold her still," Zoya barks at Pavel.

He pins Ariel's shoulders as I work. Muscle memory from field dressings and snapped bones means nothing here. The child's foot slips through my grip like smoke.

"Clockwise," Zoya snaps. "Now."

Ariel's scream shreds the storm. "You're killing him—"

"Push," Zoya commands. "Now!"

Ariel bears down. Her teeth sink into my forearm. I'm grateful for it—the pain is clean. Honest. A penance I'll wear forever. I feel the exact moment the baby turns, life itself rotating beneath my hands. Then suddenly, incredibly, a head emerges.

The child comes free, pearl-white in the flashlight's dying beam. Zoya's hands dart in to catch the mewling bundle. "Boy."

She passes the child to Belle, who swaddles him in fresh blankets and begins to clean him. Then Zoya looks back to me with a grim nod.

"One more," I say roughly. "One more, Ariel. You can do this."

Ariel clutches me tighter. "No—I can't—"

"You can."

We do it all again. Screams soaking into the ground, along with the rain, with the roots of the plants we put there together. Heaven is cracking wide open above us as Ariel pushes and pushes—and at last, our daughter slides into the world.

Her first cry splits the night like lightning. Strong. Defiant. *Alive*.

Ariel reaches, but I'm already transferring the girl to her chest. Belle does the same. Her arms close around both infants, a fortress of tangled limbs and milk-scent.

"They're perfect," she says, voice thick with tears. "So perfect."

Zoya makes quick work of the umbilical cords. Ariel is cradling both children. The boy is still loud as can be.

But my girl...

My daughter isn't breathing right.

Her lips are dusky blue, chest barely rising. Not the healthy pink of her brother, who continues to cry.

"Something's wrong," Ariel whispers, voice cracking. Her fingers clutch our son tighter as she stares at our daughter's limp form. "Sasha something's—"

I'm already moving, my notes from the Italian Lamaze class seared on the backs of my eyelids. "Give me a towel," I bark at Lora. She scrambles to comply.

Laying our daughter on the clean cloth, I tilt her head back slightly—God, she's so small, like a broken bird in my hands. Two fingers on her chest. Gentle puffs of air into her mouth and nose. One. Two.

"Come on, *malyshka*," I murmur. "Breathe for Papa."

Nothing.

Ariel's sobbing now, fumbling for our daughter with her free hand. I block her view with my shoulder. She doesn't need to see this. Doesn't need another reason to hate me if I fail.

More compressions. More breath.

"Please," I whisper. "Please."

For ten eternal seconds, the world narrows to just this: my fingers on her tiny chest, my breath trying to fill her lungs. I've killed men. Saved them, too. But never have I felt so utterly helpless as I do now, trying to coax life into this precious scrap of humanity that Ariel and I created.

Then—finally—a weak cry.

But right on its heels is the deep, splintering groan of ancient wood giving way. My head snaps up just as lightning illuminates the olive tree at the edge of the garden, its roots tearing free of the rain-soaked earth. Like God cracking his knuckles.

"Inside! Now!" Belle and Zoya each take a child. I gather Ariel into my arms, careful to jostle her as little as possible. She's limp as a rag doll, spent from bringing our children into this violent night. Against my chest, her skin burns with fever.

"The cellar!" Feliks calls over another thunderclap.

I nod. The cellar is built into the bedrock itself, with thick stone walls and a reinforced ceiling. If any part of this place can withstand nature's fury, it's there.

It withstood Ariel's fury already, not so long ago. Compared to that, the storm is nothing.

We descend in a grim procession. Pavel leads with his phone's flashlight, illuminating the narrow stairs. The beam catches cobwebs and bottles, casting strange shadows that dance like spirits on the walls.

The air down here is cool and damp, heavy with the musty sweetness of aging wine. I lay Ariel on a makeshift bed of tablecloths and jackets while Belle and Zoya tend to the twins.

"The storm's getting worse," Lora whispers, huddled against Pavel near the stairs.

As if to confirm her words, thunder shakes the foundations. Dust rains down from the ceiling.

But the old stones hold.

"S-Sasha…" Ariel's fingers find my wrist in the dark. Her grip is weak but insistent. "You have to go after her."

I know immediately who she means. "I'm not leaving you."

"Please." Her voice cracks. "She's out there alone. With *him*."

"You need me here."

"What I need is my sister alive." Fresh tears cut tracks through the dirt on her cheeks. "You did this. Now, fix it."

I close my eyes.

"She has the coordinates," I say softly. "She has Feliks's gun. She—"

"She has nothing but her pain and her rage." Ariel's fingers tighten. "And you gave her both. So you're the only one who can bring her back."

I look down at my wife: pale, trembling, but steel-spined even now. At our children, so new to this world of violence and vengeance. At the storm-dark cellar that can protect their bodies but not their souls.

"Go," Ariel whispers. "Make this right."

And God help me, I know I have to. This is my mess. My sin. My debt to pay.

I press my lips to her forehead, then each of our children's. When I straighten, my voice is steady despite the war in my chest.

"Feliks, with me. The rest of you… keep them safe."

Then I turn and climb the stairs, leaving my heart behind in that cellar as I head out to fix what I've done.

53

SASHA

The ruined church in Roccastrada stabs up from the mud like a rotten fang against the gaping maw of the storm-black sky. Rain pelts my face as I take my feet off the bike pedals, letting momentum carry me the last few yards through squelching, ankle-deep mud.

Of course it's here. When the coordinates from Kosti's phone dropped a pin on the map at this spot, I could only laugh out loud.

Almost ten weeks ago, Ariel and I sat in the pew here and I asked her to marry me.

These babies aren't your redemption arc, she told me then.

She was right. They're not. Jasmine is not. *She* is not.

But does that mean I cannot be redeemed?

Fuck if I know. It's not like my mind is clear enough to sort through things like that right now. I'm a half-drowned rat. The ride here was a wet, frigid hell and my hands still have Ariel's blood caked under the fingernails—but I could swear

I catch the milk-sweet scent of our children still clinging to my clothes.

I catch something else, too, as I leap off the bike and abandon it in the courtyard: Jasmine, slipping through the doors of the church as they loll wide like black tongues.

Feliks catches up to me and dumps his bike next to mine. "Sash—"

But I'm already chasing after Jasmine. I call her name, but she can't hear me over the storm. She disappears inside.

Fuck.

The place is dying to give up and collapse in on itself. Frescoes loom eerily in the lightning flash—saints with their eyes clawed out. The ivy-choked facade is more crack than not, with gaping holes where stained glass windows once filtered light into sacred spaces. Now, those holes just let the storm howl through like a demon's choir.

I'm half a step in the doors, hot on Jasmine's tracks, when I freeze.

"—should've stayed buried, *kurvo.*"

I'm still housed in enough shadow to stay out of sight. But halfway down the aisle stands Jasmine.

On the altar is Dragan Vukovic.

Kosti is at his side, looking more exhausted than I've ever seen him before.

Jasmine cuts a proud figure in the gloomy, rain-drenched dark. Feliks's gun shines bright in her hand, reflecting the sputtering firelight from the sconces that Dragan has lit.

I want to throw myself between her and them, but we're all spread too far. Dragan would bury a bullet in my skull before I even got halfway there.

So I start to edge around the perimeter in search of a better angle. It's slow-going, though, and with this much shattered glass and debris underfoot, one wrong step could tell them I'm here. Every step must be careful.

"You don't get to call me that," she calls out.

Dragan chuckles. "*Kurvo. Kukavico.* Daughter of a fucking corpse."

She shakes her head, wet hair slinging back and forth. "Do you feel good when you say those things? Do you feel like a man when you curse at me? When you put your hands on me?"

Kosti clears his throat. "Jasm—"

But her name isn't even halfway out of his mouth before Dragan turns and pistol-whips him with the butt of his gun.

I feel it like I'm the one who was struck. A tooth of Kosti's goes flying, followed by a spray of blood. He drops to one knee, coughing, wheezing.

Slowly, Dragan revolves to face Jasmine once again. "What do you expect to happen here tonight, little one?" He spreads his arms wide. "How would you like for this to go?"

Jasmine raises the gun. Her hands are quivering and the tip of the gun spirals wildly out of control.

Dragan smirks. "You think pointing that toy makes you brave? I remember how you screamed when—"

She fires.

The bullet grazes his ear. He laughs, blood threading his jawline. "That is about what I thought," he says with a nod.

Beside him, Kosti looks like he's aged a decade in a minute. His shoulders are a broken slump. When lightning flashes through, I catch the shine of tears on his whiskered cheeks.

"Jasmine," he whispers, "I'm so sorry. I never meant—"

"Shut up!" Her voice cracks like thunder. "Both of you, just… shut up."

The gun trembles harder. I recognize the telltale signs of someone unused to holding that much death in their hands. I'm maybe fifty feet shy of where I need to be before I can make a move. At the rate I'm going, it'll take another three minutes, maybe four, to get in position. God only knows how far back Feliks is.

"For fifteen years," she croaks, "I've lived in shadows. Jumped at every noise. Changed my name so many times I sometimes forget who I really am." Her laugh is bitter as grave dirt. "I'm remembering now."

Dragan's laugh echoes off the crumbling saints. "You think pointing a gun makes you strong? I remember the first time you tried to fight me. That little kitchen knife." He tsks. "You couldn't even hold it straight."

Jasmine swallows. "You broke my wrist."

"And yet you still made me breakfast the next morning." His grin is a jagged sickle moon. "*Slatko.* So obedient once you learned your place."

For a moment, I see her as she was fifteen years ago—bruised face, cowering in a silk nightgown, clutching a shattered rib. *Please, Sasha. Please.*

"You're nothing," she snarls. "A rabid dog who only knows how to bite."

Dragan steps closer to her. Glass crunches under his boot. "Yet here you are, *draga*, still flinching when I move too fast."

She fires. The bullet punches a chunk from the altar.

He doesn't blink. "Missed."

"The next one won't."

"Ah, but your hands shake. Like they did when you'd beg me to stop." His gaze flicks to Kosti, crumpled and bleeding. "You should thank me. Without my lessons, you'd still be that simpering girl your father sold."

"I'm not her anymore."

"No?" He takes a step forward, and even from here, I can see how she flinches. "Then what are you, *kurvo*? What are you now but the ghost of what I made you?"

"I'm what survived you," she declares. "Every mark you left, every bone you broke—I lived through it all. And now…" Her finger tightens on the trigger. "Now, I get to decide how this story ends."

But I see what she doesn't—shadows detaching themselves from the darkness behind the nave. Dragan's men take shape around her.

Jasmine notices too late. She spins, the gun swinging wildly between targets. "Stay back!"

The nearest thug snorts. "Or what, *krasivaya*? You'll miss us, too?"

She fires in a panic. Like the others, the shot goes wide, pocking the wall harmlessly. They all laugh—deep, rumbling chuckles that shake dust from the rafters. Dragan's laugh is loudest of all.

He nods to his men. "Disarm the bitch."

The largest one lunges. Jasmine screams, finger whitening on the trigger until—*click*. Empty. The *mudak* wrenches her arm behind her back. The gun clatters to the floor.

"No!" She kicks, thrashing, but another man pins her free arm. Her breaths come in ragged, wet heaves. The sound guts me.

Dragan circles her. "All these years, and you still fight like a cornered kitten." He trails a knuckle down her cheek. She flinches so hard her skull cracks against the thug's collarbone. "Remember our wedding rehearsal? You dropped the rings. I made you crawl through broken crystal to find them."

Jasmine's pupils blow wide. A tremor wracks her from scalp to soles—the same violent shaking I saw when I pulled her from his penthouse all those years ago.

"You… you held my face in the shards," she whispers.

"And you bled so prettily." He grabs her jaw, forcing eye contact. "Just like you're bleeding now."

A thin trickle of red snakes from her hairline. Her chest hitches—the prelude to hyperventilation.

"S-stop—"

Dragan feigns shock. "But we're just getting reacquainted!" He yanks her head back, exposing her throat. "Tell me, *nevjesta*—do you still wake up screaming? Still check the locks a dozen times before bed? Do you dream of me, little one?"

She can only whimper.

Dragan presses closer, lips grazing her ear. "You should've stayed dead, Jasmine. At least then, you were interesting."

Her knees buckle. The Serbian goons hold her upright like a doll.

My muscles coil, ready to spring. I'm almost there. Almost close enough. Almost. Almost…

Dragan pulls a knife from his belt. The blade catches storm light as he presses it to Jasmine's jugular. "Don't worry. I'll make it quick."

Her breath stops.

So does mine.

Now.

54

ARIEL

When did the walls start breathing?

The whole world shudders with inhales and exhales. Everything in it, living or not, sucks in a breath and releases it. Sucks in a breath and releases it.

It's all hazy—the faces hovering over me, the stone beneath my back, the burning ache between my legs. My babies' cries echo strangely, as if filtering through water.

"Ariel... *Ari...*"

Hands pin me down when I try to sit up. A hundred hands. A thousand hands. Soft hands. Gnarled hands.

One of those many, many hands holds a cup to my lips. I swat it away. Ceramic shatters.

"Ariel, you need to lie down. Your babies are okay. Everything is—"

Nothing will stay still. My mother's face melts like Dali

clocks—chin dripping onto Gina's shoulder, eyes floating in Lora's coffee cup.

Am I dead?

I look into my mother's arms. The twins aren't crying anymore—they're singing in Sasha's voice, harmonizing. They have angelic voices.

"Ari! Ari! You can't get up—"

I leap up, fly up, levitate up from the pile of blankets. I'm weightless.

Am I dead?

A monster with too many faces—Lora's, Gina's, Zoya's, Pavel's, Marco's, Mama's—chases me. I run.

All around me, shadows rise from the floor as I run. They lengthen, stretch, become fingers reaching for me. Baba's ringed fingers, Dragan's scarred knuckles, Sasha's tattooed palms. I run away from all of them.

The stairs spiral up into darkness like a serpent's coiled spine. At the top, the cellar door yawns. Moonlight pours through its throat.

I fly up the stairs. My hand finds the cellar door. Or at least, it dreams it does.

The wood is solid beneath my palm. Or maybe it's mist.

I run through.

It's chaos outside. Thunder unzips the sky. Rain comes from beneath me, pouring up from the ground and into the sky.

The village, a smear in the distance, writhes and takes shape. Becomes Jasmine at fifteen, crying in her wedding dress.

Becomes Sasha, scarred throat bared to heaven. Becomes me, split open and spilling secrets into the night.

I step into the maelstrom.

Or maybe I don't.

Maybe I never left that cellar at all.

55

SASHA

I explode from the shadows.

Rainwater drips from my hair as I charge into the firelight's jagged halo. Dragan's blade glints against Jasmine's throat—a silver smile biting into innocent flesh. My pulse thrums in the scar at my neck.

Dragan tilts his head, serpent-slow. "Still playing white knight, Sasha?"

I spread my hands wide to show I'm holding no weapon. "Just making you a deal you'd be stupid to turn down."

He laughs. "These Makris girls don't know how good they have it with you. Always coming to the rescue." His knife carves deeper into Jasmine's throat. A bead of blood pearls and runs down the edge. "What deal could you possibly offer me, Ozerov?"

I stand tall, unmoving. "You want vengeance against me, yes? Then take me. Let them both go."

His tongue flicks out, tasting Jasmine's fear. "Why? You think a quick death makes up for everything?"

"No. I know better than that. But you've studied me. You know which death would hurt worse. The one that doesn't end," I say, stepping into his orbit. "Watching everything I've built burn. How would that taste, Dragan? Sweeter than this?"

He arches a brow as he considers it. Beside him, Kosti stirs, crawling through his own blood.

Jasmine hiccups. "Sasha, don't—"

I cut her off with a dark laugh. "Don't pretend you give a shit whether I live or die, Jasmine. You can hate me for what I've done. I would hate me. And even if you were noble enough to forgive me, you shouldn't. Don't offer me redemption. I'm not worth it. I am my father's son." I face Dragan again. "Let her go. Take me instead."

Dragan looks at me. At Jasmine. Then he shrugs. "So be it. Kneel."

I don't even hesitate. Maybe I would have, once upon a time. But what do I have left now to protect—my honor? My dignity? No, fuck that. Those things are beyond worthless.

I have my wife, my children, and the sister-in-law whom I have used again and again like a chisel to mold the world to my liking. I won't use her anymore. It's my time to be used.

If my death protects them, so be it.

If it must happen in the dirt, so be it.

I sink to my knees.

"You," Dragan barks at one of his men. "Give me your gun."

He turns and smashes the butt of the weapon into my jaw. I see stars as something cracks within my mouth. Bone, tooth, I can't be sure—but the hot taste of blood follows soon after.

Then he presses the gun... to Jasmine's forehead.

I freeze. He grins wide. "So hard to choose," he murmurs, "which one should go first. Do I flip a coin? Eenie, meenie, minie..."

He dances the gun back and forth, from my head to hers, from hers to mine.

"... moe."

It stays on Jasmine.

Dragan shrugs again. "This will work." He flicks off the safety.

But before he can pull the trigger, there is movement at his feet. We all look in unison as Kosti wraps his hand around Dragan's ankle.

"Don't—! Dragan, we had a deal—"

Dragan kicks him away. "Your deals mean less than dog shit now, old man."

"You said—you said if I brought you Sasha, you'd spare them!" Blood sprays from his busted lips with every gasped syllable. Kosti drags himself upright and claws at Dragan's pants. "Jasmine—Jasmine is—"

The disgust I feel for him overpowers anything else foul I can sense. *This* is the game he was playing? Feed me to Dragan to save his nieces? For fuck's sake, we could have done this together! If he'd only asked...

Kosti glances to me and sees the repulsion written on my face. "Sasha…" His voice is wet with blood and shame. He struggles to his feet, swaying. "I had to. You have to understand—

"Understand what?" I spit. "That you sold us out to this *ublyudok*? That you let him burn my city?"

He shakes his head. "I couldn't watch it happen again."

My jaw tightens. "Watch what happen?"

"Another sacrifice. Another girl fed to you wolves." He wipes blood from his chin. "I went looking, you know. It all seemed so neat and convenient. One Makris daughter dead; one left. And who should get the survivor but you? So I went looking. I dug deep—and I found how you manipulated everything. You needed the Serbian-Greek alliance to fail so that you could take Dragan's place. So you arranged it all—the marriage. The abuse. You *counted* on him breaking her. You used her pain to expand your empire."

Jasmine makes a small, wounded sound. Her eyes find mine through the rain streaming through the broken roof.

"And now?" Kosti's laugh is weak. "Now, you are doing it again. Another Makris daughter. Another arranged marriage. Another piece moved across your board." He shakes his head. "I couldn't let Ariel become another Jasmine."

"So you went to Dragan."

"At least he's honest about what he is." Kosti's shoulders slump. "You… you pretend to be better. He does not." Finally, he drags his gaze back to Dragan. "But you struck a deal, Dragan. I gave you what you want. Give me what I am due."

Again, Dragan shrugs.

Again, Dragan looks at me.

Again, Dragan says, "So be it."

Then he puts a bullet between Kosti's eyes.

Jasmine screams, knife completely forgotten. I can only watch, too stunned to so much as blink, as the man who saved me just to damn me again goes slumping to the ground, bleeding from the hole in his forehead.

Kosti's hand flops lifelessly in between us. Reaching for Jasmine, I think. He'll never quite get there.

Dragan blows smoke from his pistol's barrel. "Annoying to the last, that old bastard." He pivots to press the still-hot gun to my nose again.

I open my mouth to tell him to go fuck himself. I might die on my knees, unloved and unredeemed.

But I will die with a curse on my lips for a man who doesn't even deserve the breath. As I inhale to speak it, though, something else speaks instead.

The roar of an engine that has seen better days.

We all turn as one just in time to see two blinding white headlights pour into the church. Stone screams as the Peugeot plows through the rotting wall, blasting the last remaining stones to smithereens. The car's grille catches Dragan cleanly, inches away from smiting me along with him, slamming him into a pillar with a wet crunch of bone. Dust and debris explode outward, choking the air.

Then—chaos.

Feliks comes keening out of the corner. He hurls a knife that sinks deep in one Serbian's throat, followed by a stone that crushes the skull of another.

Jasmine drops, scrambling toward Kosti's body as his killers reel. I'm already moving—snatching Dragan's fallen pistol from the rubble, putting two rounds in the nearest Serb's skull before he gathers his bearings.

When the goons are all dead, I turn once more to see the one who remains.

Pinned between the car and the altar is Dragan. His legs are pulp beneath the bumper and blood leaks from his lips. He's still breathing somehow. Wet, gurgling sobs that speak of punctured lungs and crushed ribs.

I advance on him with the gun in my hand. "Look at you. Roadkill."

He spits blood on my boots. "F-finish it, then."

This is for Jasmine, I think as I level the gun at his head. *For Ariel. For every woman you've ever hurt.*

But before I can pull the trigger, the car door creaks open. A figure stumbles out into the rain-slick mayhem.

The storm howls through the shattered nave, whipping Ariel's hair into a Medusa's crown of wet snakes. Her wedding dress clings to her like a second skin, ivory linen now the color of old bruises. One hand grips the car door frame—knuckles white as bone shards—the other splayed low over the swell of her womb. Blood streaks her inner thighs.

She shouldn't be here. Shouldn't be *standing.* Shouldn't be anything but curled in that cellar with our children, safe.

Our eyes lock across the carnage. Her gaze isn't the shattered glass I expected—it's flint sparking against steel. I see the girl who sent back a dozen courses just to watch me sweat. The woman who fucked me senseless on a printing press. The mother who clawed her way through hell just to spit in death's face.

Dragan whimpers beneath the Peugeot's crumpled hood. I should finish him. Put a bullet through that smirk he'll wear into the grave.

But my arm won't lift. My finger won't bend.

Ariel takes a step. Stumbles. Catches herself on a pew gnawed to splinters by termites and time. The movement parts her dress's torn slit—I glimpse the bandages Zoya applied hours ago, already blooming fresh crimson.

"You," she rasps at me, voice raw from screams, "don't get to die today. Not when you have children to live for."

Thunder cracks. The church groans. Behind me, Feliks drags Jasmine toward the blown-out wall.

But all I smell is peaches.

Ariel limps closer. Rain pools in the part in her hair. She stops a breath away. Her palm finds my chest—over the wound Kosti's betrayal left.

"Look at me," she demands.

I do.

Her thumb brushes my jaw. "You don't get to quit," she whispers. "Not on them. Not on me."

"Ari—"

Then she kisses me.

It's not forgiveness—that will take time. It's not absolution—that will take penance. It's a collision of teeth and truth and every unspoken thing that matters between then and now. When she pulls back, her lips are painted in our shared violence.

"We're not done," she says. She glances at Dragan. "He is, though. Leave him here to die."

The church doors burst open. Wind screams through the hole where our future waits—broken, bleeding, but alive.

I follow my wife into the storm.

EPILOGUE: ARIEL
SIX MONTHS LATER

The twins' hungry cries pulled me from sleep before dawn today, same as every morning. I've learned to love it. The quiet early hours, the stillness, the moments of just me and them when they're too sleepy to truly put up a fuss—those are the things I'll remember when I'm old and they no longer fit into the crooks of my elbows.

We stayed at Mama's house last night, just for a change of pace. It's nice to get out of the heart of the city sometimes. Quieter out here. Prettier in some ways, too. Sunlight slants through her lace curtains, gilding the dust motes swirling above Natalie's downy head.

Nat's the easy one. She does not play when it comes to nursing time. Eyes on the prize like a wartime general, sometimes even with a fist raised in victory. Leo, my restless revolutionary, keeps unlatching to glare at the world that dared remove him from the warmth of the womb.

I look up at the wall to check the time. Mama's French

cuckoo clock, the one Sasha fixed, is perfect down to the second.

Leo frowns and starts murmuring at the shift in my posture. "Shh, little man," I whisper, stroking his cheek. "Your sister's being so good. See?"

He sighs and settles back in, thank God.

Once they're comfortably nursing again, I return my attention to my computer screen, where a Word doc has my story waiting for today's words. It's hard enough to type with one baby, much less one in each arm, but I find a way. Feliks calls it "double dribbling." I think that's a basketball joke, but I'm not completely sure. To be honest, I don't think he knows, either.

My fingers hover over the keys as I stare at the scene I'm trying to write. The church in Roccastrada looms dark in my memory—rain and mud and broken saints watching from above. Hard to believe these same babies entered the world in such chaos. Sometimes, I wake up gasping, thinking I hear thunder. But then I feel Sasha's arms around me, hear the twins breathing in their bassinet, and reality settles back into place.

I look down at my children—*our* children. Natalie with her father's ice-blue eyes, Leo with my green ones. Both of them with Sasha's nose and my stubborn chin. They're our best story yet, written in flesh and blood instead of words.

My fingers fly across the keyboard again, weaving fiction from truth. Some details, I keep exactly as they happened— the weight of Sasha's hands as he helped me breathe through contractions, the way Jasmine's violin sang just before our world imploded.

Others, I soften, blur, transform into something less sharp-edged.

The truth is in there, though, between the lines. In the spaces where I pause to remember. In the moments when my hands go still over the keys, and I simply watch my children nurse, marveling at how something so gentle could come from so much violence.

The clock ticks on, keeping perfect time. Outside, Brooklyn wakes up slowly, but in here, it's just us—me and my babies and our story, unfolding one word at a time.

Leo's fist raps on my sternum. "I know, *agapi mou,*" I murmur, adjusting his angle. "The world's unfair. Write a strongly worded letter to management."

Natalie pops off with a satisfied smack. I shift her to my shoulder, patting the gas bubbles she'll deny having. The motion jostles Leo again, who retaliates by clamping down.

"*Malysh,*" I hiss through clenched teeth, "we talked about this."

Footsteps creak in the hall. My mother appears with two mugs, her silk kimono whispering against the doorframe. "They're conspiring against you," she remarks, setting my coffee down for me.

I sniff the steam—hazelnut creamer, heavy on the cinnamon. "They're Sasha's children. Scheming's in their DNA."

She hovers, because doting is in *her* DNA. Her fingers twitch toward Leo's wayward foot. "Do you need—?"

"You can steal them from me once they're done."

She grins guiltily, caught red-handed in Grandma Mode, then nods and slips back down the hall. When the door clicks shut, I exhale slowly. Natalie's head lolls against my neck, milk-drunk and dreamy. Leo's grip on my thumb loosens as sleep claims him, too.

The cursor blinks, waiting.

Eventually, I run out of both words and milk. When Mama knocks on the door to check on me, I offer her the children. She scoops them both up with obvious glee and starts singing as she ferries them away.

Time to do some of my other work. The screen is a maze of notifications, mostly from The Phoenix's Slack channel, where Gina and Lora are tag-teaming updates about our latest story's impact. Our exposé on Midwest Pharmaceuticals' price-fixing scheme has exploded. Major networks are picking it up, citing our reporting. My chest swells with pride. Twelve months ago, The Phoenix was a sleazy tabloid printing celebrity nip slips. Now, we're making corporate giants sweat.

A message from Gina pops up: ***CNN wants an interview!!!! Call me when the tiny humans release you from boob duty.***

I can't help but unleash a goofy grin, even though I'm all alone in my mother's den. They've been invaluable—Gina's razor-sharp editing, Lora's surprising talent for following money trails. Who woulda thought that Lora the Ditz knew accounting so well?

Together, we've built something meaningful from the ashes of the trashy rag Sasha bought me.

Speaking of meaningful transformations, there's a text from Feliks: ***Latest sweep came up empty. No sign of the Serbian snake anywhere. If he survived, he's long gone.***

My fingers tighten around the phone. Part of me wants to believe Dragan died in that church, crushed beneath that poor, tortured Peugeot that the rental company will never see again. But bodies have a way of turning up —or not—in our world.

Still, six months of silence speaks volumes. I choose to believe he's gone for good.

I scroll down to find a video in the family group chat from Jasmine. She's at her new studio in Manhattan bright and early this morning, helping a young student correct their bow grip. The difference between this Jasmine and the one who fled to France is stark. Her shoulders are straight, her smile genuine as she guides small hands into proper position.

First student showcase next Friday, reads her caption. *You're all coming, right?*

"Of course we are," I murmur. Teaching violin might seem like a small thing compared to running from demons, but I know better. Every note her students play is another brick in the wall between her past and present.

I sit back and look around me. The room glows in that fragile hour between dawn and true morning, pale light rinsing everything of colors. But even when I'm this calm, this meditative, I still don't hear Sasha until his thumb brushes the nape of my neck.

"Ah!"

He laughs and bends down to kiss where he just touched.

He smells like New York in winter—diesel exhaust and snowmelt clinging to his leather jacket—with an undercurrent of the vetiver soap I bought him after Dr. Nguyen suggested we incorporate anchoring rituals into our daily routines. His scar catches the screen's blue light as he leans over my shoulder, reading.

"Still fictionalizing me as the brooding antihero?" he asks.

"That's fiction?" I minimize the document before he can spot the paragraph where his hands are described as *'twin oaks grafted from war and tenderness.'* The last thing he needs is an ego boost. "You're here early. I thought you said you had Bratva business until noon."

One shoulder lifts in a half-shrug. Snowflakes float from his collar onto the keyboard. "I figured wife business was more important."

I pull him down for a proper kiss. "You figured correctly, sir. We've got... fifteen minutes, maybe, until Mama needs reinforcements. So...?"

He groans hungrily, but when I reach for his belt, he tucks my hands back in my lap instead of doing what I wanted, which is banging me senseless on the closest flat surface. "You don't know how bad I want that. But fifteen minutes isn't enough for me, Ariel. I need so much more time with you. Tonight."

His palm cups my jaw, guiding my gaze to his. Therapy has sanded some edges off his intensity, but the core remains— that fractured-bright gaze cataloging my every microexpression.

"Fine," I say, pretending to pout. I can't be too upset, though. Sasha has never, ever let me down when he's promised that *"later, there will be more."*

I trace the puckered scar along his ribs through his shirt. "Dr. Nguyen said you skipped yesterday's one-on-one. Everything okay?"

His pulse leaps under my fingertips. "Had a... visitor."

"Another dream?"

When he hesitates, I thread our fingers together—Dr. Nguyen's grounding technique #3. His exhale warms my temple.

"It was Moliets-et-Maa again," he rasps. "You in that alley, Dragan's knife at your throat. Only when he turned... it wasn't Dragan. It was Yakov."

I run my finger through his hair. "You should've woken me."

"Not a chance; you were actually asleep for once." His forehead meets mine. "My vow stands, *moya zhena*. Your nightmares take precedence."

I like when he reminds me of the promise he made me in that garden. Who has to be shadow and who gets to be light. Some burdens in this life can be shared. Some can't. But that's okay. We always have each other to lean on.

I let him pull me into the wingback chair, his legs pillowing mine. Dawn pinks the room as I curl into him. As we breathe softly together, just enjoying each other's touch and company, the muffled notes of Mama's singing float down the hallway toward us.

"It's a good life we have, you know," he murmurs suddenly. "It's a good, good life."

～

The steam from Zoya's feast rises in swirls, staining the air with the tang of beets and nostalgia. I watch Sasha's scarred thumb swipe a dollop of sour cream from Natalie's chin—a gesture so ordinary it steals my breath. Our daughter giggles, smearing borscht across the Ozerov family crest tattooed on his wrist.

"Careful," I warn the little princess as I pass my husband and claim a seat at his side. "That's a historic artifact you're defacing."

"Not much longer for this world," he agrees, glancing at the crest again.

Feliks snorts. "You keep saying that and I keep not believing it."

Bouncing our daughter on his knee, Sasha looks as serious as ever. "I mean it. The Ozerov Bratva has lived long enough. It's time for it to die. That's how we make room for now things."

"I know, I know. I get it." Sighing, Feliks shakes his head. "I'm mostly upset about having to wear a suit to work every day, now that we're actually legit."

"I'm not upset about that in the slightest," cuts in an obscenely pregnant Gina. "Suits are like lingerie for men." She cups Feliks's cheek, the light overhead flashing in the depths of the emerald engagement ring she's been showing off all night. It's big enough to require its own mining permit.

Feliks picked well. He knows his woman, I'll give him that much.

Across the table, Leo squirms in Jasmine's arms, making grabby hands at the dumplings on her plate. My sister deftly redirects his attention with a spoonful of pureed carrots. "There we go, *agapi mou*," she coos, her voice gentle in a way I never thought I'd hear again. "Just like that."

Belle appears at my shoulder, ladling more soup into Sasha's bowl. "Eat," she orders him. "You're skin and bones again."

Zoya comes in and thunks down a carafe of kvass. "Skin, bones, and bad decisions."

"But my bad decisions match my tie." Sasha flicks the silk monstrosity that Lora gifted him for his birthday—neon pink with dancing tacos that are saying, *Guac Out with your Tac' Out.* Leo grabs for it, shouting with glee.

"It's such a beautiful tie," Lora sighs. I'm pretty sure she missed the joke, but that's okay.

Pavel, holding her hand dutifully, just shakes his head. He knows better than to intervene.

The empty chair at the end of the table looms large. It's for Kosti, though no one says his name out loud. There's a rule at Sunday night family dinners: No talking about ghosts. We set places for them instead. Let them linger in the clink of spoons against porcelain, in the way Feliks still pours two shots of vodka—one vanished, one consumed.

My uncle made bad choices. But he did it out of love. If that's an unforgivable crime, then I'd never be able to live with the man who gave me his name and his children. Because he made bad choices, too. But he loved us all hard enough to make up for them.

Kosti didn't get the chance to leave his sins in the past. Sasha did, though—and he tells me every single day how grateful he is that the world showed him mercy that he never showed the world.

Gina leans into Feliks' shoulder, her voice carrying. "We're thinking of a Halloween wedding. With costumes! I'll dress as Medusa; he'll go as the idiot who looked at her."

"Romantic," I deadpan.

"You're one to talk."

I laugh and rest my head against Sasha's shoulder in a silent *touché*. Natalie bangs her spoon in agreement, splattering beetroot across his taco tie.

Suddenly, her little face screws up and she starts to wail. Sasha looks down and sees that she slammed her fist into a fork tine and opened up a tiny little cut.

"Ah, poor *malysh*," he croons as he rocks her until her sobs calm down. Zoya hands him a Band-Aid from the cabinet and he puts it on our daughter's hand. "Better? There, there, that's so much better."

He glances at me and winks. "Like mother, like daughter," he murmurs, and suddenly, I'm back in that Met bathroom, watching him tend to my injured hand with such unexpected gentleness.

Who was that woman, so determined to resist him?

Who was that man, so certain he could never love?

Who are we now?

That answer remains unclear. But I do know where we are and what we're doing. We are in a warm kitchen filled with food and laughter, surrounded by love. We are watching our children grow, building something neither of us thought possible.

We are healing. We are hoping. We are happy. We are *here*.

Sasha's hand finds mine under the table, his thumb tracing the scar on my palm where it all began. "Penny for your thoughts?" he asks softly.

I squeeze his fingers, watching as a miraculously healed Natalie tries to grab his nose. "Just thinking about the beginning."

His laugh is quiet but real. "It was a touch-and-go start."

"Nothing about us has ever been straightforward," I reply, leaning into him as Belle starts passing around more bread.

Babushka's Lap glows golden in the setting sun, filled with the sounds of our cobbled-together family—Feliks's barking laugh, Gina's snort of derision, Jasmine humming as she coaxes another spoonful into Leo's mouth. Even the empty chair feels less like a wound and more like a reminder that love persists, complicated and messy as it may be.

I rest my head on Sasha's shoulder. It's mint. Cedar. Home.

I tried to fight all this, once upon a time. I fought it tooth and nail, kicking and screaming. I'm not fighting anymore. I surrendered.

That's how I know it's real.

EXTENDED EPILOGUE: ARIEL

Click here to check out the exclusive Extended Epilogue to
10 Days to Surrender:
https://dl.bookfunnel.com/3cmi6297ta

ALSO BY NICOLE FOX

Oryolov Bratva

Cruel Paradise

Cruel Promise

Pushkin Bratva

Cognac Villain

Cognac Vixen

Viktorov Bratva

Whiskey Poison

Whiskey Pain

Orlov Bratva

Champagne Venom

Champagne Wrath

Uvarov Bratva

Sapphire Scars

Sapphire Tears

Vlasov Bratva

Arrogant Monster

Arrogant Mistake

Zhukova Bratva

Tarnished Tyrant

Tarnished Queen

Stepanov Bratva

Satin Sinner

Satin Princess

Makarova Bratva

Shattered Altar

Shattered Cradle

Solovev Bratva

Ravaged Crown

Ravaged Throne

Vorobev Bratva

Velvet Devil

Velvet Angel

Romanoff Bratva

Immaculate Deception

Immaculate Corruption

Kovalyov Bratva

Gilded Cage

Gilded Tears

Jaded Soul

Jaded Devil

Ripped Veil

Ripped Lace

Mazzeo Mafia Duet

Liar's Lullaby (Book 1)

Sinner's Lullaby (Book 2)

Bratva Crime Syndicate

Can be read in any order!

Lies He Told Me

Scars He Gave Me

Sins He Taught Me

Belluci Mafia Trilogy

Corrupted Angel (Book 1)

Corrupted Queen (Book 2)

Corrupted Empire (Book 3)

De Maggio Mafia Duet

Devil in a Suit (Book 1)

Devil at the Altar (Book 2)

Kornilov Bratva Duet

Married to the Don (Book 1)

Til Death Do Us Part (Book 2)

Heirs to the Bratva Empire

Can be read in any order!

Kostya

Maksim

Andrei

Princes of Ravenlake Academy (Bully Romance)

Can be read as standalones!

Cruel Prep

Cruel Academy

Cruel Elite

Tsezar Bratva

Nightfall (Book 1)

Daybreak (Book 2)

Russian Crime Brotherhood

Can be read in any order!

Owned by the Mob Boss

Unprotected with the Mob Boss

Knocked Up by the Mob Boss

Sold to the Mob Boss

Stolen by the Mob Boss

Trapped with the Mob Boss

Volkov Bratva

Broken Vows (Book 1)

Broken Hope (Book 2)

Broken Sins *(standalone)*

Other Standalones

Vin: A Mafia Romance

Box Sets

Bratva Mob Bosses (Russian Crime Brotherhood Books 1-6)

Tsezar Bratva (Tsezar Bratva Duet Books 1-2)

Heirs to the Bratva Empire

The Mafia Dons Collection

The Don's Corruption

Made in United States
Orlando, FL
21 March 2025

59688168R10249